MW01106551

The Reluctant Warrior

by

Ty Patterson

Copyright © 2014 by Ty Patterson

This is a work of fiction. Names, characters, businesses, places, events and incidents are either the products of the author's imagination or used in a fictitious manner. Any resemblance to actual persons, living or dead, or actual events is purely coincidental.

All rights reserved. This book or any portion thereof may not be reproduced, or used in any manner whatsoever without the express written permission of the publisher except for the use of brief quotations in a book review.

Books by Ty Patterson

Warriors Series

The Warrior, http://amzn.to/1kP8Q1c, Warriors series, Book 1

The Reluctant Warrior,http://amzn.to/1mFvHwZ, Warriors series, Book 2

Coming soon: The Warrior Code, Warriors series, Book 3

Acknowledgements

No book is a single person's product. I am privileged that *The Reluctant Warrior* has benefited from the inputs of several great people.

Christine Terrell, Jean Coldwell, and Kathryn Moody for their awesome constructive critique, Donna Rich for her proofreading, Pauline Nolet (http://www.paulinenolet.com) for her proofreading and editing.

Dedications

To my wife, who is my anchor and my sail; my son, who is my inspiration; my parents who never stopped giving; and all my beta readers and well-wishers.

Part 1

Chapter 1

The boy woke up as soon as he heard his father stirring, and peered out from under the edge of his blanket.

He saw his dad do his usual routine of looking across the small bedroom, from his bed to the children's beds to see if they were awake, and then step cautiously to the window overlooking the street and scan it.

His father had been doing this for the last few months. One day he had asked his father what he was looking for. He had been brushed off.

They had moved to Brownsville not long ago, just over a year back. For him life had been long periods of moving about followed by short periods of stay and calm, and so far Brownsville had been one of those short periods of calm. He looked across at his sister sprawled across the edge of her tiny bed, legs twitching spasmodically in response to some dream in her eight-year-old mind. He wondered if she enjoyed moving so much; maybe for her it was normal, since she hadn't experienced anything else. His eyes went back to his father, still standing at the window, and wondered what he was thinking about. The boy gave up wondering after some time as sleep dragged him into oblivion.

Shattner knew his son had been awake and watching, from the changed timbre of his breathing. The apartment was just a single-bedroom apartment in Brownsville, a New York neighborhood well-known for its crime.

William Shattner was a loser and looked like one. His thin brown hair, narrow face, angular body, shifty eyes and hesitant manner didn't inspire any confidence.

His father ran the only grocery store in a small town in Ohio, and by the time young William turned fifteen, Shattner Senior had realized the family's livelihood couldn't be entrusted to his son.

William didn't want to run a grocery store. He didn't know what he wanted to do in life. He had a vague idea about seeing places and doing the kind of exciting stuff girls fell for, but those were hazy ideas in his mind that never got translated into ambition. He had his eureka moment when he saw an army recruitment advertisement on TV and enlisted on his eighteenth birthday. His parents, both in poor health by then, wished him well and were secretly glad that they were no longer responsible for him.

The army shaped Shattner to some extent, but it too realized the extent of his capabilities. He had an ability to repair broken equipment and also had a liking for record keeping, and this got him a career in the Ordnance Corps. His vague dreams of seeing places materialized when the corps deployed him to various hot spots of the world.

A slightly more mature Shattner married his high school sweetheart, Coralyn, when he came home on leave. Marriage didn't turn out the way it was promoted. Coralyn had more aspirations than Shattner and demanded a lifestyle that Shattner couldn't afford. Not on a sergeant's income.

His two kids, Lisa and Shawn, were the best things to have happened to him, and in order to give *them* a comfortable life, Shattner found the means to support Coralyn's demands.

He started selling military weapons in the black market.

He didn't know how and when he crossed that moral divide; Shattner wasn't given to introspection, but he found that the illegal activity came easy to him, and for a while his life was back to as normal as it ever was.

Till the time he was found, court-martialed and discharged from the army.

His marriage had ended by then, and Shattner, using all his meager savings, fought for and got custody of his children. Then followed years of drifting from job to job, living out of run-down apartments, and trying to earn enough to raise his children. Those jobs often involved selling small firearms on the black market – a life on the dark side, the only open door for Shattner.

When the faint possibility of redemption arrived, Shattner grabbed it.

Shattner stood in the shadows and watched life pass in the street. It had become second nature for him for as long as he could remember, to look out for anything out of the ordinary on the street before he stepped out. Nothing struck him, and he headed towards the door of the apartment.

His son would wake up, make breakfast for his sister and himself, get both of them ready for school, and then the two of them would walk a couple of blocks to school. After school, his son would collect his sister and do the routine in reverse. By the time Shattner returned from work, his son and daughter would have finished their dinner and be ready for bed.

His son, a mature adult in an eleven-year-old body, had never experienced boyhood and had never enjoyed all the small things that childhood was about. For the briefest moment, the darkness of despair flooded his mind before he ruthlessly shunted it aside.

Shattner walked several blocks to the car repair shop where he worked. He could have taken a bus to the garage, but he preferred the walk, even if it was a long one, since it gave him the freedom to breathe.

On returning home he picked up a tail.

A short stocky man was trailing him from a distance. He was good, but Shattner's life in the army had left him with vital survival skills, and he picked up the tail immediately. He sat down on a bench, bought some nuts and ate them leisurely, taking the time to subtly observe the reaction of the tail and also to think the situation through.

The tail hung well back, and finishing his nuts, Shattner decided to do nothing about him. Those who employed the tail already knew where he was living and everything else about him. If he took on the tail, it would only tip them off that he knew. His apartment was on the third floor on Blake Avenue in an apartment complex that housed many like him for whom hope and a future were alien. He could hear the excitement in Lisa's voice as she talked with her brother, the voices audible through the thin door of the apartment. He stepped in silently, and the rest of his world fell away.

'Daddy,' Lisa squealed as she rushed across the room and jumped into his arms. 'Shawn helped me with schoolwork.' Her voice came out muffled as she buried her face in his shoulders.

'Had dinner, princess?' He looked over at Shawn questioningly.

Both nodded.

'How was school, princess?' he asked her as he went to their small bathroom to shower and change, listening to her momentous day. For an eight-year-old, every day was noteworthy. Shattner allowed her voice to wash over him, leaving him refreshed.

He spent an hour with her, telling stories, and as her breathing deepened into sleep, he sat there for a long while, his mind empty, as empty as the future he saw for himself. *They will have a better future*, he promised himself.

'Dad?'

Shattner turned from the refrigerator to see Shawn tousled with sleep.

'Dad, will we ever have a normal life?'

Shattner heard the refrigerator door shut behind him, the soft thud drowned by the beating of his heart as he felt his son's eyes on him. He took a couple of long strides and crouched down in front of his son.

'Two to three months at the most, Shawn. And then we'll live like any other normal family. We'll celebrate birthdays, go on holidays, and have loads of friends... trust me, buddy. Okay?'

Shawn nodded, his eyes dark, the faintest sheen of tears in them.

Shattner pulled him close, crushed him in a hug, and walked him to bed and sat beside him till sleep claimed him.

He checked his phone after dinner and saw the text message silently winking at him.

It was the one he was dreading.

'Tomorrow.'

Short, terse, like the sender.

He went to his gun cabinet, a grand description for a wooden drawer high up in the closet in the bedroom, and removed his Glock 30 and cleaning materials, and carried them to the drawing room.

He stripped the gun, wiped the parts clean, and then started a more thorough job of lubricating them. The smell of gun oil filled the room, a comforting smell, bringing back good memories. He assembled the gun, loaded its magazine, and chambered a round. He didn't think he would need the gun the next day, but it never hurt to be prepared.

Chapter 2

Jose Cruz owned Brownsville Autos, the used car dealership and garage where Shattner worked. The garage had a staff of six, a diverse mix of East Europeans, Hispanics and... William Shattner.

Jose Cruz was also regional kingpin of 5Clubs, the fastest-growing gang in New York City that had outmuscled all other gangs and ran its criminal empire like a business.

Cruz, the head of the Brooklyn chapter, was ruthless, ambitious, and rising fast in the gang.

Cruz owned Brownsville; not a single deal went down in Brownsville without his knowledge and involvement, or permission. Brownsville Autos was a legitimate business and gave him the façade to operate from.

It had been surprisingly easy for Shattner to join the gang. Later, he realized, that was one of their strengths. Making it easy to join, and making sure no one ever left.

He had been walking along Tapscott Street late one night soon after moving to Brownsville, real late at night, drifting in and out of the dark shadows, when he saw the holdup. A dark sedan had been parked on the other end of the street with five men leaning against it.

They were not leaning.

Two of them were being held at gunpoint by three others; one of the three was waving a gun and gesticulating, the other two slapping and kicking the one against the car. Shattner didn't stop to think. He wore rubber-soled shoes, dressed in dark clothes, and wasn't spotted by the group till he was a few feet away. By then it was too late.

Before the gunman could turn and train his gun on Shattner, he had gone down with a kick to his kidneys, followed by a blow to his throat. As he fell down choking, the two held up against the car turned on their attackers and felled them brutally.

A couple of minutes, that's all it had taken. Once Shattner's breathing slowed and the adrenaline subsided, he took stock of the two he had rushed to help. Hispanic was his first thought. Short, swarthy, one of them bent to retrieve a bag from an attacker and kicked him in the head for good measure.

'You guys okay? Shouldn't we call the police,' Shattner addressed them.

'No. No police,' the guy bending down replied as the other walked around the car, searching for something.

'Are you sure? These guys might file a report, and it's better if we get ours in first,' Shattner persisted.

The bent guy straightened up, holding a brown paper bag, which was half open and filled with small baggies. He glared at Shattner. 'You dumb or something? We said no police.'

The other man came around the car, tucking a pistol in his waistband, and looked appraisingly at Shattner. Perhaps he's wondering if he should shoot me, Shattner thought.

'Gracias,' he said. 'If you need anything, come here.' He handed a card to Shattner, and they left without another word or a backward glance. The next day he hoofed it to the garage and handed the card to a teenager in the reception.

'Two men gave this to me last night. They asked me to come here if I needed help. I need a job. I'm a good mechanic.'

The teenager stared at him disbelievingly for a long time – the garage wasn't exactly a career magnet – and then placed the card on the counter. 'Dude, there are thousands of these cards in the city. We don't offer a job to anyone who just walks in, hands over one of them, and tells a fantastic story. In any case, we're not hiring.'

Shattner stared back at him. 'Son, don't you think this is way above your pay grade? Why don't you get the manager and let me speak to him?'

Back and forth they went till a side door opened and one of the two men came in, the one who had spoken to him last.

'You? What're you doing here?'

'Looking for a job.'

'Why here?'

'Why not? You did ask me to come here if I needed help. I need a job. I am a good mechanic. Mechanics work in garages.'

The man looked at Shattner for some time and then jerked his head.

'Come.'

Shattner followed him, and the man introduced him to Jose Cruz.

15

Cruz was as tall as Shattner, an inch over six feet, lean and sinewy, a hatchet face with eyes that were probing all the time. He looked Shattner over as Diego, the other gang member, fired off a fusillade in Spanish at him.

Jose barked at Diego and turned away without acknowledging Shattner. Being the boss had privileges.

Diego grabbed Shattner by his elbow and took him to a windowless room, and Shattner's interrogation commenced.

The night before, Shattner had worked out that he'd crashed into a gang takedown and had thought long and hard about approaching the garage for a job. Two things had finally persuaded him – he needed a job and his savings had nearly run out, and jobs weren't easy to find for one with a criminal record.

He had also matured and believed that being a loser wasn't a lifetime sentence.

What he had not expected was meeting Cruz so easily. He had thought gang bosses were harder to meet, but he later came to know that Cruz oversaw every aspect of his business with manic attention, personally recruited every gang member, and enforced discipline ferociously.

There was a gang member who'd had ambitions of his own and started dealing on the side. One afternoon Cruz had him brought to his office, where the gang member was rewarded by the sight of Cruz raping his wife and seven-year-old daughter. When he had finished, he shot them and then sat down to have his supper. He hadn't uttered a single word to the gang member, who by then was in a state of catatonic shock. The gangster was never seen again. There were many such stories surrounding Cruz.

Cruz's gang was large, more than fifty members; the six in the garage were kept separate from the gang. The gang members seldom came to the garage, and if they did, it was after the garage had closed for the day and the mechanics had gone home. Shattner was by far the best mechanic they had; he often stayed late working on the cars, and over the months he could identify the gang members and had developed a conversational relationship with many of them – if greetings and grunted acknowledgements could be called a conversation.

The first time Shattner got involved with the gang was four months after he joined the garage. One evening he could hear loud voices from Cruz's office, Diego and Jose going at it vowel and syllable. He heard a door slamming, another opening, and Diego stood before him, scowling.

'You? Can you drive?'

When Shattner looked at him stupidly, he made a steering motion with his hands and asked again, 'Drive?'

'Come here at eleven. Night, not day,' Diego told him when Shattner nodded.

The garage was dead when Shattner returned that night, all the lights off. When he stepped inside the parking lot, Diego stepped out, followed by another, a tall, swarthy man with a teardrop tat under his left eye, carrying a brown paper sack. Diego tossed car keys to Shattner without saying a word.

It was the same dark sedan as the night of the holdup. Diego and the other man got in the back, carrying the paper sack, and Shattner drove them down Lott Avenue and parked behind a school. Diego and the other guy, Rajek, spoke occasionally but ignored Shattner.

They were gone nearly an hour, supplying street dealers Shattner surmised, and when they returned, Shattner powered the car up and waited for them to seat themselves. Diego touched his shoulder just as he was pulling away.

He stopped the sedan and turned back to see the barrel of a gun pointing at him, a couple of inches away from his face.

Diego looked back at him impassively, his finger on the trigger, and beside him Rajek grinned silently, exposing teeth that were strangers to a dentist.

'You know who we are and what we do?' Diego asked him.

'I'm not stupid,' replied Shattner.

Diego swung the barrel against his head viciously, drawing a thin line of blood from his temple. When the ringing in his head had stopped, Shattner found the black bore of the barrel against his face, steady, Diego's eyes black and empty looking back at him.

'Young hoods are desperate to join us. Some rob, some sell drugs, many sell their sisters and mothers. And some kill. To prove themselves to us. You just walked in. Not logical. Jose does not like things that are not logical.'

He paused, his eyes black holes in his face.

'I'm an enforcer. You know what that means?'

'People shit in their pants when they see you?'

Diego hit him again on the other temple. A thicker stream of blood started running down Shattner's head.

'You think you're smart. How come I'm holding this gun and you're at the other end?'

Diego extended his forefinger and touched the blood streaming down Shattner's face. He inspected it for a while and flicked it away.

'That's my business,' he said, nodding at the copper droplets flying away.

'I am number two. I am also the enforcer of our chapter.'

He paused, enjoying the fear in Shattner's eyes.

'I looked into your past, your history, and your time in the army. I spoke to your previous garage in New Jersey, your landlord... everyone who knew you. You are a criminal, just like us. But I told Jose, better to kill you. Your joining us did not feel right,' Diego continued without any inflection. He could be reading the weather.

'But Jose is smart. Smarter than me... is why he is boss. He said we need Anglos. Less suspicious.'

'He said we didn't need to worry about you. You got kids. Lisa very pretty, no?' Diego smiled a feral smile.

Shattner went cold.

Diego smiled thinly. 'Relax, Anglo. You are alive; your kids are safe... for now.' He leant back in his seat and gestured at Shattner to drive.

Rajek clicked his tongue and looked disappointed. Maybe happiness for him was Shattner's brains splattered over the windshield.

His involvement in the gang increased. He was used the most as a driver, but soon started distributing baggies to the street vendors and making collections for the gang.

The garage, while a front, was not very successful. The people who brought their cars in were known to the gang even if they weren't gang members themselves. Shattner figured out the hierarchy of the gang over time. Cruz ruled it at the top, with Diego as his second in command as well as its chief hit man. Then came a handful of Rajeks — the senior members of the gang, and then there were the doers... those who ran the drugs, the rackets, the women.

In his arms trading, Shattner had dealt with many gangs, but this one was different. This one ran like a smoothly oiled machine, a strong chain of command linking the hierarchies and utter ruthlessness shown to those who disobeyed or challenged the gang. Like a military machine. Shattner learnt over a period of time that most of the gang members, including Jose, Diego and Rajek had military experience, some in European armed forces, some in South America or Africa.

Most of those armed forces must have been happy to see the backs of these guys, he thought.

A month after his close-up with Diego's gun, he drove Diego to a hit.

Chapter 3

It was at two in the morning.

He drove Diego to an office block, killed the engine, and nervously waited for instructions.

Diego was silent and motionless, his dark eyes seeing nothing and seeing everything. His phone beeped after half an hour, and after a murmured conversation, Diego straightened. In another fifteen minutes, they saw a car make its way from the opposite end of the street, stop about a hundred feet away, and kill its lights.

Two people stepped out of the car and approached theirs, and Diego met them halfway. He bumped fists with them, took wads of cash from them, gave them baggies in return, turned his back on them, and returned to Shattner.

Ten feet away from them, he turned smoothly and drew.

So smooth and balletic was his movement that it took Shattner a couple of seconds to make the gun in his hand. The two reports were muted, hitting the other two in the back of their heads. Shattner didn't hear the bodies falling; he saw Diego step up to the bodies and fire into their heads again for good measure. He grabbed the baggies and walked back to Shattner leisurely, a thin breeze ruffling his hair slightly.

Shattner felt the cold touch of the barrel to his neck when they reached the first set of lights on their way back.

'You are too calm, chollo. Maybe you're a cop?'

Shattner broke. He swerved into the darkness between streetlights and turned back to Diego.

'A cop? Wouldn't I have brought the whole force on you guys by now? Remember I've seen a lot of shit you guys do and know a lot.'

Diego didn't say a word but continued pointing the gun at Shattner.

Shattner leaned forward and pulled the gun to his forehead. 'If in doubt, pull. That's your motto, isn't it? Go on, then. Pull.'

Black pools of nothing stared back at him, and then slowly the barrel moved.

'You have got balls, chollo. Si, I grant you that. Now drive.'

Shattner drove back in silence, gripping the wheel hard to hide the trembling in his hands. Diego sat motionless behind him, expressionless, bars of light and dark moving across his face as the car made its way to Blake Avenue. Probably thinking when he can kill me, Shattner thought savagely.

The next week, two gang members were busted by the police as they were selling drugs to street vendors near a school. The same school Shattner had driven Diego to. The week after that, a gang member was arrested as he was carrying out a hit on an MS-13 gang member.

The first arrest was shrugged off by the chapter as the price to be paid for being in business; the members were soon bailed. Just like most businesses of this size, Jose had lawyers and PR agents on retainers. The second incident caused uneasiness given its proximity to the first.

The third arrest happened in the subsequent week.

Ten gangbangers were flushed out after the police ran an elaborate sting operation on a prostitution racket owned by Jose. The uneasiness exploded into suspicion.

There was a snitch in the gang.

And Shattner was its newest quasi member.

Diego was with Shattner on every gang business errand now, watching him from behind his lizard-like eyelids. He didn't care if Shattner knew he was under suspicion.

The gang still used him, and he wondered about that. Maybe all the members are known to the cops and they're using me as a foil, *he reasoned.*

His phone vibrated on the table, bringing him out from the past. The text message stared back at him.

'Tomorrow.'

He went to the bedroom window and stared into the dark street below him, wondering if he would return home the next day.

He had heard rumors of a large deal, and it was likely Diego wanted him as the getaway driver.

That, or the summons was for his execution.

He washed his face in the bathroom and stared back at his reflection in the mirror. His hair was even thinner now, his cheeks hollowed out, and there were dark circles under his eyes. His hands trembled constantly, and he had to jam them in his pockets whenever his kids were around.

He took a deep breath, pushing away his constant fear, squared his shoulders, and stepped out of the bathroom.

Diego was awaiting him at the garage entrance the next day, sitting inconspicuously in an anonymous Toyota Corolla. Passersby did not give him a second glance, unaware that they were a few feet from the most ruthless killer in Brooklyn.

He jerked his head at Shattner, indicating for him to get in and drive, and Shattner obliged, taking them down Rockaway Avenue, onto Linden Boulevard and into a deserted industrial area on Wortman Avenue.

He parked beside a Ford Transit, and as soon as he had turned off the ignition, the rear doors of the Transit opened.

Rajek jumped out, followed by another heavily tattooed and armed man. Diego stepped out and opened the trunk of Shattner's car, and Rajek and the other man started loading burlap sacks in the boot from the Transit. Shattner stood for a moment watching the activity and then helped the transfer. He reckoned there were two hundred kilos that got loaded in the car, and from the smell, he suspected the sacks contained crack.

Rajek and his companion drove off without a word, but not without Rajek grinning at Shattner. Maybe he was wondering how long Shattner had to live.

'You think this is a picnic?' Diego growled when Shattner stood staring at the back of the Ford Transit.

Shattner got behind the wheel and followed Diego's directions, taking the Belt Parkway, moving out of the city and southwards.

His suspicions were confirmed when they took the I-95 and merged onto the New Jersey Turnpike.

'New Jersey, huh?' He turned to Diego and received a stony look in return.

He shrugged and continued driving without stopping at any of the services. Conversation wasn't Diego's strongest point.

Southport in Gloucester City, New Jersey, on the Delaware River was once the site of a nineteenth- century shipyard and later was an industrial site. Now it was abandoned and fenced off, industry and shipping deserting the city, and this was where Shattner guessed the crack was heading to.

A brilliant choice for a deal to go down since law enforcement never ventured there, and the only people that visited were the odd fisherman or jogger.

They drove through the city, driving normally so as not to attract any attention, and Diego relaxed beside him. Relaxed like a snake. Down they went on Klemm Avenue and through to Market Street, the town, a very small place that industry forgot and where everyone knew the other.

On Water Street, Diego made him drive all the way from the waterfront to an abandoned industrial site where power stations, chimneys, and buildings defined desolation.

Shattner parked in front of an enormous opening to a long, dilapidated structure that ran for a mile on either side of the entrance, its roof partially blown away, exposing an intestine of girders and frames. From the inside of the structure came the sound of an engine revving, and another drab Ford Transit emerged from the maw of the building and rattled across towards them. The Transit reversed so that it was back to back with Shattner's car.

Four heavily armed men emerged from the rear of the Transit and headed towards Diego.

Through the rearview mirror Shattner could see the men sported assault rifles and handguns; one had an M203 grenade launcher hanging from his shoulder. All four of them sported the tattoos of 5Clubs; Shattner suspected this was a trade between Cruz's chapter and whichever other chapter these four belonged to.

Diego opened the trunk, and the four men swiftly began transferring the crack to the van. He stood at one side, talking into his mobile, his gun hand casually resting inside his jacket.

Shattner, taking his cue from Diego, felt around his back, pulled out his Glock and placed it in his lap. He angled the mirrors so that he could see everyone behind him.

And then everyone heard it. Their arrival could be heard a long way away, the throbbing of powerful engines approaching fast.

Chapter 4

One of the armed men ran out to the road leading to Water Street, jerked his head both ways, and came back shouting urgently. Diego started yelling back, and the tension ratcheted up.

Shattner couldn't make out the shouting from inside the car, but the men speeded up the transfer. He stepped out of the Toyota as, at a sharp command from Diego, the four abandoned the transfer and ran towards the Transit.

'Cops,' shouted Diego to Shattner, and that was enough for him to follow Diego into the back of the van.

The van was already moving when they reached it, and rough hands drew them in the back. As soon as they were inside the van, it took off, its tires squealing in the dirt. The van careened on the road and then righted after a tight right took it onto Water Street, away from the industrial site.

Through the half-open door, Shattner could now see the reason for the escape; three New Jersey State cruisers were about half a mile away, their bars flashing, followed by a Police Command Vehicle, the roar of their engines growing louder by the second.

The air in the van felt thin to Shattner, everything jacked up and tight, and sound came to him at a distance, adrenaline drowning out normalcy. The cruisers turned on their sirens when they spotted the Transit making a getaway, and a loudspeaker called out, but the commotion in the van drowned out the words.

Shattner held onto the side of the van desperately as it rocketed down the street, its souped-up engine releasing all its horses. He glanced nervously at Diego, who was directing the men to fire at the cops.

Shattner shouted above the racket, 'You're not going to fire at them, are you? That will make this worse.'

Diego looked at him contemptuously, and before he could answer, the gangbangers opened fire. They didn't see if their shots had any effect as the van turned a corner and then immediately slipped into another street and took yet another turn, where it slid into an open slot. The four men jumped out, took the remaining stash, and ran away, disappearing in the traffic.

Diego pushed Shattner ahead of him, the two walking briskly but not noticeably hurrying, blending in the ebb and flow of the street. He nudged Shattner into a park, where they sat, outwardly relaxed, till it grew dark.

Smart move, thought Shattner. *Parks won't be the first place the cops look at.*

They broke into a run-down Honda Civic when night set in, and drove out of Gloucester City.

Diego hit his phone as soon as they were clear and back on the I-95, calling several numbers, speaking rapidly and angrily in Spanish.

'How many kilos did we leave behind?' Shattner asked him once Diego had fallen silent. Instead of answering, Diego pulled his gun and pointed it at Shattner.

'How did they know?' he screamed. The sudden move made Shattner swerve, and when he finished steadying the car, Diego screamed again. 'Are you the snitch? How did the pigs know?'

'I don't know, and fuck you, I'm not a snitch,' Shattner screamed back.

He turned to face Diego fully, ignoring the car, ignoring the traffic.

Rage flooded through him, string-tight nerves and adrenaline needing a release. 'Kill me, you bastard, and get it over with,' he screamed, spittle spraying on Diego.

'You are the enforcer, right? Hot-shot hit man, feared by all? You all suspect me of being the grass, don't you? Come on, kill me, you motherfucker.' He pushed his face to Diego's, forcing the barrel tight against his head, his eyes looking into the killer's eyes.

Diego's finger tightened on the trigger as Shattner looked at him fully, one hand on the wheel, one foot hovering over the precipice.

A long-haul truck overtook them in the fast lane, its horn blaring contemptuously, penetrating the car and cutting through the adrenaline.

Diego lowered the gun and said, 'Drive,' and fell silent.

Shattner turned to the road, his hands trembling slightly against the wheel; if Diego noticed them, he didn't say a word. After a while Diego wiped his face with the sleeve of his jacket.

'If you spit on me again, I will kill your son and Jose will fuck your daughter in front of you,' he said matter-of-factly.

It took a long time for Shattner's heart to start beating normally after that.

Diego made him drive all across Brooklyn, making random turns as he resumed his calls, speaking in a calmer voice.

It was past midnight when they reached the garage, no lights burning and no movement. Yet, when they entered the garage, a shadow detached itself from the other darker shadows.

Jose Cruz.

Diego went over to him and had a low conversation while Shattner waited in the Honda. Shattner didn't know what to expect now and had his Glock between his thighs, his hand on its grip, ready in case either Diego or Cruz or both opened fire on him.

They didn't.

After a very short conversation, which featured no cursing or yelling, Diego came over and got in. He made Shattner drive to Coney Island, to a car-recycling and salvage yard that Shattner suspected the gang owned. Diego disappeared in the depths of the yard and came back with a can of lighter fluid.

They doused the interior of the car with the fluid and lit it with a match.

It was the early hours of the morning by the time Shattner got to his apartment. He entered quietly and paused outside the bedroom, listening to Shawn and Lisa asleep, both of them accustomed to his absences, his children fast-forwarding to adulthood without him.

The weight of the day and the sight of his children brought him to his knees. He dimly wondered why he'd not been shot by the gang. If he was in their place, he would've shot a suspected snitch without a second thought.

Maybe I'm not the only one under suspicion. Or Diego wanted a white face around him to get away from that place, and now I can be killed.

He sat there for a long while trying to think in their shoes, and then gave up and dragged himself to the bathroom to clean up, and when he came out, his children were up and getting ready for school.

Lisa ran over to him, and he scooped her up, crushing her tight, feeling her small heart beat against his. 'I missed you, Daddy.' Her voice was muffled against his neck.

'I missed you too, princess,' he replied, his face in her hair, and the warmth of her breath and the fresh smell of her hair brought back the cold determination to set things right for them.

Once Shattner walked them to school, he made his plans. He wasn't sure how long his employment at the garage would last. He smiled grimly at that thought.

Heck, he wasn't sure how long he had to live.

He returned to their apartment, to the closet in the bedroom, and pulled out the lowermost section, right out of its slide. Taped to the rear of it was a thick wad of cash. He pulled out the drawer above it and removed another Glock 30 taped to its rear and three magazines of ammunition. He went to the kitchen and removed another stash of cash, another gun, and more ammunition.

He packed them in an anonymous satchel and caught the subway to Manhattan. He stowed one cache at a baggage locker near the Port Authority bus terminal and another at the cruise ship terminals. He then went to his regular small arms supplier and bought extra magazines and other odds and ends.

He would try to stick it out at the garage; he needed the money. But if necessary, he was ready to wage war.

Chapter 5

The garage was closed the next day.

Shattner peered above the gate and saw that the garage was deserted, with no movement from within. He looked to see if there was any notice put up about the closure; there was none.

After an hour of hanging about, he gave up and made a call to Diego. Diego didn't pick up, and after several rings his call went to voice mail. Shattner didn't leave a message. Diego wasn't into voice mail. He called the office number for the garage and, after several rings, got the teenager's recorded voice stating the opening times for the garage.

He hung around for another hour, trying Diego's number repeatedly with no response, before making his way slowly back to the apartment. The absence of any information was eating away at him, his mind conjuring various scenarios when the terrible thought struck him.

He stood still on the sidewalk, oblivious to the cursing of the pedestrians who were forced to flow around him.

He pulled out his phone and called the children's school. After a five-minute harangue with the receptionist, she put him on hold, and after a million years, the cool dry voice of Mrs. Harwood came on.

'Ah, the missing father. What's so important, Mr. Shattner, that you had me dragged out of a lesson?' Sarcasm. A New Yorker's birthright.

He breathed deeply, oxygen filling his mind, trying to blow away the mist in his head and mute the roaring in his ears.

'Mr. Shattner?'

'Mrs. Harwood, are my kids in school?'

A pause. 'Why wouldn't they be, Mr. Shattner?'

He squeezed the phone tightly as if by doing so he could get a better reply from her. 'Mrs. Harwood, are they in school right now?'

The cool voice went cold. 'I taught Lisa earlier today and saw her with her brother later. Is there something that the school should know?'

'Mrs. Harwood, this will sound insane, but could you please go and see for yourself that they're both in their lessons right at this minute? I'll hold. Please?'

'Mr. Shattner, I have seen both of them earlier today. Now, I have a lesson to teach, and I'm hanging up.'

'Mrs. Harwood, please. I shall never ask another favor of you, but please do me this one. Please check on them right this minute and let me know. Please!' Desperation cracked his voice and singed and burnt the air around him.

She went quiet for a minute and then said, 'Mr. Shattner, I don't know what's going on in your life. I'm not sure I want to know, but I have to ask. Are they in some danger? What exactly is happening that you have to ask this?'

'Mrs. Harwood, just this once, please go check on them.' Cities, continents, sun, life disappeared. Existence was reduced to the voice in his ear.

He heard nothing, just an empty line, and feared she had hung up on him, but no, there wasn't a dial tone. Just an empty silence. He crushed the phone harder to his ear as if that would bring her back, and then through the fog surrounding him, he heard her voice in his ear.

'Mr. Shattner? Mr. Shattner, are you there?'

He licked his lips and forced sound through his parched throat. 'Yes.'

The coldness was replaced by cool dryness. 'I'm happy to say they're both in their respective classes. Would you like me to message you a picture to your mobile?'

He cleared his throat once, then twice. The planet started spinning again. 'No, that won't be necessary. I apologize for the trouble and can't thank you enough.'

A pause and with it came the slightest softening in her voice. 'If there is some trouble, we might be able to help, Mr. Shattner.'

'No trouble, Mrs. Harwood. I was missing them, that's all.' It sounded lame even to his ears.

'Very well then,' came the brisk reply, 'I have to go back to my students, who no doubt will be thinking and behaving as if it was Christmas come early. You have a good day,' and she hung up.

Shattner stood there, the darkness disappearing, New York sprouting around him, making its presence felt again. He walked unsteadily to a nearby wooden bench, drawing huge gulps of air, a dead man revived. He sat there till the world had righted itself and then started thinking, analyzing, planning.

Clearly something had happened for the garage to shut down and Diego to go off the radar. He tried Diego's phone again a few more times and got no reply. He had to check if the gang was still operational, but first he had to drop off the radar, just in case.

He walked towards Thatford Avenue, taking care to check for tails and finding none. He stopped at a store and bought a change of clothes for the kids and himself and headed back to the school. He camped outside the school, a concrete structure that looked pretty uninspiring for a school – but most schools were these days. Drab on the outside, yet expected to churn out geniuses.

A burger and a bag of peanuts gave him brief company. At three p.m. the school regurgitated its contents, children streaming out of the gates and into the open doors of their parents' cars.

Through the crowd, Shattner spotted Shawn holding tightly to Lisa's hand, his daughter skipping and talking excitedly to him. Shattner held back, just drinking in their sight, feeling his skin and insides warm, and then stepped forward into Shawn's vision.

'Daddy,' his daughter screamed and hurled herself into his arms.

'Hello, princess, I wanted to surprise you,' he replied over her excitement. She kissed him on the cheek and started telling him about her day. He set her down and looked both of them in the eye.

'I have a surprise for you both, but I can't tell you what it is,' he told them solemnly.

Lisa started dancing on her toes and tugged at his hands. 'What is it, Daddy?'

'He said it's a surprise,' Shawn said in his big-brother superior voice.

'Daddy, won't you tell me, please?' Lisa pleaded with him.

Shattner shook his head and took their hands and started walking away from the school.

'I won't talk to you then, Daddy,' Lisa said in her most serious voice. They walked in silence for a minute, and then she burst out, 'Daddy, I mean it, if you don't tell me, I won't talk to you.'

Shattner grinned down at her and winked at Shawn. 'I heard you the first time, princess.'

She pouted and flounced along and then burst into giggles as he tickled her. He drank in her laughter greedily, drawing sustenance from it. He walked them to the subway at Rockaway Avenue, Lisa barely able to contain her excitement as they walked down the subway stairs and bought the tickets.

'Are we going somewhere, Dad?' This time it was Shawn who could not contain his curiosity.

Shattner smiled and nodded and directed them to the platform going towards Manhattan. He looked around discreetly, noticing nothing out of the ordinary. They were part of the anonymous commuting populace, merging into their inescapable routine. During the subway ride, Shawn kept Lisa entertained while Shattner organized his thoughts and planned his next steps. The motion of the train lulled his children to sleep, and he held Lisa in his arms as the train sped from light to dark and light again.

He roused them when the subway was approaching the Upper West Side and got them off on Eighty-Sixth Street. He checked them into a run-down but still decent hotel, paid in cash, and settled them in their room.

He arranged the children's stuff in the wardrobe in the room, the highest shelf holding his bag with his gun and phone, its battery removed. He let the kids have a shower and freshened himself up quickly and then set up the takeaway dinner they had ordered from a diner.

Lisa was barely awake when they finished and went to sleep soon after he had changed her clothes. Shawn was tired but awake, knowing that something had happened to make his dad change their routine.

When Lisa was asleep, he sat up in the narrow bed and looked at his father expectantly. Shattner ruffled his hair. 'I'm taking you out of school for a few days. I have some work in this part of the city, and once I finish it, we'll go back and start school.'

Shawn's mouth opened in an 'O' as he processed all this.

'Dad, how many days will we miss? Mrs. Harwood will have to be told.'

'Done.' Shattner ticked in the air. 'I told the dragon about it and made her feel nice about letting you both have some days off. And we'll be here two or three days, at the max.'

Shawn frowned as another thought struck him. 'What will we do when you're away, Dad?'

'Oh, ye of little faith.' Shattner pulled him toward his chest. 'Your superman dad has taken care of that too. There's a daycare center here that's very good. I've checked both of you in for

38

tomorrow, and you can spend the whole day there. You'll enjoy it. My buddies rate it highly.

'No dragon, no schoolwork, just fun and games all day,' he continued.

Shawn pumped his fist and whispered loudly, 'Yes! I can't wait to tell Lisa.'

He grinned widely at Shattner, his dimples pronounced. 'You were planning this all along, weren't you, Dad?'

Shattner nodded, his heart clenching, and sat with him till he fell asleep.

And felt like the smallest person in the greatest city on earth.

Chapter 6

He awoke in the morning without conscious thought and lay on his bed for a while, orienting himself.

The city made itself known through the constant growl of traffic coming through the thin windows. He got up and did his customary survey of the street below through his hotel window and then went to the wardrobe and turned on his phone again.

No messages, no voice mail, no missed calls.

He looked across the room to check if his children were still sleeping and then called the garage first and then Diego. He got no response from either of the numbers and pulled apart the phone again and slipped it into his pocket.

He woke his children and spent a couple of hours with them, pushing back the real world as long as he could, but finally it was time to get them to the daycare center and check them in.

An hour later, he was driving a yellow cab, after paying its driver handsomely for the day, driving back to Brooklyn. In the passenger seat was a map of Brooklyn with six red crosses marked on it.

5Clubs had stashes for the crack and meth and stuff they moved all across the borough, and those red crosses were the stashes that Shattner knew of.

If the warehouses were operational, the gang was operational.

The stashes were not your conventional warehouses. They were apartments in which families lived.

The occupants were usually gang families or connected to the gang in some way and got to live free in the apartments in return for having the drugs stashed in their homes. It was a neat setup by Cruz and worked so well that not once had any of his warehouses been raided. His genius lay in the location of those apartments. Some of those were in the most run-down, deprived neighborhoods of Brooklyn, such as Brownsville, and some were in the wealthiest neighborhoods, such as Brooklyn Heights.

Shattner drew up to the first address, a single-family home that housed a gang member and his wife and three kids, a two-storied building off Christopher Avenue and Newport Street in Brownsville. As soon as he drove on Newport Street, he realized this was a bad idea.

He was the only white male driving a cab in the neighborhood, and if he stepped out of the cab, he would stick out and be remembered. He drew near as slowly as he could without drawing attention, spotted the house on his left ahead, and slowed down further.

Nothing. No one.

He debated coming back up the street for a second pass, but discarded that thought and headed to the next cross.

He made his way past upmarket cafés and bistros till he came to an imposing apartment block in Brooklyn Heights. The apartment was on the third floor and was occupied by a lawyer who represented 5Clubs. The apartment was guarded whenever it housed a load.

Shattner parked his cab a block away and hoofed it across to the apartment block, grabbing his caffeine fix on the way. He walked past the block, his cap pulled low, and peered inside the entrance through the corner of his eyes, but couldn't see anything. He knew the block had CCTV coverage, and he reckoned he could make a couple of more passes safely before he attracted attention.

It was on his third pass, when he had almost given up, that he saw Aleksander, one of the gang's hit men, talking with the concierge in the entrance. Aleksander was a nasty piece of work; Shattner had seen him casually break the knee of a bystander near the garage just because Joe Bystander had stopped in his tracks to make a phone call and Aleksander had bumped into him from behind.

Aleksander's presence indicated the gang was still operational, so the garage was closed for other reasons.

Maybe Shattner was suspected of being a snitch by Diego and Cruz, and hence the garage was closed till Shattner was taken care of. Shattner didn't know and didn't waste time speculating. He glanced at his wrist. Just past noon and still time for his next visit, one he was not looking forward to.

Elaine Rocka was born with a scowl and an opinion and never failed to display either or both at the slightest provocation. Which explained why she had run through three husbands and had no children. Husband number three had left her a sprawling five-bedroom home in the Bronx where Elaine now lived with a couple of cats and dogs for company. If her opinions bothered her pets, they didn't let on.

Elaine Rocka was Shattner's sister-in-law.

She had never liked him and hadn't ever hidden that dislike. She thought her sister had ruined her life by marrying him.

Elaine Rocka had one redeeming quality in Shattner's eyes.

She loved his kids and never lost an opportunity to keep them with her. Shattner drove the cab to Pelham Bay in the Bronx and wove his way to Laurie Avenue. He parked outside the short driveway, climbed the few steps and banged the knocker, fully knowing she didn't like it banged. He could hear the deep silence in the house, and then a dog barked from its deep interior, and he could hear steps approaching the door.

Elaine flung open the door, robustly built and elegantly dressed; her scowl threatened to split her face apart when she saw Shattner.

'Prick,' she said by way of greeting. She turned her back on him and polished the brass knocker, which was shining brighter than a mirror, with a cloth tucked away in her waistband.

'What do you want?' she asked coarsely. 'Ran out of bread and come begging again?' referring to the one time Shattner had asked her for financial help after his discharge from the army.

'The kids,' Shattner replied, stuttering a little in her formidable presence, 'could you keep them for a few days while I sort out some issues at work?'

Her eyes narrowed. 'In deep shit again, are you? Right, I forgot. That's where you wallow normally, don't you?'

'Elaine, please... I need your help. Can you take them in just for a few days? I wouldn't have come to you if I could put them up with someone else.'

A wrist shot out and grabbed Shattner's shirt. 'Put them with someone else, would you, you prick? Where are they?' Her eyes moved past him and searched over his shoulder.

'They aren't here. I'll bring them in the evening,' Shattner replied as he tried to pry himself loose from a grip that was suffocating him.

'What about that tight bitch? What have you told her?' Elaine asked him, politely referring to Mrs. Harwood.

'That they're unwell and that they're visiting you for a few days.'

'Six p.m. Don't be late. They need to be fed,' she said as she stepped back into her home and started shutting the door in his face.

Shattner dug into his pocket and brought out a roll of bills and handed them to her. The heavy hand pushed him back, and he stumbled on the steps.

'I don't need your wad, you prick. Only the kids.' The door slammed in his face, her dogs barking a contemptuous chorus in farewell.

Shattner went to his cab and sat a long while. He observed the slight trembling of his hands, the tight band of pressure around him taking its toll. He picked up the phone to try the garage and then dropped it when it rang, the shrill tone unexpected and grating in the confines of the car. He looked at the display and saw that it was an unknown number.

He held it to his ear. 'Hello?'

'Chollo, we have to meet tomorrow, come to the place where we did the first transfer, at eleven.' Diego's voice was harsh, brooking no refusal.

'Diego, where the fuck are you, man? The garage has shut down, and you aren't picking up your phone. What's going on, man?'

'Tomorrow, eleven.' Diego hung up, ignoring his questions.

Shattner took deep breaths, calming himself, and looked at his hands. They were still trembling. They always did when the threat level went off the scale. He looked at Elaine's house and thanked himself for making the arrangement with her.

Shattner brought his kids to her house promptly at six in the evening. They were ecstatic when they heard they would be spending a few more days away from school, with their aunt Elaine.

She doted on them and spoiled them silly, and they took full advantage of that.

Lisa unbuckled and scrambled out of the car even before he had turned off the ignition when they reached Pelham Bay. By the time Shawn and he had got their bags out, she had leapt into Elaine's arms, the dogs yelping and running excited circles around her.

'Prick,' mouthed Elaine silently in Shattner's direction and then bent down and crushed Shawn in a hug.

'Cookies and milk first, homework second, and play afterwards. You know my rules,' she told Lisa and Shawn sternly, and then she grinned widely, 'and you know what I think about stupid rules!' She high-fived them and shepherded them inside and then turned back and stiff-armed Shattner outside the door as he was stepping inside.

'Not you, prick. Your job is done,' she hissed, out of earshot of the kids.

'But, Elaine, I need to—'

'You need to disappear,' she said, cutting him off and slamming the door in his face.

Shattner, his face burning, banged the door again till she flung it open, stony faced. From inside he could hear the excitement in the kids' voices as they reacquainted themselves with her dogs and cats.

'There's a mobile in Shawn's bag with some instructions. He should use the phone only in an emergency. Lisa's stuff is in her bag. I left a locker key in her bag, with some instructions. I'll be back in a couple of days and will keep you posted... I've closed the loop at school for them. Let me say bye to them,' he pleaded.

'Bye. I'll tell them.' The door slammed in his face again.

Shattner stood there looking at the door, a wave of helpless anger sweeping over him. He forced a deep breath and walked back to the car. As he turned the key, he looked back at the house, hoping to see Lisa and Shawn in the windows, but knew that Elaine's warmth had temporarily displaced him from their minds.

Elaine hated his guts, but would take care of his kids.

Forever, if she had to. If he did not return.

Part 2

Chapter 7

Broker stretched his long legs ahead of him and admired his Louboutin shoes. Broker was dressed in an immaculate gray suit, a white shirt of the finest Egyptian cotton and those shoes. With his shoulder-length shaggy blond hair, blue eyes, and executive threads, he was New Age surfer dude – equally at home in the boardroom as on the beach. He drew second glances from women and grinned unabashedly at them when their eyes met.

Broker was just that, a dealer who traded in information. The intel he traded in was sought after by governments, politicians, oil companies, intelligence agencies, security companies; in fact, just about anyone who could afford him. He had a real name, but *Broker* had stuck to him for so long that it was what he went by.

Lobbying firms came to him to know about the sexual peccadilloes of senators. Government agencies approached him to cross-check their intel on nuclear material on sale. Politicians consulted him to see which Middle Eastern leader was supportive of government policy. Oil companies wrote him blank checks to find out which African despot preferred which oil company. Russian oligarchs consulted him on which banks in the world offered the most secure and anonymous deposits. Mercenaries or private military security firms came to him to get the lie of the land in the most dangerous hot spots on the planet.

Broker was an equal opportunity vendor of information, with a few iron-clad rules. No trade with the dark side. No trade in information of any kind on women and children. No trade in anything against the national interest. Broker preferred to deal with those who used his information for the greater good, and he had often thrown clients out if he felt they were misusing his intel.

Broker had grown up in Lawrenceburg, Kentucky, with foster parents who had brought him up as their own child. They had lost their only daughter to a rare form of blood cancer when she was six, and when young Broker came into their lives, they showered all their love on him. His father was the county clerk and instilled a strong sense of right and wrong in his son, a set of moral values that were reinforced by his homemaker wife. They were the proudest parents in town when Broker enlisted, and they organized civic receptions for him whenever he visited them, much to his embarrassment.

Broker's ties to the town were severed when his parents were killed in a car accident. A drunk had lost control of his truck on an icy road and had rammed into their compact.

He had started his career as an intelligence analyst in the US Army, and his unique way of analyzing, identifying patterns and correlating seemingly disparate incidents had not only secured him a fast growth through the ranks, but also put him on first-name terms with four- and five-star generals in the Pentagon.

Broker had been one of a kind as an intelligence analyst since he also got deployed with Special Forces covert and overt missions to read the local situation. It helped that he could handle a long gun much better than the average soldier.

He had injured his leg in his last mission and still had the faintest trace of a limp. He had retired from the army after that mission, set up shop as a trader of information, and had discovered a natural flair for business that had made him immensely wealthy. He had an army of analysts working for him, and the best paid informants and hackers in various parts of the world. He still got actively involved in certain projects, and one such project had brought him to the small coffee shop in Dupont Circle in Washington.

Broker let the aroma of hot coffee and the ebb and flow of conversation in the café wash over him, creating a moment of suspended time. The white door swished in and Broker's meeting stepped in. The man took a sidestep and paused, waiting for his eyes to get accustomed to the darkened interior of the café.

Washington, D.C., was home to only two animals.

Ones who were important and others who thought they were. General Daniel Klouse belonged to the former species.

He stumped across the café on spotting Broker, pulled out a chair, and sat into it heavily, glaring at Broker. Washington was hell on his left leg.

A high-velocity concrete slab had taken a shine to it when a suicide bomber had driven through the gates of the US Marine battalion headquarters in Beirut with a truck bomb. It was many years back, but at times like this, in the heat, it felt like yesterday.

Despite his leg being nearly crushed by the concrete slab, General Klouse had dragged himself out of the rubble, using a metal pipe as a makeshift crutch, had taken command of the aftermath, and secured not only the safety of the survivors, but also had mounted a defense. His swift, courageous handling had taken him to the rarefied air in the Pentagon, and when the White House was looking to make a high-profile yet experienced appointee, General Klouse's name was the only one on the short list.

General Klouse was the National Security Advisor. He was also that rarest of animals in Washington, an apolitical one, and because of that, he was the President's most trusted confidant.

'This stuff you gave me about the North Koreans,' the General began without any preliminaries after pulling out a sheaf of papers from inside his jacket, 'where did you get it? The NSA and the others were gagging for it, threw their best at it, and came up with the big fat zero. So how come a nobody analyst like you got it?'

'General, I got a few things going for me that none of your agencies have. Mine is a private enterprise, for one. I pay big bucks for my information. And lastly, I am trusted. My sources know they will never be fingered or subpoenaed or WikiLeaked if they work with me.' Broker smiled at him.

He added, 'The Pentagon and many intelligence agencies around the world wouldn't agree with your description – a "nobody" analyst.' Broker was modest.

The General grunted and leafed through the documents. After a while he looked up. 'These are genuine?'

Broker spread his arms and gave him a what-else-did-you-expect look, but Klouse was staring off into the distance and didn't notice his gesture. Broker ordered them another round of coffees and waited for the General to finish his thinking. This meeting had been requested by the General, and Broker was curious to know why one of the most powerful people in the country wanted to meet him. Broker had given him the North Korean intel to prove his credentials even though he knew it wasn't required.

'I believe you've heard of Isakson.' General Klouse turned to him after taking a sip of his coffee.

Broker shrugged noncommittally. 'We have met.'

'That wasn't the way he put it to me.' There was a ghost of a smile on the General's face.

Broker had run into Isakson, a Special Agent in Charge in the FBI, when rescuing Lauren Balthazar, the wife of a prominent journalist, and her son, Rory, from a group of rogue mercenaries.

Broker and his ex-Special Ops friend, Zeb Carter, had been pursuing Carsten Holt, the ringleader of the rogue mercenaries, who had fled to the US after committing horrific atrocities in the Congo.

Zeb and Broker hadn't known that Holt was cozy with the FBI.

Isakson had asked them to back off when he'd found out about their pursuit, but the situation became a clusterfuck when Holt grabbed the hostages.

Zeb and Broker, ignoring Isakson's by-the-book approach, had mounted a rescue and had secured their release.

Isakson was not on Broker's Christmas card list.

'Isakson is tipped to be Deputy Director of the FBI,' the General continued, but was interrupted by Broker.

'Director Murphy signed his appointment today, in the early hours of the morning, an official announcement yet to be made. But then I'm sure you know that.'

That ghost of a smile appeared fleetingly again. 'Yes, I can see why you are so well spoken of. Isakson got appointed because of one quality of his that outweighed the better credentials of the others in the fray. Isakson is incorruptible. Totally.

'You need to talk to him again. I think he could do with some help.' The General sipped his coffee.

'I think we know Clare in common.' General Klouse nodded at him, and Broker nodded back, now knowing who had referred him to the General.

'Clare speaks highly of you... and a few other associates of yours.'

Clare was the Director of the Agency, an agency that did not exist in any form. It had no paperwork, no legal entities, no personnel, nothing. The Agency ran the most clandestine black ops in the most volatile or strategically important hot spots in the world and worked with a rarefied set of contractors. Broker and his associates were that rarefied set. Clare had the nebulous title of Director of Strategy and reported directly to the President.

'I need someone from the outside to work with Isakson and help him on a matter. Someone who has access to intelligence, who is not hampered by bureaucracy, can cut through the crap, and pull the trigger. Someone who the FBI has not used before.'

'General, if Isakson wanted to talk to me, he could have gotten in touch himself. Or Director Murphy could have. Or Clare. This is not a matter I expected the National Security Advisor to get involved in.'

General Klouse looked at him, and for the briefest moment the professional mask dropped from his eyes and impatient steel shined from within. They hooded over quickly as the General considered his words.

'Would you have taken Isakson's call? Or called him if Clare asked you to?'

Broker remained silent.

'I thought not,' continued the General. 'This matter is important, so important that I requested this meeting. Isakson needs your help. Talk to him, please.'

Broker still said nothing, but nodded almost imperceptibly.

General Klouse sat back and finished his coffee. 'Have you heard anything different up for sale in your network? Anything so unusual that it pinged your radar?'

'Such as? Help me here, General.'

'Such as drones. Nuclear-powered drones. Highly sophisticated drones capable of flying themselves for all practical purposes, reducing or eliminating the need for the operator sitting thousands of miles away.'

Broker was aware of research into such drones, but the research hadn't resulted in military-use drones in the field. The government had shelved development plans because of public opinion over the use of such drones. If such a drone crashed, it effectively became a dirty bomb. However, if such a drone could be made so reliable that it flew itself and could protect itself... Broker's brain raced.

He shook his head. 'Nope. Nothing even remotely resembling that. Believe me, General, that kind of intel would have had me hotfooting across to my old friends.' He indicated in the direction of the Pentagon.

'May not be a drone in its full form. Could be their designs, their power cells, guidance systems, and weapons systems... anything related to them.'

'No, sir. I always keep my eyes out for such sensitive information. There has been the usual stuff about enriched uranium, nuclear warheads, Hellfire missiles... the usual assortment, but not the slightest whisper of drones or drone related. Is there–' He stopped to rephrase his words. 'Have any designs or components gone missing?'

General Klouse shook his head. 'Thank Christ, no. However, they are high on the shopping list of the Chinese, the Russians, the Iranians, the Indians, the North Koreans. Heck, all the armies in the world want a nuclear-powered drone or two, or want the design blueprints. The National Security Agency has heard the odd rumor or two that quite a few countries are going all-out to lay their hands on a prototype or the designs. Now such rumors always go around, but the source of these whispers made the NSA flag this and bring it to my attention.'

'Sir, do such prototypes exist?' Broker asked carefully, looking the General in the eye.

The General looked weary, looked his age. 'Son, you've been in this game long enough. You know our government's stance on such drones. I can't say anything more on this.'

Broker finally punctured the long ensuing silence.

'Sir, don't the Chinese have a drone program already? Wouldn't they develop their own nuclear-powered drones? Why would they want to steal ours?'

'They do. All countries having a drone program probably have some research going into such drones. However, we've always been decades ahead of any country in military research and arms development, and stealing research or prototypes from us would bridge those decades for them.'

Broker leaned back in his chair to take it all in, making the National Security Advisor lean forward.

'I want you to be on the alert for any intel on this. Anything. A mouse squeaks "drone" in Siberia, I want to hear it. You hear Arabic whispers about blueprints, you come running to me. You come *only* to me. No one else wants to be seen working with private intelligence contractors except Clare, and she does things her way anyway. Me, I don't care for appearances or political niceties. I took an oath to defend this country, and the more ears I have on the ground, the easier I can sleep.'

Broker grinned humorlessly. 'Sir, I'm not sure if Clare has said this, my business is selling intel to whoever is buying, but I have some rules. I do not sell any intel that goes against the country and neither do I trade in intel on women or children. I would have gone to the Pentagon anyway if I had gotten any intel on drones of any kind.'

The grizzled veteran softened. 'I know, son, and Clare has briefed me fully on you as well as your associates. I am aware of some of the assignments you guys have undertaken.'

He removed a card from his jacket and scribbled a number on its back and pushed it across to Broker. 'My direct number. Call me anytime, you need anything or if you're having any problems with Isakson.'

Broker nodded. He knew the General meant it. He was old school. He had never married, had no children, and had no life other than serving his country.

As he was leaving, he patted Broker on the back and smiled at him fully for the first time. 'Call Isakson, son. That takes priority over anything else. Don't let this meeting go in vain.'

Broker sat there for a long while thinking over the meeting. There were a million other ways a meeting could have been arranged with Isakson. The fact that the National Security Advisor had come in person indicated that whatever shit Isakson was dealing with had a stench so strong that it had reached the White House.

It also meant that the NSA was figuring on cultivating his own private intelligence source and wanted to assess Broker in person for that.

In the end it didn't matter. Broker would meet Isakson and hear him out, but would take his time about it.

Isakson and he had history. Isakson's slow-footed approach and bungling in the rescue of the hostages had cost Broker dearly.

Broker had lost his best friend, his brother operative Zebadiah Carter, in that rescue. They had secured the safe release of the hostages, and Holt had been killed, but Zeb hadn't survived the rescue.

Never a day passed that Broker did not miss Zeb.

The barista behind the counter had been flirting with Broker all day. She was several years younger than him, but he appealed to her. There was something to him, and she had been planning to slip him her number when he came up to pay the check.

She glanced at him from the corner of her eyes as she was serving another customer, and her heart skipped a beat. Gone was the humor in his face, and in its place was a cold, dark look. She looked back to her customer, smiling brightly. On second thoughts, he reminded her of a wolf, best left alone.

Chapter 8

Broker caught an evening flight back to New York, and it was close to midnight by the time he reached his apartment on Columbus Avenue, near Central Park. His apartment also doubled as his office; in fact, he had a couple of other such establishments across the downtown area. One never knew when one apartment would be compromised, and in his line of business, redundancy always paid.

The door to his apartment was wood, with a plain finish; inside the door was armored steel that was thick enough to stop everything thrown at it short of a rocket launch. The steel could retract in the frame of the building if needed, turning the door to a more ordinary one. To the right of the door was a DNA and iris scanner under a concealed flap. Broker stepped in and turned off the invisible lasers and all the other nasties in store for an intruder. He headed to his office and booted up his machine after pouring himself a rich black coffee from the Jura on a corner table.

Broker spent the next couple of hours tweaking the spiders he had on the Internet, which were his ears to all the chatter that passed online. Other programs overlaid the chatter with real-time events, such as the visit of the Iranian Defense Minister to North Korea, Somalian pirates capturing a Pakistani merchant vessel, China buying mines in Australia.

Werner, his artificial intelligence engine, brought all these together and came up with various hypotheses. His analysts then took the hypotheses and correlated those with the humint and created the finished product – the most sought-after intel that had made Broker the best known intelligence trader.

The Pentagon and the National Security Agency had tried to buy Werner several times. Broker wasn't selling.

After a nap, Broker called a couple of numbers late in the morning.

'This had better be good,' growled a voice from the first number he called. Bear – six foot five and as wide as a barnyard door, all of it hard muscle, and sporting a thick beard, which was why he was called that – was never a morning person when he was in between assignments. Bear and his partner, Chloe, specialized in close body protection. Amongst other things.

'And a good morning to you too.' Broker smiled.

'Hell, man, you know me by now.' Bear yawned hugely, looking out at the sun bathing Los Angeles. 'How's the chatter business?'

'Still pays my bills. What are you guys up to now? Chloe around?'

'She's gone for her 10K run. You know how she is with her running and walking. I've told her many times that the Good Lord let man invent wheels for a reason.'

Broker chuckled. Bear was as fit as any top operative, but never saw the point in not taking it easy when he could. Chloe, a physical contrast to Bear with her petite, dark-haired frame, ran a 10K on days she took it easy.

Afghanistan was where they had met, the heat and the mountains providing a backdrop to their wordless romance.

Born an army brat, Chloe Sundstrom had moved from base to base all over the world, and had seen her father retire as an E-8 in

60

the 101st Airborne. A single child, she was treated as an adult by her parents at a very early age, and Master Sergeant Sundstrom's 'No sweat, no cake' motto in life, became hers too.

Joining the army was a natural choice for her, and determined to see active duty, she was also hell-bent on going farther than her dad. That determination drove her through college ROTC with a scholarship, through Airborne School at Fort Benning, and the 82nd Airborne got a newly minted Second Lieutenant.

Operation Allied Force in Kosovo was Chloe's first major deployment, when the 2nd Battalion, 505th Parachute Infantry Regiment was sent to the Albanian Kosovan border to support NATO's bombing of the Serbian forces in the Former Yugoslav Republic.

The battalion later became the first ground force to go in the Balkans. Army women weren't supposed to be deployed in combat roles... in reality they got in the thick of action just as male soldiers did; it just wasn't public knowledge. Chloe was a battle-hardened veteran by the time the 82nd's soldiers were deployed to Afghanistan for Operation Enduring Freedom. Afghanistan was a country ravaged by decades of war, a land where tribes frequently fought each other, a land where hope struggled to survive.

It was also a land of great beauty, dotted with villages where time moved much slower. Chloe fell in love with the towering stillness of the Hindu Kush Mountains first, and the rest of the land won her over.

It was the country where she fell in love.

The Special Operations teams from the 5th Special Forces Group (Airborne) were stationed in the same base as hers, and it was hard to miss Sergeant Bozo (Bear) Parvizi.

The Special Forces teams tended to keep to themselves and carried an aura around them. Bear didn't need auras. With his height and presence, Bear just was. He had noticed Chloe, her liquid ease in the heat of Afghanistan, her cool glances when their gazes met, a magnet in the mess hall.

They spent their entire time in that hot spot without uttering a word to each other, but had a heightened awareness when the other was in proximity. Chloe had tracked Bear down when they both left the army – it wasn't difficult, since Bear was searching for her too – and the mute romance found its voice.

Bear was the middle child in a family of five and had to compete harder for attention from his parents than his other siblings. In a family that was loud and raucous, Bear was different. He was an introvert and had no interest in joining the family business in Saint Paul. The family ran a wildly successful take-away business, the only one in the city that combined Persian and Italian cuisine. Bear's dad was of Persian origin; his mother of Italian descent.

While his brothers manned the counter, took orders, helped in the kitchen, or drove through the town, delivering, Bear dreamt of wider spaces, of places where he was accepted for who he was.

A bright student, he crushed high school, and just as his parents harbored ambitions of him being a doctor or a lawyer, he broke the news to them that he'd joined University of Minnesota's ROTC course.

They spent months bitterly arguing with him, trying to get him to consider other career choices, but Bear was adamant.

Bear's relationship with his family never recovered, and at his annual commissioning ceremony, he was the only graduate who had no family attending. Bear swallowed his disappointment, squared his shoulders, and 2nd Lieutenant Bozo Parvizi made the army his family.

'And no, we aren't doing anything. A few jobs have come up but weren't interesting enough. You got something for us?' Bear asked with a hopeful note in his voice.

'Someone has reached out to me. Might be nothing, might be something. Stay loose.' Broker gave him some more details and then hung up.

The second number that Broker called rang for a long time before being picked up.

'What?' barked a voice.

Broker looked at his phone for a moment. Phone manners. He blamed the Internet for their death.

'That cost me a five-pounder, so get on with it,' growled the voice without waiting for Broker's acknowledgement.

'Where are you guys?' Broker finally got a word in.

'Broker? Hell, why didn't you say so. Your number didn't show.' The voice lightened.

Broker rolled his eyes. Before he could answer, he heard another voice in the background shouting.

'Rog, what the fuck are you doing there? You can talk to your girlfriend all day later. Come over here and help me,' said the voice irritatedly.

'It's Broker,' Roger shouted back.

There was a pause, and then the voice shouted back, 'Does he have work for us?'

'Bwana asks if you have work for us,' Roger dutifully reported back to Broker.

Broker laughed. 'I heard. Not yet but maybe soon. Where are you guys?'

Roger ignored him and called out, 'Nope, he says maybe soon.'

'Well, then, hang up and get over here.' Bwana's voice rose again.

'Hell, you're doing fine without me. Let me talk to Broker,' Roger replied back.

'Why am I not surprised? The black guy ends up on the shit detail always,' grumbled Bwana, his voice fading away as he got back to whatever he was doing.

'We're down south, near the Mexican border, our side of it.' Roger got back to Broker. 'We were in Mexico a few weeks back, on a job for their government, and since that finished, we've been on a fishing holiday, drifting our way upwards. How're you doing, and where are Bear and Chloe?'

'I'm good, and they're in L.A. They too are between assignments. Listen, do you have anything lined up?'

'Nope. You know how we hate hard work! We might start looking out for some work once we reach the Midwest, but for now, we're good.'

'Fab. I might have something for you shortly. There is something bubbling away, and it might come to a boil soon.'

Roger turned serious. 'Broker, you just have to say the word and we'll drop whatever we're doing and turn up. Shooting, if necessary.'

'Yup, I know. Stay cool,' Broker replied and hung up.

Broker leant back in his chair in satisfaction. He had his team.

Clare had set up the Agency to take on the deepest black assignments that no other intelligence or defense agency would undertake. Taking down terrorist cells, tracking down stolen nuclear warheads, infiltrating intelligence agencies of rogue nations, rescuing high-value hostages, and sanctioned assassinations... the assignments were varied and were *all* deniable.

To maintain deniability and anonymity, she wanted an elite team who was comfortable with living and working in the shadows. She had come across Zebadiah Carter because she knew his sister, Cassandra, who had been her roomie at Bryn Mawr. She'd been intrigued when Cass had casually mentioned her brother as being some kind of Special Ops superman, and when she'd read his file – which only a handful of people had access to – she'd been impressed.

Zeb Carter had quit the Special Forces and was a private military contractor. A mercenary for those who didn't believe in political correctness.

Zeb was a merc with a difference. He took on only those assignments that fit his tight moral code, and one of those codes was nothing against the national interest. The other was no war on women and children.

She had sounded him out about working with her, and it was Zeb who'd suggested that they create a team of elite agents who were all mercenaries, but whose first allegiance was to the Agency. She had left Zeb to build the team, knowing that he would not only handpick the best from the best, but also those who shared his moral code.

Zeb came back to her with the profiles of Broker, Bear, Chloe, Bwana and Roger – all of them ex- Special Forces and in Broker's case, ex-Ranger – and the Agency was in business. Zeb was their leader, and Broker his right-hand man. She had once laughingly referred to them as her Warriors.

The name stuck.

Broker picked up the tail easily the next day. They were a two-man tag team who alternated every couple of blocks as Broker strolled down Fifth Avenue toward Lower Manhattan. They were good, but they stayed on him a bit too long before alternating. Broker's radar pinged in the second block, and he casually slipped on a pair of shades.

These weren't ordinary shades.

Broker had taken a pair of Ray-Ban Aviator shades and had outfitted them with the tiniest pinhole cameras looking rearward. The cameras projected tiny images on the inner lenses, images that the eyes could read easily. The cameras projected in either video or still mode by flicking a tiny switch on the hinge of the shades.

Broker made the operatives easily once he reached East Thirty-Fifth Street. He ambled into a café and nursed his caffeine fix as he thought. They were well dressed, but not expensively dressed so not from a hotshot security company and neither were they from rent-a-cop. He went through the assignments on his plate currently, and whilst all of them carried a significant risk, he didn't think any of those assignments had led to these tails. They could be onto him because someone was interested in knowing why he'd met the National Security Advisor, but Broker was reasonably sure who these tails were and why they were following him.

He walked out of the café and looked in the direction of the tails. One of them was reading a newspaper, or pretending to read, in front of a salon, and the other wasn't visible. Broker was sure he was hanging well back, maybe as far back as Thirty-Eighth Street, the two in radio communication constantly. Broker went back into the café, picked up his half-finished drink, and walked in the direction of the tail. He approached the tail and made eye contact and held it till the tail looked away. Broker noticed the barely discernible tensing in his body. The tail pulled the newspaper closer to his face and pretended to read. Broker stopped about ten feet away, leaned against a lamppost, and sipped his drink, keeping his eye on the tail.

He knew what would happen next, and sure enough, the tail half turned away from him, and Broker saw his lips move. Calling out to his counterpart and control, no doubt.

The black Suburban came by twenty minutes later. It rolled up a few feet from Broker, and a figure stepped out, followed by a couple of others behind him from the rear.

Broker knew him well.

Deputy Director of the FBI, Isakson.

Chapter 9

The two tails were FBI agents put on him by Isakson, Broker guessed. He kept quiet and let Isakson approach him.

'We meet again, Broker,' Isakson greeted him.

'The General said you would call, but I had a feeling you wouldn't. When nothing came from you in the last couple of days, I had to act, and hence these two.' He indicated the two agents.

'You realize they were tailing you noticeably so that you could spot them,' Isakson continued after a slight pause when Broker still kept silent.

'What do you want?' Broker asked him finally after Isakson had run out of what passed for small talk, for him.

'We need to talk.'

'We have talked. All of five seconds. Five seconds too much. We're done now.'

'Broker, we need your help. I wouldn't have reached out via the National Security Advisor if it wasn't important.'

'Say your piece.'

'Not here. Let's go to Federal Plaza.'

Broker thought about it for a moment and gave a short nod. He got into the second row of seats, and the agent sitting there moved to the rear, joining the other two. It was a silent ride back, and Broker made no attempt to break the uncomfortable silence.

It was Isakson who had requested this; it was he who had to make all the moves.

Broker turned down Isakson's offer of a coffee when they reached Federal Plaza and sat silently in an expansive office bearing Isakson's full title on the door, waiting for Isakson to get to it. Isakson took his time, helping himself to a drink from an expensive-looking coffee maker. *My tax dollars at work*, Broker thought silently.

'How have you been?' Isakson asked him politely when he had seated himself.

Broker waved him away impatiently, but still didn't say anything.

'I know what you think of me, and if I was in your shoes, I'd probably think the same. But I couldn't have acted any differently in those circumstances,' Isakson said, referring to the hostage situation in which Zeb was killed.

Broker took a deep breath and interrupted Isakson. 'Let's not go there. You have fifteen minutes to tell me what you want to tell me. You'd better make best use of those fifteen minutes.'

If Isakson had kept Zeb and Broker in the loop and worked with them, as Holt was sucking up to the FBI, the rescue attempt would have turned out differently; Zeb would still be alive. But Isakson did everything by the book and didn't see life any other way.

A dull flush spread across Isakson's face, but he held his temper.

'We suspect a traitor in the FBI, and we need your help in finding him or her,' he said bluntly.

Broker leant back in his seat and allowed it to sink in. 'And why do you think you have one?'

Isakson laughed humorlessly. 'Broker, we're not as incompetent as you make us out to be. We can connect the dots when operations get sabotaged, or when a tightly controlled takedown returns empty-handed because the assholes got wind of it.'

He took a deep breath. 'Let me start at the beginning.

'The crime scene in New York has changed for the better over the last couple of decades. As you might well know, it peaked in the early nineties and then has been reducing each year. Not many people believe that crime is so low and seek various explanations when they see the statistics. The simple reason is better policing, better procedures and systems, such as the adoption of CompStat – a management process for improved policing – have led to crime reducing over the years.'

He paused to stand up and walk around in his office. Broker noticed it was bare. No family photographs, no awards, no photos with important people, no posters, no slogans, nothing. There was just one creased poster on a wall – Sherpa Tenzing Norqay atop Mount Everest, the date printed at the bottom: twenty-ninth of May in nineteen fifty-three.

'Organized crime,' continued Isakson, 'also declined. There were many Mafia prosecutions in the late nineties. The clashes between the Bloods and the Latin Kings diminished. Everything was good. And then, five years back, a new gang turned up.

'The thing with gangs is that most of them are based on some ethnic affiliation or some shared story. Bloods in New York had

71

their origins on Rikers Island. Latin Kings have mostly Hispanic members.

'This new gang has no ethnic affiliation. They have black members, white, Hispanic, East European, Asian... The shared story they have in common is military service. Many of their members have served in the US armed forces, South American forces, or NATO forces. Many are mercenaries who have seen action in Africa or Europe or the Middle East... obviously these guys are not your Pentagon four-star material. They are the dregs, the scum, court-martialed bastards. Several of them are deserters, some discharged from their forces under a cloud.'

'You're talking about 5Clubs, aren't you?'

Isakson nodded grimly and leaned against the window overlooking the street below, thick glass separating sound and silence.

'Their service experience gives them an advantage over every other New York gang. Organization and discipline. These guys just cut through the other gangs like a warm knife through butter and took over a sizeable part of the city in just five years. Oh, and they're ruthless too. One Latin Kings' chapter had its entire management wiped out one evening... their heads were adorning the gate of one of their offices.

'Small businesses are acquired overnight. If a garage owner defies them, his wife and daughter are raped in front of him. And then shot. The hapless owner is left alive. As you can imagine, they're in every conceivable illegal trade. Drugs, girls, gambling, protection, human trafficking... you name it, this gang owns a significant piece of it.

'And that's not all. Their genius lies in their invisibility. When you mention gang, Joe New Yorker immediately thinks of the Mafia or Latin Kings or Bloods... this gang has managed to stay out of the mainstream consciousness, yet they are the single, most organized, successful gang in the city today. They have managed to stay invisible by doing their dirty business most professionally. Even the ruthlessness hasn't captured the public because they relied on us – the FBI, the NYPD – to hush up the gory details. And the fuckers were right about that. Why would we want to make public that organized crime, on a downward trend for so many years, has shot up again?'

Broker allowed impatience to show. 'All this is most interesting, but what does it have to do with me? Or with you, for that matter?'

Isakson nodded. 'This gang came to our attention because of the scale of their operations and the speed of their growth. The FBI went after this gang, and we used all our intel to bust them, but the funny thing was that most of the time we went to no-shows... a deal was supposed to go down; we put everything in place – people, wheels, tech – the deal never happened. The few busts we made were small; the guys we got were strictly small-time street dealers, nothing to connect them to the gang.'

He paused to allow that to sink in. 'We wondered – shit does happen, but not as regularly as that – but we were nowhere close to pressing the panic button.

'This went on for about eighteen months, and then we decided to change tactics. The NYPD and the FBI have a Joint Organized Crime Task Force, JOCTF, that goes after gangs, and 5Clubs was already on their plate, but we created a smaller cell, calling it 5JTF, within that task force to go after just them, headed by me.

We figured the 5JTF, with an exclusive focus, backed up by resources of the JOCTF – more resources, more feet on the ground, different perspectives – would lead to better results.

'We started building a more complete picture of the gang, with all that additional muscle. What we found was this gang ran like a commercial entity, each chapter head had the freedom to get into or out of any business they wanted. A conglomerate of illegal activity, business principles being applied with military efficiency.

'Then we started getting results. Thugs, admittedly low level, but higher up the food chain than the ones we'd arrested before. But these thugs didn't talk. Or rather, they didn't talk enough. Many of them were bailed or our charges thrown out on flimsy reasons. The gang had expensive lawyers on retainer, and we suspected they might have had a few judges in their pocket, but we never pursued that angle. Too much on our plate as it was.

'The tech route was deployed in parallel, phone taps on suspected gangbangers, remote surveillance – data analysis, cause-and-effect stuff; hell, we also threw in wheels-and-feet surveillance – kitchen sink, bathtub, the works – and for all that, we got pretty much a big fucking fat zero in return.'

He backtracked. 'That's not strictly true. We got some names, big names, more flesh on their organization structure, background on their gang leader, a shadowy East European, but just not enough meat to the bone, nothing in comparison to what we had on the Mafia, the Russian mob, and the other gangs. And to top it off, we could prosecute very few of those we arrested.'

'The others got bail?'

'Nope. Most of them got killed when in custody.

'These fuckers have the reach and the efficiency to get into our jails and have them killed within twenty-four hours or at the most forty-eight hours of being arrested. The Mafia, Latin Kings, Bloods, none of them could execute their own guys as regularly as this gang did. They were mocking us, the NYPD and the FBI, with those kills. Demonstrating that we could do jackshit to them.'

Isakson shook his head almost in admiration. 'We finally started getting some traction, long enough though it took, when we started talking to Interpol.

'They were hunting a former commander of the Kosovo Liberation Army, a mercenary who they believed had fled to the United States. Interpol had issued an arrest warrant for war crimes for this fucker and had proof of those crimes, which they laid out for us. Torture, summary executions, rape, burning children and women... this scumbag had done it all. Even the Kosovo Liberation Army distanced itself from him, and there were rumors that he was to be eliminated quietly. Evidently he got wind of this because he disappeared. Interpol traced his flight to the United States on false papers, and there is a record of his arriving here in New York ten years back, and then he disappeared. Bureaucracy and red tape between Interpol and the FBI resulted in this guy walking into the country under the guise of an American citizen and then disappearing.'

He ran his hand over his head tiredly. 'Once we got these details, we let loose our computers, and sure enough, the two stories met. The timelines matched, the snippets of info we squeezed matched, the ethnicities of some of the hoods tallied to this guy's. This guy is New York based, but never lives in one place. He moves from safe house to safe house, borough to borough, almost every night... has been living like this ever since he came to this country. Interpol said this was second nature to him. He lived like that in the KLA too. This guy is now a US citizen under a false identity, and running the most successful criminal empire in New York.'

Isakson paused and reflected for a moment, the room quiet but for the ticking of a clock on his desk. He shook his head in reluctant admiration. 'His gang has close to three hundred fuckers operational in each borough of the city and in a couple of counties in New Jersey. He's also muscled in on the illegal border traffic out West. You know, between Mexico and Arizona, Texas and California, running drugs and aliens.'

Isakson said grimly, 'Once we got his real identity from Interpol, we ran our databases and got his assumed identity. And then we got lucky. A couple of years back, we caught a chapter hit man red-handed in a shooting. And then offered him witness protection and shit loads of money to start a new life. He started singing.

'Agon Scheafer is the head scumbag, the name the KLA commander now goes under; he's one of our most wanted. He has five close lieutenants who run the New York chapters.'

Isakson opened a file and placed six photographs in front of Broker.

Agon Scheafer was tall, taller than Bear and Bwana, six foot seven, and was huge, built like a tank, with close-cropped dark hair, clean shaven, and no other distinguishing features other than his size. Broker scanned the other photographs of the chapter heads and saw the close-cropped hair, the narrow eyes, and a resemblance to the military bearing.

Broker pushed the photographs back. 'You want my help in catching Agon Scheafer?'

'Nope. We can find him ourselves, however long it takes. We want you to identify the rat-bastard mole in the FBI.'

Chapter 10

Broker leaned back in his chair and crossed his hands behind his head, utterly relaxed. 'Tell me about him. The mole. Why do you think you have one?'

Isakson counted on his fingers, making his case. 'Eleven deals that the FBI acted on, with intel that we alone resourced and had access to, and eight of those were duds. No-shows. A lot of manpower and effort watching warehouses, street corners, wherever they were supposed to take place, and nothing happened. The three busts we made, we got street dealers who were so low down the food chain that they weren't worth the hassle.'

He extended another finger. 'Another ten deals, this time with the 5JTF, and this time slightly better results, if that's what you can call them. Four resulted in ten gangbangers arrested, six were the same waiting-for-stuff-to-happen deals. Of the ten arrests, six were killed, two bailed, the remaining two were so low level that they're worthless and are now clogging our prisons. These twenty-one deals went back almost three years.

'Of the six killed, one was the hit man who gave us Scheafer's identity.'

Isakson sat down. 'One of those deals was through a grade A snitch whose juice had been good to take to the bank. Fifty Ks of smack was to change hands in the Bronx, in a gang-controlled auto garage in broad daylight. We checked with other snitches, other info, chatter that we picked up off the street, social media — you know some of these fuckers use Facebook and that shit — and all said the same. The deal was good to go.

'We did what your friendly neighborhood task force would do – stakeout, an invisible one, with the NYPD's Emergency Service Unit, ESU, and a SWAT team from Quantico in attendance. We sent undercover cops to service their cars at the garage that day. Some of us hung around doing what those hanging around do… thing is, that day, if a flea farted in the shop, we were aware of it. Nothing happened. We hung around till the shop closed and then scattered around all night, watching the shop from all ends. Nada. We drew a big fat zero.'

He paused, expecting Broker to ask questions. Broker didn't.

'We squeezed the snitch but didn't get much joy there. The snitch stuck to his story, and we couldn't do much about it. We put it down to just one of those things.

'This happened a second time, and this time there were no snitches involved. This time we got juice off a phone tap on one of the junior gangbangers. Another drug deal, this time in Brooklyn near a school in broad daylight.

'We followed the same pattern and set up surveillance. Agents carpeted the school and its surroundings. Result was the same. Jackshit.

'By now tempers were flaring, and a lot of fingers were being pointed at me and my management of the 5JTF. Remember, we're the FBI, and we always get our guy. This was making us smell worse than rotten food and dirty laundry. Worse, it was making the NYPD look bad. Any task force is also a political body, and the usual political shitstorm you would expect in such circumstances was raging, and boy, was it raging hard! And then we had the third deal.'

Isakson's voice had gone hoarse from talking. He poured himself a glass of water from a pitcher and offered one silently to Broker, who shook his head.

'I suspected that the mole might be in the NYPD, even though the previous duds were just with the FBI, so I decided to withhold intel from the NYPD and go to a bust without them. That was the next exchange.

'This one came to us through another snitch, and it was a month away. We threw everything at filtering the intel. We got agents shadowing the top gangbangers in the chapter, bugged them, used parabolic mics, email intercepts, mobile intercepts... everything. And all that we gathered pointed to a huge motherfucking deal going down in an industrial warehouse at night in Harlem. We then got together and corroborated it and picked holes in it. Squeezed the snitch. Threatened to shoot his balls off, send him to Gitmo, all that shit. The story held. You know how these things are. There is no foolproof intel. But this was as good as it got. And we ran the paranoid test to see if we were being played. The analysts came back and said it smelt of roses.

'So then we planned the operation, and come the night, we had eyes on the warehouse from all possible locations, SWAT on standby... everything in place to hit the bastards.

'The deal didn't happen. Déjà vu. The warehouse was cleaner than a newborn baby ward in a hospital. And this time, the heat on me was nuclear. We went back to the drawing board and relooked at the intelligence, and we didn't think we were being played. We got the experts to analyze all the taps to see if they could detect lies, and they couldn't. Once you have eliminated the impossible, whatever remains, no matter how improbable, must be the truth. Sherlock Holmes, right?

'We had a mole. All this just confirmed it. Of course, this conclusion wasn't public knowledge. I discussed it with the Director and a few others… not more than five others in the agency were privy to this.'

'That's it? That's all you have to go on? Fuck, man, there could be a million reasons why all those deals never happened. You're dealing with gangs here, not exactly the most rational guys on the planet. I can't believe I'm wasting my time listening to this shit from you about some mole based on this crap!' Broker growled and made a move to get up.

Isakson held a hand up. 'That warehouse had graffiti all across it, like it was a museum for street art. You know how it is with graffiti – there's so much of it, you stop paying attention to it. But in all that spray painting, one stood out. Not because it was exceptional or anything like that. It was just a smiley face, two eyes, a curve, that kind of thing. Nothing that would worry Picasso, if he were alive, or that Zephyr guy. You'd forget it, thinking it was the work of just another frustrated street artist.

'Except for this.'

He removed a file from a filing cabinet, removed a sheet of paper, and handed it over to Broker.

Broker saw what Isakson meant by the crude image. Two large eyes and grinning teeth were what identified the shape to be a face. Underneath, circled, presumably by the FBI, was the inscription, 'Better luck next time. 5Clubs.' The spelling left a lot to be desired, but the message was clear.

81

He looked up at Isakson and handed back the sheet.

'Remember, I had held back this deal from the NYPD and the 5JTF... the SAC and I were the first to the scene, the first to see this.'

There was a long silence as the two of them mulled it over.

'Of course we put our best forensic team on that, and they said the image had been drawn about eight hours earlier. We had started our surveillance of the warehouse about four hours before the deal. The spray used was a very common variety, and we didn't get very far with that.'

He returned the file back to the cabinet, leaned back, and looked at Broker.

'You know there was supposed to be two hundred Ks of crack to change hands that day... we did see an increased supply in Harlem and the Bronx for a few months after that, so we know the exchange took place. We went hard on our snitches and even collared a few gang members, but we got clean and innocent from them, and we had to let them go. Their sneering faces... I still remember them.

'I went back to the auto shop and all the other sites and tore them apart. All the locations over the thirty months had graffiti, and all of them had this smiley or traces of it. Enough traces left to fill the gaps.

'I ran a search for all such graffiti in drug deals or any deals of any kind, especially where the deals had gone sour... and I noticed that over the last two years, many of the "turkey deals" had such gang graffiti affiliated to some gang or the other left at the sites.

Get this – not a single NYPD bust where they acted alone had such images. Only our busts had.

'That time window is important. I studied all our reports, photographs, and even those that came to us from the NYPD and JOCTF, and before that window, the success rate of the FBI and the NYPD was much higher than what it was. We took drugs off the street, put badasses behind bars... with 5Clubs, we got small fry, and they walked soon, but we got their drugs. In those thirty months, the success ratio just dropped, the number of no-shows rocketed.'

Isakson swallowed his bitterness and continued.

'We quietly disbanded the 5JTF, saying that it was redundant since the JOCTF was already doing the same thing. We, the FBI, still did the things we were supposed to do, arrest, busts and all that, and we still ended up holding nothing. Then another drug bust went wrong.

'This time we walked into a trap, a booby-trapped warehouse. Lost two agents. Good guys, with families, the kind of agents the FBI is built on. The gang just blew them away with a dirty bomb, no smileys, no messages this time. The bomb was message enough.

'I was pulled off my normal duties by the Director and tasked with working with our Internal Investigations Section, IIS, to find the rat. By then, everyone knew something was off, but were too scared to vocalize it. We had been through this before. We had Hanssen, who spied for the Russians for twenty years, and whenever there was an Ames or John Walker at other agencies, we went through extensive procedural upheaval, making sure we were secure. We became a paranoid organization for some time

83

during such periods, suspecting everything and everyone, and no one wanted those days back. But they were here.

'The Director said I would be reviewing our processes and security systems, but those in the know were aware that the IIS and I were on this mission. I became Mr. Unpopular – the guy tasked with investigating agents. You know what we found in one year of investigation? A big fat zero. We went through hundreds of agent files, grilled them, aggressive interrogation, went through case files, tapped agents' phones, followed agents. Nothing. No clue, no hint, nothing. Everyone came clean.'

Isakson rubbed his face wearily with both hands, but when he removed them, his eyes were bright and hard. 'The Director declared that everything was good with us, and I was back on active duty. Investigation closed. Morale improved almost immediately after we spread that message, and today we're in a much better position than we were a few years back.

'In reality, I was still running a solo investigation, reporting only to the Director... and getting nowhere.'

He smiled grimly. 'The asshole is still out there. Investigations still turn to crap, maybe one or two a year. And this is an equal-opportunity asshole – all the shit is gang related, but not limited to any one gang. 5Clubs, Latin Kings, the Crips, Bloods... busts involving all of them have gone south. Different gang smileys turn up regularly – though of course, given 5Clubs' hold over the city, most of the drawings refer to them.

'This is where you come in. We need your help. Director Murphy has given me a free hand and unlimited resources, but I don't want to use anyone from the FBI. Been there, done that, didn't get anywhere.

'But I might have a chance if I use outside contractors. I went to Clare to see if her Agency could help, and she flatly refused. She said it was a good idea to take on outside help, but she has enough on her plate without helping us wipe our own ass. Can't blame her. I then asked her if she could recommend any contractors, and at that she basically threw me out of her office.'

He laughed a genuine laugh. 'I can see why you guys have a lot of time for her. That lady has the biggest, brassiest pair of balls I've ever seen.'

Broker pondered for a moment and asked the obvious question.

'You haven't told me anything about the JOCTF and 5JTF; how many in each of those, how many had access to the information flow?'

Isakson raked his fingers through his hair, a man who knew the enormity of the task at hand, maybe even its futility.

'Task forces are clearing houses for information in the first instance, and that information goes to a *lot* of people. Unit Chiefs, Section Chiefs, Associate Directors, SACs – Special Agents-in-Charge, ASACs – Assistant Special Agents-in-Charge, Special Agents... a lot!'

'Give me a number.'

Isakson said reluctantly, 'Including the Field Agents and the SWAT teams who went on the busts, thirty on our side. The juice came to about ten of us and then got disseminated.'

'These thirty have been on this investigation since the beginning?'

'Since time began.'

Broker looked out of the window. *That's one hell of a number, and those thirty could have further spread the word, pillow talk, water cooler gossip, no way that could have been contained to just thirty.*

He watched a bird fly past the window, forage its only concern.

'You investigated all thirty.' It was a statement, not a question, but Isakson nodded.

'Turned them inside out, made them take polygraphs, aggressively interrogated them, all under the guise of routine internal investigations, not that they bought it. We didn't stop at that. We dug into their phone records, financial records, mortgage statements, credit cards, cash transactions, linked accounts, put their children under the scanner, checked out their schools, put tails on all of them, tracked their Skype or messenger chats, followed their wives, went back to their birth records, parents' records, girlfriends, partners, all of those in their immediate orbit. We put them through psych evaluations... I got to know those guys better than I know myself. If they stopped at a Walgreens, I knew about it and why. If they went to a strip club, I knew what they did there, who they talked to. If they argued with their wives or girlfriends, we knew about it! Got enough reports that if I had to print them and convert them back to trees, we would have a brand-new Amazon forest.'

'All these in electronic form?'

'Most of them, say ninety-percent, the rest, paper files in a secure storage only the Director and I know.'

He pushed a slip of paper at Broker containing names, titles, contact details and demographic details of all thirty agents.

Broker skimmed through the list, swiftly noting the three married women and five single men, divorcés.

Isakson saw his pause, read the names upside down, and commented, 'Yeah, I focused on those divorcés, seeing how they could fit a traitor profile, but they came clean too.'

'Too clean? Any of them?'

'Look.' Isakson's voice rose in frustration. 'They came clean to me. However, I can't keep second-guessing my investigation and its findings. There are quicker ways to insanity, if that's where I want to go. Hence, I need a neutral pair of eyes, which is where *you* come in.'

He looked at Broker. 'So?'

Broker shrugged. 'Of all the gin joints and so on, why me? There must be a million other contractors out there who can help you, *and* who like you a damned sight more than I do.'

Isakson leaned forward. 'You guys are trusted by Director Murphy, who has heard of you via Clare. The National Security Advisor likes you. Makes my job easier to work with someone my bosses trust. Your dislike for me has nothing to do with it.'

Broker got up and turned to leave. 'I'll give it some thought and get back to you. But if I was you, I wouldn't be holding my breath.'

'You would be doing your country a favor by helping us.'

Broker swung round at the door, and Isakson felt the full force of cold blue eyes. 'Save it. My associates and I are the last people you should be using the patriotism card on. Your bosses know what we do, who we do it for, what motivates us. They wouldn't hold us in such regard if we were your average Joe Mercenary. I'll think about your request and get back to you.'

The two agents who followed Broker were hanging around outside Isakson's office. Broker glanced at them as he brushed past them. 'The next time you follow me, I'll break your legs.'

Chapter 11

When in doubt, coffee, was Broker's motto, and the Jura brewed him a hot black one when he reached his office. He leaned back in his chair and allowed the aroma to clear his mind. If he was honest with himself, he could help out Isakson. There wasn't anything on his plate that his analysts couldn't handle. He had already activated General Klouse's project, but even that didn't require his all-day attention. He'd let Isakson stew for a couple of days and then tell him he was on board.

That decision made, he went over his analysts' reports, looking for mentions of any out-of-the ordinary military hardware and didn't find any. He checked Werner to see if the spiders were configured correctly, and saw that they were. He patted it. Of course patting it made it work harder! This was artificial *intelligence,* after all. He then pushed everything out of his mind and turned his thoughts to Isakson's revelations.

His computer chimed softly. Isakson had sent him the dossiers of the thirty agents and the key surveillance summary sheets and findings. He shook his head at Isakson's persistence and then smiled. Broker would have done the same in Isakson's situation.

He opened the files and started reading them swiftly, keeping his mind blank, letting it make any associations unconsciously.

Seven hours and four refills later, Broker leaned back and stretched with a satisfying grunt. He could read nonstop, without moving, and had done so from the moment he clicked his mouse. The pad in front of him had scribbling on it – Venn diagrams, models, graphs crudely drawn – and in the center were nine names: Charlotte Adams, Becky Pisano, Emily Santiago, Kory

Refus, Claude Beucamp, Rick Stonehaus, Eric Yarbrough, Floyd Wheat and Chris Slinkard.

Women didn't fit the traitor profile, and that was precisely why Broker had jotted their names down. The next five names were the divorcés and the last, Chris Slinkard, a Special Agent in a strong marriage with two kids, was perfect material for FBI recruiting posters.

Broker had picked the women and Slinkard because they *didn't* fit the profile, and the single men just had to be included. He would turn Werner loose on all thirty, but those nine would be his starting point. He would compare whatever Werner threw up against Isakson's reports and look for anomalies, coincidences, patterns, spreading the net wider with each search.

Broker was rinsing his coffee mug when his mind turned to the FBI's previous traitor.

Robert Hanssen, a veteran FBI agent, had been spying for twenty-five years for Russia before his arrest in 2001, and was the most destructive traitor the FBI had known. Hanssen's betrayal had led to the execution of two KGB double agents, the imprisonment of a third, and thousands of pages of highly classified material to land in Russian hands. Hanssen's betrayal still haunted the FBI, and the slightest whiff of a mole made the organization paranoid.

Broker had been in the intelligence business for a long time and knew that every intelligence or investigative agency in the world was susceptible to betrayal from within. All that the best agencies could do was constantly reinvent their security protocols, minimize the damage when a rat was discovered, and relearn and reshape themselves. He could imagine the suspicion hanging in the air in the FBI corridors and, for the briefest of moments, felt sympathy for Isakson. He shook his head, snorted, and polished his mug extra hard.

Being a double agent in an organization such as the FBI was not easy. It required leading a double life and layers to be maintained for many years. Successful double agents were able to make the life layers a habit, as ingrained as brushing teeth in the morning. Such agents got exposed because they either got betrayed by another double agent or in some cases got careless, or overconfident, and made mistakes. Robert Hanssen got exposed because the FBI tapped a former KGB agent who gave evidence that led to Hanssen's arrest.

Isakson's traitor was yet to make any mistakes, which meant that the traitor was so seasoned that the double life *was* his life. *Or* that Isakson had not picked up his mistakes. *Or*, and this was a possibility, that there was no traitor – that all that happened could be coincidences, even the messages at the warehouses. Broker would start his investigation fresh; he didn't want to be contaminated by Isakson's thinking, assumptions and judgment.

Broker also realized that there was no one who was beyond suspicion. With that in mind, he glanced at his watch and made a call. It was early, very early, but the person at the other end took calls at any time.

Broker met Clare in a drab office near City Hall the next day.

'Keeping busy, Broker?' Clare greeted him.

'Can't complain, ma'am. There's enough wickedness in the world for me to earn a living,' replied Broker.

91

Clare poured him a coffee and waved at him to continue.

'I met Isakson yesterday—'

'I heard,' Clare interrupted him with a ghost of a smile.

Why wouldn't she? She's head of the most secretive and well-informed Agency in the world, Broker thought and continued, 'He wants my help in an investigation of his.'

'I think I know which one.'

'Do you think his theory has legs?'

'I'm sure you know the answer to that one, Broker. The FBI has been traitor-free for several years now. Either that situation is too good to be true, or it *is* true. No organization is immune to rats. In any case, I heard that there is some evidence to back his theory, so he's not shooting in the dark. Are you going to help him?'

Broker nodded. 'Yes, after letting him swing in the air for a day or two more. Unless you have some assignment for me and the rest...' He trailed off.

Clare shook her head. 'Nothing right now. But even if something comes up, I'm sure you can multitask well. Besides, they' – she nodded, referring to the FBI – 'know I have dibs on you.'

'I need to talk to Director Murphy,' he told Clare.

Clare laughed. 'Ah, *that's* why you wanted to meet me. You want to know how Pat would react if you investigated him too?'

Broker spread his arms wide in acknowledgement.

'He's been in the investigation game for a long time. If you didn't put him under the scanner, then he'd think you're the wrong person for this. You aren't. There's no one more qualified to help the FBI than you guys. In some quarters, you are viewed as *guns for hire*, or rather my private army, but I know he's aware – General Klouse, and a few select others as well – of the full extent of your skills. You don't need to be worried about Pat. Go investigate, and see if you can crack this and identify the mole, if you think there's one.'

'Thank you, ma'am. That's what I wanted to hear. Could you arrange for me to meet him?'

An eyebrow lifted up. 'You don't want Isakson to set that up for you?'

'Nope. If I get involved in this, I want to do it my way. If they have a mole over there, he'll get wind of Isakson setting up my meeting and might be able to figure out what my role is. My way – I'm just another meeting the Director of the FBI has.'

Clare nodded. 'I'll set it up. You'll get a call from someone.

'You'll be looking at Isakson too?' She knew what his answer would be.

Broker grinned. 'That's the bonus in all this.' He paused. 'You mentioned no agency is immune... you've had rats too?'

A small enigmatic smile came and disappeared quickly. 'Surely you don't expect me to answer that, Broker?'

Broker nodded in acceptance and understanding. In an agency that didn't exist, any mole, suspected or the real article, had a short shelf life. As he was leaving, she asked, 'How are you guys coping? I met Bear and Chloe sometime back, and they were holding up well.'

She was referring to Zeb.

Broker turned back to her, all the humor gone from his face. 'There isn't a day that we don't miss him. But the pain is becoming manageable now.'

He smiled suddenly and fully, the smile that made many hearts skip a beat from Wall Street to Wushan. 'He would give me the Zeb look if he heard that,' he said and stepped out.

Clare – Director of the most powerful agency in the world, Keeper of Secrets, as many called her – sat staring at the door through which Broker had passed.

Zeb had been her protégé. His absence hurt her as much as it did Broker. She sighed deeply and made the call to Pat Murphy, Director of the FBI.

'I'm in.' Broker called Isakson a few days later.

'Thank you. I'll–' started Isakson, only to be cut off by Broker.

'Send me all the rest. I want everything, notes, scribbling, doodles... if anything was put to paper or on a computer, I want it,' said Broker and hung up.

He waited, and his phone rang minutes later. Isakson. He let it ring a few times and then answered it.

'Broker, we don't work like that. I would like you to work out of a secure office I can set up for you–'

Broker interrupted him. 'Deputy Director, *I* don't work like that. Send your stuff to me, and I'll come to you if and when I have something or I want something. If Clare comes up with an assignment for me and my team, I'll drop everything I'm doing, including this investigation, and do that job. Those are my terms.'

He heard Isakson go quiet for a long while, and then he responded stiffly, 'Very well. I'll send everything we have, and get you security clearance, and fix up any meetings you need.'

'The first two, yes. I'll fix my *own* meetings,' responded Broker and hung up on Isakson.

The other call came minutes later.

Chapter 12

Director Pat Murphy was a pugnacious Irish-American who had grown up in the Bronx back in the days when its streets were mean. After law school, he had started his career working in the corporate sector and then had moved to public service and risen to be the Attorney General of the United States before being appointed as the Director of the FBI.

Director Murphy was fiercely protective of the FBI and was determined to weed out the mole, if one existed, and restore the pride of the agency. When Isakson had reached a dead end in his investigation, he had listened to General Klouse and Clare and suggested that Isakson seek outside help.

Isakson had heard of Clare's team several times, but hadn't met any of them previously. He had readily agreed to meet Broker when Clare had called him since he wanted to assess him personally.

Broker breathed deeply as he walked to the J. Edgar Hoover Building on the most famous avenue in the world. Spring in D.C was good, but he was a New Yorker and refused to accept that any other city was superior in any way to NYC. He noticed that there weren't as many people doing stuff on their phones while walking – street pizza-meat he called them – as in New York, but he resolutely pushed away such traitorous thoughts.

Director Murphy studied him as Broker was ushered in the room. *Showboat*, he thought and then erased that from his mind. He hadn't risen to his role by making snap judgments. He gestured for Broker to seat himself and rasped, 'So, mister, I hear you're going to find our mole?'

Broker grinned. 'Are you sure you have a mole, sir?'

'That's what everyone tells me. You telling me something else?' Murphy's eyes narrowed.

'Nope. I don't know enough to tell you anything at this stage. All I'm saying is that it's easy to get sucked into a mole hunt when in reality all that happened was just random chance.'

'Isakson's a good agent, mister, which is why I've made him the Deputy Director. He's not the kind to go after windmills. I know you don't have the highest regard for him, but *I* do. And if he says there's a mole, I've no reason to disbelieve him. I can go with random luck to an extent, but that doesn't explain the warehouse messages.'

Broker nodded. 'Yeah, that's the one thing that makes the case for a traitor. Only, I wonder why a traitor would be so stupid as to leave messages like that.'

Director Murphy waved his hand impatiently and growled, 'Don't you think we haven't considered that? We think it's not the traitor, but some stupid punk in those gangs that left those messages. Agreed, it's a weak theory, but nothing else makes sense. Now, *you* tell me how you're going to help us. You are, aren't you? You didn't come all the way here to show your mug, I hope?'

'I'm in, sir. I mentioned that to Isakson. I wanted to meet you to get your views on this and–'

Murphy held up a hand, interrupting him. 'Isakson's views are my views. The two of us are on the same page.'

Broker inclined his head in acknowledgment. 'I also wanted to manage your expectations. These hunts can take months and even years. If this mole is really good, he'll be buried so deep, covered so well, that only a mistake or a betrayal will expose him. It doesn't look like he's made a mistake yet.'

'I know how long this can go. I've been involved in a few hunts and cleanups myself,' Director Murphy said brusquely.

Broker leaned forward. 'Sir, how're you protecting operations till such time as we find this bastard?'

Murphy broke eye contact for the first time, looked away and back again. 'Mister, there isn't much we can do on that front. We can't cut back on operations. Isakson and a select team reviewed our policies, and we have implemented all the recommendations from that review. Our most sensitive operations are handled by agents handpicked by me – agents who are thoroughly and rigorously vetted regularly. Our information is always on the strictest need-to-know basis and our systems and policies have come a long way from the days of Hanssen. I am proud that we run the tightest investigative agency in the country.'

His voice hardened. 'Which is why it burns me to think of some bastard sitting in some office of mine, wrecking yet another operation as we sit here. Mister, find me that bastard. I want to rip his balls off, pickle them, and display them in a jar on my mantelpiece.'

'I'll do my best, sir, but you know very well that I can't promise any results. We might well end up investigating for years with no happy ending.'

Director Murphy replied, 'Your best is what I want. I can deal with whatever shit comes out, even if nothing comes out.'

'Sir, you know I'll have to investigate everyone...' Broker trailed off.

Murphy smiled grimly. 'Mister, I would have been disappointed in Clare's judgment if you didn't investigate Isakson *and* me. If you come up with something interesting in our lives, let us know. Our lives have forgotten what interesting is, these last few years. Has Isakson sorted out everything for you?'

Broker nodded and stood up to leave. Director Murphy leaned across to clasp his hand, his grip as hard as concrete.

He looked in Broker's eyes, and his voice softened the slightest. 'I'm sorry about your loss. You know Isakson couldn't do anything else.'

Broker bent his head just once and left.

Director Murphy didn't have to say that, he thought, but it showed the kind of person he was. Didn't mean Broker's opinion of Isakson had changed.

He stood at the corner of the avenue and whistled for a cab. Nothing happened. He shook his head. Of course nothing would happen. This wasn't New York. His confidence in New York's superiority restored, he hoofed it to the nearest Metro and made his way to the airport.

He called Bear the next day.

'You guys still chilling out there?'

'Hell yeah,' Bear answered in a monotone.

'You don't sound that enthusiastic.' Broker laughed.

'Man, everything is so perfect here. Perfect blue sky, perfect beaches, perfect teeth, bodies, hell, Broker, I'm perfectly bored. Get me out of here. Do you have a job for us?'

'Nada.' Broker was still chuckling. 'Where's Chloe?'

'Oh, she's gone on a perfect run!'

Broker burst out laughing. 'Bear, you need to relax, maybe go for some yoga, discover your inner chakra or some shit like that. It's a fucking holiday for the two of you!'

'I need to do all that like I need a hole in my head.' Bear snorted. 'This holiday has outstayed its welcome.' He sighed deeply. 'Anyway, why did you call, Broker?'

'How many feet could Chloe and you round up for some surveillance?'

'How many do you need? Maybe ten, fifteen good guys. Really good.'

Broker shook his head, not that Bear could see. 'I might need much more than that. Maybe fifty or seventy.'

'Jeez, Broker, how many bodies you want followed? Sounds like a whole army! What's this about? Something Chloe and I can help you with?'

'Maybe, but not yet. Things haven't yet fallen into place or heated up. Do me a favor. Start warming up as many feet as you can but also manage expectations. This is not the first line of approach for me, and it might not go anywhere. All I want to know is if I need feet, I can get them.'

'Will do, Broker. Stay safe and stay cool.'

Broker hung up and checked his mail. There was an encrypted memory stick from Isakson, which had several files on it, reams of data on the investigation Isakson had conducted, files and notes of agents he had put on the scanner, and details of the various operations that had gone south.

Broker studied the files for hours, and when it turned dark, he closed the folder, leaned back and stretched. This wasn't the approach he would take. Repeating the investigation Isakson had conducted would be pointless.

He would attack this problem from the other end. It was time he put his own badasses to work.

Chapter 13

Two thousand five hundred miles away, Roger sighed and looked up at the night sky barely visible through the thick blanket of the forest.

They had made their way from Copper Canyon in Chihuahua, Mexico, northward and crossed the border a while back and then drifted toward Coronado National Forest in southeastern Arizona, not far from the Mexican border and Nogales, Sonora, in Mexico. They had spent several days here, drifting through the vast forest that covered more than a million and a half acres, soaking in the solitude and wilderness... and fishing.

This was the life – fat fish lining his belly, a comfortable sleeping bag, the vast emptiness of the forest surrounding him, silence echoing around him... A clanking behind him disturbed his thoughts, and he twisted around to see the source.

A tall, sinewy black man was washing up after their dinner, his body language expressing disgust. Bwana glanced at Roger. 'Hey, Rog, you know this is called *camping*. When two guys go camping, they share stuff. Stuff like work. It's called distribution of work. I thought you, having gone to college, would know all about this.' He banged a saucepan and plate together to make his point.

'Hold on right there, buddy,' Roger drawled, rubbing a palm through his close-cropped brown hair as he adjusted his lean and muscled frame on the sleeping bag. He twisted on his side, propping himself on an elbow. 'I thought we agreed on alternating the work. Me doing the fishing in the morning, you cooking and cleaning in the evening, and the next day we alternate. It's called rotation. I studied that in high school football, not in college. I'm sure you had some schooling, didn't ya?'

'Rotation is fine when the chores are evenly distributed, but they aren't. You eat like a hog, actually you eat like three prize hogs celebrating their birthday, and I end up doing more work.'

'I can't help it. I'm a growing boy; I need all the nourishment I can get. Besides it's your fault, you cook so damned well.' Roger laughed.

Bwana glared at him and then chuckled. He finished drying, tidied the campsite, laid out his bag on the other side of the bank of glowing coals, and settled down.

Silence crept over them, both of them perfectly comfortable in the silence, perfectly comfortable in the dark.

Bwana Kayembe was born to a Congolese father, a school teacher, and an American mother, an aid worker with an international charity, in Luvungi, in the Democratic Republic of the Congo. His earliest memories were of the lush green canopy of forest just a stone's throw away from the huts in the village, and of the towering hills weeping rain as they overlooked the village.

Robert Kayembe, his father, a forward-thinking man, had witnessed the birth of an independent Congo after years of Belgian rule, but independence did not bring stability or peace to the country. The country was in a state of constant strife, with tribal rivalries and ever-present rebels resulting in the land going through two presidents by the time Bwana was born.

Robert migrated to Shelby County, Tennessee, along with his wife and four-year-old Bwana, having decided that the intelligent and inquisitive child deserved all the opportunity he could get.

Bwana grew up with a long gun on his arm in their farm in Arlington, hearing stories of faraway lands and different people, and this fueled a desire in him to see what lay beyond the horizon.

The Army ROTC course at the University of Tennessee set off a chain of events that eventually led to his joining the 5th Special Forces Group (Airborne) and driving with four others in a Mine-Resistant Ambush Protected vehicle (MRAP) through the valleys and mountains of Eastern Afghanistan one wintry morning.

The MRAP was designed to deflect and nullify the improvised explosive devices (IEDs) that the insurgents used, and numerous soldiers owed their lives to it, but it lacked maneuverability and was like a drunken boxer when driving in rocky, mountainous terrain in 'Stan.

The valley was full of mines, and the vehicle had to stick to a well-rutted path, but the steep turns and bends resulted in such slow going that Bwana jumped off the vehicle and guided it around bends, fully knowing there were snipers about.

The first few turns were navigated safely, and then came the fourth turn, a particularly steep one, and as Bwana rounded the bend, he came across the goats. His attention was half focused on the width of the road, and he was calculating angles and distances for the vehicle grinding behind him when he stopped short on seeing them.

Goats. There were about thirty of them, a hundred yards away, some of them lying down, some feeding on the grass off the mountainside, doing all the things that goats did, with not a care in the world. Bwana backed up slowly, alert for an ambush, scanned for a goatherd, and found none. He could hear the engine's revs dropping as they slowed for his return, and he waited, his M-4 coming to his hand as naturally as he drew breath.

He risked a quick glance around him as he heard a shout from the MRAP, calling out for him; he was alone, just him and the goats, the vehicle and its occupants a few yards around the corner, a galaxy away.

He opened his mouth to respond, and the first shot rang out from ahead on the slope of the mountain, missing him by several feet, the sniper not taking his time. Seven, no, eight men rose from amidst the goats and trained their guns on him and opened fire.

Bwana had already dropped to the ground, roaring, 'Ambush,' the stock coming smoothly to his cheek, his first shot taking the man on the left.

He started crawling back urgently, seeking shelter behind the turn, firing in short bursts, making them duck behind the animals, and then one of them raised his upper body, clutching something in his hand. Grenade. Goodbye, Bwana. It was a good ride while it lasted.

The man's head exploded in a red mist, the flat bark from behind coming to him simultaneously, and then a louder, larger noise, the I-6 diesel of the MRAP drowning them all out and rifles opening up at once, taking out all the ambushers now exposed by the scattering goats.

The cluster of rocks ahead — the sniper's hide — exploded, clouds of mud, blood, and stone rising in the air, shimmering in the thin sunlight before dissipating slowly as the echoes of the guns died.

Silence crept up on them, broken by the bleating of the wounded animals, their cries cut short by single shots as Roger moved grimly among them, ending the misery of those wounded beyond help. He was flanked by two others, checking and confirming that the ambushers were all dead.

Bwana still lay prone, his M-4 trained on the sniper hide till he felt a hand clasping his shoulder.

Roger smiled down at him. 'Don't go to sleep down there, partner. The day's still ahead of us.' He rose, offering a hand to Bwana, helping him rise to his feet, that clasp of hands unbroken to this day.

Bwana looked at the dark shadow that was Roger on the other side of the coals. Roger never spoke about himself. Bwana knew he was an orphan and had grown up with a foster family who couldn't wait to see the back of him, and had no one else to call family.

That was enough backstory for Bwana. The past didn't matter, the now and the future did. Family? *He* was Roger's family.

Roger didn't know what woke him, but one moment he was in a deep, dreamless sleep and the next he was awake. He lay still, allowing the night and forest to envelop him. He turned his head towards Bwana and saw the dark shapeless shadow of his bag. He glanced at the dull green numerals on his watch. Two a.m. He lay still, listening, trying to sense what had woken him.

It wasn't any sound, he decided, nor was it any presence.

'Yeah, I can feel it too,' murmured Bwana from the other side of the banked coals.

Roger grinned soundlessly and got up from his bag, Bwana doing the same; two wraiths rising, the still air bending itself around them – habits nurtured in the Special Forces, practiced in far-off dusty lands and now like breathing to them.

The woods had gone silent; the customary sounds of the nightlife deadened – *that* had woken Roger and Bwana.

Their camp was north of Pena Blanca Lake, in Peck Canyon, and was located in a thicket, caution and the habit of blending in guiding their choice of camp. They were right in the middle of Peck Canyon Corridor, a route for herding illegal immigrants from Mexico to the United States; the Corridor stretched from border crossing points, across the Pajarito Mountains, Atascosa Mountains, and the Tumacacori Mountains... Peck Canyon divided the Atascosas from the Tumacacoris.

The border between the United States and Mexico, about two thousand miles, had steel and concrete fences at places and infrared cameras and sensors at others, supported by about twenty thousand US Border Patrol agents and drones in the air.

This still didn't deter the flow of illegal immigrants. About half a million of them crossed into the United States each year, many of them guided by coyotes – smugglers who were often armed – who shepherded the illegal immigrants across the border for a fee. Many criminal gangs organized and controlled the flow of illegal immigrants across the border, and most of the coyotes worked for some gang or the other. What the physical and the virtual fence had done was move the flow of immigrants to remote, inhospitable terrain such as Peck Canyon Corridor.

Roger and Bwana were fully aware of the immigrant traffic in the region but hadn't encountered any during their camping.

Roger crossed to his kit and buckled his Kimber Target II in his shoulder holster, slipping extra mags in his pockets. He strapped a Benchmade to his ankle, slung a pair of night-vision goggles around his neck and stuck a comms set in his ear. He looked across at Bwana, and he was tooling up similarly; Bwana was a Glock man, a Glock 21 tucked away in his shoulder holster, and as Roger looked on, he slung a Heckler and Koch MP7A1 compact submachine gun over his bag. Bwana didn't believe in doing things by halves.

They looked around, and Bwana pointed to a very faint glow in the skyline about a mile back and headed off at a rapid pace, Roger following. The silence grew louder as they approached, and then as they slowed, they heard it.

It was the shuffling of a large body of people moving stealthily in the night.

Bwana glanced at Roger and quickened his pace, making as much noise as a shadow. He slowed down and faded into the bole of a tree, Roger finding another large trunk to shelter behind – they were two hundred feet away from the human mass.

The dim lighting they had spotted was caused by high-intensity flashlights held by six guards, who were in a rough U-formation around forty people. The bright beams were carefully turned

108

away from the mass of people, and Roger couldn't make out the details. He looked at Bwana, who shook his head. *Coyotes,* he thought. *There goes our sleep, just our fucking dumb luck.*

They let the group get a lead and tracked back to scan for a rear guard – there was none.

'Illegals crossing the border,' murmured Bwana. 'Thing is, do we let them go or do we play the heroes?'

'Let's warn the Border Patrol,' replied Roger, and they slowed down further, and Roger powered up his phone. 'Shit, hardly any bars on this. How about yours?'

Bwana checked his phone and shook his head. Roger dialed a number and held it to his head and then gave up after a while. 'No ring going out.'

He fished out the sat phone they used to communicate securely with Broker and Bear, and shook his head disgustedly when he saw they'd forgotten to charge it.

They followed the group for over a mile and noticed two other coyotes in the front who were acting as scouts. All the coyotes were heavily armed, and even in the darkness, through the distance, they could see the dim outlines of AK-47s and AR-15s on the three closest to them.

'Is that standard wear for coyotes?' muttered Bwana.

Roger shrugged; the weapons didn't bother him. 'How long are we going to follow them?'

'You got anything better to do? Other than sleeping?'

Roger shook his head silently, and they pressed on. It was dark and cloudy, but the light reflecting off the walls of the canyon gave them enough visibility to follow. They weren't able to make out the details of the group from behind, but noticed that they were of average height and some of them were female, from the long hair. The coyotes took care not to direct the light on the group as they hustled the group along at a rapid pace. They prodded the slow ones with their rifles or slaps and muttered curses. One slap felled an illegal to the ground, and the coyote grabbed an arm, dragged him upright, and slapped him again to prod him on.

Roger tightened inside and drifted closer to the group, a hundred and fifty feet separating him from them.

The group turned around a large rock outcrop that narrowed the track, and they lost sight of the mass momentarily. They slowed down their pursuit... it was a good place for an ambush. Roger tried his phone again and after a while put it back in his pocket in disgust. Bwana crept forward, hugging the far end of the ravine, and peeked beyond the outcrop. After a while, he made a hand signal, and they surged forward.

The main body of people was flagging – they had probably been on the move all night, and the heat and the pace was telling on them. The coyotes were growing increasingly angry, and the frequent sounds of slaps and curses punctuated the air. Bwana looked across at Roger expressionlessly. He would have the same expressionless face if he was breaking the arms of the coyotes.

Roger looked at the group, looked back at the trail, and what had been gnawing away at him became stronger. He came to a halt and dug into another pocket and drew out a military compass and checked his bearings. He pictured their location in his mind and placed the compass on it and then zoomed in and out on his mental map.

He frowned, looked up to signal Bwana.

Three shots rang out.

Chapter 14

There was a haze of dust in the air, further dulling the visibility. But the aftermath of the shots was clear, even from their distance in the dark.

Two illegals lay on the ground; a couple of others hunched over them.

The coyotes were loosely strung out and were threatening the group of illegals with their guns. All eight of them. The rest of the illegals were huddled together, cowed.

Roger couldn't make out the expressions on their faces, the darkness and distance rendering the faces into pale blobs, but none of them were showing any signs of aggression. Roger and Bwana hugged the rocky outcrop, invisible against its dark shadow beyond the dim light of the flashlights.

One of the illegals crouching over the dead, a woman, sprang suddenly at the coyotes, shrieking, her arms outstretched. The heavy closest to her stepped back without a word, upended his AK-47, and with a lazy, casual swing hit the woman across the face. The woman fell back and then collapsed in an untidy heap without a sound, and seconds later the dull watermelon-like thud of the impact reached Roger and Bwana.

The coyotes shouted and prodded the rest of the group who resumed shuffling along the corridor. The coyote who had felled the woman hawked and spat on her body and stepped across her as he followed the group.

The gang started hazing and herding the illegals, urging them to go faster. The last one bent over the fallen woman and felt something on her body. He then rose and fired a short burst into her body. Point blank. He then stepped across the body, went to the wall of the ravine, hitched his shirt up with a loud sigh, and urinated a long stream. Just another day in a coyote's life.

Roger felt loose and light. He could smell and taste each molecule of air that brushed his face and feel the blood steadily pulse inside him. He looked across at Bwana. He knew Bwana understood. Nothing needed to be said.

They moved like a well-oiled machine, countless missions in hot spots of the world perfecting every step they took. They drifted along, flanking the group from both sides, narrowing the gap.

Bwana was closest to the last gangbanger, the one who had fired into the prone woman.

One moment the coyote was trotting to catch up, his AK-47 held loosely in his left hand, feeling deeply satisfied with the night's activities. The next moment, a steel band whipped across his throat, and a knife pierced his ribs. Before his neurons could transmit and his brain could decode, Bwana's rocklike arms snapped his neck.

Bwana dragged the body to the side, lengthened his pace, and drew abreast of Roger.

The coyotes had not yet realized that one of theirs was missing, and were still loosely bunched together behind the illegals. Roger smiled grimly as he counted seven of them. None of them had gone ahead of the group.

The rough track had started widening, and the coyotes started pushing the group faster, shouting and cursing. Roger glanced at Bwana briefly. With the terrain opening, the risk of one or more of the coyotes heading to the front of the group increased.

One of the illegals stumbled and fell, and the coyote closest to her roared and lifted his rifle to strike her.

'*Hola, amigos,*' Roger called out softly and immediately stepped to his right.

The coyote froze, and the others jerked as if burnt and whirled. Flashlights stabbed the night, rifles leveled, and a query of voices rang out. Roger could make out English, Spanish and a few other languages that he didn't recognize.

The gunmen squinted against the lights, peering in the darkness, trying to see past the shape and shadows of the valley.

One of them let loose a fusillade at where he thought the voice had come from.

Bwana took him out with a head shot and dropped down prone.

Roger stepped sideways again, his Kimber coming up smooth and fast, the lights painting bull's-eyes on his targets, six shots roaring death in the ravine, double taps that felled three gunmen. He fell prone, rolled a few feet away, his gun tracking the group, and saw the remaining three drop as Bwana got them.

He kept the fallen heavies in his sight as Bwana approached them cautiously, not in a straight line, and confirmed the dead.

He joined his companion, and they walked around the group of illegals, who had come to a stop and were watching them vacantly. Bwana went up close to a few of them; they didn't step back, just looked at him. He shook his head and approached a few more and got no reaction.

Roger watched for a moment and then looked around for the woman who had attacked the gunman. He found her deep inside the group, shivering violently as she stared at him.

He approached her slowly, his arms spread wide, harmlessly.

'Hello.'

She didn't respond to his greeting but stood there motionless, shivering and watching.

'*Hola*,' he tried again and got no response.

'*Ola*.' Nope, just shivering and a blank look back at him.

He scratched his head and tried in French and got nothing in return. He cursed under his breath and shrugged out of the jacket he was wearing and went forward to drape it across her shoulders.

She flinched as he went closer, but did not utter a word when he had wrapped it around her. She pulled the jacket closer and stared back at him.

Roger realized she was young, maybe in her mid-twenties. With sudden shock he looked harder at the rest of the group, pushing his way in deeper – he had given the group only cursory glances till then since he had been focused on the coyotes.

All of the illegals were young white women. All of them maybe in their twenties.

He sought out Bwana, who nodded when he met Roger's gaze.

'Yep, I noticed it too.'

'Are they carrying any drugs?'

'Nope, but then I didn't search them,' replied Bwana. He checked his phone again. No signal still.

'Yours?'

'Nope. No idea how big the dead area is,' Roger said, referring to the lack of mobile coverage. 'We'll press on to the nearest town and hand these women to the police. Why don't you try talking to them and see if you have better luck than me?'

Bwana drifted over to the group as Roger went to the dead bodies and collected all the rifles and smashed their barrels on a large stone. He went to the nearest body and removed the jacket the illegal had been wearing.

You won't need it. Not where you are now, he thought and, dumping all the magazines in it, fashioned a rough rucksack.

He stood up as Bwana approached him, shaking his head.

'No luck. All of them are drugged to the gills. Not a single word from them. We need to get them to civilization quickly before the effects of the drugs wear off.'

Roger pulled out his compass from his pocket, and then it came back to him in a flash.

'These folks were all heading the wrong way.'

'Wrong way? What do you mean?' asked Bwana quizzically.

'They were heading TO Mexico. Not stateside!'

Chapter 15

Bwana looked at the group and then at the trail they had come from.

'Are you sure?'

Roger nodded, pointing in the general direction the bandits and illegals were heading. 'That way is Nogales. Nogales, Sonora, in Mexico.'

Turning back, he waved his hand. 'And that's where all the aliens and drugs head to. The I-19 from Nogales to Tucson distributes product, whether human or drugs. These guys were definitely heading *toward* Mexico, not deeper into the US. That's not the normal route for illegal immigrants to take.'

There was a pause as Bwana digested this. His face grew grimmer. 'Young white girls being smuggled to Mexico. We can guess what for. I'm glad we erased them. But more likely, they're part of a gang.'

He went to the bodies and started searching them. Roger joined him, and they went through the eight bandits thoroughly.

Half an hour later, they had laid out the results of the search on the ground. Wallets with no identity documents, a mobile phone, keys, loose change, magazines for the rifles, handguns, knives, but no documents, nothing that said, 'Mr. Coyote, Gangbanger.'

Roger investigated the phone. 'Burner phone. Just one number that has been dialed from it. No signal on this either.'

He slipped it in his pocket and turned to Bwana. 'Some of them look European, which would be a bit unusual for gangs doing this. You notice the mark on the wrist?'

Bwana nodded. 'Never seen it before, but then I am yet to do my PhD on gang tats. Looks like a playing card, a five of clubs.'

Roger thought for a moment and then shrugged. 'Nothing we can do till we get a mobile signal. Let's press on. Nearest town should be Rio Rico, that away, so let's get going now.'

The gangbangers had carafes of water with them, which Bwana and Roger shouldered. They went to the group of women, who were standing passively, watching them, and silently offered the water to them. Some of them drank thirstily, others just stared back blankly.

Bwana went ahead of the group and said, 'Let's go,' and the group moved obediently. Roger took one last look at the dead guys and made a mental note to wreak grievous bodily harm to any other gangbanger he met, and followed the group.

The bandits had clearly been following a well-trodden route and probably had a rendezvous with others at some point – others who would start pressing silent panic buttons when they didn't show. Bwana and Roger kept a careful watch and rotated the lead between them, but encountered no one else.

A couple of miles further, dawn broke, bathing the valley in silence, the vast and towering landscape making them feel like the only living beings on the planet.

A mile on, they got a mobile signal.

About forty-five minutes later they heard the Customs and Border Patrol chopper, which on spotting them swung low, and a loudspeaker came on, asking them to follow it to a clearing.

The chopper settled down in the clearing, and three heavily-armed Border Patrol agents jumped out and spread wide as they approached the group. Two other agents covered them from within the chopper, their H&K UMP .40 submachine guns tracking them. Bwana and Roger kept their hands empty and relaxed, conveying a nonthreatening message.

One of the agents walked up to them, his hands free but close to his H&K P2000 holstered pistol, while the other two circled the group of women and started offering water. Roger noticed one of those two was also carrying a medical kit with him.

He drew his attention back to the agent in front of him.

'Supervisory Border Patrol Agent Gonzalez,' the agent introduced himself. 'You guys had a long walk, it looks like. Need anything? Water? Chow? Medication?'

'We're good,' Bwana replied and introduced Roger and himself.

Gonzalez chewed slowly as he looked them over and noted their weapons. 'Never heard or seen such a thing happening before, two guys, ex-Special Forces, right? We checked on you. You guys took down eight bandits and rescued forty-odd hostages. They would have been sold into sex slavery, and once they had outlived that, would have been used as drug mules. All these women seem white American or European... at a casual glance, anyway. We'll process them once we take them to Nogales and start the investigative process as well as inform their kin.'

He scratched his head. 'We've busted some human-trafficking runs before, but not this large nor have we put down so many bandits. This has gotten the entire Border Patrol buzzing. You guys are going to have quite the reception when we get to Tucson.'

'Tucson? Not Nogales?' Roger asked him.

'Nope, we're going to Sector HQ in Tucson – this is big.' He paused. 'So why don't you tell me all that happened right from the beginning?'

Roger and Bwana were expecting this and talked him through their camping trip and the happenings of the night.

'Sir,' one of the agents shouted at Gonzalez, 'these women are drugged and are in a stupor. We need to move them fast.'

'Load them up and take them to base, Brodell. All of them won't fit, so we'll need to make two or three round trips. I'll stay with these guys till we're all done here.'

Brodell acknowledged with a thumbs-up and started leading the women to the chopper. Gonzalez watched as Brodell led about fourteen women to the chopper while the other agent led the rest to shade and tried to make them comfortable.

He then turned back to Roger and Bwana and saw they had drawn a map in the earth and hunkered down. Roger stuck a stick in the earth. 'This is where we were camping. Still got our gear there. Woke up in the night, sensed something was wrong—'

'Sensed how?' Gonzalez shouted over the roar of the chopper lifting off.

Bwana shrugged at him. 'We've lived with danger a long time. Knowing when something is off is second nature to us.'

Gonzalez nodded, expecting the answer, and waved at Roger to carry on.

'So we woke up, scouted around a bit, and saw this glow in the night, followed it and came across these guys.' He stuck another stick in the ground. 'This is where the bastards shot three women, and then we took them all out and led the women here, about four miles from where the action happened.'

'And if we track back, we'll find the bodies?' Gonzalez asked them.

'Danged right, but you'd better get there before buzzards and animals make short work of them. You'll also find their rifles, smashed, and if you go back further, our gear.'

'We'll be obliged if you get our gear back,' Bwana said straight faced.

Gonzalez laughed. 'We'll try.' He looked at the sheet of paper Bwana handed over to him.

'Coordinates of all the points Rog marked over there,' Bwana explained.

Gonzalez nodded in thanks, stood up, and used his radio to check where the chopper was. He then walked over to the women, tried talking to them, and walked back defeated.

'Have seen this before. The bandits drug them to the eyeballs and then make them walk the trails. Makes it easier for them to manage. By the way, did the bastards have any markings on them? Any gang signs?'

'Had a playing card sign on them. Here.' Bwana pulled out his phone and brought up a photograph and showed it to Gonzalez.

Bwana scrolled through a few more pictures and showed them to Gonzalez.

Gonzalez whistled as he swiped through the pictures. 'I dunno how well you guys are clued on gangs operating on the border, but these guys, 5Clubs, are an upcoming gang who've muscled in and started taking over the drug and human-trafficking business. This is the first time we've busted one of their runs.'

He looked up. 'Once we get you back to Tucson and sort out all the formalities and paperwork, will you come back with me to locate the bodies?'

'We're good to go right now,' Bwana replied.

Gonzalez shook his head. 'I wish we could, but paperwork is paperwork. Still let's see if we can grease the wheels and turn it around quickly.'

They heard the chopper returning and looked up.

'There's another behind it,' Roger commented.

'Yup, I want to get the women back to Tucson and medical attention as soon as possible,' Gonzalez said as he approached the women and got them organized.

Roger and Bwana followed him and helped him to split the women in two groups and get them aboard the choppers.

'We'll be turning back as soon as you meet the DCPA and debrief,' Gonzalez shouted over the racket of the chopper.

'Deputy Chief Patrol Agent Hugo Fernandez,' he clarified on seeing Roger's and Bwana's quizzical looks. 'El Jefe in Tucson, for the moment.'

Roger nodded and stared out of the chopper. He knew what was coming: briefing after briefing, to bureaucrats. He looked at Bwana, who read his mind and shrugged.

They were greeted by a phalanx of ambulances, doctors, and agents, who rushed to the group of women and took them away. Gonzalez led Roger and Bwana to the DCPA's office, who rose from his seat and strode around his desk to greet them. The room was bare of decoration except for a few awards and framed pictures of the President, and one of a uniformed person who they took to be the Chief of the Border Patrol.

Fernandez was short, stocky and mustachioed, with a weather-beaten face that had seen everything on the border. He sharply assessed the two before him and ushered them to their chairs.

'Gentlemen, Gonzalez would have told you we've rescued many men and women from human-trafficking bandits, turned away many illegal Mexicans, busted many drug runs, but this beats them all. I've no idea whether to call you heroes or lucky fools, but whatever you are, our thanks go to you.'

Roger and Bwana nodded silently.

'Now,' rasped Fernandez, in a voice sandpapered by the sun and the border, 'why don't you tell me everything right from the start.'

123

Bwana and Roger narrated their story once again as Fernandez silently handed over a couple of sheets to Gonzalez. *Our military records*, guessed Bwana. When Roger had finished, Fernandez strode over to a large map of the border on the wall behind him, took a box of flag pins with him, and grunted, 'Again.'

He started sticking pins on the map as Roger went through the events and walked them through the route they had taken. He turned around when they had fallen silent. 'This route is known to us, and we routinely patrol it, but budget cuts have taken their toll on our ability to man it as well as we would like to.

'This new gang, 5Clubs, is a lot smarter than all the others. They track us and seem to know when we are going to patrol the Corridor and lie low at that point. It wouldn't surprise us at all if they had snitches in Nogales and Tucson who monitored our movements, our choppers, everything, based on which the gang moved people. I mentioned before – this is the largest people bust we have made – but this is also the first time we have busted a movement going to the *other* side. In addition to that, it's the first time we've struck at this gang, and believe me, we've been itching to do this for a long time,' Gonzalez chimed in.

'Despite all our technology, all the choppers, sensors, satellites, all the geek shit we can throw at it, there's no way in hell we can seal the border totally, and thus drugs and people still get smuggled across the border.' Fernandez looked resigned for a moment and went quiet.

Bwana and Roger sat silently, allowing Fernandez and Gonzalez to blow steam. They had seen firsthand the enormity of the border and knew how difficult the task of patrolling was.

Fernandez collected himself, gave a last look at the map, sat down at his desk, and scribbled on a notepad. Tearing the sheet off, he handed it to Gonzalez and looked at the two men in front of him. 'You will go with Gonzo and recover the bodies and your kit.' It wasn't a request.

'We can leave once we've done that?' Roger asked him.

Fernandez nodded. 'Yup. No call to hold you guys. If it was me, I would have pinned a fricking medal or two on your chests.'

'Speaking of medals,' he continued, 'you don't have any shortage of those, do you? I made some calls when we first got your message. Got your sheets sent to me... you guys come recommended from so many places, so high, that my poor old head goes dizzy just thinking of those heights.'

Bwana shrugged. 'All those medals, they're a past life. We just got lucky in those days.'

'Not so past, so I've been told.' Fernandez looked at him shrewdly. 'I've also been told not to ask you guys too many questions about what you do now.'

'Why? We just fish now, sir.' Roger laughed and stood up to leave, Bwana following suit.

'One last point.' Fernandez halted them as the trio was heading to the door.

'This bust is so big that in no way can it be contained. The media will be all over it, and truth to say, we like our fifteen minutes. It makes the jobs of all these guys worthwhile and makes them feel recognized.' He waved broadly, meaning Gonzalez and the Border Patrol.

'Question to you – we can spin this to take all the credit, or we can share credit with you. If we share credit with you, your names will be public. The danger with that is that 5Clubs might hunt you down. They have a reputation for being ruthless and for meting out punishment… and seeing that you have wiped out a good amount of them and caused them a serious loss, they might want to treat you extra special.'

Roger grinned wide as he pointed at Bwana. 'Heck, mention our names. We're not shy. Besides, he's getting fat and lazy with all that fishing and sleeping. Time we had some excitement in our lives.'

'Are you sure? If they come after you, it'll be open season. They're known for it. There was this guy in Nogales who was suspected of being our snitch. He wasn't – we take care of our snitches and hide them well – but the rumor mill and the media somehow made this guy to be a snitch who fed us juice on 5Clubs and other gangs.

'This story broke out one evening. The next day, the guy was found dead at home, hanging from a ceiling fan. On closer inspection, his head was pinned to the fan with a stake. Driven through him when he was alive. Around him lay his family, all butchered, three generations of it.'

Fernandez paused. 'So, think about it. It could mean war if you guys are mentioned as being responsible for this bust and killing all those bandits.'

Bwana replied quietly, 'War is our business, sir.'

Chapter 16

Roger and Bwana followed Fernandez and Gonzalez outside the Border Patrol Office on Swan Road – a swarm of news vans and reporters awaited them. They spent the next hour answering the reporters and then made their escape with Gonzalez to the chopper awaiting them. They were accompanied by six more Border Patrol agents. *To get the bodies back,* thought Roger.

'I'd rather face twenty hostiles barehanded than go through that again,' grumbled Bwana as he belted himself in the chopper.

'What, and lose the chance to be known all across the country as the baddest man not to be crossed?' Roger grinned at him. Bwana gave him the finger and leaned forward to guide Gonzalez and the pilot, not that any directions were required, since they had coordinates to all the locations.

The chopper settled down at the same place that it had picked them up from, outside the canyon – that was the closest the chopper could get. Forty-five minutes later, as the sun was casting long shadows in the stillness of the canyon, they reached the bodies. What was left of them.

A few vultures lazily flew away as they approached, and Bwana shooed away the last coyote. Gonzalez went over the seven bodies again and discovered nothing – Roger and Bwana had handed over all that they had collected from the bodies. Gonzalez produced a camera and took several photographs of the bodies and the 5Clubs markings on all of them. He took a few other photographs of the surroundings and then beckoned to his agents. They'd brought large black body bags with them and in a short while had all the bodies wrapped. The six agents paired up and carried the bodies back to the chopper.

'Might be quicker if we helped,' Bwana murmured.

'Not his fault. Blame his folks. They brought him up to never be idle, not even for a few seconds,' Roger sighed, addressing the air, and followed Bwana.

An hour later, the bodies were stacked in the chopper, and Bwana led the way to the remaining bodies a hundred yards away. There was a risk that the gang would send more bandits to check on the missing, and Bwana and Roger were alert, but they were the only ones moving in the ravine. Other than the shadows.

Gonzalez approached the fallen women first and circled around them, his camera working rapidly. He knelt in silence next to one of the bodies, the woman who had been felled by the bandit's rifle, and noted her deformed head. His face was grim when he arose, and looking over at Roger and Bwana, he uttered a silent *thank you*.

Roger didn't know if that was for helping the agents or for taking care of the bandits. It didn't matter. He pointed silently to the coyote lying in the distance, his chest punctured by Bwana's knife.

Once Gonzalez had snapped away to fill his memory card, they placed all the bodies in the chopper, taking more care with the victims.

Roger turned to the Border Patrol agent once they were done. 'We can hoof it from here to our camping ground and recover our gear.'

'And how'll you get back?'

'The way we usually do. Hoofing it and hitching rides whenever we can,' drawled Bwana.

Gonzalez shook his head. 'The least we can do is help you recover your gear and get you back to Tucson.'

'It's about three miles away from here—'

'That's nothing. We've walked longer and in harsher conditions, and sometimes under bandit fire.' Gonzalez laughed and signaled to his men to follow them.

Bwana shrugged and led the way. The canyon was now throwing longer shadows as the sun began its daily descent. They moved with care, not disturbing the silence of the surroundings, keeping a sharp lookout for other bandits or any seek-and-destroy mission by 5Clubs. But other than the towering walls looking down at their insignificant forms, and the occasional wildlife, they encountered no one.

Probably realized discretion is the better part, thought Bwana, of the rest of the gang.

They found their camp near Pena Blanca Lake, in the thicket, undisturbed except for their pots and pans in disarray.

'Birds and wildlife,' surmised Roger and set about packing them up.

They always travelled light – just their camping gear and their weapons – and within half an hour, they had turned back to the trail to the chopper.

Ninety minutes later, in Tucson, they helped offload the bodies into anonymous vans. 'The media is still buzzing, and we don't want those assholes to follow our vehicles and hence these.' Gonzalez nodded at the vehicles when he saw Bwana's raised eyebrows.

'Dez wants to meet you and wrap things up,' he continued as he led Bwana and Roger to his Dodge Charger and eased into it with a satisfied grunt. Roger spotted a sticker across the wheel: '*We Do it For God and Country – And for the A/C too,*' and on cue, Gonzalez turned up the cooling.

'Thanks for the help, guys,' Fernandez greeted them when they went to his office. 'Hopefully we'll be able to identify the bodies and start working back to how the women got abducted. It should be easier to identify the bandits if they're from this side of the border. Chances are they'll have a record. Gonzo, why don't you do the honors?'

Gonzalez removed the memory disc from his camera and plugged it into a computer that was connected to a projector. He narrated the trail and their activities as he brought all the pictures up on a bare section of the wall.

Fernandez leaned back in his chair once Gonzalez had finished. 'Gotta cover that section of the canyon more.'

'We've done as much as we can, Dez. That section of the country is laid out so that only two legs can cover it, and we don't have the manpower to patrol it more often. Which is why those coyotes use it,' said Gonzalez as he let off frustrated steam and raised his hands heavenwards.

Roger and Bwana silently watched the byplay and then turned to each other with a *why're we still here* look.

Fernandez noticed the byplay, and his lips twitched. 'Yup, I would be getting itchy feet too if I were in your place. Like I said, you guys are well connected, and someone wants to talk to you. Apparently you guys have turned off your phones or they've run out of juice, and hence my office is the only place to make contact with you.'

Bwana and Roger simultaneously reached into their shirt pockets and dug out their phones.

Roger was first off the mark. 'Ran out of battery. You know who called?'

The phone rang, stilling Fernandez's reply. He lifted it, grunted in it, and handed it over to Roger.

'Get your butts over here,' came Broker's baritone. 'I swear, the moment I leave your side, you guys end up in trouble.'

Roger grinned broadly. 'Aye, aye, sir. As soon as we book our flight.'

'If you head over to the JetBlue desk, you'll find a couple of tickets for you and that worthless friend of yours.'

Roger looked over at Bwana and mouthed, *He called you worthless.*

'Forgive him, My Lord. He knows not what he does. Or says,' mumbled Bwana.

Fernandez started drumming his desk loudly, which was the cue for Roger to hang up and stand up.

'We'll be on our way now. Thank you for helping us recover the gear.'

Fernandez waved his thanks away and walked with them outside the office, where Gonzalez revved up the Charger to drop them off at the airport.

Gonzalez clapped his hand on Roger's shoulder. 'Watch your backs, guys. 5Clubs are not to be taken lightly, and chances are, they'll be seeking to get even.'

Bwana looked sideways at him with a face granite could be sharpened on. 'We're counting on that.'

Chapter 17

A whole night and half a day later, they knocked on the door of Broker's large apartment overlooking Columbus Avenue in Manhattan. Broker greeted them with a, 'Took you long enough to get here.'

'We would've been here sooner if you'd got your fingers out and invented time travel,' snarled Bwana and headed to the shower.

'Has he always been this cheerful and sunny?' Broker asked Roger, staring at Bwana's broad back.

'Ignore him. He hasn't killed any badasses in twenty-four hours. You know how cranky he gets. So what's cooking? Why did you get us here?'

Broker held his palm up for patience. 'All in good time. Bear and Chloe are in town too and should be here shortly. All will be revealed then. Now how about filling up those skinny frames of yours?' He laughed as Roger's stomach growled loudly on cue.

Broker regarded himself as a mean cook and never passed up an opportunity to treat his friends to his culinary offerings. He was a good cook, but they would rather have their nails pulled out with pliers than acknowledge that.

Broker led the way to his kitchen, where he had several chicken breasts and legs baking, coated with a mix of bread crumbs, lemon zest and thyme. He laid out cutlery on the dining table and, when Bwana walked in from his shower, bowed elaborately and gestured to their seats. Bear and Chloe came in from their walk just as Roger and Bwana were seating themselves. Hugs, fist bumps, and a bottle of Sauvignon Blanc later, Chloe turned to Roger and Bwana.

'So, guys, have you started getting calls from Hollywood? The channels have been reporting you as the modern-day version of S.H.I.E.L.D.'

Bwana shrugged embarrassedly. 'Chloe, don't believe all that shit they report. We just happened to be in the right place at the right time.'

'Or the wrong place at the wrong time, for those assholes,' chimed in Roger and then chuckled as he noticed Broker's slack-jawed expression. 'Yup, Bwana did blush then. You don't get to witness that sight often.' He ducked as Bwana swung a punch.

Turning back to Broker, he turned serious. 'I presume that's why you got us here? To deal with whatever this gang, 5Clubs, might throw at us?'

Broker swirled the wine in his glass and took a deep swallow. 'That's one part of it. The other part started a while back when the National Security Advisor requested a meeting with me.'

Roger choked on his food and, once his coughing fit had passed, exclaimed, 'You mean General Klouse?'

'None other.' Broker passed the bottle around, leant back and narrated his story.

A couple of hours and a second bottle later, Bear frowned. 'So we have this gang, 5Clubs, giving Roger and Bwana a gentle workout, and over here on the East Coast, they just might have cultivated a mole in the FBI. But if all the intelligence and computer shit at your disposal isn't able to find that mole, how exactly are we going to help?'

Broker leaned back in his chair, the light catching his shaggy hair, Surfer Dude with a halo.

'You know, Robert Hanssen was caught because the FBI went about trying to buy informants who knew his identity? They couldn't identify him as the mole through all their conventional investigation.'

'So we're going to buy this mole's identity? Shit, that'll require truckloads of the stuff. I know you're rolling in it, but do you really want to go down that route?' Bear was incredulous.

'Nope, I thought we would take a simpler approach.' Broker paused theatrically and sipped his wine slowly.

Chloe rolled her eyes. 'Out with it, Sherlock.'

Broker chuckled. 'Why, we'll just ask them politely.'

The pregnant silence lasted a few minutes, and then Bear guffawed as it hit him. Coming off his frame, it sounded like rolling thunder.

Broker looked searchingly at Roger and Bwana, who weren't displaying any particular reaction.

'You guys okay with this? This could get nasty, for a very long time. In fact' – he turned to Chloe – 'are you both on board with this? Me, I don't have anything to lose, but you guys have each other, and Roger and Broker have been partners for far longer than all of us have been working together for Clare.'

Another silence fell in the room, and this time Bwana broke it with a growl. 'I haven't known you to ask before, Broker, what gives?'

'I think I've become wiser ever since we lost Zeb and hence asking you guys to jump into this fully knowing that taking on 5Clubs will be a war, not a battle, and a war that we cannot win. We will never put out any gang. At the most, we'll put a dent in their operations.'

He passed the bottle around. 'And know this. It's perfectly okay to back out of this. There'll be other assignments – hell, there'll be a lot – which we *will* work on together.'

Chloe looked at him in disbelief. 'I can't believe this is the same Broker. We have *always* worked together, have never backed out of any assignment, never refused an assignment, however dangerous, whatever the threat... even if it meant we lose one of ours. So what the fuck has changed now?'

She slammed her palm on the table so hard the bottles jumped.

Broker smiled. 'Cool down, Chloe. I'm asking, because we lost Zeb and we never lost anyone before. I'm also asking because this is the first time we have assembled after Zeb, and I wanted to get a feel for your thinking on this assignment.'

Chloe snarled at him, her petite frame quivering with anger. 'Nothing's changed, Broker. We were a team, we are a team, and we'll *always be* a team. If Zeb's loss means anything, it's that we never fight alone. We are the best elite black-ops team in the world, which is why Clare employs us. We are fucking proud of that.'

Bear mumbled in his glass, 'Remind me never to piss her off,' and winced as Chloe slugged him in the shoulder.

Bwana cracked a wide grin. 'You're getting old, Broker. That's what this is all about. You can't handle the stress of working with us on an assignment anymore. Stress-related fear happens to many in the field. There's nothing to be ashamed of. You were a good operative once; you can be proud of that. Why don't you tend to your machines here and let us do all the heavy lifting?'

Broker gave him the finger. 'I'll stop to smell the roses and dawdle next time your sorry ass needs rescuing. All right, guys, it looks like your stupidity levels haven't diminished, so let's get serious. Clare doesn't have anything for us and knows we'll be helping Isakson on this.'

Roger pinched his nose as if to ward off a stench and said nasally, 'Keep that pile of shit away from me, will ya, Broker? Else I just might have a go at him.'

'You'll be joining a long line, believe me, but let's put aside what we feel for him for the time being. If there IS a mole in the FBI, and all signs do point to there being one, then let's uncover the bastard and stamp him out.'

He went to his study and returned with a sheaf of papers and laid out the six photographs in front of them.

'Agon Scheafer is the chief badass, the guy who put together 5Clubs. Scumbag was some hotshot commander in the Kosovo Liberation Army, but with a penchant for torturing women, raping them, raping kids too, driving stakes through people... that kinda shit. He became too hot for the KLA to handle, and just as they were going to put a bullet in him, he fled to our shores, adopted a new identity, and started this gang.'

He looked down at the dark eyes staring back from the photograph. 'He makes Holt look like Snow White.'

Chloe placed her hand over Broker's, bringing him back to the present, back from Zeb. 'Doesn't matter how ruthless he is. We'll get him to hand over the mole.'

Bwana raised his glass in a silent toast. 'Who're the other fuckers?'

Broker laid out the images in a row and pointed to each one of them. 'Jose Cruz, heads the Brooklyn arm; Martin Kelleher, Queens; Jorge Sancada, Bronx; Dieter Hamm, Manhattan and New Jersey; Pancho Morales, Staten Island. Agon looks after the activities on the West Coast himself. He's got some hood on the ground, who's chief hood there, but he's not a chapter head. Scheafer is based somewhere in New York, but never stays in the same place for more than a couple of nights... the usual shit these guys follow just to stay invisible.'

'We going to knock out all these guys?' Bwana asked hopefully.

Broker laughed, shaking his head. 'Let's not lose sight of what we want to achieve. We want to find out the identity of that mole – that doesn't mean we're going to start offing these assholes left, right, and center. If we did that, we might never find the mole.'

Bear looked up from his glass, which he had been looking at thoughtfully for a while. 'Is this the only way?'

Broker nodded. 'Werner' – he pointed to his desktop – 'has been running on this ever since I met Isakson and so far hasn't come up with anything. I've gone through the FBI investigation, and I can't fault it. Our way is an unconventional way, which no one will expect. But if you guys have other ideas, I'm listening.'

The five of them went quiet, and then Bear shook his head. 'You've had the most time to think this through. If you can't come up with any other way, then how the hell would we?'

'What I thought,' Broker said and handed slim dossiers to all of them. 'Those have more details on the gang. Go through them, memorize them, and get a feel for the top dogs. How are you guys for kit?'

'We have a cache, but we're open to topping up. There's no such thing as too much kit,' Bwana replied as he skimmed through the file.

'Right, we'll go to Bunk's for kit. You all know him, right?'

'Heard of him, but never had the pleasure of meeting.'

Broker noticed Roger frowning heavily. 'Something on your mind?'

'Yeah. How is this going to work? Which chapter are we going to go after? We going to stay together or split up?'

'We'll try the Manhattan bastards first. As for splitting up, nope. You both should be known to them by now, so safety in numbers and all that shit. Also, I don't want to pass up on any opportunity to keep your sorry ass from being shot.'

Roger smiled sardonically. 'Okay. Now what?'

'Now you finish that bottle and tell us some dirty stories. Tomorrow we'll head to Bunk's and indulge in some gun porn. The day after, we start a war.'

Chapter 18

'Where's this Bunk fella?' Bwana asked as he shoveled boiled eggs in his mouth for breakfast the next day.

'A town called Newburgh, an hour and half, two hours north of here, in Orange County. Badass country. The city was called Murder Capital of New York State, and remains one of the most crime- ridden cities in our beloved country.'

'Why?' Bear paused his chewing.

Broker set a plate of freshly boiled eggs on the table and sat down. 'The usual reasons − high unemployment, illegal immigrants, poor density of law enforcement, and lack of growth, investment, and development.'

He reached out for the eggs, but Bear's massive paw got there a shade earlier. He looked heavenward. 'It's breakfast, Bear, not a fricking competition.'

'I know, but my frame needs more nourishment than yours does,' said Bear witheringly.

Roger burped politely. 'So why's our guy there?'

'It's ideally suited for what he does. He's an arms supplier to gangs on the East Coast and some on the West Coast too. He also supplies to mercs, private contractors such as us.'

'And the law hasn't bagged him?' asked Bwana skeptically.

'That's a very good question. Your proximity to my brains is showing.' Broker grinned.

'Boys, calm down,' Chloe warned as Bwana gave Broker the finger.

'The law is fighting a losing battle in Newburgh. Its small alleys and narrow streets make it easy for gangbangers to get away fast, stage sieges, and all that shit. Now, the reason the law and the Feds have let Bunk operate is simple. He's a carefully cultivated snitch for them.'

Roger, who had been silently attacking his eggs and bacon, looked up at this. 'Say what?'

'He passes gang information to the Feds and the NYPD, has been doing so for a long time. Makes sense if you think of it. Given where he's based and what he does, he's ideally placed to provide juice. In return they let him deal with the gangs. Of course, they do keep tabs on what he sells, just in case he slips a nuclear warhead across the counter.'

He munched for a while. 'But he's really one of the good guys. Zeb was the one who found him. He was digging for possible associates of Holt and came across Bunk. Ex-Seal that he was, he'd trained with Holt and been on a few missions with him. I met him during Zeb's funeral service, and we've kept in touch since.'

He pushed back from the dining table. 'Right. Let's get your lazy asses rolling and spend some of my hard-earned dinero.'

Chloe went to one of the floor-to-ceiling glass windows and looked down at Columbus Avenue in the distance. 'Gee, Broker, you do like to live the high life, don't you?'

'It's part of the façade, Chloe. The people I sell to want to see a successful businessman, not some seedy-looking guy who operates out of his briefcase.

'Not that I'm complaining about all this.' He waved his hands to indicate his apartment, and his laugh bounced off all the glass as he led the way to the basement.

Broker's drive for the day was a heavily-customized Range Rover, extended at the back to make more storage, panels at the back of the seats for guns, a wireless network, armor plating and bulletproof glass, run-flat tires, radar, ejection seats. 'All the gizmos money can buy and some that it can't,' was how he put it.

Bwana leaned back into the plush leather seats with a contented sigh. 'Can you leave this to me in your will, Broker?'

Broker grinned. 'You'd just trash it when you went camping. And use it to store your fish.'

Roger chuckled. 'You got that right. Which is why we never take his car when we're travelling. A few moments in it and fish would wrinkle their noses up.'

'Should we swing by the Manhattan chapter's digs before we go to Newburgh?' Bear asked as he watched New York flow past the window in a heavily muted stream of color and motion.

Broker shook his head. 'Not now, not before we're fully kitted out. There's stuff in the Rover, but I'd prefer us to have our kit of choice before making any move. Maybe on the way back.'

They fell silent as Broker navigated them through the force of energy that was the city. Chloe looked up at the towers that pierced the skyline, Chrysler Tower peeking out in the distance, and murmured, 'This is why we do what we do.'

Bwana, draped over the last row, lifted his hand in a silent salute, stretched his legs, and prepared to snooze. 'Wake me up when we get there, Rog. Never been to Newburgh and want to see these guys that have Broker scared.'

Roger shook his head mournfully. 'See what I have to put up with? No wonder I end up doing all the work.' He pulled out a pencil stub and rummaged in the glove compartment for a notepad.

'Right, who wants what?'

Broker slowed down as he entered Newburgh an hour and a half later and nosed his way through the town. He deliberately took a circuitous route to show them around. Glancing briefly through his rearview mirror, he smiled when he saw all of them glued to their windows.

Chloe broke the silence finally as they passed yet another run-down street and homes hollowed out of hope. 'Bear, we are not coming *here* for our holidays.'

Bear shook his head. 'This is a town where hope has no hope.'

'That's right,' Broker commented. 'Now, I can go right to Bunk's parking lot, and we can hop to his store from there, or if you guys are hankering for some more atmosphere, I can park a little way out and we can hoof it.'

'Hoof it,' came the unanimous reply.

Broker grinned. 'You don't need to be macho all the time, you know? The wise man knows his own strength and doesn't need to flaunt it.'

Bwana looked balefully at Roger at that. 'Do me a favor, Rog. Shoot me the day I start uttering such horseshit.'

Broker found a parking space on Broadway a few hundred yards from Bunk's storefront, and they walked to the store from there.

Hoods lounging against walls and fences – attired in mandatory hood gear: sleeveless T-shirts, hoodies, hipsters hanging so low Newton would have rewritten the laws of gravity, and smokes dangling from stained teeth – straightened and gave them hard stares with eyes that had seen it all. Some of the hoods crowded around them wordlessly and fell back slowly as they advanced without breaking stride.

The hoods sported intricate ink, and many of them had teardrops with numbers beside them – the kills they had made.

Roger's lips barely moved. 'Punks. Half of them won't see the year end.'

'The other half, the next year,' muttered Bwana.

A distant bell rang from inside the store as Broker pushed the door open and led them inside. They spread out and stood stock-still, their looks making Broker laugh.

'Wow. Is this dude a gun dealer or a museum caretaker?' Chloe exclaimed.

The store had immaculately polished, gleaming wooden and glass cabinets everywhere. A horizontal running cabinet ran the length and breadth of the room, containing antique arms ranging from Roman knives to flintlock pistols, all neatly laid out and labeled. Hugging the walls were tall vertical cabinets featuring muskets, Civil War rifles, British shotguns, firearms of all makes and kinds dating far back into history.

Roger and Bwana crowded around a beautifully maintained muzzle-loading Baker rifle that had its ancestry chronicled on a handwritten note.

'Rog, I would like to marry that rifle,' Bwana said in a hushed tone.

Chloe snorted on hearing him. 'Any offspring aren't going to be better looking than you, Bwana. Let's not inflict such a crime on the world.'

Bear looked up from the second-generation 45 Colt single-action revolver in the cabinet in front of him. 'Broker, surely we aren't taking on 5Clubs with these?'

'Those aren't for sale,' came a voice from a door at the far end of the room. Bunk Talbot – as tall as Broker, slim, wiry, with close-cropped brown hair, dressed in a brown T-shirt tucked into a pair of faded jeans – strode into the room and bumped fists with all of them and then hugged Broker.

He grinned at Broker. 'Been a long time, bro. Good to see you're still kicking.' He cast an appraising eye on the rest of them and turned back to Broker.

'These them? The black ops legends?' The black ops world was a rarefied world, and there were rumors about ghosts – Clare's team – who trod where other special ops agencies feared to go.

Bwana lifted his hands heavenward. 'Hallelujah. Fame! Can the riches be far behind?' He turned to Roger. 'We need a money manager. And an agent.'

Roger studiously turned his back on him as Broker chuckled. 'Dunno about famous, Bunk, but crazy as loons for sure.' He introduced all of them to Bunk and then handed over the shopping list Roger had written.

Bunk studied the list and lifted an eyebrow. 'Starting a war, Broker? Aren't there enough already?'

'Insurance, my friend, just insurance.' Broker's baritone rumbled through the glass.

'What's the story with these?' Chloe asked Talbot, indicating the vintage and antique weapons.

'I've always been interested in old weapons and had started collecting stuff from when I was in the Seals, from all over the world. The collection just built up, and then when I got into selling arms, it became a very neat cover for my business. I sell vintage weapons also — though these are my private collection — and that's a perfect reason for all kinds of folks to meet me.'

He laughed sardonically. 'Hell, even the Latin Kings buy vintage weapons from me. They see those as instruments for investment. Of course that's not the only arms they buy from me.'

He waved the list and disappeared back into the depths he had come from. He returned an hour later wheeling two large duffel bags, placed them in the center of the room, went to the entrance and shut it, and then opened the bags.

Roger and Bwana crouched over the bags and pulled the weapons out and started ticking them off the list. They had ordered several M41As carbines, MP5A3 submachine guns, Glock 19s, Beretta M9s and the ammunition to go along with them... these now lay silently gleaming, filling the room with the smell of new weapons and gun oil.

Bwana dived into one of the bags and whistled softly as he lifted his favorite weapon, the Barrett M107A1 .50 caliber sniper rifle. 'Saved my ass many a time,' he murmured and sighted the Leupold Mark 4 scopes. Roger laid out stun grenades, body armor, combat knives, medical kits, and encrypted wireless comms equipment along with the base receivers.

'Used by the Secret Service,' commented Talbot as he watched the two work swiftly and surely. Bear and Chloe joined the two crouching and began putting the equipment back into the bags.

Talbot looked at them for a few more moments and then nodded at Broker. 'Privileged.'

Broker nodded back. He knew what Talbot meant. His guys were not *just another* elite force. They commanded the respect of even battle-hardened Special Forces operatives.

'What do you know of 5Clubs?' he asked Talbot as the others zipped the bags up and stood up.

'Nasty, ruthless, professional, and my biggest customers,' came the prompt reply.

'Are they active here? In Newburgh?'

'Nah. This town is for lesser gangs. 5Clubs runs New York City, large parts of New Jersey, and I heard they were looking to control the Mexican border.'

Something in Broker's posture made him narrow his eyes. He remembered fragments of conversation between some of the 5Clubs gangbangers, and the tumblers in his mind clicked. He looked at Broker with a question in his eyes and got a smile in return.

'You aim to wipe them out?'

'Nope. We want a piece of information from them. A name.' Broker grinned. 'All this is in case they refuse to play ball.'

'Do they know you guys yet? Have you commenced the game?'

Broker grinned wider. 'They don't know of us as this black ops team or such shit, but these guys have upset them a bit.' He nodded in Roger and Bwana's direction. 'You caught the news about girls, women, rescued in Arizona?'

Talbot looked in their direction in silence and then snapped his fingers. 'Fucking hell. You wiped out how many? Six? Seven?'

'Eight,' Chloe replied when Roger and Bwana remained silent.

Talbot shook his head in reluctant admiration and then sobered swiftly. 'This name you want – it's that important?'

'Yup.'

'Then get some more guys. I know enough operatives, good guys, who'd love to join you. The five of you ain't nowhere near enough for a gang of that size and that kind.'

'Nah, we'll manage.'

Talbot fell silent, opened his mouth to say something, and then closed it again. Then he blurted, 'Broker, I hope that's not ego speaking. This is not a run-of-the-mill gang of nasties. These guys are as professional as they come, with combat experience. Five of you against three hundred? Not enough.'

Chloe wiped her hands on a piece of linen she had in her rear pocket. 'We've enough ego to know our strength, but you're looking at this problem the same way everyone else will, and hopefully even the gang.'

She leaned against the long running counter. 'We're going to engage in guerrilla warfare, and our size is our strength. Secondly, just because they've seen action doesn't mean jack. They have been out of combat for a long while, and you should know what the lack of training does to an elite soldier's skills. Why, Bunk, you've seen combat. Do you think your skills today are still as good as they were back then? We train with the Seals, Delta, the Marines, Rangers, the Special Ops guys, all manners of black ops folks, and the Mossad's baddest guys when we're in between assignments. We know exactly how good we are and how bad they are.'

She didn't wait for him to reply. 'You said they're professionals. If they're as professional as everyone makes them out to be, they'll come to the table. And talk. Once they've worked out their cost-benefit-risk-loss analysis.'

Talbot looked at her in the growing silence, and a small smile tugged his lips. 'Why aren't you running a fancy corporation instead of whiling away with these bums?'

She chuckled. 'I run these bums – more interesting.'

Broker protested. 'Hey, I thought I was boss-man!'

She winked at Talbot. 'See what I mean? Such delusional people need someone like me.'

'Damned right,' Bear muttered and lifted his hands in apology when Broker mock-glared at him. Broker turned back to Talbot.

'You could do us a favor. Spread the word that we're after their hides.'

'Hooah. I know how you guys play that game now,' replied Talbot.

Roger and Bwana shouldered the large gun bags with effortless ease and headed to the door. Bwana looked at Chloe as he was passing her. 'I get to do the heavy lifting like always?'

'You're the only one we can rely on, Bwana,' Chloe replied sweetly.

Bwana straightened, squared his shoulders, puffed his chest out, and marched out, their laughter following him.

They walked back to Broker's Range Rover, the hoods in the street bunched together loosely, following them with their hard stares and contemptuous looks. Bwana looked back at the hoods through the window. 'Their mammas taught them one thing at least.'

'What's that?' Bear asked, puzzled.

'Discretion is the better part of valor.'

Chapter 19

Bunk stood in the door, watching them drive away, and then looked at the hoods watching the disappearing Rover. *I think I'll lose some of my clientele.* He grinned and, remembering Broker's request, went back inside the store, turned off the lights, turned on the alarm, and made his way to his favorite watering hole.

As he walked past the hoods, one of them shouted out, 'Yo, Bunk, who them bitches? Niggas walked like they owned this place.'

'Should've set them right,' spat another.

'They're all right, fellas. They're mercs.'

'Shoulda shown us some respect. Held back just because of you, Bunk, else we would've spanked their asses.'

Lucky for you, you didn't. Bunk put distance between them, turned into Liberty Street, and walked into the bar and was greeted by a nod from the bartender, who silently served him his first Grey Goose of the day. Talbot took a long pull, let its magic work, and looked around. He nodded to a few of the regulars and spotted another customer of his, a contractor who took on protection gigs in Africa.

He took his glass and headed to his customer's table and clinked his glass. 'You still here, Mack? I thought you were catching a flight to Somalia.'

Mack, a balding veteran who had served in the Rangers, took a generous sip of his beer, wiped the foam off his lips with a hand the size of a baseball mitt and hard as a shovel, and grunted in reply. 'Enjoying some beer that tastes like it before I head over there. Had to make arrangements for the stuff I got from you.'

151

They sat in companionable silence as they each demolished a fried steak. 'Say, Bunk, my gig will be over in about a month. I'll be needing another when I return, but this time, I would rather be stateside. Can you put the word out?' Mack's voice could drown a John Deere Monster Treads Tractor, but a whole steak inside his mouth acted as a muffler… for which Bunk was thankful.

'Hooah.' He nodded. 'Any particular kind of gig and location?'

The baseball mitt waved in the air, nearly decapitating Bunk. 'Nah. Am too old to be particular. Am thinking of hanging up my boots next year, and want these last few gigs to be here.'

'Say, you heard what happened to Kelton Pahle?'

Bunk shook his head and wondered if he had made a mistake joining Mack. Mack was known for his gossip, and Bunk was dreading he would be stuck there for a long while.

Thankfully it was only an hour later that he surfaced from his listening mode at Mack's, 'What's happening your end? Anything new?'

'There's this bunch of Special Ops guys that I know from way back. They're into something big, really big.'

Mack leaned forward, and the wooden table creaked in protest. 'Huh? What kinda big? Government stuff? Protection stuff? Celebrity protection? What?'

'Bigger than that. They're taking on a gang, the fastest-growing gang in these parts.'

Mack sat back and worked it in his head, and then his eyebrows disappeared into the creases on his forehead. 'You mean…'

'Yup, the same hoods.'

Mack whistled softly. 'Why? Do I know these guys?'

Bunk shook his head. 'Not a fucking clue why. And you don't. Hardly anyone knows these guys. They're ghosts.' He wiped his hands, left a hefty tip, and stood up.

'Hey, give me a frigging clue. Who are they? Can I run with them?'

He grinned at Mack. 'I gave you a clue, Mack, not that it'll help you much since only a handful of people know them. They're a tight-knit group – don't work with anyone. Hell, even I don't know them. They just buy stuff from me, and this stuff is something I overheard when they thought they were alone.'

He waved his hand at Mack as he left. 'I'll put your name out and send you word.'

The Watcher was sitting nearby, wearing a New York Yankees cap and dark glasses. And a thick beard. He had looked back when the waitress had stared at him, a *glasses-in-broad-daylight-and indoors-too* stare, and she had hurried away. He had slipped in when Bunk had seated himself with Mack, and rested himself a couple of tables behind Bunk. From there, he could easily overhear most of their conversation. *With the way Mack was going, some of it could be overheard on Mars.*

He'd ordered a blackened chicken sandwich and, placing a half-folded newspaper beside it, proceeded to demolish it. And listen.

He leaned back from his plate when Bunk left the bar, and looked across at Mack. Mack was well on his way to getting smashed. He waved his hand in the air, caught the bartender's eye, and indicated another beer for Mack.

'Bro, I couldn't help overhearing Bunk's comments. Did he say which gang those ghosts of his were going after?'

Mack looked up blearily and then at the cold beer that had appeared by magic. 'Nah. You know Bunk?'

The Watcher nodded silently.

'You know how he is. Tighter than a clam, the bastard. Never gave me any names of the ghosts. I woulda loved to join their action.'

'What about the gang?' the Watcher asked patiently. Talking to a tractor took patience.

Mack blinked, and the Watcher could hear the brain cells moving sluggishly as they attempted a response.

'Gang? Nah, man. He clammed up on that too.'

From the depths, his brain cells dragged out a memory.

'He did say it was the fastest-growing gang. 5Clubs is who I think they are. The bastards are growing faster than mushrooms on steroids. You in the game?'

The Watcher shook his head. 'Just a boring accountant.'

Mack bent down and chased thick potato wedges with his fork. 'Dunno why Bunk's so fucking tightlipped. I'm sure I coulda been useful to those ghosts.' When he looked up, the Watcher had gone.

'Fucking ghosts everywhere,' Mack grumbled and disposed of the wedges.

The Watcher stood in the shadows of an alley near the bar and looked the way Talbot had gone. He walked halfway down the street Bunk had come up and turned into a narrow street that led to where his truck was parked.

Two hoods accosted him in the street.

One of them, black and heavily tattooed, teardrops marking half his face; the other with a shaven head and a permanent leer on his lips.

'Now, who do we have here, Kano?' Teardrop rumbled.

'Looks like fresh pussy. Ya think this nigga is with them other bitches?'

'Nigga, we asking you something,' Teardrop asked impatiently when the Watcher stood silently, motionlessly.

'You think he deaf?' Teardrop queried his friend when the silent standoff continued.

'Mebbe he blind too, what with them glasses,' replied Kano.

Teardrop chuckled and then laughed loudly, exposing stained teeth and breath that a corpse would have fled from. 'The bitch have a bitch dog to guide him, then. Can't see any other bitch here, though.'

The Watcher looked at them a few more seconds and then started ahead, making his way between the two of them.

Teardrop dropped a huge hand on the Watcher's shoulder. 'Hey, muthafucka, we talking to—'

The Watcher flowed, a single move that started at his heels, moved up his body, through his shoulder and down his arm to his hand that gripped Teardrop's hand, removed it effortlessly and clamped it tighter than a vise and twisted Teardrop's arm, dislocating his shoulder. The Watcher kicked his feet away, and Teardrop fell heavily, his shriek echoing in the neighborhood.

The Watcher leaned down, hooked his hand through Teardrop's hipster, and threw him bodily into Kano's body, whose head was still processing what his eyes had seen. Teardrop's head smacked deeply in his midriff, and both went down untidily. The Watcher stamped Kano's right hand, crushing his fingers for good measure.

He stripped both of them of their weapons – a couple of Czech pistols and a wicked, serrated knife. He removed the magazines from the guns and pocketed them, and broke the knife.

Assholes could have just walked on, and their day would've turned out differently. He looked down at them moaning softly, and then around. The street was quiet and undisturbed. Newburgh had seen and heard far worse than daytime shrieking to be bothered about it.

He walked on unhurriedly to his truck.

He had been drifting north to south along the Eastern Seaboard, down the I-95, when the clutch on his Dodge pickup reached its end of life. He had then drifted inwards seeking a replacement. He could have had the clutch replaced at any number of garages, but he was picky. He wanted a mechanic who didn't want to engage him in any conversation... not about football, baseball, politics, nothing. A mechanic who grunted when he took on a job and grunted when he finished. The Watcher didn't like conversation. He knew such a one in Newburgh and didn't mind the detour.

After all, there was no schedule to keep.

He was off the grid. No phones, no laptops, no email... the nearest thing he had to an electronic device was his electric razor, and that was dead. Nobody could contact him, and nobody knew where he was, which was not very surprising. Only one person on the planet knew who he was, and that person was not expecting any contact from him for a while.

An hour later he was speeding in his truck towards New York.

Speeding was a word used loosely since he could see white-haired grannies overtaking him in their Lincolns as he chugged along in the slow lane. A few even gave him the finger and inched faster when his dark glasses swung their way.

He coaxed as much juice as he could from the Dodge, without it falling apart, and settled back in his seat. Time hadn't been an issue earlier; it was now.

He knew who the ghosts were and what damage they could do.

Chapter 20

The Watcher hit George Washington Bridge a couple of hours later and headed south on Henry Hudson Parkway, down West Side Highway, and slowed as he reached the outer edges of the Garment District and headed east. He found a crowded parking lot and nosed his truck between an equally decrepit Toyota and a Ford Explorer. Taking his sole possession, a rucksack, he headed to a self-storage on Thirty-Sixth Street. He headed out of the storage an hour later, his rucksack weighed down by his Glock, magazines, other stuff a good ghost carried, and a hunting knife.

He headed to the nearest pay phone and dialed a number. He knew how the other person would react. *Look at the number, frown, think about ignoring it, think again, and turn on the speaker.*

He spoke one sentence, ignored the exclamation of surprise, and listened. Ten minutes later he was heading north. He knew what was happening and what he had to do.

Broker headed into the city once they crossed George Washington Bridge and drifted into Harlem. 'You guys wanted to check out the Manhattan Chapter?'

He headed deeper, past Hamilton Heights, and then headed south on St. Nicholas Avenue and headed east again, the neighborhood sprouting auto repair shops, computer shops, barbers, any number of small businesses. 'Harlem's gotten better in the last few years... fewer gangs and safer streets... but still a long way to go.'

He slowed a little and pointed to a large walled compound on the left, and as he neared it, they could make out the name of a garage fronting a wide entrance. Several cars stood in the forecourt, and they could see a hive of activity in the garage.

'This is where they hang out. Dieter Hamm, a few shooters, the top hoods. This is where they do business.'

Roger noted the security cameras and tapped Broker, who speeded up slightly. 'You want one more pass?'

Roger shook his head. 'Let's work out what we're going to do, and then we can come back tomorrow. I'm sure the moment we make another pass, we'll get flagged, if they have any decent security shit.'

'They will,' Broker said grimly. 'They're hoods basically, but not stupid hoods. Let's not reveal ourselves tonight.'

They reached Broker's apartment in near silence, and as they were going up the elevator, Chloe broke the silence. 'The first time we met, you said we'll just ask them. That's what we'll do. We'll go to that garage and ask this Hamm.'

Bear bowed extravagantly. 'Your wish is our command, milady.'

She snorted. 'That would be good if it wasn't a one-off. And you better be packing heat tomorrow. We're not going to Sunday school.'

Bwana looked up hopefully. 'We off-ing Hamm tomorrow?'

She shook her head. 'I am surrounded by idiot savages.'

Broker used the same Rover the next day. 'If we're declaring our hand, they might as well know our ride.'

The car shop was busy when they arrived. Broker parked, the Rover facing its entrance, with a clear lane for exit, and led the way inside. Bwana strayed from the group and paused to watch a couple of mechanics work on a Mustang. *Seem to know what they're doing. This is a very good front for the gang.*

He went into the reception, a large, white-tiled square that had a desk at one end and posters of cars all over the walls. Broker was talking to a short, bald mechanic with greasy fingers; the others were casually spread out.

'Dieter Hamm. We're here to see him.'

'No one here by that name, man. You got a car to be looked at?'

'No, we're here to see Hamm. Could you tell him we're here?' Broker, patient, coming across as the Wall Street executive.

The first trace of impatience came into the mechanic's voice, and his voice roughened. 'Told ya, no one by that name. And if you don't have a car to be looked at, you're wasting our time.'

'Who's your manager? Let me speak to him?'

The mechanic opened his mouth and then shut it and looked over Broker's shoulder. Broker turned to see a tall man in a well-tailored suit glide forward, his tanned skin stretched across his face, his head bristling with a steel gray buzz cut.

He stopped a few feet in front of Broker and made an eye signal to the mechanic to leave.

'Can I help you?'

'Not if you aren't Dieter Hamm. We're here to see him.'

'I think Enrique's told you already that we don't have anyone by that name here. Now if you don't have any vehicle to be repaired, I suggest you leave. As you can see, we're busy, and you're eating up billable hours.'

Roger shouldered forward. 'Let's drop the shit, shall we? We know this is a front for 5Clubs, and we know Dieter Hamm runs this chapter. We want to see him. Tell him we're here.'

Suit looked Roger up and down and then at the others. 'Gang? 5Clubs? You've got your facts wrong. I own this business, and I've nothing to do with gangs. Now I suggest you leave, or I'll call the cops for harassing us.'

Broker pulled out a business card and handed it to Suit. 'We'll be back tomorrow and will expect to see Hamm.'

Suit took the card carelessly and placed it on the desk without looking at it. 'You'll be wasting your time.'

He stood in the center of the floor watching them leave. Bear lingered and looked him over. 'You were a Joe?'

Suit shook his head, his lips moved in a sneer. 'Marine.'

Bear nodded and left silently, Suit watching him.

Suit made his way to an inner office that overlooked the forecourt and parted the window blinds to watch their Rover leave the garage.

He picked up his phone after activating a scrambler. 'Some guys came asking for you. Four guys and a woman. They didn't give a reason and didn't believe that you weren't here.'

He listened in silence and then described them.

'Hold on.' He put the phone down to fetch Broker's card.

'Business card says Broker and has a number. Nothing else on it.'

He spelt out the name and a New York number. 'He said they'd be back tomorrow.'

He listened some more and grunted and put the phone down.

Hamm tossed the phone, leaned back in a plush chair covered with lizard skin, and stretched. His body rippled and flowed in the chair, the long snake tattoo on his forearm curling and flexing. 5Clubs had a flat hierarchy with no layers separating the bosses from the hoods. Quinn and a few other managers, in effect the enforcers and shooters, had easy access to him. The gang also had an impressive early warning system. Anything out of the ordinary got reported upwards immediately, however small.

That the garage was a front for the gang was known to very few in the business – even the NYPD had no knowledge of this – it troubled him that the façade had been uncovered so quickly by these strangers.

He picked up another phone, a burner phone that would be crushed at the end of the day, and called a number that was burnt in his memory. That number would change the next day, and he would have to memorize the new one. He was allowed to make only one call a day to the number.

The phone at the other end got picked up after precisely five rings. Always five rings, no more, no less, at any time.

The person at the other end didn't say anything, just filled the line with silence.

Hamm recited what had occurred in short precise sentences, unemotionally. The listener didn't say anything for a long minute after he had finished. 'You trust Quinn?'

'Yes. Served with me. Good guy, not imaginative, but will die for the gang.'

'Call me in two hours.'

Hamm nodded. 'Okay.'

After two hours he got his orders. Meet the strangers and find out what they want. Have them followed. Bugged if possible.

The next day, the garage was the same scene, except for the presence of several hoods loitering around, alert, trying to fit in and failing.

Suit approached them as Broker led them inside the office. Suit was in decent shape for his age, but the well-cut jacket couldn't hide the thickening of the waist.

Broker greeted Suit before he could open his mouth. 'Hamm going to see us?'

Suit gestured to a few chairs and disappeared wordlessly into the snugly fit door he had come from.

'Power games,' mumbled Broker to Roger, who was closest to him.

'Who's the fucker? Bear said he was a Marine?'

Broker nodded. 'Name's Quinn. Nothing special in his record. Except for a dishonorable discharge. A temper that gets worse when drunk, and he gets drunk often.'

Broker looked over at Bwana and frowned. Bwana and Chloe were looking up at the ceiling. If you looked hard enough, you could just make out the concealed camera. Bwana stuck his finger up and grinned silently.

'Cut that shit out, Bwana. This is a public place.'

Chloe gave a last look at the camera. 'Maybe Bear and I should wait in the Rover?'

Broker nodded in their direction, their ride had to be secure, and settled down to wait, Roger and Bwana leaning against the opposite wall. An hour later they were unmoving, all three of them, with their eyes shut. They heard various customers drift in and out of the office, the clunky sounds of the garage at work, and then the inner door opened.

'Come.'

Broker opened his eyes to see Quinn beckoning at him. He flowed out of his chair and approached Quinn, Bwana and Roger falling in behind him.

'Not them. Just you. This is not a fucking convention.'

Bwana and Roger resumed their Zen meditation as Broker disappeared behind the inner door.

It was a simple office. There were millions of such offices in millions of garages around the country. Untidy piles of paper littered the desk and the filing cabinet in the corner, posters and certifications hung on the wall, a coffee pot bubbled away in the corner.

Millions of garages around the country did not have Dieter Hamm, chapter head of 5 Clubs, seated lazily behind the desk. Hamm was wearing a blue shirt hugging his muscular body, the sleeves rolled up to his elbows, exposing veined, hairy, tattooed forearms. His eyes were dark and hooded as he watched Broker cross the room and seat himself after being expertly patted down by Quinn.

He tossed Broker's card across the desk. 'You demanded this meeting. What do you want?'

Broker leaned back in his chair and contemplated him, and a broad smile split his face, a chuckle coming from deep inside.

Hamm's hooded eyes didn't change; his expression didn't change. 'Something funny?'

Broker waved his hand to encompass the room. 'Yup. This. You. You're just a punk. All right, a punk who dresses well and speaks well, but still a punk. And look at your airs!'

Quinn shifted on his legs behind him, his shoes creaking above the muted sound of the garage. Hamm blinked. 'You're wasting my time. What do you want?'

'I want the mole you guys have in the FBI.'

Hamm regarded Broker curiously. 'Mole? FBI? I don't know what you're talking about. Why would I have a mole in the FBI? What does a garage have to do with them?'

Broker smiled, but no mirth reached his eyes. 'Look, Hammy. I'm so glad you didn't pull that I'm-just-a-small-business shit with me. I know who you are, and doubtless you have done some research on me. Let's not act virginal about this FBI mole crap. I know you have one there, you know it, and the Feds know it. All I want is the scumbag's name, and I'm out of your life. I am least interested in your gang and your activities.'

Hamm continued regarding him curiously. 'Is this where the threats come in? Where you say you'll destroy us if we don't give up this hypothetical mole?'

Broker's sunny grin filled the room. 'Hammy, don't be dramatic. You guys are what, three, four hundred at last count. How can three or four of us destroy you? Nope. I think you'll listen to reason.'

Hamm's brow furrowed. 'What might that reason be?'

Broker had to restrain himself from rubbing his hands together. 'Those guys outside, they're the reason. See, two of them are known to you. They came across your guys on the border... you're short a few hoods over there, aren't you?

'You might want to check their faces against the news bulletins from Tucson,' he added helpfully.

He heard Quinn leave the office and allowed the silence to build.

'Those two don't like hoods. Hell, none of us do. You guys are parasites. But as you know, I am a businessman. Live and let live is my policy.' Broker believed himself. Almost.

He nodded his head, indicating the guys outside. 'I had a tough time restraining those two. They not only share my dislike for

166

hoods, they carry a torch for the vulnerable. Like young girls. Women. Children. They wanted to start a war in Arizona and California and take down all your guys there. The Border Patrol talked them out of it. Luckily. For you.

'So, they're the reason. Them and the other two.' He sat back, case made.

Hamm held up a calloused hand, the fingers slender and rock steady. 'I'm trembling. Wetting my pants.'

'I didn't think you would be. You're a shit. But you're a shit that's survived the toilet paper. But I also think you, and all you cruds and your chief crud, Scheafer, are businessmen and understand risk and reward, cost and benefits.'

'You really thought you could come here, insult us, demand this nonexistent mole, and we would bend over?'

Broker smiled genuinely this time. 'Nope. This is exactly the reaction I was expecting. My guys will be glad. They're getting fat and lazy.'

He headed to the door and pulled it open and turned back. 'You're lucky. Bwana wanted to take you out today.'

Hamm stared at the door as he heard muffled voices from behind it. It swung open abruptly.

Bwana and Roger took a step inside silently and looked back at him.

Roger finally spoke. 'We'll save you for last.'

Chapter 21

'What now?' Chloe demanded as they reached the Rover. She had to shout to be heard over a power hammer and compressor.

All of them were wearing shades, the specially modified Ray-Ban Aviators Broker had outfitted with rear cameras. Broker turned on his shades and noticed the hoods bunched together watching their departure.

'Any trouble?' he asked Chloe in return.

'Nope. They would be stupid to do anything in broad daylight,' she replied impatiently.

'Hey, no one said hoods were geniuses.' He rolled outside the exit, and once they hit Nicholas Avenue, his eyes met Bwana's in the mirror.

'Let me know if you can spot them.'

Bwana nodded silently and went back to watching through the darkened rear window.

Broker glanced sideways over his shoulder at Bear and Chloe and answered her finally. 'Now we sit tight for a couple of days and then hit one of their warehouses. We rinse and repeat. We remain on the move always.'

Bear broke his usual silence. 'You know where they stash their drugs?'

Broker grinned. 'I can find some of them. But let's not go just after the drugs. They run a whole lot of operations, drugs, girls, porn video shops, you name it. Let's distribute the pain.'

Roger looked at the rearview mirror on his door, and no vehicle stood out. 'Why wait a couple of days? We've warned him already.'

Broker nodded as Chloe cut in, 'Yep, but waiting will dull their alertness. That's assuming they take us seriously.'

'They will if they've got enough intel on us.'

Silence descended on them, a comfortable silence born out of working together, fitting perfectly, and knowing that each of their lives could, and *had* depended on the others.

'Five o'clock, tan Toyota Camry. Been with us for a while now through the lights and traffic. I make two in the front. Driver and passenger. Can't make their faces,' Bwana said, looking at the tiny images on his shades, then looking out the back.

Roger removed his Aviators and adjusted the mirror on his side. 'Got them.'

'We lose them?' he asked Broker.

Broker looked at the series of traffic lights strung out ahead of them in the distance and sped up a notch, keeping in the outer lane.

The Toyota followed and cut across the lanes lazily and positioned itself a couple of cars behind them.

Broker drove steadily, following the weight of the traffic, and as he approached the third light, he slowed down and then punched the gas as it turned red, cut across the lanes dangerously, and pulled a tight illegal U-turn, leaving rubber and furious honking behind.

The Toyota was stuck at the light, its driver burning holes through their glass as they headed in the opposite direction.

Broker punched a button on the wheel for a number.

'Yeah?' a laconic voice answered.

'Tony, we'll be there in twenty. Everything set?'

'Yes, boss.'

Broker hung up and relaxed back.

'We switching?' Chloe asked.

'Yup. Switching where we stay too. We'll keep changing locations now.'

Broker drove to the financial district and into a basement parking lot of a towering office block. The lot was empty except for a black Ford Taurus in the far corner.

Tony, skinny and with thinning hair, jumped out of the Taurus and approached them when Broker parallel parked. He stroked his thinning hair. 'I swung by your apartment and got all your kits packed in separate go bags.'

He blushed as he turned to Chloe. 'Uhhh, ma'am, I put together some stuff for you too.'

Chloe smiled at him reassuringly. 'We'll do just fine, Tony. Thanks for your help.'

They transferred their weapons from the Rover to the Taurus, and Broker tossed its keys to Tony. 'Get it back to the basement, Tony. I'll be on my satellite phone; we all will be on ours, from now on.

170

Hold the fort and run past my apartment every now and then. You know the drill.'

Tony nodded and gave them a salute as he drove the Rover away.

'Good guy. He's my number two. Don't let his appearance fool you. Ex-Ranger. He's ice cold under pressure and a master marksman who's seen combat.' Broker nodded in his direction. 'All my guys are either ex-police or ex-military… cool heads when things hit the fan.'

He noticed Roger rummaging through his go bag. 'Problem?'

Roger shook his head. 'On the contrary. How the hell did he know my favorite stuff?'

Broker was incredulous. 'I am in the *intelligence* business, Rog.' He shook his head in despair as Roger disappeared behind the Taurus to change into a pair of jeans.

'Why're you changing?'

Bwana jumped in disgustedly, 'Hell, he's like that. Changes four or five times a day. Has to look as if he's stepped out of *GQ*.'

Roger folded his discarded clothes, stuffed them in the bag, and approached them.

'What?' Bwana asked him, seeing the expression on his face.

Roger held out a phone. 'I found this in my jeans. I was wearing them in the valley.'

Bwana frowned as he inspected the phone. 'This must be from one of the bandits. We were searching them, and you must have slipped it in your pocket and then forgotten about it.'

He powered it on. 'Nada. No juice.'

Broker took apart its battery and put it back again and powered it up. He shook his head. 'Deader than that frog in my biology class in high school. This is a pretty basic phone. We'll power it up later and see whether we can retrieve any numbers or messages off it.'

Roger looked at him doubtfully. 'I think there was one number on it, but I don't remember it.' He looked at Bwana, who shook his head. 'Shouldn't we ship it to the Border Patrol?'

'We will. *After* we have played around with it.'

He clapped Roger on the shoulder. 'Good find, even if it was a late discovery. Now let's hope it yields some dirt.'

Chloe had been inspecting her bag and looked up impatiently. 'Can we get out of here now? Broker, I presume you've arranged digs for us?'

'You presume right, Chloe. A seedy place – an hourly hotel, between Little Italy and Central Park, will be our palace for a few days. Not exactly the Mandarin Oriental.'

He drove out of the basement lot and merged into traffic, which was moving slowly, dragged down by the after-office commuters.

The hotel was as seedy as Broker had promised. A wad of cash flashed by Broker ensured that the desk clerk didn't glance at them, hardly looking up from the lurid magazine he was thumbing through.

Broker pulled out his iPad once they had settled in and assembled in his room. 'One of their stashes.' He enlarged a section of the map of Harlem. 'About half an hour drive from the garage, the other end of Harlem, near the river. The gang bought a dilapidated plot having a couple of semi-detached houses a few years back and converted it to a storage and distribution center. They deliberately let it run down on the outside and on the inside demolished the separating walls and made it one large warehouse.

'They receive drugs here, unpack them and pack them into smaller units for street distribution. They usually have fifty Ks there, and that's just coke. They have other nasties there, meth, PCP, 2CP, all kinds of stuff people inhale, inject, and consume.'

He pulled up a series of images of the warehouse. 'The warehouse is basically a long rectangle with one of the smaller sides facing the street. It's surrounded by a wall, and there's a gated entrance at street level. Front door is solid oak, a few inches thick, opens outward. Has a sliding slat that covers a peephole. A couple of barred windows either side of the door, a bit high up, and three windows each on the side walls. The rear is exactly the same as the front. Just the two exits, front and back. All windows are barred. Four corners of the house have CCTV cameras. As far as Joe Public is concerned, this place is some sort of civic or community center. A couple of heavies always at the gate to discourage Joe Public and to ensure that the *right* community enters the warehouse. Not that it's a street Joe Public would frequent. It's gang territory, and they know enough to keep away.'

Chloe frowned at the images. 'What about the surroundings?'

'Low-income apartment blocks, where a lot of single-parent families, broken families, reside. This is not exactly the neighborhood where you'll find moms and kids or couples going

173

for a stroll. If there's anyone loitering on the street, chances are they're hoods.'

'How come the police haven't pulled this place down? If you know of this, surely they do too? In fact, how did you know the chapters operate from all those places, that garage, for example? If it was so easy to find where the gang holed up, surely the cops would have been on them like a ton of bricks,' Bwana asked him.

Broker counted on his fingers. 'One, the cops cannot act until they have probable cause, for which they have to mount surveillance, monitor various gangbangers, all that shit, which can take days, weeks, months or years. Just because they *know* that the garage is Hamm's office isn't worth jack.

'Two, the chapter headquarters are properties owned by the gang through a series of shell companies, which have offshore accounts. The cops need warrants and have to cut through international red tape to tie all those together and lead it back to the gang. Werner' – he nodded at his computer – 'doesn't need all that shit. Werner goes where he wants to' – the program was a living being for Broker – 'does what he wants, and leaves no trace. I have some incredibly smart guys all over the world, like the Ukraine for example, who put the pieces together. There's a lot of technology that goes into gathering such info. Using gangbanger sightings at various places, correlating street chatter, drawing radii of influences, running facial recognition programs, analyzing Facebook posts, reading financial statements... lots of geeky stuff.'

The middle finger came out. 'I shared my dossier on the gang with the cops a long time back, and I'm sure the intel in it has helped their organized crime task forces, but like I said, they've got their constraints.'

Broker made a disgusted face. 'One of my analysts came across *this* warehouse by accident when he was gathering juice on illegal arms shipments in the city. I fed the NYPD this intel, and they never did anything about it. I took it up with Clare, and she said the NYPD had politely told her that I should mind my own business. So I did.'

Roger looked up at him. 'Are you sure the gang still uses the warehouse?'

'Yup. Tony has been watching it for a few weeks now. In fact, there's possibly a stash there; he saw stuff being unloaded. Came two days back and the gang hasn't shipped out whatever came in yet.'

Chloe scrolled through the various images. 'How many bandits?'

'About eight heavies work inside the warehouse and cover it, two or three park their asses on the street usually. But Tony says now there are anywhere from twelve to fifteen inside and five outside. Guess Hamm must have told them about us.'

'Shouldn't we tip the cops?' Roger asked.

Broker grinned. 'Done. I've a friend there who's pretty high up; I've told him. Have also asked him to give us a few hours before they hit the warehouse. We go a long way back, plus Clare has pulled strings. Dunno what yarn she has spun, but he knows juice when he hears it.'

Bear cracked his knuckles. 'What's the plan?'

Broker grinned. 'We do some distribution ourselves.'

Chapter 22

They hit the warehouse at noon the next day.

Bwana cruised down the street, driving a bright red Ford SUV with dark windows, wearing a red cut-off tee that showed off his heavily muscled arms, a black bandana covering his head. His windows were rolled down, and music blasted away, audible at the next planet. Not exactly a gangbanger look, more like *dad-banger*.

'Five hoods outside, three to the left of the gate, two to the right. All wearing our favorite gang tats. Gate is wide open. No signs of activity outside or inside,' he murmured into his collar mic.

'Roger,' came Broker's voice through the flesh-colored earbud.

Bwana glanced disinterestedly at the hoods and drove slowly on. Once past them, he arranged his inside mirror and made eye contact with Roger and Bear, who were in the rear of the vehicle. They gave him a silent thumbs-up, having heard his call to Broker.

Bwana drove around the block and re-entered the street again, driving slowly. 'All clear, except for the hoods.'

'Roger. You can see us now.'

From the other end of the street an identical SUV approached, heading his way.

The hoods had clocked the Fords, but their postures hadn't changed, their butts firmly parked against the compound wall. Bwana's gaze passed over them casually. *No weapons visible, but those lowriders are weighed down with something.*

He drove past the first couple of hoods and idled to a stop a wheel length ahead of the three hoods. They straightened and stared balefully at him. In his mirror he could see the two hoods behind them looking their way.

He leaned his body across the seat, stuck his head out the window, and shouted above the music. 'Say, bro, this where 5Clubs hang out?'

'What?' the one closest to him shouted back, stepping closer.

Big mistake.

His left arm blurred, a brown explosion of muscle and sinew, grabbed the hood by his tee and smashed his forehead against the A-pillar.

The other two hoods moved towards them, their hands darting inside their pockets and then jerked and fell to the ground as twin streams of electricity shot out from Roger and Bear, who had come from behind the SUV.

They turned off their Tasers, pulled out plastic ties, and cuffed the hoods' hands and legs, and then duct-taped their mouths. Bwana got down from the vehicle and did the same for the hood whose face he had smashed. The three of them threw the three hoods in the SUV, slapping away their attempts to kick them.

The two hoods on the other side of the gate had started running towards their brothers when Broker slowed and Chloe slid out of their ride. The heavies were running too fast for her to unload the Taser, so she stood her ground and let them approach her.

A smooth step to the left, ducking beneath the gun that had appeared in the first hood's hand and his wild thrust, she grabbed his wrist on its outward swing, twisted his arm, nearly dislocating his shoulder, and thrust him in the path of the hood behind him.

Both went crashing down, and swift kicks in their nuts took them out of combat. Broker hopped out and duct-taped their mouths, muffling their groans, and a minute later the two hoods were in the vehicle, immobile.

Broker looked up and down the street and across it. The street was quiet. No one came out of the apartment blocks opposite. *Probably seen and experienced enough to mind their own business.*

He looked down the street at Bwana. 'All done here,' he said into his collar mic. Bwana gave him an acknowledging nod and climbed into his Wagon.

They drew the SUVs to the next street, where Tony was lounging against a large NYC Department of Transport truck parked sideways and sectioned off by traffic cones. He guided them to park in a rough triangle when they approached, closing the view to onlookers. Tony, dressed in blue overalls with the DOT's logo, rapped the driver's window. Another stringy man climbed out, similarly dressed, bumped fists with Broker, and silently helped them transfer the five hoods.

Broker took hold of the legs of the last hood and Bwana, his shoulders. 'Don't ask. That's Eric, another of my guys,' he replied when Bwana looked at the truck and back at him.

Tony drove away when they had finished.

'He'll keep driving till we tell him to RV with us,' Broker said and then grinned at Chloe. 'That was smooth work. You had them down before I could join you.'

She chuckled. 'You're old, Broker. You wouldn't have been of much help in any case.'

Bear cut in before he could reply. 'Let's hustle, shall we? The gang will soon notice the absence of their street patrol.'

They climbed in Bwana's ride, and he pulled off, merging in the traffic unobtrusively.

Bwana stopped a couple of buildings away from the warehouse, on the opposite side of the street, and stepped out. They had a clear view of three of the CCTV cameras on the corners of the warehouse from that spot. 'Broker, you're the one they would have seen the least of, since Chloe and you were away from the sight of the front door and windows.'

Broker got out without a word and then stuck his head back in the window. 'Ageist, that's what the lot of you are.'

He turned his jacket inside out in the shadow of the vehicle – most people tend to remember upper clothing – and walked down the street, which was still empty. An hour had passed since their first entry in the street, but it was still deserted. *Kids at school, guys either stoned or at work, moms at work.*

He looked at the warehouse from the corner of his eyes as he walked past it and thought he detected sounds from inside and distant movement deep inside the window, but he couldn't be sure. He went down to the far end of the street, pulled out a rolled-up newspaper from his jacket pocket and read it as he walked back. Nothing had changed in the second pass.

179

The other four were standing in the shade of the SUV when he reached them. All of them had turned their jackets inside out, and Chloe had tied her hair up and tucked it under a baseball cap. All of them were wearing dull-colored combat trousers with large pockets. The jackets concealed their guns in their shoulder or hip holsters, and carried their spare magazines, and their leg wear had large and deep pockets down the thighs, knees, and legs, for more magazines, a backup gun, duct tape, plastic ties and first aid kits. Each one of them had blades strapped to their chest or down their backs or trouser legs.

Bear and Chloe dug out road barriers and signs and each walked two hundred yards down and placed them across the street. On top of the barriers they hung large 'Road Temporarily Closed' signs.

Bear adjusted the sign at his end and looked at it critically for a moment. *Broker said the NYPD would stay out of this. Wonder if they're watching.* He stopped thinking about it and placed smaller signs at the entrances to the apartment blocks on the street.

Roger and Broker watched them while keeping an eye on the warehouse.

Bwana climbed inside the SUV from the passenger side and lifted a long, heavy case from behind the seat. He unwrapped a Remington M24A3 sniper rifle from the case and put it together with practiced ease. The Remington, along with the Barrett, were his sniper rifles of choice, and as he slapped a Leupold Ultra M3 scope on it, he remembered the last time he had used it had been in Iraq.

The target then had been a planner and banker for terrorist organizations and was the brains behind several suicide bomb attacks in Europe and Africa.

Clare had green-lighted the assignment, and a three-man team had followed him from country to country before deciding on the hit in Iraq. The target had been paranoid about his security and had never stayed in the same country for more than a month and, even then, stayed only in apartments for less than a week, places that his organization had vetted and secured.

Broker had picked his trail up by tracking down his advance team, who went to the apartments and secured them by paying cash and, on the rare occasion, by card – a mistake that Broker gleefully capitalized on.

The three-man team had worn white dishdashahs, the long, one-piece dress traditionally worn by men, covered their faces with gutrahs, the headpieces, and had followed the target in a Toyota Saloon that had seen better days. Three days of sweltering heat in Dora, Baghdad, choking dust, and endless traffic, and they were no closer to finding a pattern to the target's movement or a spot for the hit. The target's apartment was surrounded by gun-toting men all day and night, and was struck off immediately as a take-out site.

Conscious that the target could leave the country at any time, they finally decided to take out the target the next day.

There were two constants in the target's movements – one was the street he took in his heavily armored Land Cruiser once he exited the apartment. This street led to a crossroad where the vehicle took any exit randomly.

The crossroad would be the site of the hit, since the vehicle slowed down almost to a stop to allow for oncoming traffic.

The other constant was the target's seating in the Land Cruiser. The target sat in the rear, next to a window, directly behind the driver.

The sniper's hide would be the flat roof of an apartment block – apartment block was being generous to the bombed-out building – behind the target's building, taller than it, with a clear view of the street.

The bullet would have to traverse a shade over two thousand yards in the heat of the day, a temperature of around a hundred and ten Fahrenheit and a wind speed of eight meters/second. Difficult shooting conditions, but Bwana had shot in those conditions before.

The challenge was to get the target to lower his window, which was made of toughened, bulletproof glass.

The three-man team occupied the roof of the building at dawn the next day. The building was deserted, a hollow shell, through which the ghosts of the dead wandered.

Bwana and his spotter surveyed the roof and positioned his Remington on the site that afforded the fullest view of the street. Bwana set the Harris bipod up, put together the rifle, took wind and temperature readings, and then did what the best snipers did – lay down prone and willed his metabolism to slow and went inside himself. His spotter did the same.

The third man went down to the street and did a check of their comms – barely detectable earpieces and microphones that were covered by the folds of the gutrah.

At eleven in the morning the Land Cruiser swung in front of the block and waited, its engine ticking over. The man on the street whispered in his gutrah and got an acknowledgement from Bwana and the spotter.

At half past eleven, the target's bodyguards came out, forming a protective circle around the target. One of them opened the door for him, and Khalid Ashraf, the target, settled into the window seat with a satisfied grunt. The Toyota set off.

A hundred yards later, the Toyota slowed, and Ashraf squinted through the window at the large white banner on the side of the street. 'Salaam Alaikum, Ashraf,' read the banner in large Arabic script.

Another hundred yards, another banner. 'Ashraf, we have a secret for you.'

Ashraf leant forward, ignoring everything else, and his eyes grew wide as the next banner approached, 'Pay attention, Ashraf.'

The Toyota was approaching the crossroad and was slowing down in anticipation. Khalid ignored everything else on the street and yelled out to the driver to go slower as he spotted another banner on the street. The banner became his universe.

He squinted harder to make out the smaller lettering. He couldn't.

He squashed his face against the glass and tried again. No luck. He wiped the glass with his sleeve and tried again. The letters still remained unreadable. The banner was almost in line with his window now.

He cursed and lowered the window.

'I have a message for you, Ashraf,' it read.

And Bwana took the shot.

The spotter continued watching through a pair of Steiner binoculars and then patted him silently on his back and stood up without a word. Bwana took apart the rifle swiftly, without haste, and looked up at the spotter when it was neatly packed. Bwana acknowledged only one other sniper as his better.

That sniper was Zeb, his spotter on that day.

Roger tapped the roof, bringing Bwana out of his reverie. He folded the rear seats, set up a tripod and mounted the rifle on it. He made small adjustments and murmured, 'All set,' in his collar mic.

Broker went to the front passenger side and leaned casually against it while Roger fiddled with something stuck in the rear wheel. Chloe and Bear were still on the street, on opposite sides, making sure the street was clear, Bear drifting closer to the warehouse.

'Now,' Broker said and leaned inside and turned on a cell phone jammer. An NSA classified device — he had gotten hold of it through his channels — it had an effective radius of a kilometer, which was enough for them.

Bwana took a deep breath and released it and then swung the driver's side passenger door sideways. He now had a view of the warehouse and, more importantly, the three CCTV cameras.

He crouched down, and the first camera jumped at him through the Leupold. A moment to allow the rifle to become an extension of his arm, the trigger, a sixth digit on his hand, and the camera to the right disintegrated. Bwana swung the rifle steadily to the left and shot that one.

When Broker saw the third camera explode, he nodded at Roger. Roger straightened and, wiping his hands on his trousers, reached inside the SUV and picked up a small satchel. He walked swiftly through the gate of the warehouse and made his way to the corner on the right.

He glanced back and saw Bear heading to the corner on the left with a similar satchel. He hugged the wall and ran to the first window. It was glassed and barred and a foot above his head. He paused for a moment and heard movement and muffled voices from inside. None of the voices appeared to be shouting or strained.

His Glock slid smoothly in his hand and, reversing his grip, he extended his hand and rapped the glass firmly. *Highly unlikely anyone's near the windows. They'll be packing and unpacking and doing whatever shit hoods do inside.*

From the satchel he took out a couple of cylindrical objects, a stun grenade and a CS gas grenade, pulled their pins, and tossed them through the broken window in an overarm arc.

He heard the first bang from the stun grenade when he reached the second window, and then he heard shouting. A second bang followed, and he smiled thinly. *Bear.*

He broke the next two windows and tossed devices through them and sprinted to the rear of the warehouse. Pandemonium had broken out inside the warehouse, the flash-bangs, shouting and screaming becoming a wall of sound. *More than ten inside, closer to fifteen, and likely this is their first experience of flash-bangs. How does it feel, assholes?*

Half a minute from entering the gate, he navigated the rear corner and stopped suddenly.

The rear door was wide open, and five hoods were outside.

Three of them were armed, one had an AR-15 rifle and two of them had Skorpion machine pistols. The other two were in no position to offer any resistance. One was retching against the wall, and the fifth was kneeling down, holding his stomach. The three with guns were looking through the open door in amazement and shock.

AR-15 spun round on hearing Bwana's approach, his loose shirt stretching tight across his stocky frame, the barrel coming up.

'The fuck you are? What…?'

Roger flowed from a standstill, all thought and speed, moving under the arc of the rising rifle, twisting his body to the side, grabbing it with both hands like a javelin, and jabbed back, hard, catching the hood flush in the face. He collapsed in a heap; another jab and he was out of the equation.

Roger turned to look at Bear and saw that he didn't need any help.

Bear had two facing him with the Skorpions, but he had the advantage of surprise and training. It also helped that the two were bunched closely together. He moved swiftly, turning, keeping one hood between the other and, coming inside the firing arm of the first hood, kicked his knee out. As the hood fell, losing his gun, Bear picked him up bodily, a hand on his collar and one at his belt, and threw him at the second hood. He hit them with a Skorpion and swiftly bound their hands with the plastic ties.

He bumped fists with Roger, and the two of them picked up the three hoods and threw them inside the warehouse. The two affected by the stun grenades were still dazed and stumbled inside the warehouse without offering any resistance when Roger and Bear frisked them for weapons and then pushed them inside.

Roger took a quick peek and saw the rest of the gangbangers were lying incapacitated and dazed, some of them crying.

'Better be sure,' he said and picked up the fallen AR-15 and fired a burst in the ceiling of the warehouse.

He stepped to the side immediately, slammed the door shut, and wedged the AR-15 against it. It wouldn't hold against a determined and concerted assault from inside, but they weren't expecting one and were prepared for that eventuality too.

Bear opened his satchel and brought out a thick steel mending brace, a battery-operated screw driver and drill set, and with Roger helping, sealed the door against the frame with the brace.

They collected the Skorpions and the AR-15 and with a last look around, headed back.

'On our way,' Bear said in his mic and got an acknowledging 'roger' from Broker.

Bear threw the last of the flash-bangs and CS gas grenades through the windows as they left, for good measure.

Roger looked at him quizzically, and a grin parted the thick beard. 'Mamma always said I should finish my lunchbox at school.'

He trotted to the rear of the vehicle and removed the street signs, and Chloe did the same at the other end.

'All quiet here,' Broker commented when Roger removed the magazines from the guns and dumped them in the SUV and joined him at the front. 'Not a peep from anyone within the warehouse. If they had, Bwana would have fired at and through the door, and that would have pegged them back.'

'What about spectators from the apartments?'

'Nah. I think they have learnt to leave well enough alone.'

Roger left him to help Bear and Chloe load the signs in the rear, and they all climbed in, a tight fit this time with Chloe perched on Bear's lap, since Bwana was still manning the Remington.

Broker powered the ride and reached down to turn off the jammer. He twisted around to check they all were aboard and then called a number.

'No names. You know who I am. It's time to ride and claim your headlines,' he drawled when he got a reply. 'About ten, no thirteen or fifteen of them,' he corrected when Roger mouthed at him silently.

'Of course they're alive. We don't believe in killing,' he said piously. 'You'll need to hurry, though. Those bastards are passive at the moment, but that might change, and also the gang might send more hoods.'

'How're they passive? Well, I dunno. Hoods have a siesta in the afternoon, don't they?'

The phone squawked, and Broker cut in. 'That's all I can share. The headlines are all yours for the asking if you move immediately,' and he hung up.

'NYPD?' Chloe asked him as she loosened her hair and tied it again and replaced the cap over her head.

'Deputy Commissioner. I've done him enough favors for him not to ask too many questions.'

'What're we waiting for now?' Chloe asked. 'We shouldn't be here when the NYPD arrive.'

'We'll wait till we hear their sirens,' Bear replied in a muffled voice, Chloe's back squashed against his face.

'Huh, and who asked you to talk?' she said, jamming her back further against him.

Bwana fired and reloaded immediately, the muffled clap of the shot loud in the confines of the vehicle, cutting off any further talk. He reloaded.

All of them peered at the warehouse. 'Got someone?' Roger broke the silence.

Bwana continued keeping his vigil through the scope. 'Wasn't aiming to. Saw a face at the slat and shot well high to discourage them. I don't reckon they're still in any shape to attempt an escape.'

He glanced sideways at Bear and Roger. 'That brace will hold, you reckon?'

Roger nodded. 'They'll need a heavy battering ram to rip it off the door, and something tells me those guys in there are in no shape to lift a battering ram, let alone use it.'

No other faces appeared at the slat, though a few times some gangbangers fired from inside. That came to a stop soon enough when Bwana placed his shots in a tight grouping at the top of the door. Another ten minutes and they heard sirens coming closer, and Broker rolled the SUV.

He drifted down the street while keeping an eye on his mirror, and when he saw the first flashing lights, he sped off. Just as he turned into the next street, he rang another number and put the call on speaker.

The phone rang five times before being picked up. There was silence at the other end, though they could hear the person breathing in the distance.

Broker chuckled. 'Hamm, is that how they teach you to create an aura? By keeping silent? You guys should write a book, *The Badass Guide to Intimidating People*. It would be a best seller.

'But maybe not. I plumb forgot that reading isn't exactly at the top of a hood's hobbies.'

Silence still.

'By the way you guys have a warehouse in Harlem, don't you?' He gave the address and got no response in return.

'You *had* that warehouse.' He hung up and drove.

Chapter 23

The Watcher stretched in his hideout and put down his scope for a moment.

He had a vacant apartment in the block opposite the warehouse, with a good view of the entire street and the warehouse. He had broken into the apartment at dawn, padlocked it from the inside, and had then set up his hide.

A Barrett mounted on a bipod, a Leupold scope and binoculars, water and rations, and he had everything he needed for the whole day. He had seen the five hoods make their way to the street, with a lot of backslapping and low-rider tugging, and park themselves against the wall. They frequently adjusted their guns and privates as women passed them by, and their loud and lewd comments reached him even over the distance.

He had seen Bwana and Broker driving up and the smooth taking down of the hoods. When they returned, he had trained the Barrett on them, adjusting the scope so that the crosshair was bang on target. He could have taken them out any time he wanted to. He lip-read them whenever they were on his side of the truck, and from their actions and the snippets of conversation, he knew what they planned.

It hadn't been difficult to track them down. The voice on the phone had been most informative, and the Watcher had found Broker's apartment block on Columbus Avenue easily.

Breaking in was out of the question since Broker's security was unrivalled. The Watcher studied the block and Broker's apartment overlooking the avenue, and a half day and several coffees later, he was still struggling for ideas.

He drifted off to a Thai food truck, and when he returned, he noticed the window washers abseiling down the apartment block.

Maybe there isn't a need to break in.

He studied the livery of the window washers and hung around to see what time they clocked off work. They left their equipment on the roof after work each day, a bonus for him. A couple of days later, he approached the block wearing the livery of the window washers, rappelling harness on top of his coverall, walked past the concierge, who barely registered his presence, and after using a cloned access card, went to the roof.

The scaffolding rig was already in place, locked down, with weights loaded on it. He picked the lock and moved the rig across the roof to above Broker's apartment and secured it. He donned the rest of his abseiling kit, and after attaching and securing his ropes, he rapidly dropped two hundred feet down.

Thick sheets of dark blue glass, twelve-feet-high and across the entire breadth of the apartment, fronted Broker's lounge and a large bedroom. The Watcher dug out a small object the size of a dime, covered it in a sticky putty the exact shade of the glass, and stuck it in one of the upper corners of the lounge window. He walked across the face of the window and stuck a similar voice-activated bug in the other upper corner and stuck two more bugs, for good measure, in the two upper corners of the bedroom window.

The sticky putty, which muffled the radio waves emitted by the bugs and rendered them undetectable by the most sophisticated

192

equipment available, looked like chewing gum and was the brainchild of NSA's ANT division. It was so deeply classified that even Broker hadn't got hold of it or was even aware of its existence.

The Watcher walked up the face of the block and secured the receiver to the underside of the air-conditioning unit on the roof, and attached a transmitting device that would take the signal from the receiver and broadcast it to a wider range.

After moving the rig back to its original location, he took a last look around before heading down to the basement.

Broker's Rover was in a brightly lit corner of the basement facing a ceiling-mounted CCTV camera.

The Watcher rolled up the collar of his coverall and donned a baseball cap that he pulled low over his face. He pulled out an unlit cigarette and walked casually across the basement toward the Rover.

When he was six feet away from the vehicle, he stuck another putty-covered bug to the front of the cigarette and blew on it. The bug flew from the cigarette-shaped blowpipe and stuck to the roof of the Rover, looking like debris from the road. So long as Broker didn't remove the debris or take the Rover to a car wash, the Watcher would have ears on the vehicle.

Having eyes on his movements was easier given that Broker's vehicles were fitted with custom LoJacks.

LoJack was a well-known manufacturer of vehicle tracking and recovery systems that enabled stolen cars to be recovered. The manufacturer installed small radio transceivers in vehicles that emitted a signal to tracking units. The NCIC, National Crime

Information Center system used by federal and state law enforcement agencies, talked to the LoJack database, and thus stolen vehicles could be quickly tracked and recovered by the cops.

The Watcher, while walking across, had another NSA gadget in his pocket – a battery-operated miniature spectrum analyzer that rapidly scanned thousands of frequencies in milliseconds. The NSA had the frequency ranges used by manufacturers such as LoJack, and by the time the Watcher had passed the Rover and exited the building, he had the frequency to the vehicle.

The Watcher put his eye back to the scope to see the last of the police roll out their tapes across the gate and the door, and drive away leaving silence and an empty warehouse behind. He waited. The sounds and smells of dinner being prepared drifted through the block, the liquid laugh of a woman wafted and hovered and slowly broke up, and still he waited, the silence of the apartment a second skin.

It was close to midnight when the sedan nudged its way through the street and stopped in front of the warehouse. Doors opened and thumped shut quietly, and through the scope he saw three figures head to the warehouse.

Forty-five minutes later, the figures returned, the two on either side of the central figure doing a lot of nodding and head shaking. The Watcher zeroed in on the central figure, Hamm, who turned to his left, to Quinn. *Find them. Put the word out.*

Quinn nodded. *What about the other warehouses and businesses?*

You'll get more people.

He slid inside the rear of the sedan, doors thumped again, and the sedan drove off.

The Watcher waited a couple of hours more, and in the deep of the night, he left the apartment as soundlessly as he had entered, the rifle folded neatly in a noise-and-shock-proof sling across his shoulder, a smaller backpack resting on his back.

He approached the warehouse in the shadows, vaulting over the wall in the furthest corner, approaching the rear. The rear door was still intact, the brace gleaming in the dark. He turned on a red nightlight and saw that it would take too much time, make too much noise, to remove it.

He walked around the building, pausing in the shadow of the front. The night slept. He ducked under the tape and, stepping to his left immediately, hugged the wall.

The warehouse smelt heavy; fear and sweat mingled with the odor of CS gas and the flash-bangs. Mingled with it was the smell of drugs. Furniture was strewn across the floor, large tables lying on their sides, some of them smashed, cardboard cartons and rolls of unused baggies strewn all over.

The Watcher reached into his backpack and removed four time-delay incendiary flares and, setting the delay on them, tossed them in the corners of the warehouse.

He had reached the end of the street when the warehouse went up with a loud whoosh, outlining his form briefly before he merged into deeper shadow. He walked on without breaking stride and pulled out his phone.

'911? Reporting a fire.'

He flipped his untraceable phone shut. *That was a good move by Broker. Switching vehicles. Where could they be?*

Bwana and Roger were wolfing down sandwich rolls for breakfast in a Subway a block away from their hotel when Broker, Bear, and Chloe joined them the next day. Bear and Bwana filled the café with just their presence.

Chloe looked at the roll in Bwana's hand and grimaced. 'Bwana, you do realize it's called breakfast for a reason, and not lunch?'

Bwana took a larger bite. 'Yup. But I'm a growing boy and need all the vitamins. You're all growed out, so you don't need them.'

Bear stifled a chuckle at Chloe's glare and headed to the counter to get nourishment for the rest of them.

Broker had his laptop running when he returned and was replying to Roger. 'We lie low for a day or two while we decide which other place to hit.'

Bear paused while handing out their drinks. 'What about Isakson? Is he in the loop? Does he know about yesterday?'

Broker shook his head. 'Nope and nope. He might put two and two together, but we have carte blanche to do things our way. That was the condition I insisted on for helping him.'

He went back to studying his laptop. His intelligence business did not need his full-time presence, and he used a light touch with managing Tony and his other managers, but he still studied all the intelligence reports that were collated overnight, and commented on them before they got distributed to various clients.

His phone rang, interrupting his reading. He glanced at it and picked it up. 'Tony? What's up?'

He listened for a moment. 'Did the NYPD approach you?'

'All right, keep me posted.' He leaned back and gazed out of the window for several moments, not registering the inquiring glances from the rest.

Chloe finally broke the silence. 'Spill it, Broker. We've been properly respectful for long enough.'

He turned to look at her, grinning. 'If you guys had been really respectful, you'd have allowed me to speak first.'

He turned his gaze on Bwana and Bear. 'The warehouse was burnt at night. Late night. The NYPD suspect it's arson. They've found traces of incendiary devices at the site, and the official line is that they're pursuing all lines of inquiry. Unofficially, they don't give a damn. They've got the gangbangers, they've got a shit load of drugs, and they've got the limelight. The case will be buried and closed later.'

He held his hand up to forestall them. 'That's all we know, guys. Tony is looking into it and will let me know if he has more intel.'

'Could 5Clubs have razed it to the ground?' Bwana asked curiously. 'Maybe they'll claim damages from insurance.'

Broker shrugged halfheartedly. 'It's possible. I'm just wondering why they'd want to bring attention to themselves, if that's what they've done.'

197

They went at it for a few more minutes without any theory taking shape. Bear said disgustedly, 'They wouldn't be a gang if they acted rationally, would they?'

And on that, they put it behind them.

Broker folded his laptop to tablet mode and pulled up Google Maps. He zeroed in on three addresses – in the Meatpacking District, East Harlem, and in Midtown West.

'The first is another crack warehouse, very similar to the one we busted. The second is a gas station in East Harlem. They own this station… a lot of their customers end up reporting card fraud. They probably use card skimmers to rip the numbers. They use the gas station to also consolidate their daily take from their local businesses. The last one, in Hell's Kitchen, is a high-end strip club. Business types from Wall Street, corporate honchos, media guys… you know the kind, they all head there.'

Bwana tilted the tablet toward himself to see better. 'Why don't we hit all three?'

Bear shook his head immediately. 'Let's turn the screw slowly. Let's do one and then another a few days later.'

Broker nodded approvingly. 'What I figured. So, guys, which place do we go for?'

Chloe grinned when hers was the only finger resting on the strip club. 'I thought you guys wouldn't pass on the opportunity to see some flesh. Are you being righteous on my account?'

None of them replied.

Chloe looked back at the map and frowned. *What did I miss?*

'Gotcha. More innocents at the strip club.'

Bear's lips twitched, though it was hard to make out with his thick facial hair. 'I wouldn't call patrons of a strip club innocent exactly, but yes, more people there.'

They went back to studying the map as Broker zoomed in on the gas station. 'On Second Avenue and has exits to the street on two sides. Other two sides are walled up. A Spanish restaurant, a saloon, and a grocery store opposite, on the other side of the street. All with a clear view of the service station.'

'We watch tomorrow?'

'Yup. In turns, every two hours from four p.m. in the evening to midnight. You and Bear go first, then Bwana and Roger. I'll go last, with Tony. After six hours, we change partners, you pair with Bwana then. We're looking for one vehicle with a couple of guys, maybe three, though I think two is the most they'll send. One to drive, the other, the bagman. If they don't fuel up but drive right to the glass door, one guy going in and coming out very quickly with a bag or case of some kind... those will be our boys. One of our pair will idle in a car nearby.'

Bwana shook his head mournfully. 'Not even a contest.'

Chapter 24

Bear and Chloe walked down the block on Second Avenue the next evening and, after one pass past the service station, crossed the avenue and headed to the eating joint. The place was empty, the lull between lunch hour and the evening traffic giving it a sleepy feel.

Chloe rummaged in her bag and spread out a large map of New York and started circling the attractions while talking about their plans for the next day, tourists filling in every available minute with things to do and places to go. Bear moved around to sit with her and look at the map better, and watch the gas station across the street.

'I was thinking we'd struggle to kill two hours. I shouldn't have worried,' Chloe commented when their orders arrived. Bear's tray was overflowing with food, whereas she had ordered just a salad.

Bear grinned, his eyes softening. 'I'm compensating for you.'

She laid her phone in front of their trays, the head of the phone facing the street. It was a Broker gadget, a long-distance video recorder whose lens was built in the head. 'I doubt we'll see them on our watch. Too early.'

Bear nodded silently. His silences had never been an issue in their relationship, Chloe was the talkative one, and he was the listener. Well trained was how Chloe described his silences.

The only excitement during their watch was when an overweight drunk lurched in the pizza joint and waved a long, wicked knife at the cashier, a blade that caught the lights and looked scarier than it was. Weaving on his feet, he shouted at the teenager to open his cash register. The joint was nearly empty, just Bear and Chloe and another couple, and in the sudden silence, the drunk's loud, labored breathing sounded like the wind across the windows.

The drunk looked around when he felt a hand on his shoulder.

'Let me take this. Someone might get hurt.' Bear smiled down at him, his hand gripping the drunk's fist like a vice. He twisted the arm around, kicked his feet back, and leaned the drunk against the counter. The drunk offered no resistance, and by the time the teenager had overcome his trembling, the owner, who was also the chef and his dad, rushed in from the kitchen.

He stopped short when he saw the drunk. 'Not again! Mike, I thought you had quit drinking.' He scolded the drunk in Spanish, who was now weeping, and then turned to Bear. Bear realized this was not a genuine holdup and released Mike.

'*Gracias, Señor*. Mike is my brother, and he does this a few times when he's drunk. But he had sworn on our mother that he'd quit.' He whacked his brother on his head and pushed him to the teenager, who led him away.

'No police?' Bear asked mildly.

The owner shook his head furiously. 'No, *Señor*. This is family. Mike is harmless. He'll be alright once he's sober. Thank you for helping.'

Bear went back to Chloe, who had kept a watch on the gas station. 'Anything?'

Chloe shook her head and smiled faintly. 'That's low profile?'

Bear grinned. 'For me, yes.'

They left half an hour later after the owner had waved away their attempts to pay the check. They passed Bwana and Roger on the street and exchanged the barest of nods with them.

It was late in the evening, nearly nine p.m., and Broker and Tony were playing cards on a bench in front of the restaurant when a black BMW sedan circled the service station twice. Broker threw down a card. 'Maybe something here.'

The BMW went away, returned after half an hour at an idling pace and nosed inside the forecourt, reversed and backed up against the glass doors. A slim man in a loose shirt slipped out of the passenger side and headed inside. They could see him talk briefly to the pimpled guy behind the counter and return to the waiting car with two bulging plastic shopping bags.

The BMW sped off, and a few minutes later, Broker saw a dark Ford SUV merge in the traffic three cars behind it.

'He's checking something in the bags... maybe counting.' Roger's voice was clear in their earbuds over the hum of the traffic. 'Bear, Chloe, where're you guys?'

'Behind you, four car lengths away. You can't see us, but I can see your black top.'

Broker looked at his cards. 'Keep behind them. My guess is they'll collect a few more takings before heading to Hamm's garage. Tony and I'll be here just in case we've got the wrong car.'

'What if we've got the wrong car? Might be Joe Public picking up stuff?'

'We'll flash a wad of cash and make good any hassle.'

They hadn't got the wrong vehicle.

The BMW stopped at another service station and a strip club and then headed downtown, taking the East Side Highway.

Broker and Tony folded their cards. 'Take them.'

They all donned black masks, Chloe tucking her hair in, as Roger closed the gap on the Beamer, tailgating the cars ahead till they dropped off, and saw Bear overtake them from the corner of his eyes. The last car stubbornly remained in place and gave way only after Roger drove to an inch of its rear, but not before the driver rolled down his window and flipped them the finger.

Bear's brake lights flared red ahead, and Roger surged, motion and machine slamming into the Beamer, ramming it against Bear's truck. The Beamer was strong, German engineering at its best, but it was no match for a Ford SUV sandwich, its hood and trunk grating and buckling under the impact.

Steam and smoke roiled and shadows moved, and the shadows became Bear and Bwana.

They loomed silently, looking down at the hoods, who were dazed and slapping away at the deflating bags and the powder in the air. One of them, Loose Shirt, reached for his waist, and Bwana smiled against his mask – he'd spotted the 5Clubs tat on the thug's neck. He smashed his Glock in the man's mouth. 'Don't.'

Bear bored his gun in the driver's temple and gestured silently for his weapon and handed it to Roger without a backward glance. Bwana disarmed Loose Shirt and reached down and hauled the bags out.

'You fucks–' the driver started, and Bear slashed his jaw. The driver looked in his eyes showing through the holes in the black hood and saw a world of hurt and kept quiet.

Cars and trucks slowed down and then sped off when Chloe's hooded face trained on them, her gun shining and hard and visible under the streetlights.

Bwana tossed plastic ties across the roof to Bear. 'Hands,' he said to Loose Shirt.

Loose Shirt hesitated for the slightest moment, then put his hands forward, and Bwana secured them tightly with the ties. Bear cuffed the driver, pulled open the glove box, and riffling through the papers, pocketed them. 'We're done here, bro,' he said to Bwana.

Their trucks were dented, but the engines turned over smoothly, and they disappeared into the night.

Broker counted the bundles in the bags. 'Enough to buy an apartment downtown. Whoever said crime doesn't pay didn't know shit.'

They were having dinner after checking into another anonymous joint and handing over the SUVs to Tony and his stringy colleague. The vehicles had untraceable number plates and, after being wiped down, hosed, and valeted, would be left on a crime-ridden street with the keys in them. And would be stolen.

Broker took a long pull of his beer and settled in his chair, the dim light shining off his hair. 'I made some calls. NYPD picked up those guys within fifteen minutes of your leaving. They got a description of three hooded men and nothing much else to go on. They've diligently noted their report and have assured them they'll investigate the holdup. They'll probably check camera feeds and ask for witnesses to come forward, but will get nowhere. If we'd left their guns behind, those guys would have some explaining to do their own selves.' He grinned. 'We've got our first report filed against us, you know.'

Chloe shrugged. 'I'm sure it'll keep us awake at night.' She nodded at the bags. 'What do we do with those?'

'What do you suggest?'

'Maybe some charity can have a pleasant surprise tomorrow?'

'You got it. Name your charity, and we'll leave it on their premises at night. Now something else. Remember that phone Roger picked up in Arizona? I juiced it up and went through its history, directory, everything that it had.'

He took another swig, letting the silence build and, when Chloe rolled her eyes, continued. 'Wasn't much in it, other than a few numbers. Four numbers, in fact.' He nodded at Roger and Bwana. 'There were three other numbers you guys didn't spot. Two of those were numbers in L.A., one of them a New York number, and the last was a voice mail number.

'Now the two L.A numbers belong to a scrap dealer... a junkyard where they make scrap out of old bangers. This junkyard is owned by 5Clubs; the LAPD know about it and have a watch on it.

'The New York number is an untraceable one, most likely a disposable one. And the last one is interesting, a mailbox number. I think that's how they pass messages, by leaving messages on a voice mailbox that everyone can access.'

'Have you tried these numbers?' Bear asked him.

'Only the New York one, and that turned out to be a dead one. Shall we try the others?'

Bwana's emphatic, 'Hell yeah,' made him chuckle. He dug into his pocket and pulled out the phone, a Nokia model that smart phones had rendered almost obsolete.

Bwana picked it up and scrolled through the history. He frowned. 'This isn't...' and the phone rang.

He turned on the speaker and placed it in the center of the table.

A young voice came out, tinny and hesitating. 'Zeb?'

Part 3

Chapter 25

They filled Elaine Rocka's dining room, Bwana silent and large at one end of the table, Bear bookending at the other end, and Roger, Broker, and petite Chloe in the middle.

Elaine sat in silence, her eyes narrowed, her dogs, German shepherds, sitting either side of her, ready to attack at a word. Shawn had called the number every day, increasingly in despair than hope, and she had seen his face transform when the phone was finally answered.

'So run it past me again. Just who the fuck are you?'

No one was going to meet her babies without her approval.

'Ma'am, we're friends of Zeb. We all served in the army together, and once we left the army, we set up a security services firm.' Broker was economical with the truth with strangers, and this was the strangest situation he could recall having been in.

They had blurred through the city after hanging up, each one of them lost in their own worlds.

'Zeb's phone was dead and lying in my room for ages. Looks identical to the phone Roger had. I must have charged it by mistake and brought it with me,' Broker said after a long while.

No one replied, and he sped faster, allowing the traffic to imprint itself back on them, keeping the memories at bay. His phone rang just as they reached the Bronx.

'Tony, what've you got?'

'Elaine Rocka, early forties, lives alone in the Bronx, owns her house. Divorced several times, received quite a payoff from the last one. No kids. Works part-time in the mayor's office, in the payroll department. Now, get this. This is where the connection could be.

'Has a sister, Coralyn Rocka, who was married to one William Shattner. Shattner was an E-5 in the army... was dishonorably discharged. Served in Iraq *at the same time* as Zeb.'

Tony paused and carried on when there was no reaction. 'Shattner and his wife separated when he was in Iraq; she's now in Miami with some other dude. Shattner got custody of the kids, two of them, a boy, eleven years old, and a girl, eight years.'

Chloe broke in. 'Tony, any specific connection to Zeb? We had enough feet there to populate a small city, and Zeb would have interacted with many.'

'As of now, nothing's come up. Will keep digging and call if I get anything. Broker, let me know if you need anything else.'

Elaine Rocka lasered Broker. 'So why isn't this Zeb here?'

'He's dead.'

Elaine Rocka didn't like it one bit. It showed in her face, in her body language, and the dogs sensed it. One stood and walked around them, the other growled.

'So if he's dead, why are you fuckers here? You could have said that on the phone.'

'Ma'am, we wanted to see what the connection to Zeb was. Why would the boy call Zeb?'

'He called because the SOB who passed for his dad left him a message to call this Zeb if anything happened to him. He doesn't know anything else.'

'Did he say how he knew Zeb?'

Elaine Rocka shook her head. 'You aren't hearing me, mister. Shawn doesn't know anything else. The prick, his dad, didn't say much in his entire life.'

Broker chose his words carefully. 'The boy's father, he's not around?'

'Prick disappeared three months back. Left the babies here and said he had some work to attend to.' She snorted. 'Work! Asswipe never did an honest day's work in his life.

'Not a peep from him since then. No way to contact him. My babies... just as I got them on the mend, you fuckers show up.' Her look burnt the air around them.

Broker kept his voice neutral. 'He's been missing for three months? Ma'am, have you reported his absence to the police? Do the children know he's missing?'

If a glare could burn, Broker would have been ashes.

She spat. 'William Shattner is a thief. He was sacked from the army for stealing and selling arms. When his wife, my sister, broke up with him, he conned the judge into granting him custody of the kids. He drifted all over the country with the kids in tow, never stayed in one place for long, doing odd jobs. I kept track of him because I wanted the kids, wanted to bring them up. He started dealing in arms again, supplying them to gangs.

'When he brought the kids here, they came *home.*' The word filled the room.

'I go to the police, they're going to want to speak to the kids, go to their school... you think I'm going to subject my babies to that? I'll tell the police in good time. *My* good time.'

Chloe broke the silence gently. 'Elaine, we're here just to understand the connection to Zeb, not say or do anything that will hurt the children. We aren't here to change any circumstances. Perhaps we could speak to them? Talking might help them remember.'

The lasers turned on Chloe. 'Honey, I work in the mayor's office. I deal with smooth-talking scumbags all the time. I know all the tricks in the book and those that aren't. I know what you're doing with your sweet-as-syrup voice. Won't work. You aren't talking to my babies. I'm going to make life good for them, not remind them of that worthless piece of shit, their dad.'

She glared at each of them, the dogs barking once to punctuate her.

Roger's voice rumbled in the room, surprising them all. 'Ma'am, we lost Zeb over a year back, and while we are moving on, the pain is still fresh. If you were in our place, wouldn't you want to know what the connection was?'

'Just what do you guys do? If your Zeb was that no-account's help line, then I'm guessing you guys are up to no good too.'

Broker was unruffled. 'Ma'am, I'm taking a leap of faith here. We are a Special-Ops unit... we do stuff that cannot be done by any government agency. Commissioner Forzini and Deputy Commissioner Rolando know us and know me personally. I can give you more references if you wish.'

Elaine Rocka studied him, thinking it over. Shawn and Lisa meant the world to her, and her rage at the way the kids had been brought up was matched by her determination to give them a happier life. Broker had mentioned those names easily, an ease that came with familiarity. The quicker she got them out of her house, the sooner she could get back to her kids and restore normalcy, and maybe it was the only way.

She got up abruptly and left the room, signaling the dogs to stay behind.

She came back shortly leading a tall, brown-eyed, brown-haired boy with her, holding his hand. The boy walked hesitantly and glanced up at Elaine, who smiled at him reassuringly.

Bwana leaned forward, a broad smile splitting his face, lighting up the room. 'Hey, I'm a Yankees fan too. This guy here' – he glanced pityingly in Roger's direction – 'he supports the Sox.'

Shawn relaxed immediately and, patting his sweatshirt, grinned in return. 'All of us can't be perfect, I guess.'

Bwana chuckled and exchanged high fives with Shawn. 'Damned right.' He apologized immediately. 'Excuse my language, ma'am, Shawn. What can I say! These heathens with me lack refinement and try their best to drag me down to their level.'

Broker had his game face on but smiled inside when he noticed the almost imperceptible relaxing in Elaine Rocka. *That was almost an approving nod.*

Bwana introduced all of them, Broker last. 'Yes, he's really called Broker. He peddles information, so we all started calling him that, and the name stuck.'

Broker deadpanned, 'They couldn't remember my real name, had to call me something.'

'Does your dad have any nickname for you, Shawn?'

He shook his head. 'He says he wouldn't have named me Shawn if he wanted to call me something else.'

Elaine Rocka shifted subtly in her seat, the pleasantries were over.

'Honey, what did your father tell you about Zeb?'

Shawn's smile faded. 'Dad left a note along with a phone in my school bag. It said if there was any trouble and he wasn't around, I should call Zeb. He would know what to do. He wrote Zeb's number on it.'

'Did he mention where he was going, Shawn?' Chloe asked him.

Shawn shook his head, his eyes glimmering. 'No. He worked in a garage and tended to keep late hours, but he never went away for days. He said there was some work stuff he had to attend to and got Lisa and me out of school so that we could stay with Aunt Elaine.'

He bit his lip to keep it from trembling. 'I waited a couple of days to hear from him, and when I didn't, I told Aunt Elaine, and she

213

said we should try calling Zeb. We've been trying for more than two months.' He looked accusingly at Broker.

Broker looked pained. 'Shawn, your aunt might have mentioned, Zeb died over a year back. After that, I just stopped charging his phone. I juiced it up by mistake yesterday and got your call.'

He gave Shawn a searching look. 'Your father say anything about how he knew Zeb?'

'No. He never talked about his past. He said just once that if there was anyone in his life who he would go to for help, it was Zeb. I asked who that was, but he didn't say anything. Is he really dead?' His voice trembled slightly, his eyes bright with unshed tears.

'Yes, honey, he died a while back,' Chloe said gently. 'Where did your dad work? Did he leave you with anything else, other than the phone?'

'He was a mechanic in Brownsville Autos, over in Brownsville.'

The bright eyes turned to all of them, struggling to find hope in a world gone bleak. 'I don't know what's happened to my dad... Lisa cries at night and asks me, and I tell her he's gone for work.' His hands balled into fists and angrily brushed away the tears rolling down.

Elaine Rocka crushed him in a hug, her eyes shut tight, and when they opened, she reduced all of them to the size of insects.

Chloe cleared her throat, meeting her eyes, hoping she understood, but knowing she didn't care about their reasons. She turned to Shawn. 'Honey, I'm sure there are good reasons why he's been away. We'll ask at the garage. Maybe they'll know.'

The battle-axe broke her silence. 'Did. They've shut down. Checked records.' She nodded in the direction of One Police Plaza, the NYPD headquarters. 'They've disappeared.'

She glanced down at Shawn. 'Shawn, why don't you go play with Lisa? I'll finish up with these people and join you soon.'

He stood slowly, glancing at them, hope dying in his eyes, knowing what that usually meant in adult-speak, and turned to leave. He stopped when he saw the head peeking through the door.

They all turned to look.

Blonde curls framing her expressive eyes, Lisa asked them, 'Will you find my dad?'

Chapter 26

'Brownsville Autos is 5Clubs owned.' The words hung in the air, sinking slowly in them, as Tony turned his laptop screen toward them, showing them a complicated ownership trail of the garage he'd drawn that led back to the gang.

They had driven back in near silence from Elaine Rocka's home, each lost in their thoughts, Broker breaking the silence once to call Tony to, 'Get off your ass and earn your money.'

They were in another café, the 'don't-even' vibe around them keeping the waitress away.

'Jose Cruz, the chapter head, was based out of the auto shop till a few months back when the garage closed abruptly. About the same time as Shattner went missing. I haven't yet been able to find out why, nor where the gang is working from now.'

He held a hand up to forestall Broker. 'I'm working on it, boss. Hold your horses.'

'Did you get anything else on Shattner?'

'Pretty much what Ms Rocka told you. An E-5, he had an ordinary service record till the time he got transferred to Iraq during Desert Storm. There, he was a Unit Supply Specialist in Iraq during Desert Storm and started selling small arms on the side. During his army trial, he said he did this out of desperation since he needed funds to fight his wife over the custody of their kids. He was discharged, but get this, he *retained his pension*. How he swung this is not recorded, but I suspect this is where Zeb stepped in. You know how he was.'

'No obvious link to Zeb, I guess?'

Tony shook his head. 'They were in the same base, but other than that, no record. I'm speculating obviously, but I think it was Zeb's intervention that got him his benefits. I have left a few messages for those who were involved in Shattner's case, but haven't heard back from them yet.'

'So we've got squat,' growled Bear and grinned suddenly as Tony's shoulders tightened.

'Relax, Tony. Not aimed at you.' He looked at Broker. 'Does the why of the Zeb-Shattner connection really matter?'

Broker returned his look. 'Nope. It'll come to us eventually. We're going to find Shattner, aren't we?'

Chloe's answer was low and fierce and spoke for them all. 'Hell yes. If Zeb was involved, so are we.'

They bumped fists, and Broker took charge.

'Tony, keep digging and let us know. Also dig more into Elaine Rocka.'

Bwana ventured, 'You don't think—'

'I don't, but intel never hurt us. We should keep the pressure on the gang, and I'm thinking the four of you should take down the strip club. You can clear out the club so that there is no collateral damage.'

'You'll not join us?' Roger asked him.

'I need to work the street, talk to some junkies I know, and see what they can tell us about the Brooklyn chapter.'

Roger looked at him doubtfully. 'Alone?'

'Yeah. These guys will clam up at the sight of strangers.' He grinned. 'I *can* take care of myself... don't forget I've saved your butts many a time.'

Bwana nudged Roger. 'And he'll never let us forget that. Broker, about those kids and Elaine Rocka... I really think the cops should be informed about Shattner's absence.'

Broker nodded in agreement. 'We need to persuade her, but let's go back to her after a few days. I didn't press her today since her defenses were all up and we'd have ended up in a confrontation in front of the kids.'

The Watcher was deep inside another café, across the street, a baseball cap pulled low over his head, shades covering most of his face, the collar of his thick jacket rolled up. A crossword puzzle in front of him, he had the air of a man in no hurry and no particular purpose.

He had found them the previous night after hours of driving past cheap hotels and run-down neighborhoods that hope had left behind. He had cut downtown into grids and searched, looking out for two vehicles that were on the right side of anonymous and were company owned. With his laptop running on the passenger seat, he had driven for hours, taking his chances on Broker staying in hotels that didn't come with basement or valet parking, and therefore the vehicles would be street-parked.

Company-owned, anonymous cars were aplenty, but the Watcher was seeking transport that was owned by a series of shell companies, and when he finally found two of them in the early hours of the morning, he kept watch on them.

When the group came out and surveyed the street, they didn't spot him. He was prone in his car, several car lengths away, watching them through the mirrors, and when they left, he merged in their wake.

At the Rocka residence, he'd briefly considered approaching the rear of the house to overhear them – briefly considered and rapidly discarded when he noted the proximity of the houses and the barking from inside.

He looked up Rocka, covering the same ground Tony had, and pieces started falling into place. He dug out his phone and called the garage and got nothing. He was politely turned away at Rocka's workplace. He looked down at his scribbling, at the various names he'd written. He called the next number, a school, and the jigsaw was complete.

Bwana led them out of the café, and he paused, scanning the neighborhood. Nothing unusual stood out, yet his radar was uneasy. He didn't feel followed, yet he felt something. His shoulders moved in the smallest shrug when the street gazed back at him blankly, intent on its own course for the day.

'Yes, I've felt it too,' Chloe said behind him, 'and I haven't spotted anyone. Bear too. If we're being followed, it's by a ghost.'

'I'm sure the gang is searching for us, but I'm also pretty sure they haven't found us yet,' Broker commented as he led them to the Wagon. 'I had Tony search our Rovers for bugs, and he didn't find any. There aren't any on the Wagons. This other player can see us, but not hear us... let's wait till he shows his hand. If he's real!'

He noticed Bwana grinning, sunlight across the dark man's face. 'I know. To you, the bigger the party, the better.'

It was late evening when Broker approached Snarky in Brooklyn, when schools and offices closed and apartment windows were lit, and different beasts roamed the street.

Snarky was a junkie who teetered on the edge of the precipice, knowing enough when to back off, but not having the resolution to walk away. A part-time dealer and user, he was a frequent partaker of the NYPD's hospitality, and after one such sojourn, Broker had tapped him. The NYPD squeezed him for juice when it found him, for Snarky had one redeeming quality in its eyes – he knew the streets better than any cop or junkie, and was quick to part with it and get back to the street.

In Broker, Snarky found a better paymaster, and someone who didn't judge him and treated him with respect. Respect. Snarky found that the word warmed him and stirred something deep inside him in a way Broker's money didn't. That too helped, though.

Snarky was lying where he usually lay, sprawled against the shutters of a long-dead store in Lorimer Street, a trilby covering his face, legs and arms sprawled out. He was king of his section of the pavement. He was singing, what *he* called it, and waving a bottle in a brown wrapper when Broker passed him. Broker thought it might have been a popular tune, but he could be wrong. Alcohol and Snarky's abilities had a unique way of reshaping songs.

Snarky twitched when Broker passed him — Broker had never figured out how he recognized passersby with the hat covering his face — and lurched to his feet and followed at a shambling pace.

Broker entered a bar, a slight improvement from a hole in the wall, very slight, and had ordered drinks for Snarky and himself by the time Snarky's body odor announced his presence.

'Snarky, you know there's such an invention as a shower?'

'Conserve earth's resources, that's what they say at the home,' replied Snarky piously, in his thin, reedy tone. Snarky frequented a shelter for the homeless when he wasn't dealing or housed at the NYPD. 'Besides, it's my shield. No one willingly gets close to me.' He laughed, and Broker was reminded of hyenas barking.

Snarky had surprisingly perfect diction, and Broker had occasionally seen dog-eared books on philosophy in his pockets.

They drank, the pleasantries over. 'Which gang runs Brooklyn?'

'Gangs, they're a dime a dozen. They come and go. No one rules any place for long. There's always another bigger, stronger, dirtier that comes up. Way of the jungle and all that.'

You had to be patient with Snarky. He got to the point, but not in the way a crow flew.

Broker seated himself more comfortably and listened to a mix of science and philosophy, and eventually Snarky addressed his question.

'Only one gang. 5Clubs. Came from nowhere, and now nothing happens without their knowing or permission. Ruthless. They want to be feared, and they are.'

'They've a chapter here?' Broker knew, but he wanted to hear it from Snarky.

Snarky nodded. 'In Brownsville, which, as you know, is not exactly where you'd want to bring up your kids. Guy's called Jose Cruz, and he has one real badass dude by his side. Diego, his enforcer. Real bad, that hombre.'

He reflected for a moment. 'You know, I've been here a long time and seen gangs come and go. *These* guys are different.'

'Different in what way?' Broker moved his seat back a couple of inches. Everything was fair in a battle against odor.

'They've written the book on best practices for gang survival. I've heard that this gang recruits from the military, but they've adapted to survive on the street.'

Broker didn't reply. *This junkie probably knows the gang better than the JTF.*

Snarky edged closer to Broker. 'What's your interest in them?' He paused and then continued when Broker didn't answer. 'Keep your distance from them. They're scum, but they're disciplined about it and all the more dangerous.'

'Where does this Cruz hang out?'

Snarky pushed the trilby back fully, exposing gray stubble and sunken eyes. The eyes were sharp. 'They hung out in a garage a while back, but moved to the edge of Brownsville recently. Was that your doing?'

'Where?'

'A Laundromat. A big one. Used to be Chinese-owned one day, and the next day, Cruz and his gang had all but unfurled their flag over it. But they're keeping very low-key about it. The garage saw a lot of their heavies coming and going, and some of them were always there... this one here, they've just three guys or four all day, and Cruz comes irregularly. Most of the time he comes at night.'

Broker dug into his pocket and pushed a roll of bills toward Snarky. 'I need more than this drip feed. I want to know who and how many exactly is at that place, how often Cruz appears, who's with him... the works. You know the drill.'

Snarky eyed the bills and wet his lips. They were enough to feed him, or his habit, for months.

'Shit, man, why did you go and do that? Tempting me like that. What you're asking me to do is too dangerous. Word gets to them about me, I'm dead. In their world, you're either minding your own business, or theirs. If theirs, you're doing it for them else you're dead. And you don't die easy. That family... I heard whispers... they've disappeared.'

He shivered and, wrapping his coat tightly around his skinny frame, tipped his bottle back and took a long pull.

His eyes shone brighter as he looked into Broker's for a long time, knowing very little of what Broker did, but knowing enough, and his shivering slowed.

'They've no idea, do they? No idea of the dragon they've poked,' he whispered.

Broker said nothing, kept looking back at him.

Snarky caressed the bills, picked them up, and smelt them. His voice was steadier when he spoke. 'How do I contact you?'

Broker gave him a number. It was a toll-free messaging number, totally unreachable by the gang. 'Call that number from a pay phone. Where are their other hides? Their businesses?'

Snarky bared his lips, his version of a smile, the roll disappearing from his hand, and recited a long list of names. Some of those, the strip club and a couple of others, tallied with Broker's intel.

Broker kept looking at his back when he left, the door swinging in the shadows.

I should warn him, but he's survived the streets a long time. He knows what he's getting into.

Broker walked back the way he came, deep in thought. Much later, that would be his excuse for not noticing the shadow across the street, behind him.

Chapter 27

The strip club had an anonymous façade, its sole distinguishing feature the full-size cutout of a nude woman. Its front had limited parking spaces, and small darkened show windows stared out either side of the large door.

The strip club had a narrow alley at one side, which led to a walled and valeted parking lot at the rear, a rear entrance linking the lot to the club. Parking was important. Business types didn't like walking, and the rear parking offered anonymity. The alley side had an entrance, presumably for supplies.

The front of the strip club merged into storefronts for salons, convenience stores, Mexican take-aways... everything that men would need on the same street.

'Three cameras facing the street, one in the alley.' Bwana was driving, Chloe was in the front, Roger and Bear were taking notes in the rear. Bwana turned left at the lights at the end of the street, another left and a right, and he was driving up the street on the same side as the entrance.

Chloe glanced inside the alley as they drove past. 'Can't see much. It's a dead end with just one drive leading to the lot. The camera is right on top of the alley entrance.'

Bwana drove to a gas station a couple of streets away and pulled into a vacant lot. He swiveled as Roger and Bear opened the building plan for the club.

'Broker said it might not be recent, but this's the only plan he could get.'

They studied it in silence for a moment. The front and rear entrances led the patrons to seating and the stage to the right, while a bar, changing rooms and restrooms took over the left.

'Three entrances, the rear doubles up as the fire exit.' Chloe traced them with a lacquered finger. 'I bet the alley entrance is also the staff entrance.'

'Night?' Bwana asked hopefully.

'Nah. Too many people and there'll be enough goons to outnumber us,' Bear replied.

'So when?'

'Evening, around four. They open at six, so that's when they'll be stocking up and have enough cash in the place, but not that many heavies.'

'I was them, I'd have heavies round the clock,' Roger commented.

Chloe turned off the iPad and handed it to Bear. 'Which's why we'll recon all day tomorrow, hit the day after.'

Roger winked at Bear. 'She bosses you all the time?'

Bear pulled a long face. 'I'm not allowed to say.'

Roger arrived early the next day driving a cab and left it parked on the street, in the opposite lane, and placed an 'NYPD. Impounded' card on the dashboard with a number on it. Broker had tossed him the keys with an all-taken-care-of grunt in the morning.

He locked the cab and walked without a backward glance down an alley and behind the street. He thumped twice on a black Escalade and hauled himself inside when it opened.

The cab had a hi-res, hi-zoom camera rigged in its advert canopy, swivel mounted, with a sixty-degree turn capability and a parabolic mic. It fed images wirelessly to base and relay stations they had mounted the previous night, leading the feed and controls to the Escalade. Bear looked up when he entered and turned back to the display and control panel. He nudged the joystick, watched for a few more minutes, and then pushed back.

'These gadgets would have saved us a lot of grief in Iraq and 'Stan.'

Bwana, lying on the rear bench, opened one eye and snorted. 'You'd have ended up fat and lazy, a bottom broader than this truck.'

Bwana caught the balled-up napkin thrown his way and went back to snoozing.

'Where's Chloe?'

'Should be back soon. Coffees and all that.'

When Chloe joined them, they seemed to be asleep, an impression that had cost many an ambusher dearly. The Warriors were used to recon and could go for hours, days, in silent stillness. *Zero to lethal in a second,* she thought as she surveyed them, glanced at the monitor, and settled herself next to Bear.

They broke off the surveillance late at night and watched the feed from the start.

The first employees at the club arrived close to midday, the kitchen staff, via the alley entrance. Then came a series of deliveries, drinks, groceries, maintenance guys, cleaners, the invisible operators of the club. At half-past three, a Camry rolled up, low on its wheels. Four toughs inside would do that. Three of them hopped off at the alley entrance, one carrying a heavy backpack. The fourth drove the car behind, to the parking lot, and disappeared from the recon cam.

Bear paused the video and zoomed in so they could see the bag, its shape and weight, and resumed the feed.

At four, the girls started arriving and a fifth heavy, who escorted them. Roger looked at the girls and started to say something... and kept silent when he felt Chloe's steady gaze on him. At seven p.m. the last heavy arrived, this time at the front entrance. He rapped on the door and withdrew red rope barriers and their stands and laid them out in the front, went back inside, and the lights and hoarding on the front came on.

The club was ready for business, and its patrons started arriving at six.

They continued watching the feed till midnight, though there wasn't much more to watch. During its busy hours, two of the thugs came to the front and acted as bouncers.

'I count about ten staff not including the girls, and seven goons,' Bwana said when Bear turned off the feed.

He looked around at all of them. 'Let's hit them when they've just the four heavies. I suspect we'll have about twenty minutes before the other goons come in and maybe backup hitters rush to the club.'

They all nodded. 'Yup. If we aren't out of there by then, we'll be in a whole heap of trouble.' Chloe tapped a polished fingernail on the laptop. 'Where would you guys position yourself, if you were them?'

228

'At the rear. Most people go for the front entrance, and hence that's always the one heavily manned. At this club, I'd go for a force at the back,' Roger replied promptly.

'Way I figured. So, assuming that, I'll take the front; Bwana, you take the rear; and Bear will take the staff entrance.'

She noticed Bear frowning. 'Don't agree?'

'They'll be expecting us, won't they?'

She nodded. 'They won't know when, but yeah.'

'Let's do the unexpected, then. Same approach, but different tactics.' He outlined his plan.

They waited for the Camry to make its deposit the next day and then made their move.

Chloe, a leather coat cinched at her waist and large shades covering her face, fluffed her blonde wig and rang a discreet buzzer on the front entrance. Lots of cleavage did the trick.

She heard rattling at the door, and it opened a sliver to allow suspicious eyes to peer out. 'Yeah? We open later.'

She tossed a grenade through the crack. The suspicious eyes tracked her, then the object, grew wide, and the door slammed shut. From inside she heard a muffled shout, sudden voices, and the door was flung open.

The people rushing out reversed suddenly, and the door slammed shut even quicker when she fired just above their heads, pockmarking the door horizontally.

'Back,' someone screamed from inside.

The back had Roger and Bwana, in their trademark black and masked.

The rear entrance was shut when they approached it. Positioning themselves either side of the entrance, Bwana, on the left, knocked on the slat. It opened a few minutes later.

Roger wordlessly tossed three grenades inside and stepped back, away from the line of sight of the door. Bwana stayed where he was, hugging the wall.

There was deep silence for a second, and then they heard the first deep yell from inside, and others followed.

The double doors flew open, and the stampede began, all of them screaming and cursing. Bwana let the staff go, grabbed the first thug by his collar and rammed his face in the side of the building. The second thug turned around, startled, his mouth wide open in a silent shout, his eyes seeing but not comprehending, and he folded when Bwana's Glock met his temple.

Roger joined him and pulled the other two bouncers from the fleeing crowd. The first one didn't give him any trouble once his mouth had opened to receive Roger's SIG; the other needed a little more persuasion, like a knee in the nuts.

Minutes later they had the four thugs lying on the concrete, plastic-tie cuffed. Bear and Chloe, having sent the staff home by pointedly waving their guns, joined them and wordlessly hauled the men up to sitting positions and looked at Bwana, giving him the cue. Bwana nodded at Roger, who disappeared inside, and minutes later they heard the sound of furniture crashing. He came back lugging a heavy plastic sack. 'Stuffed with bills, mostly small notes. Emptied the till under the counter too. Retrieved all the grenades.'

They gave one last look at the four. One of them had his nose smashed and was bleeding heavily, another was looking at them with glazed eyes, and a third was doubled up and moaning softly.

The fourth glared at them balefully. 'Feel like men, huh? Guns in your hand, bet you do?' he sneered.

Roger tossed one of the grenades to Bwana, who held it up in the air for the four to see. 'Feeling stupid that you didn't notice its pin was still in? Bet you soiled your pants.'

They often used sudden, simultaneous attacks to create pressure-cooker environments that left no time for rational thought. Animal instincts, fight or flee, kicked in. Even battle-hardened soldiers lost the fighting instinct when they saw a grenade clattering in, and these were thugs. Former soldiers, but still thugs.

The man flushed angrily as Bwana's words registered. 'If I wasn't—'

Bwana didn't allow him to finish. Tossing the grenade back to Roger, he glided across, and hauling him up, he cut him loose.

He pushed the man forward. 'Tell you what. Since you're such a man, I'll take you on. No guns, no knives, nothing. Just you and me.

'You man enough for that? Or do you prefer fighting women?' he goaded the heavy. 'If you beat me, we'll let you go free. Not only that, we'll cut all of you free and walk away. Without all that money.'

The gangbanger was gym fit, his arms and legs heavily muscled, his shirt tight against his chest. He boxed and honed his skills whenever the gang needed to control a recalcitrant victim. He had a couple of inches over Bwana's six-three, and he was confident. He bared his lips and feinted.

Bwana stood still, watching him through half-lidded eyes. A bee buzzed in front of him, decided it wanted no part of him, and flew off.

The man feinted again and swung a tentative left and, as Bwana ducked easily, snapped a wicked right... at the air.

'What's the matter, boy? You ever been in a real fight? A fight for your life?' Bwana asked him softly.

Jab, hook, jab, feint, and still Bwana floated lazily, not even raising his hands. Through the corner of his eyes, he saw Chloe look at her wrist and drop it. The man advanced again.

And Bwana didn't retreat.

Approaching the man swiftly, he dropped suddenly to his hands and executed a blurring, crouching spin kick, knocking the thug off his legs. Completing his kick in one smooth, round motion, back on his feet, he reached out and grabbed the falling man by his left hand, pulled him forward and, with his right hand, slapped him on his face, open palmed.

Two hundred pounds of Bwana, all loaded at the end of his arm, met his face, delivering the most humiliating blow a man experiences, rocking his head sideways, staggering him two, then three steps back.

He fell and lay there, offering no resistance as Bwana cuffed him again and dragged him back to the other captives. Roger, who'd been interrogating one of the heavies, looked up and nodded.

They met trouble as they were leaving.

Chapter 28

Bear was nosing their Yukon out of the alley, joining the street, when a tan Ford and a black Nissan surged from their right, the Ford edging ahead of them. Faces swiveled in their direction, eyes widened as they took in their masks, the driver gesticulating furiously at his companions.

Its rear window rolled down, and they could see hands reaching down or inside jackets and shirts.

Bear T-boned them.

Thousands of man-years of workmanship had gone in the Ford, but it crumpled like a crushed can against the Yukon, and shuddered again when the Nissan rammed it in the rear.

Bwana slipped out of the reversing Yukon and roared out loudly in a voice that could wake the dead, 'NYPD. Stay down.' Cops didn't wear masks, but the more deception, the more distraction.

He reached back inside, tossed two of those mock grenades through the rear window of the Ford, and shot out its visible tires. The Glock in his right hand was steady and looked like a cannon to those in the Ford, but they weren't offering resistance, the shock of the crash bleeding it away.

Roger was running to the Nissan, whose rear doors had opened, and two men were climbing out. Running and then flying as he launched in an aerial kick that took out the closest one to him, and landing on the roof of the Nissan, he slashed with his SIG at the second, and again, this time a reverse swipe.

Roger leapt back to the rear as the two in the front shot blindly through the roof of the car, and then the Nissan's windshield shattered first and then its windows as Chloe fired, double and triple taps, extreme penetration, bonded bullets first punching holes in the windshield, spiderwebs around it, the other bullets following through, hours of practice of firing against different targets and combat experience coming together without conscious thought.

And then they were away, Bwana and Roger leaping to the running boards of the reversing and then surging Yukon, silhouetted for just a moment against the concrete and glass storefronts of the street, their forms slicing through the air, and then the Yukon disappeared in the traffic and they in it.

Tony removed his hand from his backpack, pulled his door shut, relaxed, and tasted his coffee. It had gone cold.

Broker had sent him as insurance, and he had watched the takedown from his anonymous van parked down the street. He'd parked early in the morning, his van bearing the signage of a utility company, his coverall bearing the same signage. He'd a work order clipped to a board in the passenger seat in case anyone was nosey enough to ask.

He wiped his palm against his coverall and let his backpack slip and fall to the floor of the van. It fell with a muted thud, a Colt 45, spare magazines, stun grenades, a flashlight, blood pack and emergency kit weighing it down.

If the Yukon had been attacked, he would have let loose with his Colt, a gun not for stopping people, but disintegrating them. He thumbed a button on the steering wheel, and when the phone connected, he said simply, 'All clear,' and fired the van up.

235

'Roger,' Broker answered and smiled. The others didn't need to know that Tony would have been their cavalry, if required.

On the other side of the street a tramp shuffled to his feet and staggered away. The street had thin traffic, which had further dispersed on Bwana's warning. The drunk had lain against a storefront through all the action, heedless of uncaring bullets, gripping his half-empty bottle as he stared sightless.

He bounced against storefronts and half fell into an alley and straightened and dropped the bottle in the nearest trash can. The Watcher wiped his face and slipped on shades from deep inside the blanket over his body.

Tailing them was easy now, though not required. His bugs did that job, and even when they switched vehicles, he was onto them. He walked a couple of blocks to the nearest subway and smiled inwardly when he got a seat despite the rush hour. *Funny how BO can clear space.*

Broker had a bemused look and was putting down his phone when they went to his room.

'What?' Chloe asked him.

He shook his head and poured coffee for them, taking his time, allowing their adrenaline to subside, the sounds and smells of a crowded and hot city to calm them down.

'Any problems?'

'Nah.' Bear took a long gulp of his drink, letting it burn his mouth. 'Some gangbangers showed up as we were leaving. We read them the riot act, and they calmed down.'

Broker grinned. 'And the take?'

'About fifteen thousand dollars. Big Brothers Big Sisters will be happy tomorrow. So what happened here? Why that face?'

'Got a message from Snarky.' He explained who Snarky was. 'He had info on the chapter and was getting to it when the call got cut. He *did* say he was running out of change. Guess I'll have to go and meet him.'

'Is that safe?' Roger asked him doubtfully.

'Safer than your walk in the park.'

Broker left their company after dinner and made his way to the same street and heard Snarky before he could see him. Snarky was slaughtering Nat King Cole's 'When I Fall in Love' enthusiastically, yet his hat was gleaming with coins. Broker shook his head in disbelief and dropped his loose change in the hat.

He was well into his Newcastle Brown Ale by the time Snarky joined him, downed *his* beer in a smooth swallow, and pushed his glass toward the bartender for a refill. The balding bartender, a dirty towel across his shoulder, looked questioningly at Broker and filled one for Snarky at Broker's nod.

'Took you long enough to get here,' Snarky accused Broker. 'I called you, like, hours back.'

'If you had some change with you, we wouldn't be having this conversation,' Broker shot back.

'Man, you know how I am with phones. They're spying on us, besides if I used my change for calls, what would I use for drinks?' Snarky fervently believed that THEY were spying on all of them and every phone in America was tapped. He went a bit vague when pressed about THEY.

'Get to it,' Broker reminded him.

'Cruz comes around midnight, with about five guys, stays for a couple of hours, and then leaves. He's with his enforcer always. The two are never seen alone. Man, they're evil. The things they've done and will not stop at doing...' His voice trailed away.

'So why did they move there?'

'A deal went wrong, cops came to the party. Hurt them a lot. Next day garage's empty, laundry got new owners.'

It was good to have Broker's jigsaw being corroborated.

The third beer flowed inside Snarky and so did the bills Broker slipped in his palm.

'One other thing.' His eyes cleared the way they did when they needed to. 'They lost a strip club; some masked hoods came and took it apart. That you? If so, they're madder than a hornet and are looking for you. Word's out on the street. They know your name and are also looking for a black guy, a woman, and some others, along with you. Those with you?'

Broker was unperturbed. This was something they were expecting and, if anything, were expecting the gang to have discovered them earlier.

'That's all right, don't answer. Wouldn't be surprised if it's not just you they're looking for. They could have found I was asking... guess I'll have to find another empty storefront to rest my ass against.'

Broker laughed incredulously. 'Snarky, if they're looking for you, you need to get the hell out of here. Leave town. Disappear.'

'And what? Be a drunk in another town? I'll take my chances here. Besides, if they're looking for me, what do I know about you? Your description they already have. I guess I could give them that number you gave me. Much good it'll do them.'

Broker persisted. 'Your life won't matter to them. Get out of town. Now.'

Snarky shrugged. 'Maybe I will, and maybe I won't. I've lived my life on the street and survived. Whatever kind of bad these guys are, I can handle it.'

He turned away and stopped short suddenly.

The bar had cleared out silently and in the dim light stood two men facing them. Both olive skinned, one short and stocky, and another bald and thin. Baldy was smiling thinly, knowing they had the advantage over a drunk and an older dude.

Broker followed Snarky's gaze and then whipped back to the bartender. No one.

The two spread out, and Shorty signaled with his hand. 'Come with us.' He looked at Baldy. 'Call the–'

Broker hurled his glass at Baldy, and Snarky rushed Shorty and tackled him. Broker was moving even as the glass hit Baldy over his right eye. Skin split and blood flowed freely over his face, and then Baldy doubled over as Broker's knee sank into his belly. Broker followed it up with an uppercut, and Baldy was out of action.

Snarky's initial advantage was long gone, and Shorty had gripped him by the throat and was squeezing the life out of him when a bar stool broke over his head. Broker smashed another bar stool over his head for good measure.

He looked down at the two. *Not bad for an old guy and I'm not even panting. These are my bragging rights for a month.*

He shoved a heaving and wheezing Snarky outside the door and fast-walked him a block away and stopped in the shadow of a poorly lit street.

'Get out of here. Go someplace else and lie low. You might be a drunk in another city, but you'll live to have more drinks.' He shoved another roll of bills at Snarky, who had sobered by then. Snarky pocketed them and swayed for a moment.

He grinned. 'Don't you worry about me. I'll surface somewhere like those Whac-A-Mole creatures. Maybe we'll take down some gang somewhere else.'

Broker stood in the darkness, thinking back to the bar. *Bartender must've called it in. I wasn't followed... would have been difficult to shadow Snarky, given that he lay there most of the day.*

He pulled out his phone. 'Get outta there, now! Tony or I will call you with rendezvous details.' He hung up on Chloe, knowing they would act. He dialed another number.

'Tony–'

Tony interrupted him. 'Boss, they're looking for you. Chatter is high.'

'They found me, got out with my skin intact. We need to move. Can you find us a place, a different one now, not the kind we've been staying in so far.'

'Roger. You okay?'

Broker chuckled. 'Never felt better. Kicking ass, kicking *young* ass, always feels good.' He told Tony briefly what had gone down and took his time walking back to a subway station. At the subway, he caught trains randomly, switching them at whim and taking any line that caught his fancy. He was sure he hadn't been followed, but precautions never hurt.

It was while riding the Red Line downtown that his thoughts turned to Zeb.

He liked riding the rails, especially at night. The play of light and dark as the train moved, the blur, the crowds and the space… he liked them. He used to say you were always alone in your bubble in the subway, no matter how crowded or empty it was. That was Zeb. He never spoke much, but when he did, there would be a universe of meaning.

The subway car was empty that night save for Broker at one end and a cuddling couple at the other. She noticed Broker, a bit older than them, but the strength in his body, his carriage, his hair, drew attention. She saw him faintly smiling at something, and her lips curved in a small smile involuntarily. They stepped out at the next stop, and she turned back to glance at him again.

She noticed his cheeks were wet.

Broker was wrong. He'd been shadowed.

The Watcher had followed him once he had left the others. The Watcher's technique was simple and the most difficult to master. He kept his *Ki,* his life force, so low and muted that it merged in the Brownian motion of six million other people. The inner radar of those he was shadowing, so finely tuned, failed to spot the Watcher, and the only moments when they felt a twinge was when the Watcher had to come closer or when his Ki had risen.

The Watcher had spent a long time observing Snarky before concluding that he was just that, a drunk. And Broker's snitch.

He had seen the gangbangers enter the bar. There weren't two. There were three.

The last one was a couple of steps behind, and just as he was entering the bar, he had been grasped by the collar and sucked back, a giant vacuum pulling him. The Watcher rammed his face on the wall, glanced indifferently at a passerby who was standing shocked, and dragged the now unconscious man away. He found a trash can and heaved the man inside it. He had seen Broker dispatching the other two heavies and, seeing no other gang members nearby, had made himself invisible.

He lip-read Broker. *Not the kind we've been staying in so far.* The Watcher didn't need to know where they would be staying.

They could hide their trail better than anyone; they were the best.

The Watcher was better.

Chapter 29

'All white guys, a father and son in one room, and single occupancy in the other rooms. This way, they hack the hotel, they won't find a couple and a black guy.' Tony handed Broker his room card and stifled a yawn. He had found them an upmarket hotel very close to Central Park, had checked in, using their names with a few other guys, and had stayed back to hand them their room cards so that they would have no interaction with the desk.

The hotel had a fancy restaurant, and Bwana and Roger were attacking it the next day when the others joined them. Breakfast was a serious business to be attended in silence, and it was much later when Bwana, with a wooden face, asked Broker, 'Heard you nearly got your ass whupped?'

Broker growled, 'You heard wrong. My well-shaped ass could handle two like those in its sleep. They could've sent three and wouldn't have made any difference.'

Bear wiped his mouth with a napkin and stretched in his chair, which creaked in protest. 'What do we hit today, and who do we shoot?'

'We visit an old friend tonight, and tomorrow we go back to Elaine Rocka.'

Chloe grinned. 'We shooting her?'

Broker rolled his eyes. 'Nope. It's time we asked her to go to the police. The NYPD will turn a blind eye to our doings, but we still have to report the missing man. They also have more feet on the ground and more resources and will be able to help.'

'And who's this old friend we're meeting?' Roger asked curiously.

'Connor Balthazar.'

Connor Balthazar was a journalist, but he was no ordinary journalist who reported on snowstorms and 'dog bit man' stories. Connor headed the International and Special Features desk at the *New York Times*, where he oversaw the largest stories in the national and international editions.

It was Connor's wife and son, Lauren and Rory, that Broker and Zeb had rescued from Carsten Holt. Connor knew what Zeb had meant to them and also knew some debts just *were* and could never be repaid.

Connor passed a bottle of Shiraz to Broker, who studied it, nodded and handed it back to Connor. Connor, his dark curly hair thinning but still thick enough to frame an intelligent face and piercing eyes, went to the sideboard and took his time pouring the wine in their decanters.

They had been greeted with heartfelt warmth when they arrived, Rory rushing into Bear's arms when his frame filled the door. Despite their protestations, Lauren had taken charge and had insisted on their staying for dinner.

'You're all growing boys, I know.' She had laughed in Bwana, Roger and Bear's direction.

Connor knew this was no social call and had waited for his wife and son to go to bed. 'Looks like you're all loaded for bear.' He chuckled mildly.

'Nature of our job.' Broker smiled briefly and handed over a slim folder to Connor, who skimmed through it quickly. 'I know most of this... common knowledge. Proof, of course, is a different matter, and hence the NYPD hasn't been able to do much.'

The folder was a summary of the gang's activities and structure in the city.

'You cover them still?' Chloe asked him.

'Not me personally. I'm more of a desk jockey now, but we've got reporters who cover them. You need some info on them?'

Desk jockey or not, Broker knew the reporter in Connor was very much alive and loved the scent of a big story. 'You know this place they operate from downtown. It might be worth getting your reporters to keep a close eye on it for the next few days.'

Connor waited for more and got none.

'Something's going down?' he asked carefully. He knew who they worked for and the sensitivity involved.

Broker nodded emphatically. 'Something will go down and, in fact, has been going down for a few days. Might be a juicy story for those newshounds of yours.'

He laughed at Connor's expression and, leaning across, filled Connor's glass.

'It started off like this...'

They were still there a couple of hours later after Broker had told him everything. *Well, not everything.*

'This can't be printed, I presume,' Connor asked him, his eyes gleaming with interest. When Broker nodded, he continued, 'And what exactly is going to happen in the next few days?'

'It wouldn't be a surprise, then,' Bear interjected gruffly, and Connor let it rest.

'What I would appreciate is anything you have on the Brooklyn chapter. Heck, anything you guys have on the gang will be useful.'

Connor laughed, and when he saw their puzzled expressions, he said, 'Broker asking instead of hacking! Got to be a first.'

The heartbeat of the city had slowed by the time they left his apartment, and dim streetlights reinforced the dark. Roger and Bear glanced once around, and then Bear slipped in the driver's seat. He waited a while before turning the key, looking at smudges of shadow in his side mirrors. When the shadows didn't move, he fired up and drew away. *Whoever he is, he's very good*, was unsaid and obvious to them all.

Just after dark the next night, the lights in the garage in Harlem flickered out. In the movies, they flickered once or twice before dying, but real life worked a bit different to the way Hollywood viewed it.

The streetlights in front went out too, and four shadows slipped over the walls of the garage. Five gangbangers who stood watch at night became instantaneously alert and pulled out their cell phones, to find there wasn't a signal. Before they could raise any other alarm, they were overpowered, cuffed and gagged.

Later, they would swear that the shadows were darkly clothed and masked and didn't utter a single word. It was as if they communicated telepathically.

They weren't blindfolded, and they saw one of the shadows scale the camera mountings and spray-paint it. Another hung what looked like banners all over the garage. The men looked at one another, their anger in being overcome so easily giving way to puzzlement. No one hung banners in a gang hideout. It was too dark to see what the banners said.

Another shadow made its way to the garage office, paused at the locked door, and returned. Two shadows took some kind of a can and climbed to the roof of the garage and disappeared. Two others spent a long time moving slowly, bent over the paved surface of the parking lot of the garage.

The shadows from the roof joined the ones on the ground, and they all disappeared as noiselessly as they had come. The streetlights were restored in minutes, but the garage remained dark all night while the night around it lived and breathed.

Phones rang in the early morning, the air turned blue with swearing, and the garage turned into an attraction for a few hours as TV and newspaper reporters crowded around the police tape and camera lenses chased anyone wearing NYPD colors. Not satisfied with the standard, 'No comment,' they ran down any passerby who approached the garage for sound bites.

A blonde journalist was breathlessly reporting, 'No one knows who put up these banners and posters over night. The NYPD has said they are actively pursuing all leads but are refusing to divulge more. Some of the cops have struggled to keep a straight face as we interview them. The garage owners have not responded to our calls and comments. The question remains on everyone's lips. Are these banners true? Or are they an elaborate joke? If you have any information, call us on...' She patted her hair down in the breeze as the camera cut in to show close-ups of the posters.

There was a giant poster on the main gate of the garage:

> **Your Friendly Neighborhood Gang has opened for business.**
>
> **Come to us for drugs, kidnapping, murder, extortion, carjacking and any other criminal activity.**

Another poster read:

> **Money Back Guarantee.**
>
> **If we fail to deliver to your satisfaction, we WILL refund your money. Call Dieter Hamm, NOW!**

Yet another went:

> **Don't steal, murder, blackmail, or kidnap to feed your drug habit. We will do that for you.**

There were many such posters all over the garage, all of them signing off with Dieter Hamm's name and phone number. There was even one that had a rate card, and this was the one Broker was chuckling over when the others joined him in his room.

They could see the southern line of Central Park from the window, office workers rushing across with no thought in mind except the day ahead, a few cyclists enjoying the sunshine, parents and babysitters letting their children play, and the usual traffic snarl. Another day in New York City.

Except it wasn't for 5Clubs.

They had returned late at night and had already made arrangements to check into another hotel, this time under different genders and ages. Broker had looked into setting up safe houses a while back but had discarded the idea quickly. Hotels had their risk, but the benefits far outweighed them for their kind of business. Anonymity, multiple escape routes, vantage points, all these had convinced Broker that when needed, hotels and motels were where they should hole up.

The others laughed at one of the posters, interrupting his thoughts.

'They'll be hunting us now with a vengeance. From now on, we travel in two vehicles and split up in two groups and stay in separate hotels. Bear, Chloe and I in one group, and Roger and Bwana, you guys in another.'

He got a thumbs-up from all of them, and as they were leaving his room, his phone rang. Not many had that number.

He frowned as he listened briefly. 'I'll be there.'

'NYPD,' he said to the others. 'They want me at One Police Plaza.'

Chapter 30

'You know anything about this?' Detective Lee Chang asked Broker, leaning casually against a filing cabinet. Chang's creased suit, thinning hair and weary eyes spoke of a detective who had seen it all and worse. Broker had heard of him and knew he was a good cop. Chang didn't jump to conclusions and allowed the evidence to lead him to wherever it took him.

Chang's partner, Pizaka, was in sharp contrast. Pizaka shone. His gleaming white shirt, knife-edged trousers and polished brown shoes hurt Broker's eyes. He donned a pair of shades and turned back to Chang.

'Detective, of the eight million people in the city, why're you asking me?'

'Cause Dieter Hamm, the owner of the garage, whose name has appeared in all the posters, has accused you,' drawled Pizaka. He and Chang were a good team; Chang lulled the suspects with his sleepy eyes and laid-back attitude, and Pizaka swooped in for the kill. They were proud of their *Tango and Cash* label.

They had called Broker in to get a first statement after Dieter Hamm and his expensive lawyer had filed a complaint and threatened to move heaven and hell – *Hell for sure*, thought Pizaka – if the NYPD didn't book Broker and his associates.

'He said you threatened him, accused him of running a gang, and tried to intimidate him and his staff – you and four others. He claimed you were responsible for a midnight raid on his garage and sticking posters all over it. Said he didn't know what beef you had with him and that these...' Pizaka's poise slipped as he tried to find the right word.

'Slander,' Chang said helpfully.

'These acts of defamation and slander are your doing. Discrediting the reputation of a respected pillar of the community and all that. Oh, I forgot, he's also accused you of trespassing on private property and attacking his employees.'

'I accused him of running a gang, of running prostitution rings, orchestrating kidnappings and being pond life and scum. That's all true; that's not slander.'

'There's the small matter of evidence and conviction,' Chang murmured.

'Which is your job, Detective. How are you getting on with that?' Broker challenged them. He grinned at the ensuing silence and then continued, 'But if this pillar of society is accusing me of putting up the truth on his garage last night, not guilty.'

'Where were you last night? And your associates?' Pizaka's Armani shades reflected the light, adding to the shine around him.

The strip club and the gas station employ goons and don't report all their income to the IRS. Bit hard to file a report in those circumstances. The garage, on the other hand, is clean, if you overlook all the gangbangers hanging around in it, mused Broker.

'Anyone home?' Pizaka asked again, bringing Broker back.

'Oh, yeah. We were in Atlantic City, in the Gold Rush Casino. Went in the afternoon yesterday, returned today, just a couple of hours back. Pamela was our cocktail waitress. She should remember us,' Broker smiled innocently.

251

'Why should she remember you?' Pizaka took the bait.

'You mean this is not reason enough?' Broker gestured at himself, grinning. 'We must have made a pleasant change from her usual customers, most of whom are trying to look down her neckline or groping her.'

When Pizaka and Chang didn't react, he continued. 'We were pretty much the only people she was serving. My associates put away a lot of food and drink.'

'You could have paid her to be your witness.'

Broker nodded. 'I could. I guess I could've also paid Gold Rush's security people to insert our images in their camera feeds.'

Broker employed hackers, no ordinary hackers but some of the best on the planet, who could run circles round those employed by the NSA. His hackers were based in the Ukraine and Serbia and were utterly loyal to him. They had been disappointed with Broker.

'Is that all? We could move some of their money for you...' one of them had complained.

Chang straightened, and Broker knew it was over. He and his partner had nothing on them, and the purpose of the interview was merely to make a statement to him. As Broker was leaving, he couldn't resist. He turned back to them, both of them sporting shades now, the shades reflecting multiple images of Broker.

Broker aimed two fingers at his eyes and reversed those fingers at Pizaka first and then Chang, in the classic B-movie gesture. 'No? I thought we would have parted with you doing this. Isn't it in the Suave Detective Handbook?'

He glanced casually to his right when he stepped out of the interview room, closely followed by the two. There was a bunch of people milling around several feet away, and something about them caught his attention. He gazed sharply and then recognized Hamm accompanied by a smartly dressed middle-aged man, his lawyer.

Broker stepped across to them, ignoring the sharp breath Pizaka drew behind him and Chang's whispered, 'Don't.'

'Had some trouble, Dieter?'

Hamm's lawyer leaned in and whispered something, and Hamm's bunched shoulders relaxed, his eyes watching Broker like a cobra's.

'That rate card...'

Hamm lunged toward Broker, his hands reaching out, and Chang and Pizaka hurled themselves between the two, and that wasn't enough. Hamm came to inches from Broker's face and whispered, 'You're a dead man walking.'

Pizaka twisted his face back at Broker. 'Get outta here.' If he had heard Hamm's comment, he ignored it.

Broker looked at Hamm and grinned even wider, feeling light and carefree and utterly dangerous. 'Listen to your lawyer, Hamm. Don't do or say anything stupid. Scheafer wouldn't like it. As it is, I'm sure he's not very happy with your incompetence.'

Hamm stilled, the surging force in him stopping and subsiding, and the two looked at each other, and the others became inconsequential. The spell broke as Hamm turned and walked away, his lawyer trotting fast to keep up with him.

Broker walked outside, things coming back into focus, the murmur of voices growing louder, and when he reached outside, he paused to let life normalize. He could have crushed Hamm's larynx and left him dead in seconds. Crushing Hamm wasn't the objective.

Taking a deep breath, allowing it to run through him and calm down the motor neurons and synapses, he dialed a number. 'Meet me at Rocka's.'

Pressure, relentless pressure. That was the objective.

He drove out, knowing that three other vehicles would fall in behind him.

A fourth vehicle detached itself from the rest of New York and followed them.

The Watcher.

'Why?' Elaine Rocka glared angrily at them.

They had grouped in two Tahoes and reached her home before she had returned from work, and had waited for her return. Her Subaru eased into the driveway an hour later, but rather than going inside, she strode – walking was not for the Elaine Rockas of the world – down the sidewalk and returned half an hour later with Shawn and Lisa. Lisa was holding her hand and skipping beside her, narrating her day, while Shawn followed more thoughtfully. Boys had their standards. They didn't walk abreast with girls, even if they were their sisters.

They had waited for another half an hour, and then Broker had knocked on her door and braced himself. She had flung open the door, made a sound of disgust, crossed her arms and waited, her dogs ever watchful behind her.

Broker had outwaited her, and they had finally been admitted to her living room, but not before she had sent the kids to their rooms.

'Why?' she repeated, scraping her chair back angrily. 'You got the answers you wanted. Why are you back?'

'Shattner's absence has to be reported to the police,' Broker replied patiently. 'Ma'am, we fully understand your wish to shield the children, but a missing person report has to be filed.'

Her face turned red. 'That is none of your business. You came to find the relationship with your dead friend; you got all that we knew. Why don't you disappear and let us get on with our lives?'

'Ma'am, this became our business the day we got Shawn's call–'

'Screw your business,' Elaine Rocka shouted, glanced around her, and lowered her voice. 'Just go.'

Broker sensed Chloe's gaze on him and looked at her and nodded briefly at her expression. He walked out of the living room without a word, the other men following him.

'Think she'll go for it?' Roger asked after a while.

'If Chloe can't persuade her, none of us can,' growled Broker, his calm exterior breaking to reveal his impatience. 'He's been missing for months now, for crissakes. Surely she understands that at the very least she's got to lodge it with the NYPD.'

Roger didn't answer, and Broker turned to glare at him, and then his glare dissolved.

Lisa had her face scrunched against the window and was drawing circles on the glass; Bwana was drawing smileys in them, making Lisa giggle. He traded glances with Roger and Bear and firmed his shoulders resolutely and turned back inside just as the door opened.

'We're going in half an hour,' Chloe announced, 'as soon as she gets the kids ready.'

'How did you manage that?'

'That's between women.' Chloe smiled and then answered seriously, 'She doesn't have a lot of choice. We could have gone directly to the police, and then she would have been in deeper trouble; the Office of Children and Family Services could get involved.'

A tornado burst out the front door and glared at them. 'We're ready,' Elaine Rocka said through clenched teeth, and then her face relaxed as the kids came through the door. Bear pulled the door shut behind them after an abrupt nod from her.

Bear opened their Tahoe's door with a flourish and bowed deeply as Lisa and Elaine climbed in. 'Milady.' He gestured grandly at Chloe, indicating she join them in the rear.

Chloe nudged Lisa. 'He's never opened doors for me before. Stick around with us, honey, and maybe we'll get him to shave that beard.' Lisa giggled when Bear caught her eye in the mirror and winked at her.

After dropping the dogs off at friends of hers, Broker led them to a safe house, the setting sun bathing Triborough Bridge in gold, time standing still momentarily for nature's work.

Far behind them, but keeping them in view, Tony pressed his earbud. 'On the move.'

'Roger,' came back another voice belonging to a stringy man driving a compact a couple of car lengths behind Tony. Their job was to keep the lead vehicles free of tails, or warn them of any.

At One Police Plaza – Chang had wanted to meet them there once Broker had called him – Pizaka led them to an empty office, empty save for Chang. He shut the door after Bwana, Roger, and Shawn joined them, and crossed the desk to join Chang.

Pizaka and Chang were professional and ran through Elaine Rocka's statement, disappeared for a few minutes – *Checking on the school, Elaine Rocka's manager and the garage*, Broker surmised – and returned with an air of finality, indicating the interview was nearly over.

When their aunt led the children away, Broker lingered back. 'You know the garage Shattner worked in was 5Clubs run? It was Brooklyn's epicenter of crime. I'm sure you guys were keeping tabs on it.'

Chang's sleepy expression didn't change, and Pizaka had his game face on.

Broker shrugged. 'Just saying. Shattner kept a journal, we just learnt. Wouldn't be surprised if it turned out to be hot.' He cut himself short when Pizaka and Chang looked over his shoulder; he glanced back and saw Shawn looking at him curiously through the half-open door.

An hour later, Elaine Rocka's stony visage was still the same, though her stiff shoulders had relaxed fractionally. It was hard to relax when Lisa frequently blew the shiny whistle she had hanging around her neck. 'Lee said I should use it if I'm in trouble, and they'll come with their sirens.' Lee. Detective Chang and her were besties now. Her friends at school would be so J.

Broker got sucked into meetings with other cops, intel that he'd passed helping their cases, and it was several hours before they could head out of the building.

'Broker, why did you say that? Dad didn't leave anything with us.' Shawn glanced up at him.

'I know, son, but I want them to work hard in finding your dad, and I'm dangling a carrot for them.'

Shawn nodded, unconvinced 'Do you think...?'

'I have dad's key,' Lisa said.

Broker stopped so abruptly that Bwana, a couple of steps behind him, ran into him. He knelt down. 'Say what, honey?'

'Dad kept his secret stuff in his locker. He gave me the key and said I should not give it to anyone.'

'You're lying. Dad always told me everything. He gave me his phone. He would have told me about his locker,' Shawn said angrily. He had always been the custodian of his dad's secrets, and it looked like now he wasn't.

Lisa's lower lip trembled, and her eyes filled. 'It's true. He gave it to me when he took us out of school. He made me pinky swear and stuck it inside my school bag.' She brushed away a tear with her face and ran to the comforting embrace of her aunt. Elaine Rocka glared at them. *See what you've done.*

Bwana knelt beside Shawn, dwarfing him even then. 'Do you trust your dad?'

Shawn nodded wordlessly, his eyes betraying his hurt. 'Then you should accept that this doesn't mean he didn't think you couldn't keep a secret. He had a good reason for this.' He kept looking at Shawn till the boy nodded again, slowly and reluctantly.

Bwana patted him on his shoulder and rose. He knew a lot about trust and faith. They didn't need to speak about it; it was just there, like sunlight and air.

Lisa had fallen asleep, the rush of traffic lulling her, when Elaine Rocka finally broke her silence. 'Do you think he has anything in the locker?'

Broker shrugged silently, the thought was uppermost in all their minds. 'We won't know unless we—'

'DOWN.'

'DOWN.'

His window exploded.

259

Chapter 31

Eric, driving the compact, had flagged the bike to Tony, who in turn had relayed it to Bwana and Broker.

Broker had kept an eye out for it and had spotted it as it came in the range of his mirror, just as Bwana's, 'Watch your seven,' came over his earbud.

A few blocks later, the bike was still tailing him and evasive action was called for, when the bike sped up and came alongside, the figure all in black straightened a right arm, and Broker shouted, 'DOWN.'

Broker stomped the brake, hard, and swerved *into* the bike. The bike wobbled, not expecting the maneuver, straightened, and the bullet flew wide, puncturing Broker's window, puncturing Bear's window, disappearing in the darkness, its lethal flight in vain. Rubber howled and burned in protest, but listened to its master, and the Tahoe came to a stop, nose across the lane divider, shutting down both lanes.

'Clear,' said Bear, crouching down in the well in the front, legs braced for impact, left hand steady on the steering in case Broker was hit, right holding his Glock.

'Clear,' said Chloe, lying on top of Elaine Rocka, who in turn was lying on Lisa, who was prone on the floor.

'All clear, he's gone,' came Roger's voice softly, something in his voice saying anyone approaching them now had better approach slowly, carefully *and peacefully*.

Broker looked in the mirror and saw them parked two car lengths down, both of them on the running rails; one had his gun trained behind, the other had the front covered.

He inspected his window, a round hole in it surrounded by spidery cracks, the exit on Bear's side similar, the holes large. *Large caliber. Shooting like this is iffy; deflection, angles, speeds all play hell. Gunman probably thought of pumping several shots to make at least some count but didn't get an opportunity.*

New York blew in through the holed windows, horns baying, drivers cursing, fingers sticking up in the air as the traffic bent and straightened around them. Some of them slowed; drivers rolled down their windows to swear at Broker, saw something in his face, and sped on to home and a beer.

The first of the NYPD cruisers came and then another and another, and the night became flashing red and blue.

Chang and Pizaka came. They checked on Rocka and the kids, who had moved to the second Tahoe. Lisa had gotten over her fear and was drinking it all in, *Millie would die when she heard*; Shawn kept looking around him, then at Bwana and Roger, and kept pulling on his serious face, but it fell and the grin came back on, it was all one big thrill for him. Elaine Rocka opened her eyes just once to look at Pizaka and say simply, 'This is why,' and closed her eyes and shut them all out.

'Got a description?' Pizaka asked Broker as he looked over the vehicle. Bear, removing shards of glass from Broker's face, glanced in Pizaka's direction and answered, 'Black. All black and hooded.'

'We didn't ask his name,' Bear added, sarcasm dripping.

261

Pizaka was as immaculate as ever, not a hair out of place, the crease sharper than a Jimmy Lile blade. *He must have cloned himself.*

'Number plate?'

Roger recited a number, not that it would do much good. It would be a throwaway, and the bike was probably already in some scrap heap somewhere. 'One of the sergeants said he would put a BOLO out.' Roger nodded in the direction of the police who were the first to the scene.

The detectives kept quiet. Broker and his companions knew how the system worked, how investigations such as these worked. Seven out of ten times, a hit-and-run such as this was never tracked down, not if false plates were being used, there was no workable description, and no credible witnesses or camera footage.

Broker patted his face with a wet tissue gently and inspected the tissue in the light. No glass. Satisfied, he asked the two detectives, 'This guy, Shattner. Was he one of yours?'

Both shook their heads simultaneously.

Chang said, 'We don't have anyone inside with that name. Heck, we don't have anyone inside the gang. Tried it a few times, and lost a few good guys. First time we heard his name was today. We ran him through the system when you guys left, and got arrests for dealing – unlicensed firearms, narcotics – that sort of thing. Strictly small time, and this was soon after his release from the army. After that, nothing. We haven't heard back from the FBI yet, if they have anything on him. We requested his army file, but that'll take time. You got anything to tell us?'

Broker briefed them, but there wasn't much more to Shattner. He was what it said on the tin. One of life's losers who got caught in a gang's grip. His children were now paying the price for that.

'You mentioned a journal. What's in it?' Pizaka asked them.

Broker faced him squarely, the two of them filling his vision. 'Now that. There isn't a journal. I mentioned that to get a rise out of you guys... to see your reaction.'

They looked at one another a long time, silent but for the traffic and the police working to keep the crowd and the television vans at bay. Roger and Pizaka digested what that meant, and their faces tightened, but they didn't say anything else. *The attempted hit went down just hours after mentioning the journal to the cops.*

Pizaka jerked his head back at the second Tahoe. 'You're aware you've put that family in danger by mentioning a nonexistent journal?'

'Yes,' Broker replied shortly. He didn't need reminding about it.

They had a long discussion about this before going to the Rocka home and had all felt that this was yet another way of piling pressure on the gang. *So long as Elaine Rocka and the children stayed with them till the heat died down.*

They had looked doubtfully at one another when *that animal* raised its head. Knowing Elaine Rocka, they had decided it was best to be upfront with her and see whether she would be willing. Chloe had told her everything about themselves — their investigation, their course of action, their preference and the rationale behind it. To her utter surprise, Elaine Rocka had agreed to go along with their proposal.

Seeing Chloe's bemused expression, she said fiercely, 'I want to make him a hero in their eyes. No child should think less of their dad. Not one. If this can help...' She walked out of the room without another word.

Maybe we've misjudged the battle-axe, thought Chloe as she looked at her departing form.

'Ms. Rocka? She's aware of the danger?' Chang dug out a toothpick from his rear pocket, tore the paper wrapper, and started chewing away, his eyes as hooded as ever.

'Yeah. And before we start, we know you won't be able to spare bodies for their protection. We'll take care of it.'

'Well,' drawled Pizaka, 'we never said that. Of course we can spare a warm body or two. We have many trained in close protection, and most of the time they're just going to fancy dos. This'll be real work for them.' The NYPD close protection division had the best trained close protection agents in the business, who were assigned to visiting heads of state and politicians of a certain rank. The division's reputation had ensured it had a growing 'private sector' business, VIPs and celebrities, that earned it a good revenue for far lesser risk involved.

Broker laughed and declined the offer with a polite shake of his head. *No way are they going to place a CPO, Close Protection Officer, with us.* 'In case you've forgotten, we've done this before. They'll be safe with us.'

Pizaka looked at the controlled chaos around him; several cops were taking witness statements, a few others were clearing the asphalt of shards, making the street ready for the usual onslaught of traffic. The legwork would begin now, going through the witness statements, seeing if any cameras had captured the bike, following various stolen bike reports, chasing down 'bike found' leads. They needed a lucky break, but he wasn't confident this time they would have much luck.

Broker read their body language. 'Perhaps you should focus closer to home.' Meaning the possibility of a mole in the NYPD.

Chloe asked quietly once they were on the way again, 'Pizaka and Chang, how're they?'

Broker met her eyes in the mirror, knew what she was asking. 'Not them. I've heard of them and have looked at them myself, in the past, for another assignment. It would be too obvious in any case.' In Broker-speak, look meant extensive background checks. 'The gang has either a dirty cop or has hacked into their system. No other way could they have mounted an attack so quickly. Once they knew we were all at One PP, it would have been easy to have a hit team follow us.'

'That wasn't a very professional hit team.' Chloe chuckled.

'I think what happened was they knew we were with the cops, didn't have a hit team ready, got someone to tail us, and that someone, a low-level guy desperate to earn his stripes, took a shot,' Bear rumbled from the front, keeping his voice low.

'Been thinking about it,' he said defensively when they all turned to look at him. His reasoning made sense, and they didn't have any other ideas, so they went with it.

'All the more reason to keep away from the cops and FBI,' Bwana muttered, echoing their thinking.

They had taped the window together as best as they could, but wanting clear vision, had left the hole in either window open. Lisa and Rocka, wrapped in a thick blanket, had fallen asleep finally, the adrenaline and the hush of tires lulling them.

Broker looked in the mirror at them and met Chloe's eyes. Their mission had expanded now; it included keeping the family safe and finding out what happened to Shattner.

'Tony?' he murmured in his collar mic. Tony and Eric were still behind and had remained in the background throughout the attack and the subsequent questioning by the police. Broker had kept his mic open, and they'd heard everything go down.

'Boss?'

'Where's the apartment?'

'Five bedrooms, five baths, a rooftop swimming pool, uniformed concierge, the works... Bit embarrassing to call it an apartment, but that's what they call it. You'll love this place. Any guesses where it is?'

Broker blinked at Tony's cheerfulness. 'Tony, I've been shot at, interrogated, sworn at, and have been Elaine Rocka-ed. Let's keep this simple. Why don't you tell me where the danged place is?'

Tony laughed. 'It's smack dab in the middle of Marine Park, which is as good as cop town, lot of cops and firemen live there. The gang tries anything there, they're likely to get a warm reception.'

Broker smiled slowly. *That's why he's my number two.* Tony had been working the phone ever since they left One PP, hunting accommodation for all of them, and this ticked all the boxes. Marine Park was in southeast Brooklyn, bounded by Flatlands Avenue and Gerritsen Avenue, next to the borough's largest park. Its lack of subway access and small community ensured that newcomers would be quickly spotted.

Chloe settled Lisa's head on her lap and stroked her hair as the girl shifted restlessly in her sleep. 'You guys will retrieve her backpack tomorrow?'

'Bwana and Roger will. We'll stay back and go through some ground rules with–'

'Boss,' Tony broke in urgently, 'another bike coming up on your seven.'

'Got him. On his tail. Close. Real close.' Bwana's voice came through their earpiece; he could've been reading the weather for all the excitement in his voice.

Bear glanced back at Chloe and saw that she was wedged by the sleeping forms. Coming to a decision swiftly, he reached below the seat and pulled out a Mossberg shotgun. 'Let them sleep. *We'll* go on the attack.'

He swung his door open, stuck his left hand out on the railing above, and uncoiled out of the Tahoe smoothly, the Mossberg a toy in his right hand. A deadly toy.

267

He spotted the bike behind them, making its way straight between the flowing lanes of traffic on either side, the rider, clad in black leather, his dark helmet gleaming in the shadowy light, looking straight ahead.

If the rider was aware of the Tahoe looming large and close behind him, he gave no indication. If he saw Roger standing on the rails, his shooting arm as steady as if he was stationary, his Glock tracking the rider, he didn't show it. The black bore of Bear's Mossberg followed him, and he didn't twitch.

Broker slowed fractionally, and the bike came on, cutting through the traffic, *gliding* through it, man and machine one, the Yamaha's purr putting tarmac behind it effortlessly. It came on their tail and slowly crept up on them, and the universe melted away for Bear and Roger, their breathing steady, their heartbeats low, their fingers ready to pull and send damage.

The visor turned slowly toward Broker, the purr of the engine blending with the throatier growl of the Tahoe, light glancing off the visor and disappearing, just blackness looking at Broker.

The Watcher looked. Saw Broker, stubble winking in the light; saw Bear and the Mossberg, a volcano ready to explode. Through the dimness, he could just make out Chloe, her eyes large, her hand aiming her Glock, a shape across her thighs. Through the corner of his eyes he saw Roger behind him, on his five, knew there was at least another gun on him. The Watcher didn't twitch, didn't flinch, didn't react. This was him slowing time, seeing all that he wanted to see.

The visor swiveled back smoothly straight ahead, the purr became louder, and the rider became a speck and then became night.

Bear and Roger followed it till it disappeared and then slipped inside the Tahoes, and they sped up. There wasn't any other traffic at that time of night, and if any of the passing traffic witnessed the byplay, they didn't stop. Bwana presently broke the silence. 'Is it him? Our stalker?'

'Could be. Then it could also be just a curious rider.' There was doubt in Broker's voice, though. No rider would be so relaxed with weapons pointing at him. He shrugged, putting it behind them. The stalker, if that's who it was, would have to take a stake in the game if he wanted to play. Till then he was irrelevant.

The others were still sleeping when Roger and Bwana left early the next day to retrieve Lisa's bag. Roger headed to the driver's side of their Tahoe when he paused. 'Think we should switch vehicles?' We can carjack one and return it before the owner realizes it.'

Bwana looked at him strangely. 'Now why would we want to do that, partner? Why make it difficult for trouble to find us?'

That settled it for Roger, though he still took a long, circuitous route to the Rocka residence. 'No need to be stupid,' he said aloud and looked at Bwana for a reaction and got a gentle snore in return.

He didn't spot any tails, not that he expected to, and when he neared the home, he shook Bwana awake. They parked their wheels a block away and flagged down a cab and drove past the residence and then reversed and drove by slowly again. Roger noticed the driver eyeing them curiously through the mirror, looked up his name on the permit, and said, 'Relax, Miguel, we're undercover cops.' He flashed the badge Broker had issued them, and Miguel nodded once and forgot all about them, his suspicions allayed.

When Miguel reached the end of the street, Roger motioned him to a halt and, thrusting a sheaf of bills at Miguel, asked him to take a break for an hour. They drove the cab, the most anonymous car in the city, back, parked it four hundred yards away, and settled down to watch.

Three hours later they were still the only people showing an interest in the home. He looked at Bwana, who nodded.

They walked casually to the house, taking cover from the parked vehicles on the street, and split up, Bwana heading to the rear and Roger to the window in the front. Roger picked up a rock from a flower bed and, when he heard Bwana's soft grunt in his ear, swung it against the window, shattering it. He heard the rear window give way with a louder crash, ran round to the rear, and followed Bwana through the wreckage. Covering each other, they went through the house swiftly, relaxing only when the last room was 'clean.'

Bwana holstered his gun. 'Too late.'

'House was wrecked. Someone had been there before and tossed it. Totally.' Bwana glanced at Elaine Rocka and looked away when her face hardened, her fingers whitened. He poured hot water in

270

a couple of cups, inserted tea bags and, when they were the right shade of brown, handed one to Roger. He looked at her again, a glance that was part apology, part embarrassment. They should have realized the gang wouldn't have waited till the morning.

'Ma'am, we've wrapped police tape all around the house. It's a good neighborhood, so it will be respected and the gang – we're pretty sure it was them hunting the journal – have no reason to go back there now,' Roger told her gently.

She nodded, cleared her throat and forced a smile. 'It needed a makeover anyway, what with the dogs around. The insurance will cover it.' The battle-axe returned, and steely eyes looked at Chloe. 'You'll get them?'

Chloe nodded once. That had always been the plan.

Before they could say anything further, Lisa and Shawn burst into the room and climbed on Rocka's lap. She held them close, her eyes asking them not to mention the house. Chloe nodded fractionally and asked the kids, 'Right, guys, I bet you're hungry. What do you have when you're hungry?'

She jammed fingers in her ears at the loud yells in reply and grinned. 'I can't hear you. Now you'll have to get your own cereal.'

'Will you go to the locker today?' Shawn put an end to their gaiety.

'We'll hunt for it, yeah,' Broker replied, choosing his words carefully. The locker was lost to them now, the key either in the debris of the house or with the gang.

Shawn frowned, puzzled at Broker's choice of words. 'What's there to search for when you have the key.'

'They don't have it, honey. They went to get Lisa's backpack but couldn't find it. They'll go back and search again.' Rocka combed his hair with her fingers, her touch calming him.

'It's with me.' Green eyes looked at them from beneath tousled blonde curls, as if to say *why wouldn't it be*? Lisa giggled when she saw most of them had their mouths open.

Bear was the first to recover. 'Your backpack...'

'Is with me,' she replied firmly, and then her face became indignant. 'You didn't think I would leave Dino behind, did you?'

'Dino?' Broker asked for all of them.

Lisa sighed long and theatrically. Adults. They didn't come with enough training.

'Keys,' she held her hand out and demanded.

Broker looked at her blank faced, and when Lisa thrust her hand out again, he gave her the Tahoe's keys.

She reappeared minutes later with a pink backpack festooned with ribbons and badges. Reaching inside it, she drew out a tattered green dinosaur and placed it in the center.

'Dino.' She pointed. 'Backpack.' She pointed at it.

Broker closed his eyes briefly, gathering his thoughts *and his wits*. He started, 'When did you—' and stopped when she held a palm up. Adults couldn't be trusted to ask the right questions.

'I was carrying it when we left home. Guess none of you noticed.' She smiled smugly. 'Now, Broker, can you find my dad's key?' she challenged him.

Broker would willingly face off with entire gangs, but kids were beyond him, and he wisely kept quiet. He reached out and emptied the bag, glancing curiously at a pink diary with a tiny padlock, a key dangling next to it. Lisa snatched it out of his hand, saying it was her private journal. He felt the insides of the bag, then the outside, turned the straps inside out, checked the folds, and came up with nothing. He started again, slowly this time, and still found nothing. He noticed Lisa and Shawn grinning, and it clicked.

'A key and a lock go together, don't they?' he asked casually, and Lisa smiled cheekily at him. 'Took you a long time, Broker.'

He examined the key. It looked like the key to the padlock at first glance, but closer inspection showed that it didn't match. 'Your dad did this? I thought he taped it inside your backpack.'

Lisa shook her head. 'He did, but then I removed it and hung it from the lock. It looked more natural there,' she said proudly.

Chloe beamed at her. 'That was very smart, honey. Not many kids would have thought of that. Did your dad say anything when he gave you the key?'

She scrunched her face, trying to remember, and then the blonde curls bounced. 'He said I should give it to Zebra only. He would know what to do.'

They looked nonplussed for a moment, and then Shawn rolled his eyes. '*Zeb*. Zebra is that striped animal.'

Lisa was on a roll and let that pass airily. 'Whatever. And I know.' She stuck her tongue out at him.

'Dad didn't say anything else?' Shawn took the key and inspected it and handed it over to Chloe. It wasn't anything special, like a billion keys out there, its sole purpose to go in a lock and uncover its secrets – but that was possible only if they knew *which* lock it fit.

The other men inspected it, but all of them came up blank. Broker went to his bag of goodies, *his* backpack, and taking a magnifying glass, examined the key, shaking his head in frustration finally when it stubbornly remained anonymous.

He leaned back and half-closed his eyes, thinking. Zeb would know what to do. Why would he? When he opened his eyes, Bwana and Bear had rolled out a map of the city and were marking the gang's businesses they had hit. Of course.

He leaned over them and marking Brownsville Autos with a cross, drew a large circle around it. Broker fired up his iPad and read out addresses within the circle.

Storage lockers, half an hour's commute from the garage.

Far enough to have enough distance from the garage, close enough that his absence wouldn't be missed. He probably went during his lunch hour.

Zeb used to have storage lockers all across the city, where he stowed several emergency stashes of cash, fake passports, identities, clothing, and weapons. Everything that a sudden exit needed.

They studied the twenty addresses, and after some more research, Broker drew a red line through five of them. 'Not big enough. He would want someplace that was large enough for him to feel anonymous.'

It was at the eleventh self-storage unit that they hit pay dirt.

The locker was empty save for a few clothes and, beneath them, a thin notebook.

Broker ruffled the pages and saw that only a few of them were filled. He went back to the first page and read.

'If you're reading this, then I am dead.'

Chapter 32

Broker finished reading in half an hour, breathed deeply, and passed it to Bwana and Roger. They read it in silence, and in silence they headed back to Marine Park.

Shawn looked at them expectantly when they returned and smiled when Broker waved the notebook at him, the smile fading when the three of them didn't say anything. 'Nothing in there?'

'Some clues. Will need some legwork.'

Shawn looked at him for a long moment, looking past Broker's game face and noncommittal answer, fearing the answer, not ready for it. He slid out of his chair and left the room. Lisa looked at them uncertainly and then, snatching Dino, ran after him.

'Not good?' Chloe asked them.

Broker handed her the notebook wordlessly.

Shattner's journal started from his days in Iraq. He wrote about his wife, his kids, the journal sunny and cheerful, a lot of pages focusing on his 'sprouts,' and then he started writing about his marriage coming under strain, and the jottings became darker. '… marriage has become a black hole for my money. If only she worked.'

There were several blank pages, and then one started with, 'There were a million reasons not to go down that route, and I knew all of them. Giving my kids a good life outweighed them all. Keeping her quiet was worth it.' He wrote about selling small arms that were on the verge of being deactivated, his way of rationalizing.

The entries became swiftly written, the pen digging deep in the journal, words bottled in Shattner finding a release.

The next entry was dog-eared, and the page was heavily smudged, as if Shattner had revisited it again and again.

'He was an odd one. He never socialized with anyone, didn't encourage conversation, never smiled... no one knew what he did and when asked, he said, "This and that." Rumor was that he was Special Ops, working with the rebels, but no one ever knew for sure.'

Next entry.

'He caught me.' The *caught* underlined. '–saw me stuffing my duffel. One moment I was alone in the store, the next moment he was there. He didn't ask me what I was doing. He just flat out told me, with those dark eyes looking deep in me. I could see he didn't buy my explanation. I told him why and am ashamed that I cried. He didn't fucking react. I lost it and trained the gun in my hand on him. He didn't move and didn't react, just said, "Soldier, you're in deep shit. Don't dig yourself in deeper." He walked away and before I could leave, the MPs came and arrested me.'

The next entry was more than a month later.

'He spoke *for* me at the trial. Said my circumstances should be taken into account, and the insignificant value and deactivated status of the arms should be considered. He has some juice because my pension is intact.'

Another entry, three weeks later.

'I am like cancer. No one approaches me or talks to me. I sleep alone. On the last day he came and gave me his number. I asked him why, and he just walked away.'

Elaine Rocka was reading over Chloe's shoulder, and she asked them, 'Is that your friend?'

They nodded, and silence fell again as the women resumed reading.

The entries for the next few months were about his winning custody of the children – 'They're my everything and I'll be theirs' – and the challenge in finding a job.

'Everything's okay till I tell them I was court-martialed. Then the doors slam shut.'

A couple of months later, drifting around the city.

'Sold my first gun. Got it from a gangbanger, sold it to another. Food for a few weeks. Pension not enough. Lisa and Shawn need clothes, books, school money.'

The entries became further spaced out and shorter, about reviving his arms-dealing contacts, time with the kids. The writing became terse, as if Shattner didn't want the journal to question him. There was one page the two of them lingered long over.

'Both of them are smart, maturing faster than normal kids. Don't think they know, but the boy sometimes looks at me, and I hurt. Suicide? I can see why now, but not until they'll be taken care of.'

A couple of months later, just one line on the page.

'Caught by the cops in a sting. Offered amnesty in return for being an informant in a gang. 5Clubs.'

A few days later.

'Many discussions with cops. Detective Kirkus will be my contact. Met with him a few times and got my backstory from him. It's not difficult to memorize; it's not far from mine. Discussing ways to connect, phone numbers. Light appearing at end of tunnel.'

The next entry didn't have a date.

'In now. Cruz and Diego scare me. Kirkus happy. Worried that other than assurances, nothing from the cops about amnesty. Deal done with the devil.'

The last sentence was underlined twice.

The entries, brief, came rapidly now.

'Most valuable mechanic now. Kirkus not happy. Says repairing cars is worth jack shit to him. Can't exactly tell Diego to involve me in gang. Kirkus evades when I ask him about amnesty or payment.'

There were many one-line entries after that, mostly about Kirkus urging him to be more valuable to the gang.

Then, four months later.

'Shortage of drivers. Drove Diego and a gorilla, Rajek, to a small deal. Sat in car. Kirkus happy. Shawn is man of house, takes care of Lisa. My son has no childhood. Because of me.'

He had recorded the time of the deal and drawn a crude map of the location. He'd also drawn a boy's face next to Shawn's name.

Elaine Rocka sighed deeply, and Chloe started to close the book, but she urged her to go on.

They flipped through the pages rapidly, stopping only where he went into some detail.

'Drove to a hit. Diego killed a guy in front of me. Suspects me of being a snitch since I was very calm. Told the bastard to shoot me. I have nothing to lose anyway, but my kids. Kirkus found the body. Says story is gang warfare.'

He had started recording deals by then, estimates of kilos, money and other parties involved, in small writing in the corners of the pages.

'Kirkus happy with flow, finally. Says cops are busting some deals. Puts more pressure on me. Kirkus continues to evade amnesty question,' went an entry.

Bear had moved behind them and was reading over their shoulder, and noticed Rocka's shudder at the next page.

'Found a bug in my house. They suspect a snitch and obviously I'm the newest. Carrying my gun with me now.'

The women didn't notice Lisa and Shawn creeping in the room, Bwana and Roger shushing them and leading them out. They were reading about a deal in Gloucester City; Shattner hadn't written much, but they could sense his fear and relief at living through it.

The next entry was the last.

'Garage closed. Diego's asked me to meet him, not said why. My kids are safe with Elaine. Shawn will call Zeb if I don't return. He may not remember me, but I don't have anyone else. I don't know anyone else I can turn to. I have failed all my life. I should see this one through.'

They turned the pages, but there wasn't anything else, but Bear stopped them and flipped back the last few pages.

It was there at the bottom of the page, in very small writing.

'Tried to be a good father. Failed. Forgive me Lisa, Shawn.'

Chloe remained bowed for a long time as Rocka fingered the notebook, opening it, riffling the pages, as if it had more on Shattner. Bear looked around and outside, at the pool glistening in the silence, the distant sounds of the city creeping in on them, and back at the notebook.

Elaine Rocka cleared her throat. 'Now what?'

Chloe lifted her head then and looked at her, at the others, and that thing in them stirred and then leapt out and roared silently.

Chapter 33

'Kirkus died a couple of months back. Bad heart. Died at his desk. Good cop.'

Deputy Commissioner Rolando looked down the long conference table at them. They were in an anonymous civic building, Rolando flanked by Pizaka and Chang, facing the five of them. Isakson was on the cops' side of the table. He was present when the five of them arrived and said, 'I was in the city on JTF business when Bruce updated me.

'We had long wanted an inside man in the gang, and when we arrested Shattner, he fit the bill perfectly. A cover story wasn't needed because he had it all. Criminal record, ex-army, willing to do anything – he didn't bear a grudge against the army, but he put on a good act. We put him through several psych evaluations, and all came out good. High motivation levels, good liar.'

Rolando smiled briefly. 'Could handle stress and pressure, such stuff. It didn't take us long to convince him.' Rolando looked at them individually. Broker and he went back a long way, but this was the first time he was meeting all of them. He saw a compact, well-oiled machine.

'Did you intend to grant him amnesty?' Chloe asked pointedly and stared back at Pizaka challengingly as his shades trained on her.

Rolando cleared his throat after a brief silence. 'Ma'am...'

'Chloe.'

'Chloe, the way these things happen, we don't grant amnesty outright to anyone under such circumstances. We see the quality of the juice they give us, and only then grant it. Shattner's juice was A-grade, and we would have upheld our end of the arrangement.'

'How does this work? I presume Kirkus ran him, but who else got his juice?' Bear asked him.

'Running a man deep inside is not like in the movies. There are no dead drops, no call signs, passwords... nothing of the sort. Some of that happens if we have a *cop* inside, but with a civilian, especially one who has a record, the protocol is decided by the detective and the insider.'

Bear raised his eyebrows in astonishment. 'So Shattner just called when the mood struck him? Called him on Kirkus's line?'

Rolando smiled thinly. 'They *had* a secure protocol they followed. Calls at specific intervals, an untraceable number, safe words, danger words... but when a man is inside, his ability to communicate depends a lot on his circumstances.'

Broker eyed the journal that was now in front of the Deputy Commissioner. Bwana and Roger had been against informing the cops about the journal, but Broker had convinced them finally. 'After all, we are helping Isakson, and they just might know something about his whereabouts.

'Who had access to his intel?'

Chang stirred and fielded that question. 'A secure network is established for those who need to know and it goes to all those. In this case, Kirkus's reports went only to the boss.' He nodded in Rolando's direction.

Isakson shook his head when the other side of the table looked at him. 'First time I'm hearing of Shattner. Bruce kept the JTF informed, but didn't tell us the source.' The rebuke in his voice was loud.

'I'm sure the FBI doesn't tell us everything it knows, Deputy Director,' Rolando retorted. Isakson acknowledged this silently. Rolando and he got on well and the two of them had reduced the inevitable turf wars to a minimum.

Bwana brought the discussion back to Shattner. 'So no one knows what happened to Shattner? Kirkus tell you anything? Surely some *what-if* scenarios were discussed with him.'

'Kirkus told me he just dropped off the grid after the last bust. Didn't respond to coded text messages, no calls, nothing. We had plans in place to extricate him and his kids if he was in danger, but that panic button never got pressed.'

'He's probably dead, isn't he?' Bear and Chloe spoke at the same time.

'Yes. That's a real possibility.'

'Which means the gang knew he was a snitch... I wonder how they knew that?' Roger mused.

Rolando glanced at Chang and Pizaka. 'We've started looking into that. It won't be quick and neither will it be clean.

'Did he tell you anything else? How the gang was organized, their bases, how they communicated... all that stuff? My informants give me that kind of juice.' Broker addressed his question to the cops.

Rolando shook his head. 'We would have got to that, but all of us were under pressure to show results... and the focus was just on deals that we could bust.'

Pizaka spoke for the first time. 'Of course the gang could have offed him just because they suspected he was a snitch. They don't exactly follow due process.'

'Kirkus, what about him?'

'We'll start there obviously,' Rolando said with distaste. A dirty cop who fed the gang was his worst nightmare come true, and he hoped Kirkus wasn't that.

'Waste of time,' grumbled Bwana when they'd left the meeting.

Broker shrugged. 'We did what we had to and learnt that there was nothing to learn.'

He smiled suddenly. 'Think Rog and you can go ask this Cruz and Diego?'

Cruz and Diego were no longer at the laundry.

Bwana and Roger had been watching it for three days, and they saw a lot of bruisers, but not the two they were seeking. The laundry had a regular clientele, most of them office workers, but for its location, it could have been busier.

Bwana yawned and worked the kinks out of his shoulders. 'Those bruisers hanging about... if I was Office Man John Doe, I would stop coming to the laundry. Lots of other places in the city for laundry.'

Roger didn't reply, just nodded, and they lapsed back to silence. On the fourth day, they were joined by Broker. 'Making sure you aren't sleeping on the job,' was his comment, and he got flipped the bird by Bwana.

The laundry was in a long chain of stores, convenience stores, take-aways, exotic foods, salons, all of them busy but for the laundry. A week went by, and as the smell of a Chinese take-away filled the car, Roger broached it. 'Doubt those guys are here. We've been watching 24/7, and we've seen all the gangbangers in the world but them!'

'Mmm.' Broker was thinking furiously. Soon after their meeting the cops, Cruz and Diego stopped using the laundry as their base. It was entirely possible that they had stopped using it long before, but Broker hated coincidences.

He looked at the Cyrillic lettering on a grocery store, its red-lighted signage casting a glow in the night sky. 'Let's do this another way,' he said.

It took a couple of days to set up, two days when Chloe and Bear, itching for action, suggested hitting another 5Clubs business. Broker considered it; on the one hand, it would maintain the pressure on the gang who would be hurting now; on the other, a lull could relax their vigilance. 'Let's go with this first and see what comes of it.'

They met at a midtown hotel, its glass-fronted façade giving an air of respectability to the person they were meeting. That person had bought out all the rooms on the seventeenth floor and had his people stationed in the lobby, fire escapes and the service entrances. His people wore loose-fitting suits, looking like poorly dressed brawlers and bouncers, the bulges under their suits plain to see, but then they didn't care if they blended in or not. Each floor had four elevators, but that day only one stopped on the seventeenth.

The four of them, Chloe staying back with Rocka and the kids, stepped out of the elevator and were accosted by six brawlers, three behind them, three in front. There were two more men at either end of the corridor, Uzis slung casually across their shoulders. Bwana and Bear were big, but each one of these men had at least a couple of inches and ten pounds on them. The bruisers in the front of them silently frisked them and led them down the corridor to a suite at the far end.

One of the Uzi-wearing gunmen knocked on the suite and, after precisely six minutes, swung it open and ushered them in.

The suite had a huge living room with floor-to-ceiling glass windows through which they could make out the spire of the Empire State Building. They didn't have much time to dwell on the view because two more large men appeared and frisked them again silently and took away their phones.

Broker made himself comfortable on a sofa while the others ranged around the room, Bwana positioning himself next to one of the brawlers.

An Oriental girl came from an inner room carrying pots of tea, and went about making tea for them without asking their preference. *He didn't get to where he was by asking people politely*, thought Broker.

287

Vasily Oborski made them wait for another half hour before making his entry. Dressed in a tan suit, his middle-aged but very fit form, thick brown hair and a lightly wrinkled face could have easily graced a men's fashion magazine. The head of the Russian mob in the city seated himself opposite Broker and helped himself to a scone as the girl rushed to pour tea for him.

He regarded Broker over the rim of his cup, the wreaths of steam giving his face an otherworldly look. 'Long time, Broker,' he greeted him mildly.

Oborski had never been known to raise his voice.

His father had been sent to a Siberian prison for crimes against the state, leaving six-year-old Vasily to fend for a sick mother and four-year-old sister, in the bitter cold of Kodinsk.

Five years on, the mother had passed away, and the sister had died in a brutal attack by a rapist. Vasily, mature and tough beyond his years, had spent three months hunting the rapist down and one cold morning had left his insides steaming in the snow. Vasily fled Kodinsk when the rapist's friends turned the heat on him and, after a tortuous journey by cart, farm tractor and truck, reached Moscow.

The journey expanded Vasily's mind, and while Moscow was three thousand miles from Kodinsk, it was nowhere far enough for him. He roamed the city for a week and finally stowed away in a freight vessel to New York. The city got a new immigrant that year, a battle-hardened criminal, young in years and hardened by the Russian cold. Ten years later he was a gang leader and, thirty years later, was heading the city's Russian mafia.

Over the years, Oborski had eschewed the crudity of his peers and adopted a refined patina that smoothed his way to the top. The hand was no less iron just because it was in velvet; in fact, it had more of an impact when it was revealed.

Broker had found him heavily bleeding, lying in a restroom cubicle in Penn Station late one night when Oborski was still a gang leader. Shrugging off his jacket, Broker had stripped down to the waist and, tearing his Egyptian cotton shirt to narrow strips, had tightly bound Oborski's stomach. Knife wounds, he had dimly noted before rushing off to find help. When he had returned, the cubicle was empty save for bloodied footprints that led outside and disappeared in the walkway. It was months before he realized who he had saved.

The Russian mob had its hand in all criminal activities, including arms dealing, but Oborski steered it clear of one: nuclear arms trading. Russian enriched uranium, technical expertise, and nuclear weapons found their way to the underground market, and were highly sought after by rogue states and terrorist organizations. Oborski wasn't a patriot, he was a businessman, and he realized early on that such arms trading came with too much unwanted attention and had issued a diktat against such trading.

His rule had been broken once, unknown to him.

A few years back, the FBI had intercepted chatter that the Russian Mob had acquired enriched uranium and was in active discussions with a rogue state the US State Department had blacklisted. Clare had sat in the President's daily briefing and come away with the terse message, 'Find it. Finish them,' and had asked Broker to verify the chatter.

Broker had gone with his gut instinct and had orchestrated a highly unusual and clandestine meeting between Clare, the Director of the FBI, the Director of National Intelligence, and Oborski. He still guffawed loudly when he recalled that day, the most powerful law enforcers in the world and one of the most dangerous criminals in the same room.

Oborski, a master at talking obtusely, had asked for twenty-four hours. It didn't take him that long. Early in the dawn, Broker went to a warehouse where he found a gangbanger bound and gagged and naked. Broker delivered him to Clare, and he was never seen or heard again. Neither was the uranium.

Broker reined in his wandering mind and said simply, 'I need your help.'

Oborski raised his eyebrows, urging Broker to continue.

'5Clubs have taken a significant market share from you, haven't they?'

Oborski placed his cup back in its saucer carefully, aligning the handle to an angle he was satisfied with, and leaned back. 'Let's say we were doing better before they arrived on the scene. But tell me about your problem. You are generally solving other people's problems.'

'I need to know where Jose Cruz and Diego are.'

Broker saw the flicker in his eyes. *He knows them. You wouldn't head this outfit if you didn't know who your competition was.*

'Why?'

Broker grinned widely. 'Come on, Vasily. We both know how this game is played. Surely you don't expect me to answer that.'

'What's in it for me?' Oborski asked, ignoring Broker's disarming grin.

Broker shook his head reprovingly. 'You're a businessman, Vasily. What harm does it do you to tell me about your rivals?'

'Tomorrow, you might ask other gangs about me.'

Broker shrugged. 'If I have to, I will. If I have to go against you, I will.' The grin flashed again. 'I know you'll be a worthy foe.'

Oborski looked at him long and coolly. 'You sit in my presence, surrounded by my men, and say that. You've some balls, Broker. I'll grant that.' He looked over Broker's shoulder at Bwana, Roger, and Bear, an assessing glance. 'Those... mishaps 5Clubs are experiencing? That's your doing?'

'I just trade information, Vasily, as you know. You give me too much credit.'

Oborski smiled thinly. 'Maybe they gave you too little.' He continued regarding him for a long time and then looked at one of the bruisers behind them. The man went across and whispered something in Oborski's ear, staying bent, awaiting instructions till Oborski nodded once in dismissal.

'There's a warehouse in the Meatpacking District. We've been watching it for some time, and my men tell me the two you mention have been seen there recently. Seen there a lot. Of course, there's no saying that they'll continue to frequent that place.' He gave them an address, and his face took on the appearance of a lean, hungry wolf. 'You'll do damage to them?'

Broker threw up his hands in exasperation. 'Vasily. Read my lips. I deal in research.'

Vasily brushed his comment away and stood up, the meeting was over.

'Broker.'

Broker turned as he was just leaving. Vasily was looking at him, something deep and unfathomable in his eyes. 'You'd make a worthy foe too.'

Chapter 34

'You have interesting friends, Broker.' Bear broke the silence on the way down in the elevator. 'This Oborski... think even we would find it tough to go against him. Yet 5Clubs have encroached their business. Doesn't figure.'

'Oborski has rules; this new gang doesn't. That's the difference. Eventually their lack of rules will also be their downfall; surviving in a jungle needs rules.'

Broker smiled inwardly while they digested Roger's take. They were a unique bunch, not just exceptional operatives, but they also brought very high intelligence and reasoning skills to the mix. Roger read philosophy in his spare time while Chloe was a science nut and Bwana and Bear were Mensa members, a fact they guarded more zealously than their weapons.

Bwana looked admiringly at Roger. 'Always knew it. You're the complete package, bro. Brawn, beauty *and* brains.' He ducked the punch Roger threw at him.

The Meatpacking District was a twenty-square block in Manhattan, with Chelsea Market on the North and Horatio Street in the south. In the early twentieth century, the neighborhood had close to two hundred and fifty slaughterhouses and packing plants, which delivered a third of the country's dressed meat. With the improvement in transportation and distribution, the building of the interstate system, and the decline of shipping in the Hudson, several of the meat-associated businesses moved out to the Bronx or New Jersey, and the neighborhood declined. Neighborhoods don't die in New York, they transform, and replacing the meat businesses came nightclubs, restaurants, high-end boutiques, and the district got its makeover to become one of the trendiest hoods in the city.

There were still a few meat businesses remaining in the hood, and it was one of those warehouses that Bear and Chloe watched that night. Chloe had glared at Bwana and Broker when they picked up the key to another Chevy and had snatched it from them. 'Why do *you* get to do all the fun stuff?'

Bear smiled as they surrendered meekly without protest. A Chloe glare could melt tungsten.

The Chevy they were in was wearing the signage of a grocer two streets away. Tony had rustled the vehicle and the signage in quick time, and the grocer was the richer for it. They had to be on the move constantly, and switching vehicles was a must if they were to stay ahead of the gang.

Through windows lowered an inch, they could smell fresh meat as cartons of it were moved from warehouse to delivery vehicles. The watch was three hours old, and it was just past supper, no sign of Cruz, the chapter head. They had seen the odd bruiser, recognizing them from the laundry, so they knew they were in the right place, but all they saw was a lot of foot soldiers, no chief.

'The night's still young,' Chloe commented; Bear just grunted, his reclining form not moving. Chloe looked at the occasional vehicle that passed by, some of them having kids in them, the solitary couple walking hand in hand. 'You think we'd ever be like that?'

Bear opened one eye fully and regarded her quizzically. 'You would have gone bat-shit in two days... probably shot me.'

She thought about it, but knew the answer already. She wasn't made out for the white picket fence and two and a half kids. She wouldn't have joined the army if she was.

'What do you think it means?'

Bear sighed and straightened his long frame and brought his seat forward. He knew what she was referring to.

There was one last page in the journal that Broker hadn't told the cops about.

He'd torn out that page, made copies of it for all of them, and only then had handed the book to Rolando.

That page had Shattner's last entry, the day he left the kids with Elaine Rocka.

Forgot to tell Kirkus their messaging system, and now it may be too late. Our next call is not due for a few days. The system is simple. We all call a number and leave a voice mail on it and then text the other guys a password. The password can be anything, numbers or letters, or a combination, but has to have the number nine in it somewhere. Where the nine appears doesn't matter, it just has to be there. Asked Diego about it once, and he looked evilly at me, and I thought we were going to do the gun-forehead routine again. I don't know why the nine and why not any other number, but the nine in the password means that it's an authentic gang message.

Broker had thrown Werner at it but wasn't hopeful. You can't crack a code on just one facet, you need some more. 'At least this way, the gang won't know that we know... and just maybe will still have the same system. All that we need is to pick up a few brawlers important enough, knock their heads, and we'll know what it means, and then we go listening to their messages... that messaging number's the same one we found on that phone Roger picked up in Arizona.'

'Dunno.' Bear shrugged. 'Broker has that thing of his chomping away at it, so we might find something.'

'That brain of yours hasn't a clue?' Chloe teased him.

Bear scratched his beard, embarrassed. Most people looked at him and went, all that meat must mean the brain's small, and he was more than happy for them to think that. During his Special Ops days, he had learnt it was better to be underestimated than overestimated.

'I did give it some thought. Bwana too, but we didn't get anywhere. Thing is, a random number is impossible to break unless you have the context to it or clues to *that*.'

A Cherokee with blackened windows swept inside the open entrance of the warehouse and unloaded four men, not warehouse workers, unless warehouse workers had suspicious-looking bulges underneath their tops.

'Lots of them now,' Bear murmured, glancing at the clock in the dash, eleven p.m. 'I reckon about fifteen.'

At two a.m., three Patriots, all identical, with black, darkened windows and dimmed headlights, passed once down the street, Bear and Chloe squeezing themselves down below the window line. They saw the dimmed lights returning in the distance and, pushing their seats back, lay prone and pulled dark linen blankets over themselves. Just in time, as the lead vehicle turned on two spotlights on its roof, playing on both sides of the street, and moved slowly, looking for vehicles with occupants. They passed the Chevy without any break in speed, and at the end of the block they could hear the three engines fade out and then increase as they U-turned and returned. One more pass down the block, the searchlights probing and finding silent rows of unoccupied vehicles, and then the lights turned off, and the Patriots wheeled inside the warehouse.

The warehouse doused all its exterior lights, and in the darkness they could hear the soft thuds of doors opening and closing. They raised themselves up cautiously and, through night vision, saw the first set of wheels had spilled out four armed men, the last, another four. When the eight were all out, the vehicle in the center spewed its passengers – the driver, who held the door open for Diego, who was followed by a hatchet-faced man. Jose Cruz.

Seven men formed a circle around Cruz and Diego, and at a hand wave from Diego, the warehouse emptied, the men from the Cherokee herding workers to a bus outside. Some gunmen accompanied the workers, and when the last had boarded, it shuddered to life and nosed down the street, the rest of the gunmen following it in their ride.

Eleven left, must be the inner circle. Bear observed the circle, the way they stood and moved. *Forces, for sure, but slack and out of training. Wouldn't last an hour in the Farm.* The Farm was the Agency's secretive training ground, where they honed their skills, and kept up with the newest weapons, technology and tradecraft.

The circle shaped itself and moved inside the warehouse, two men staying out to roll shut the large sliding doors. The doors, well oiled, rumbled as quietly as doors their size could, shutting the gang leader and his number two from the outside world. A light turned on inside the building, silhouetting the two outside, one of them leaning against a SUV and puffing deeply on his smoke, the other circling aimlessly.

After an hour, one door rolled open a crack, and a voice asked something sharply and got an indistinct reply. Satisfied, the voice disappeared, and the door slid back. *Checking they aren't sleeping*, Chloe mouthed at Bear.

Bear reached back for his backpack and slid something in his pocket, moving carefully so that his heavy frame didn't rock their wheels. He shook his head, *Nothing*, when Chloe looked questioningly at him.

After another half an hour, he started timing every ten-minute block in his mind, and at the third block, he eased open his door and slid out, ignoring Chloe's whispered shout.

Using the wheel well and the rear mirror as cover, he peered out, waiting, counting down the ten minutes.

In the last third minute, the smoker flicked his second smoke to the ground, said something over his shoulder and disappeared around the corner of the structure. The second man laughed, and he walked to the other corner, but kept walking straight ahead till he reached the wall.

A cool night, nothing to occupy the mind except the bladder. Unzip, relieve, zip, and wipe hands, sigh, and job done. Fifteen seconds to turn around.

Bear raced across the street, through the entrance, his thin rubber-soled shoes whispering no louder than the wind, reached the first Patriot, leaned down, straightened, one single move,

298

moved to the next, and then the third, and raced back. The first guard had rounded the corner when he reached the shelter of the Chevy, and the second had joined him when he climbed inside.

He shushed a furious Chloe, who had unlimbered her gun, ready to provide covering fire if he had needed it. Each of them had tracking devices in their backpacks, fitted with a specially designed magnet. A sliding switch turned them on, and they latched on to the undercarriage of the vehicle till the end of eternity, or till they were detected and turned off.

An hour later, one of the men came out on the street and stood there looking up and down, the night light gleaming dully off an automatic rifle across his chest. He removed a flashlight from his pocket and started checking cars randomly on both sides of the street. The Chevy was the tenth set of wheels he inspected, his light reflecting off the window, revealing a pockmarked face and thin moustache. He walked on, checking cars behind it, doubling back to inspect a few ahead of it, and when he was satisfied, he rapped on the sliding door.

Cruz, in the center of the phalanx, barked orders all the way to his ride, receiving nods in return, and his gang boss duties done, climbed inside, and disappeared in engine growls and exhaust.

Silence crept down, and in the darkness, a shadow detached from behind the driver's wheel well and stood and stretched. Bear wiped his hands against his fatigues and waited for Chloe to join him. She had taken cover behind a vehicle behind him.

They walked a block in the shadows – the Chevy left behind to be part of the furniture on the street – turned a corner, walked three streets, and a Ford's door swung open.

Bwana thrust hot coffee in their palms and smiled in the darkness, his teeth lighting up the gloom. 'How many you shot?'

It was dawn when they returned to their base, Broker up and waiting for them, and when they all turned to go in, Elaine Rocka stood pointing a Colt 45 at them.

'Whoa,' Broker exclaimed, raising his hands in the air. 'We're on your side, ma'am.'

She lowered the gun. 'I heard voices and came down to investigate.' A flicker of amusement swept across her face as she read their expressions. 'I grew up on a farm in Texas. I was hunting foxes with an air-gun when I was seven and went hunting with my dad when I was ten. I can handle guns.' She turned and left and threw another over her shoulder, 'And I can make them count.'

Broker looked pointedly at Bwana. 'Maybe we should induct her in our team. Bet she'd shoot better than this lug.' A flicker of movement caught his eye, and he turned to see Tony leaning against the door Rocka had just vacated. 'Some guard you are. She came down to see what was up. Bet you were resting your ass... and your head.'

Tony grinned good-naturedly. 'Boss, I had her in my sights, was behind her. But I loved that look on your face when she pointed that cannon at you. Priceless.' He stuck his gun in his waist and jammed his fingers in his ears to ignore Broker's swearing.

'If I've made your day, why don't you rustle up coffee for us, and we can listen to what these guys have been up to?' Broker growled.

He listened silently as Chloe outlined the night, interrupting her just once to fetch his laptop and check that the trackers were active. Leaning back when she had finished, he sipped his coffee appreciatively. 'He would make some woman happy. Best danged cook I ever met.' He smiled at Tony's snort from the kitchen.

'Let's observe them for a night or two more. We don't want to be tracking the wrong car and go to Alaska.' A plan was taking shape in his mind, two plans actually, but they had to verify that Cruz stuck to his routine and used the same vehicles.

Bwana and Roger were on surveillance the next night, the six-foot-four black man almost dwarfing his companion, who wasn't short himself, an inch over six feet. They carjacked the vehicle in front of the Chevy, Roger occupying it while Bwana made himself comfortable in the Chevy. Roger whispered, 'You comfortable, bro?'

'Compared to some places we've been, this is the Ritz,' Bwana drily replied through his mic.

The black Cherokee swept in, right on time at eleven at night, and the men Bear and Chloe had mentioned unloaded. The activity level of the packers and loaders increased, and three hours later, on time again, the three SUVs repeated their passes of the street and finally went in.

Cruz and Diego stuck to their routine of the previous night, and when they'd left, Roger and Bwana unlimbered themselves, stretched to loosen the kinks, and walked back to the same block, where Bear and Chloe were waiting for them.

Broker was on his laptop when they returned, notes filled with his scribbling spread out in front of him.

'What?' Chloe asked him when she saw his expression.

'I got something.' There was the slightest trace of hope in his voice. 'Werner's narrowed down the thirty to three.' He qualified his comment. 'Werner returned twenty names in the first pass, and I refined the search and anomaly pattern, and it returned three.'

'This is based on that number nine?' Bear raised his eyebrows.

'Yup.'

'Hell, Broker, the nine could mean anything. I'm sure the number nine figures in *everyone's* lives in the world!'

Broker nodded sagely. 'Why I further refined the search and made Werner home in on the number that had more than a mundane existence in their lives!'

'So who are they?' Chloe asked impatiently.

Broker turned one of the sheets around for them to read.

Becky Pisano, Rick Stonehaus, and Floyd Wheat were underlined twice on the list. 'Pisano's youngest daughter was born on the ninth, Stonehaus's dog died on the ninth, and Wheat, his hobby is base jumping, had his first jump on the ninth.'

'Well, now,' Bwana said in satisfaction, 'shall we pick them up?'

Chloe rolled her eyes. 'We're still going after Cruz while you do whatever you have to do to dig into those names further?'

'Yes, ma'am. Nothing's changed, other than having the glimmer of a string for us to pull at and see what unravels.'

'Good.' She turned to Bwana and Roger. 'We take them down tomorrow.'

Bwana grimaced. 'Us four against them eleven? Not fair is it.'

'You have a better idea?'

'Rog and I could go. Just the two of us.'

Chapter 36

The takedown would happen outside the city, late at night, on an open road that would be clear of traffic at the time they were planning it.

Broker had arranged for two contractors they knew to stay round the clock with the family. Pieter Traut and Derek Coetzer nodded at all of them when they entered the home. The two South Africans slapped hands with Broker, Bwana, and Roger, who they'd met on previous assignments.

Broker had given them a tour of the house, introduced them to Tony and Eric, and had gone through schedules and details with Elaine Rocka, their professionalism and experience both apparent and comforting.

Chloe would be riding her bike the night of their attack, following the three-SUV party, to confirm that Cruz was in the motorcade and keep the rest of them updated.

She would also take out the last vehicle in their motorcade.

'In New Jersey, on US 130, I know where,' Broker decided as he brought up a map of the route Cruz had taken the previous nights.

'Why so far? Why not take them down in the warehouse?' Roger asked him as he calculated the distances, working out the logistics rapidly.

'We've hit them thrice now at their places of business. I don't want us to be predictable. Besides, gunshots in the city are bound to attract attention. If we take him in the warehouse, I expect a prolonged firefight, quite different from our rapid entry and exits earlier. On top of that, I want to know what's in NJ, and the closer to their destination we hit them, the quicker we'll find out what and why.'

The rest of them would be in two vehicles and would deal with the remaining Patriots. Tony and Eric had their roles to play too.

'Chloe will be alone, without backup. You okay with this?' Bwana shifted uneasily, looking at her.

'Yup. That part was *my* plan if you recollect.'

'Tony will be following at a distance,' Broker said mildly, deflating Bwana's tension. Bear looked bemusedly at him and shook his head. 'All that badass routine… you're just a softy underneath, aren't you?'

Bwana gave him a look that chilled hardcore gangbangers, but it just raised a laugh from Bear.

'What about traffic? We can't be sure we'll be the only ones on that stretch.' Roger was frowning still.

Broker's lips twitched. 'We *can*. Eric will be driving a Freightliner with a container, an empty container, and it will develop some problems, if needed, and block the highway. I've made some calls, and we will not get attention so long as we can clear up the highway in half an hour. That should be enough for us. Tony will be backing up from the rear, a distance away.'

They took two custom-fitted Escalades from Broker's garage: bulletproof glass, double armor- plated, run-flat tires, navigation system, impact proof, the works.

'I have a few.' Broker patted the roof when Bwana looked quizzically at him. They were colored a dull gray so that no shine reflected off them, and ran low on the wheels because of their weight, but the four hundred horses under the hood gave them enough muscle and torque to leave most other wheels behind.

Chloe's ride was a favorite of hers, a Yamaha YZF-R6, fast, steady, jet black, and when she wore matching leathers, with her chest-strapped Glock, Bwana gave her a wide berth.

He shook his head admiringly. 'That sight alone is enough to reform me. I pity those hitters.' They loaded their weapons, Bear throwing Mossberg shotguns in the back of his Escalade, Bwana packing his long gun carefully, and when they were done, Broker placed hampers of rations in both the vehicles.

He shut the door and looked at them. 'Let's do it.'

Chloe went to their Chevy, a familiar friend by now, inserted herself in it, and checked her comms. 'In position,' she whispered.

'Roger,' came Broker, who had headed to US 130 a couple of hours earlier with Bwana as his wingman, the two of them catching a snooze, waiting for everyone to catch up and the action to begin.

'Yup,' Bear and Roger acknowledged, in their ride a block away.

The hoods repeated the same routine, the Cherokee coming, hitters spilling out, increasing the pace of activity in the warehouse, the three Patriots rolling in at two a.m., signaling the exodus of the workers, and then Cruz and his motorcade left at just after three a.m.

Cruz was in the middle set of wheels.

Chloe waited for them to clear the block and then unlimbered herself and jogged to the end of her street, rounding it, and reached into a dark alley for her bike. The roar, when it came, was muffled, the custom silencers doing their job. She tapped keys on her dashboard, and the navigation and tracker system sprang to life. She scanned the console swiftly, noting the three red dots, and eased out on her bike. 'Bogeys identified and all rolling.' She spoke normally, the days of shouting over the wind had long gone with the technology Broker had access to.

In his Escalade, Broker queried Tony and Eric, 'You guys with us?' and nodded silently when the affirmative replies came back. They would fall behind Chloe once they left the city behind.

Chloe zipped past dimly lit streets, the rare cab or police cruiser crossing her way. This was a different New York, silent and brooding before daylight came and restored it to its cheer and energy.

Keeping the last Patriot's taillights in sight in the distance, her own lights doused, she followed them through Holland Tunnel, entering the Garden State, down Hoboken Avenue, then Newark Avenue.

'I think they're taking the US 130,' she said in the wind.

'Gotcha. That's the route they took the last couple of nights. So far they're sticking to habit, which's bad for them, good for us.' Broker's baritone came back muffled, trying to clear sticky gum in his mouth.

They hit the highway at North Brunswick, and the hoods maintained a steady pace, ignoring the call of the empty expanse of tarmac ahead of them.

The gang's motorcade took a three-hour break at a rest stop, presumably to catch up on sleep, and when they resumed their ride, Chloe followed.

The sun was painting the sky gold as suburban America fled past, places where dreams and hopes took shape, bearing names such as Cranbury Township and Windsor. Chloe started to wonder if she'd been going too fast for those behind when Broker's baritone broke in her ear. 'Alrighty, we're behind you now, rather, we are behind Eric; you should see him soon. Bear is following us.'

She glanced at her mirror, and in the distance she could see Eric's Freightliner take shape, growing larger as he ate the miles between them, the gleaming chrome grill catching the dim light. She breathed deeply, patted her gun once, and smiled when she remembered the conversation Bear and she had had. This was her life, their life... not the picket fences and children's toys in some of the homes she rode past.

The lights ahead flared suddenly. 'Uh-oh,' she commented.

'What?' came Bear's voice urgently.

'They're slowing, hang on... no, they're speeding again, now turning, the exit to US 206. I'm following them. Eric, did you get that?'

'Yo, ma'am, will follow your tail.'

Broker glanced at Bwana. 'They could have made her... or maybe that's where they were planning to go in any case.'

Bwana shrugged; he was scrolling through the navigation system. 'Works just as well. There's a lot of empty road and open country there.'

Broker swung the wheel and followed Eric's truck, Roger and Bear's ride behind them, and far behind, Tony's van fell into position.

They drew on, the road narrowing to two lanes, the surroundings becoming thicker, densely wooded, darker, the terrain preparing itself for action.

Broker looked far ahead and behind in the mirrors. 'Go.'

They accelerated, closing the gap to two vehicle lengths, and Eric stomped the gas, his truck filling Chloe's mirror, escaping it as it came alongside and drew ahead, powered behind the gang's Cherokee, and started overtaking it.

She revved, sticking close to its body not more than two feet away from its rear and using it as cover, the Freightliner's front wheels throwing fine gravel over her, pinging her helmet.

She feathered out from behind when the truck drew abreast of the last gang vehicle, eased between the sets of wheels on either side of her, the Yamaha rock steady amidst the buffeting from both sides. Through the darkened glass of the rear window, she could make out a hitter on the phone turning back to look at her, his mouth a dark oval, and his silent shout as the Glock slid whisper smooth into her hand and she shot the right, rear tire.

Their Patriot wobbled, straightened, lost speed, and she flashed past, the sight of windows cracking open and hitters shouting fading behind her. She cut across in front of Eric, who swerved into their lane, absorbing the automatic rifle fire that spat from the gang, and she was free ahead.

The pothole came up in the edge of her vision as she was scanning her mirror; her fingers instinctively reacted, guiding the bike around it, and the handle twisted violently in her grip, and she was flying, falling, landing in the woods, rolling over and over again, her helmet cracking, until she came to rest against the bole of a tree, and woods closed in on her.

Their takedown was planned for the wider highway. On a narrower road, the margins lessened, and loose gravel around a pothole was what Broker eloquently called, 'Shit happening when it doesn't need to.'

She lay in her position, allowing her brain to scan her body, sending impulses to neurons, receiving acknowledgement, and decided she was fine – bruised, dazed, but in one piece – the thick leather she wore cushioning her fall. She removed her helmet and saw she was about twenty feet away from the edge of the highway, where the line of woods started. She could see the hoods parked in the distance behind her, her bike sprawled sideways at the edge of the highway. Eric's taillights brightened as he slowed down ahead, and in the far distance she could see the two Escalades. She checked her watch, less than ten seconds since her crash.

Breathing deeply, once, twice, clearing her mind, she pressed the earbud back in and heard the urgent voices calling out for her.

'I'm fine, guys. The bike slipped around a pothole, but I'm fine. Eric, you carry on. Broker, could Tony get me?'

'I will, ma'am. I'm a mile behind you.'

Bear twisted back in his seat and took the scene in in a glance. 'Chloe, are you sure you're okay?'

'Yes,' she said impatiently. 'You guys stick to the plan. Tony and I will catch up with you.'

Bear relaxed at her impatient tone and mouthed at Roger, 'She *is* fine.'

'The lady's spoken. Let's haul ass,' Broker announced, and they floored their rides.

Cruz's motorcade was visible in the distance; it had slowed down when the last vehicle had called them, and then had picked up speed, hustling down the narrow road.

One hitter stuck his head out of an open window of the lead vehicle, shouted, his words lost in the wind, poked his head out again, and fired an automatic rifle, the bullet singing harmlessly in the air.

The lead vehicle abruptly left the highway, crashing through the undergrowth in a thinner section of the woods with waist-high grass and shrubs, the tree line about a mile away. They could see heads turning and watching them through the darkened windows of Cruz's vehicle as the two vehicles flattened undergrowth, heavy going on the soft, uneven ground. The shrub was a flat, green, dense expanse, stretching wide and deep to the tree line, with an occasional tree spearing up.

'Woods,' Bwana yelled, and Broker nodded. If they reached the tree line and vanished into the dense foliage, their hunt would be harder.

He swung hard, catching them, ramming Cruz's ride in the rear, whipping it from side to side before its driver controlled it, but not before it surged forward and grazed the lead vehicle.

The two vehicles sped up, now having the advantage over the heavier pursuers. Broker's Escalades were great for tarmac; here, they were weighed down by the armor plating and moved slower and sluggishly.

The lead vehicle angled, and two hoods opened fire from the rear windows, their bullets singing in the sky harmlessly, some spattering against their roofs. They ducked back inside when Bwana cracked his window open and loosed a long spray at them, the going too uneven for accurate shooting.

'Come on,' Broker growled, coaxing more torque, the RPM already in the red. 'Rog, can you go faster?' he shouted.

'Nope, on this soil, this is a frigging tank.'

Two hundred yards between the pairs of wheels when luck swung their way.

The lead vehicle came to a sudden stop, its follower nearly crashing into it from behind. Bwana risked a quick poke out of the window. 'Tree fallen across, long and wide.'

He paused for a beat. 'Lead vehicle will pour covering fire for the rear, and they'll make a run for it.'

'Roger, Bear?' he called out.

'Yo. We know what to do.'

On cue, the first automatic opened up from the lead, followed by three others, making time for the second vehicle to turn sideways, driver side to them.

Broker opened his mouth to shout, but Bwana had leapt out, making for the brush, rolling down beneath the stream of fire, most of it going high above them. Broker turned off the ignition and, flinging his door open, dived under its cover, into the shrub.

The automatics turned off one by one as the hitters ran behind Cruz, Diego, and their driver, their heads bobbing above the waist-height shrub.

Thirteen hundred yards to the tree line.

And then the firing opened again, steady, bouncing off the now empty Escalades, seeking them in the thick grass.

Bwana looked at Broker, beneath their ride, and didn't need to speak when he saw it in the other's eyes. *Some, maybe all five of them behind the log, providing covering fire while Cruz ran for safety.*

He felt a hand on his shoulder, Roger, and nodded at what he saw in his eyes.

Roger drifted off in the undergrowth, making as much noise as a big cat, Bear shadowing him on Broker's side. The two split wide, heading to the log from behind which the hitters were firing sporadically. They had unleashed a barrage at the green foliage and then realized they were more likely to run out of ammo than hitting anyone and had settled down to firing occasional bursts.

Bwana took a breath and leapt up once, taking in the scene at a glance. Cruz, Diego, and their driver were running to the sanctuary of the forest, trotting since Diego and the driver weren't in the best shape, and had covered about a hundred yards.

Bwana ducked back and crawled ten feet away swiftly, just in time, avoiding a hail of bullets. 'I'm good. Rog, Bear, take those guys out,' he said softly before anyone asked him.

They would flank the tree from either side, about a hundred feet away, and would either take the hoods out from whatever cover they could find, or disarm them. Bear patted his pockets, he'd enough magazines with him for his handgun, but would have preferred the M41 back in their ride. He visualized the fallen tree, mentally marked where he would come at it, and the foliage opened to welcome him. The hitters had Uzis and AK-47s from the sound of them, and they had Glocks. He shrugged mentally. Felt even to him.

Bwana crawled back towards the vehicle and rolled under it, joining Broker. Broker was fiddling with something he had drawn from his fatigues, and when Bwana looked at it closely, he saw a thin cable camera that had a phone attachment at one end.

Broker twisted the long cable, and it became a firm five-foot stalk. Plugging in the phone end, he raised it above the grass, slowly, so that it didn't stick far above the shrub.

The picture came blurry initially and then cleared, like a live video feed. The guns had gone quiet, and in the distance they could see the three who had fled had stopped and were gesticulating at one another. One of them, the driver, came running back and said something to those behind the tree, and head shakes and furious hand gestures followed.

After another round of furious hand waving, backed up by some shouting from Diego and Cruz, the driver ran backward, his hand cradling his automatic rifle. They could see heads bobbing up and down behind the log, and twin bursts of firing followed, providing covering fire for two hitters darting out, bent double, and disappearing in the shrub at opposite ends.

Bwana raised his hand and shot blindly in their direction, but knew he had missed. Broker and he crawled swiftly away, but they didn't draw fire.

'Bogeys coming your way, one each, maybe two,' Bwana said in a low tone in his mic.

He got two acknowledging clicks.

'I think all four have left the tree,' Broker told him in a low voice.

Bwana risked another quick leap and saw no bobbing heads. He crouched down and looked as Broker scanned his camera and shook his head. He hustled a few feet at an angle, in the direction of the tree, and raised his head again, gun ready. Nothing.

Cruz and his companions were making distance, and Bwana, after motioning to Broker, set off after them, his Glock held high and ready.

Bear paused and lay prone, the pungent smell of wet soil and the vastness of silence surrounding him. Another slow day in rural America to savor the sun, but for the hitters out to get them.

The hitters would know roughly where they were, and if their training was still with them, would search in sections, but keep each other in sight. Ten minutes, Bear reckoned and started counting down.

In the ninth minute, he heard something move, a long pause, and then another movement. The undergrowth wasn't one thick wall, but patches of thick and thin, and occasional bare earth sections, though from a distance, it was one rolling green wall.

Bear was in one thick pocket of green next to a small bare earth space, and if the hitters were good, they'd be coming at him at an angle, about fifteen feet apart. Closer than that and they would be one target; farther than that and they wouldn't be able to eye-signal effectively. They would come to brown earth and would be undecided which section to search. A slug crawled across slowly, came across the cold metal of his Glock, didn't like it, reversed and ambled away, enjoying the day.

The smell came to him first, cigarette smoke and sweat, clinging to the clothes of the hitters, and then came a footfall and another, and then a couple more, and a shadow fell across the opening, and then a barrel poked through the green, and a face appeared behind it, thirty feet from where he lay.

He'll be the more experienced; the second guy will be backing him up, or parallel to him, and to his right; the human eye tends to look to the right first.

Bear searched without moving and saw a slight darkening in the green, looked to the left of it, and through the edge of his eyes saw the shape of the other hitter. Another barrel poked out twenty feet away, and Bear and the two hitters made a crude upturned L, Bear the angling tail.

The hitters peered cautiously at the open space and at each other, and took a cautious step forward. Bear clicked his earbud, and Bwana, who was chasing Cruz and Diego, spun round in a full loop, firing blindly.

The hitters started and looked back, and Bear rose silently, a pillar amidst the foliage, and shot the nearest in the head. He snapped a shot at the other, missed, and dived in the thicket, ducking below the spray of bullets.

The second hitter ducked down, and silence and sunlight beat on them again. The hitter fired again blindly through the undergrowth in Bear's direction.

Bear wasn't there.

He had rolled and moved *forward* as soon as he'd landed and was now behind the hitter's right shoulder.

The hitter stopped firing suddenly when he realized it would give him away. He crawled cautiously around the open space and through the stalks of grass, saw the undergrowth bend forward and straighten slowly as weight moved over and away from it.

He fired a long burst, directing his barrel in an arc to cover the shape of a man.

From behind him, Bear rose and tripled-tapped him.

He double-clicked his mic and got acknowledgements from the others, untied the long cord attached to the thicket, and waited for Roger.

The sun, the smell of grass, the stillness made it a good day for death to come visiting.

A bird flying across the blue sky swerved suddenly, and Roger knew where they were before they came in sight. Swarthy, unshaven, the two came abreast cautiously, and he saw that the taller man was the more experienced of the two and had good tradecraft.

His eyes were ceaselessly scanning left to right, then right to left, but his partner was jumpy. His partner kept drifting closer to the senior man and retreated jerkily when the tall man gestured angrily at him.

Roger slithered back slowly, sliding through the grass rather than over it, so that from the top, the grass looked as if it swayed with the wind.

A gnarled, stunted bush, its leafy shade stretching above the canopy of the field, trembled in the sun, drawing the attention of both.

They stopped. The tall one looked at it, then around it, trying to see through the depth of the growth, looking for patches of dark and light. The other nervously licked his lips, his barrel pointing straight at the shrub, finger on trigger.

The bush jerked forward suddenly toward them as if attacking them, and the nervous one fired his Uzi wildly at it till his magazine was empty.

The tall hood placed methodical shots ahead and behind the growth – and then his gun fell silent as Roger shot him, a double-tap through the chest and a third through the head. The nervous hood went down seconds later as Roger's Kimber rolled thunder in a cloudless morning.

Roger went to the bush and freed the cord he had used to control it, rolled it up and jammed it deep in one of his pockets. He double-clicked to signal his companions and searched the bodies. He found one phone on the bodies, which he pocketed, and found no identities or papers of any kind.

Bwana and Broker were gaining on the three hoods when the last one, the driver, swung back and fired a spray-and-pray burst. They dived to the ground, and Broker raised himself to his elbow, grunted, 'Go,' and fired back at the hood. The range was too long for accurate handgun shooting, but it was enough to deter the driver, who stepped back and resumed running, ignoring Cruz's curses.

Bwana covered ground rapidly, the undergrowth bending to his will; the driver looked back at him and gaped at the sight of the tall, big, black form speeding remorselessly after them.

One hundred feet away, the driver turned back again, his barrel coming up, and Bwana dived to his left, a long sail in the air, his gun coming straight, eye to the sight, sight to the driver, and punched a hole in his shoulder. The hitter stumbled and fell, losing his rifle, and Bwana circled him wide and took him out.

Two hundred yards to the tree line and Diego and Cruz, risking a quick glance behind them, coaxed more speed from their legs.

Bwana picked up the fallen man's AK-47, looked over it swiftly, thumbed it to semi-auto, kneeled down in a classic shooter stance, and sighted. The first shot was for range, the second was range again, the third shot went into Diego's thigh and brought him down sprawling.

Bwana shifted and fired a shot over Cruz's shoulder; he kept on running still. He fired another, over his other shoulder, no effect. Cruz was weaving erratically to throw off his aim; Bwana waited and then creased his shoulder, more by luck. Cruz stumbled, recovered, and then hugged the ground and lay there when Bwana shot over his head.

Broker reached them, circling cautiously, keeping behind Diego's back. His caution was justified when Diego whirled on his back and came up with his gun, pressing the trigger. Broker shot him in his right shoulder, shooting his other thigh for good measure.

Bwana had restrained Cruz, a knee on his back, one hand pressing Cruz's right hand deep in the ground. Cruz thrashed on the ground, nearly unseating Bwana, a stream of curses filling the air. Bwana slashed his head with his gun barrel, and that drained his resistance. He removed plastic ties from his belt, and Cruz struck.

Using his grounded hand as a pivot, using the force Bwana was bearing down on him, Cruz twisted sideways and jerked back with his head, catching Bwana on the bridge of his nose. Bwana, his grip loosened, reared back as Cruz whipped a foot-long blade from an ankle sheath, twisted around on his right shoulder and slashed at Bwana.

Sharp, so sharp that it cut the light, the blade swept from left to right, a neat horizontal line appearing in Bwana's shirt that turned crimson and then black. Using the twisting motion to free a leg and get it under him, gaining leverage, Cruz swept back the blade in a wicked arc, aiming for Bwana's throat.

Bwana, half falling back, losing his balance, deflected the strike with his right hand and, with his left hand, bunched Cruz's shirt, put a knee to his middle and heaved him over his head, and threw him behind.

He rolled immediately, getting to his feet and turning around, and Cruz was up, attacking, not giving him time. He had run almost half a mile, but he was breathing normally, the knife weaving in his hand, catching the sunlight in tiny streaks.

He feinted, withdrew, feinted and attacked, a quick in an out at Bwana's stomach, and Bwana stepped back. He darted forward again, and this time the blade went horizontal and upward, a smooth controlled flow, and Bwana swayed out of reach again.

Bwana reached down for his knife, but stopped when Cruz feinted again, a long sweep of his arm, Bwana following it with his eyes, and the arm swerved suddenly up, Bwana moving just his upper body and his head, the sharp edge catching the tip of his ear.

Cruz bared his teeth in a feral grin, attacked rapidly, thrusting in short fluid motions, and as his right arm was cutting the air, the left hand, which was stretched for balance, cocked and swung at Bwana... who was ready for it, sailed under it, and the knife came back, lightning fast, parting the air, aiming for his throat.

Bwana bent back, making room and then following the blade, grasped Cruz's wrist in a lock that had crushed bricks, pulled Cruz forward, kicking him in the groin, his leg curling up in the same motion to knee him in the face, swayed to the side, still holding his wrist, twisted and dislocated his shoulder.

He threw Cruz to the ground and grasped his hair to pull his head back and break his neck.

'No,' Broker said quietly.

Bwana paused, looked silently at him, Cruz's harsh breathing punctuating the seconds, and slowly released his head, and finally cuffed and gagged him.

He stood up, breathed deeply once, twice, then thrice, to rid his head of the adrenaline and combat instinct, and caught Broker's smile.

322

'You could've shot him and saved me the trouble.' He grinned.

'I thought it was high time you took a shower, and this now gives you the reason,' Broker bantered back. He'd guessed, correctly, that the two swipes were more blood than cuts, and would heal in no time.

'Were you slow, or...?' Broker asked.

'Nope. I *wanted* him to draw blood, make him confident. Overconfident.'

He walked over to Diego, crouched down, and looked in the hate-filled eyes. The feared enforcer stared back and spat at Bwana, who ducked and smiled at Broker.

'Feisty fella, ain't he? Let's see just how long he lasts.' He pressed down on the wound in Diego's thigh.

Diego cracked ten minutes later and told them what they wanted to know.

They looked up as steps came their way – Roger and Bear, who had finished searching the bodies and stacked them together.

'What?' Bwana demanded, seeing something in their eyes.

'Chloe, she's not answering. Tony too. Eric doesn't know where they are. He thought they would be here by now.'

323

Chapter 37

The Watcher had been following Tony at a sedate pace, knowing Tony would eventually take him to where the rest of them were going. He knew they were planning to take out Cruz and Diego; the where was unclear to him.

As they headed out of the city, he figured it would be somewhere on the highway, and once they were on the US 130, he knew.

He held back, shielded from Tony's mirrors by the dark around him, his headlights doused, and was enjoying the feel of air and speed when he saw Tony's brake lights come on, slow down, then pick up speed. He drifted to have a clearer view of the highway ahead and didn't see anything.

That was his first inkling of trouble.

When Tony veered off the highway, the Watcher idled to a stop, dug out his night vision and scanned. He saw Tony step down from his vehicle and approach Chloe. When they bent over her bike, four figures sprang from behind the undergrowth and surrounded the two.

They were bundled in the Patriot. He followed them.

He shook his head at the hitters' stupidity. They should've shot the two, but then the end result would have been the same.

Traffic was increasing now; on this highway, a couple of cars half an hour apart was the definition of heavy traffic.

Onward they went, down US 130, the SUV maintaining a steady pace, down an exit, then another, more tarmac and miles, and they entered Gloucester City shrouded in predawn mist, its red traffic lights blinking at emptiness.

Klemm Avenue and Market Street fell behind, and Southport loomed, power pylons and cranes reaching up in the sky like Godzillas.

The Watcher, holding way back now, blending his ride with dark surroundings wherever he could, followed them down to the port on potholed tracks that had forgotten what tarmac was, and saw them turn into a factory site.

He turned off his bike, and in the distance he could hear iron grating rolling, the entrance to the site being shut.

He gave them another fifteen minutes as he pushed his bike closer to the site and laid it on its side in the cover of stunted undergrowth. Stripping off his leathers, he donned a lightweight backpack that he tightly secured, and resumed the chase on foot.

Hunt, he corrected himself. It was no longer a chase.

The rolling gate across the site was ten feet tall, rusted, and went from left to right where it got padlocked to securing clasps. There was no padlock on the gate, but one glance at the condition of the gate and the Watcher ruled out rolling it a foot back to slip in.

He approached the left pillar, took a running jump, levering himself off it, over the gate and inside.

Inside was a flat expanse of tarmac littered with broken crates, old containers in a corner, run-down trucks, forklifts... what one would expect to see in a factory site, except they were all still and old.

The structure in front of him was huge, as large as an aircraft hangar, with a gaping entrance large enough for a midsized plane to wheel in and out of, and through the dim light inside he could see gantry cranes and machines.

The structure didn't have windows, but had skylights, and the only way inside was through that enormous maw. Ruling it out, he ran along the side of the structure, left of the entrance, to the far end, peering cautiously around the corner and saw another large entrance in that side, two hundred yards down. The rear probably had another such exit.

He pulled a black ski mask over his head, donned dark shades and thin feel-through gloves, and paused when he heard the noise.

A woman's voice cut off abruptly by a sharp sound, a slap, and then another man's voice that, too, got cut off. The other voices started shouting again, talking over one another, their individual voices echoing in the cavernous interior.

He made out that they were at the side entrance and, if they were smart, would be in the deep interior where the light didn't reach. He couldn't risk putting any eyes inside, not even a fiber camera, without knowing how alert they were and which way they were facing.

Their shouting was a good sign, though. *They don't know where Cruz and Diego are, haven't been able to make contact, don't know if their bosses are dead or alive.* He heard further shouting, slapping sounds, and what sounded like a groan. Shouting also meant they were thinking less.

He looked round and saw a couple of barrels in a far corner of the site. He ran toward them, saw they were empty, and lifting one easily, brought it back to the corner of the building. Placing it on its rounded side, the flat top parallel to the side of the structure, he assessed the lengths of the sides of the building.

Less than two minutes to get to the opposite side.

He pulled the barrel back a few feet and set it in motion toward the open mouth and took off down the length of the building.

Three hoods were arguing loudly among themselves, the fourth trying Diego's phone for the umpteenth time as he walked circles around Chloe and Tony. Tony had fallen to the ground sideways, a deep gash on his forehead, his teeth broken, his eyes half closed. Chloe, her lips cut, stared at the circling hood steadily through her swollen eyes.

Phone guy stopped suddenly, looked at his phone, jammed it in his pocket, and gestured urgently for the others to keep quiet. They heard it then, a soft metallic, grinding sound outside. He mouthed at the driver, 'Anyone follow us?'

Driver shook his head. Phone guy motioned at him to go look outside. Driver hesitated and then took a couple of steps to the sound, now growing louder. Phone guy beckoned at another hood to follow him.

AKs gripped in their hands at the ready, they edged to the entrance, the second hood covering the first from behind. Phone guy and the last hitter took cover on either side of the entrance, their captives in plain sight through the opening.

Driver took a quick look to the right, his rifle following his sight. Nothing. He whipped to the left. Nothing. His eyes slipped lower and spotted the rolling barrel, which was a few turns from coming to a stop just at the edge of the entrance.

Driver shouted a warning and darted backward in the shadow of the factory, keeping the barrel in sight. He fired at the barrel, and bullets pinged and whistled in the air, some of them making holes in the empty barrel. It shuddered and came to a stop, jerking sporadically as bullets hit it.

The second hitter scanned the other end, saw nothing, and whispered at Driver to inspect the barrel and recce the front of the factory.

Driver stepped forward cautiously, edging wide to have an early look inside the barrel. It was empty. He whipped his rifle up and called out softly to the men inside, briefing them.

The second hitter stepped away from the building and edged to the back, taking short steps.

His rifle poked its snout around the edge of the building, then one eye appeared, followed by his forehead; the rest of his head showed itself as he detected no threat.

The Watcher lay prone, hugging concrete and cold steel, another dark stain in the darkness carpeting the shadow of the site.

His hands were stretched in a pistol shooting stance, arm and fingers melding into pistol, eye becoming front sight, front sight becoming forehead, finger depressing in response to a brain command.

The hitter's head exploded. The Watcher didn't wait to watch.

His left leg and arm sprang down, powering him up, right leg taking a long step, left leg another, right leg taking him to flight, left leg bracing against the cold metal of the side, launching him.

The Watcher flew out of the side of the structure, legs spread wide, body bent forward, his gun arm straight and steady, searching and finding Driver, who was looking eye height and down for threats. The Watcher's first bullet went wide, the second hit Driver in the left shoulder, the third tapping him in the back, and the fourth caught his head.

The Watcher landed, took three steps to slow and turn and ran back down the side of the building. Stopping in its shadow, he pulled another gadget from his backpack, an audio playback device with a timer setting, scrolled down its list of recordings and selected one. Setting the timer, he hid it under a metal overhang at the foot of the building and ran.

The hoods inside saw the men outside being blown away, and one of them stuck his rifle out and started firing blindly in the direction of the attacker. The other, older and more experienced, shouted at him repeatedly till the shooter stopped, and signaled at him to stay quiet. They needed to know how large the attacking force was without revealing their positions.

Twenty seconds of deep silence followed, broken by the creaking of metal, and then the first shot rang out, loud and echoing in the empty factory, making them duck for cover. A barrage of shots followed, pinging off the metal frame, making them step deeper in the cover of the side walls. The older guy ducked low, took two steps back, frowned hard, and he whirled round suddenly as realization hit him.

His forehead blossomed and disappeared before he could shout a warning.

The Watcher stood inside the shadow of the entrance, trained his gun on the second man, and then lowered it.

The woman had taken advantage of the distraction to run behind the second hitter, kicking him in the groin from the rear, another kick smashing his face against the metal wall. He fell heavily and stayed still as she kicked him in the head again for good measure.

The Watcher's lips twitched, his muscles unused to smiling, as he tossed a knife on the concrete and disappeared.

Chloe turned around, saw the entrance was empty, checked outside, ran back to the side entrance, past the corner, peered low, and saw the device. She'd realized the shots were phony, yet in the heat of battle, they'd sounded realistic along with the metal pings and impacts.

She went back inside to the knife and, lying down awkwardly, picked it up with her fingers, fumbled with it, and headed to Tony.

Half an hour later she was leading Tony out, away from the site to where the hum of vehicles could be heard.

Vehicles meant people. She kicked up the pace.

Harry's Diner, its faded sign swaying limply in the sky, was in a gas station and, despite the shabby exterior, was richly warm inside, the smell and sound of food, coffee, and people comforting.

She marched to the counter, where a bearded and heavily tattooed mountain stood chewing on a plug.

'Phone,' she demanded.

The mountain ran his eyes over her and jerked his head at a far wall where a pay phone hung.

Chloe picked up loose change, tips from tables, on her way, lasered the waitress's indignant, 'Hey,' with cold eyes, and dialed.

'They must have followed Chloe and somehow got the drop on her and Tony.' Bear broke the silence at last.

They were hurtling down the highway toward Gloucester City, following a weak signal emitted by a transmitter sewn in Chloe's jacket. They all had such transmitters, put there for just such circumstances.

Broker nodded, didn't comment, his foot down hard, cold rage and fear turbocharging the vehicle.

Bear glanced at Bwana, who had just smashed a massive fist against the window.

'They need her alive, Tony and her,' he said mildly. 'Till they know what's happened to Diego and Cruz, they need leverage to negotiate... and they don't know since we have their phones and have ignored their calls.'

Bwana looked at him and away, the truth in Bear's words not reducing the urge in him to strike hard, reducing the hoods to fine dust.

Roger gripped his shoulder, knowing exactly how he felt.

Silence fell over them again, their thoughts drowning the rush of rubber on asphalt and sounds of occasional passing traffic.

A silence that was broken by Broker's phone ringing shrilly. He looked at it, not recognizing it, and took it on his headset.

'Yes,' he grunted, then sat straighter, letting the vehicle slow.

'Where?' he asked and thumbed directions on his GPS system. 'Hold tight. We'll be there in half an hour.'

He hung up and turned on the gas again, ignoring the inquisitive looks the others gave him till Bwana punched him in the shoulder, a light punch by Bwana's standards, that nearly threw him into the windshield.

He grinned broadly. 'That was Chloe. She's out and safe.'

He held his hand up to silence them. 'Nope. I don't have anything more than that. All she said was she was taken to Southport in Gloucester City, and now she's free and safe. She said we should haul our asses and get her.'

'That sounds like her,' Bear said and leaned back, relaxing, little springs and nerves in him uncoiling.

They didn't spot her outside the diner, just a whole load of cars, trucks and drivers of various shapes and sizes. No Chloe. No Tony.

Bwana didn't wait for Broker to stop, lunging out of the Escalade before it had even come to a halt, covering the ground in long strides, other drivers scampering to get out of his way.

Broker shook his head at his departing back. 'Surest way to get ulcers, or give someone a panic attack.'

Bwana flung open the double doors to the diner and stood there, ignoring the scowls from the tattooed mountain behind the counter and scanned the diner. No Chloe. No Tony.

He scanned again, now joined by the others, blocking the door. No sign of them.

He walked to the counter. 'There was a guy and a woman here, half an hour back. She used the phone. Seen her?'

The man looked at him dismissively. 'Bud, do I look like someone who keeps tabs on who comes here, does what? So long as I'm paid, I don't give a damn.'

Roger joined Bwana, the others staying by the door, and smiled widely at the man. 'My friend here is not a man to rile. If you know where those two are, it's best you tell him.'

The man opened his mouth to retort, saw something in Bwana's eyes, and closed it, his eyes moving past their shoulder.

'Those two are here,' came Chloe's voice from behind them.

They turned round to see her supporting Tony, handing him over to Bear and Broker.

'Any need to barge in here and threaten violence?' she asked Bwana icily.

'I didn't. I asked politely,' he growled back, enjoying the relief the back and forth provided.

'Hell, Bwana, you walk like that without even saying a word, and mothers take their children and run to the hills,' she threw back at him.

'How's he?' she asked Bear once they were driving back. Bear was tending to Tony in the rear.

'I was a Ranger, ma'am. I'll be fine, just some flesh wounds,' Tony mumbled through cracked lips. 'Should help me land the girls now.'

Broker snorted. 'I can just imagine the stories that you'll spin out of that, Tony. Enough fodder for a few years, I reckon.'

Women fell for Tony, finding something in his average appearance and shy demeanor. It helped that once he lost his reserve, he was an incredible raconteur.

Bwana, driving, glanced balefully at Roger. 'You never told me that bruises will help with women. You always said all I had to do was dress sharp and the women would come running. I did, and none came.'

Roger looked pityingly at Bwana. 'Nothing can help you, Bwana. You've seen those Hulk movies, haven't you? You figured out that there's a reason for Hulk not having a mate?'

Chloe and Bear, listening behind them, knew this was their way of letting off their tension, helping the needle move from red to normal. She squeezed Bear's arm, conveying all that she felt in that small gesture.

Broker let them have their moment and then asked her, 'What happened? How did you get out?'

Chloe shook her head, puzzled. 'I've been trying to figure that out for some time. Those goons took us to that place and started on us when they couldn't raise Cruz. Well, both of us were going to hold out as long as we could, and then someone joined the party.'

She told them what she'd seen and heard. Which wasn't much.

'But I retrieved these.'

She dug into the pockets of her fatigues and brought out the knife and the playback gadget.

Broker inspected them for a long while and then sighed. 'The blade… millions like it sold in Walmart and Target. We won't get anywhere with that. The device is more interesting. Home-made with components from RadioShack, but those components are fairly common, and we won't be able to track the source store.'

He went silent, thinking, and finally gave voice to what had been going through his mind for a long time.

'You know, if this is our same ghost, he isn't your ordinary vigilante or gun nut who's developed a Batman syndrome.' He held the playback device. 'This is an amateur device, but sophisticated enough to have hundreds of recordings in it that play back authentically. There's shooting in a desert, shooting in a corridor to give echoes… he's got shooting on a mountain, for crissakes. The way he appears and disappears, the way he took those guys out – the first time he's shown his hand. If it's him, of course.'

'He's a professional. Like us.'

They digested his words, nodding in acknowledgement. They had reached the same conclusion.

'Better not be one of those navy boys,' Bwana muttered.

Roger waved a hand dismissively. 'Question is, why is he helping us?'

Broker got there before them and waited for their light bulb moment.

'Clare?' Chloe asked.

'Well done. She's the only one I can think of who's got a vested interest in looking after our hides.'

'If it was her, why wouldn't she tell us? And looks like this guy is so good, how about bringing him in our fold?' Bwana broke in.

'All in good time, Mr. Patience. As long as this ghost isn't in our way, he's not hindering us in any way.'

Chloe twisted around to peer in the back of the Escalade. 'Where are those two? What did you find out from them?'

Broker sobered. 'They had suspected Shattner of being a plant after several of their deals went down badly, and after the cops had barged in on their last deal, which was there' – he nodded in the direction of Southport – 'they were even more sure.

'They hadn't plugged him till then because he fit into their façade perfectly, good mechanic, white guy, all that shit. And get this – they were thinking of using him as their own double! However, when the deals started going south, they couldn't risk having him around anymore and decided to lift Shattner.

'They brought him here, maybe the same place that you were held in, going by what he mentioned in his journal, their description of it, and your mentioning it.'

'Shattner didn't break.' Broker's voice softened and slowed, his words hanging heavy in the air.

'They shot out his knees, but he stuck to his story. Diego went to work on his insides, and by then he was screaming, calling out his kids' names. He must've lost his senses by then.

'But he didn't break.' Broker wiped his face with his hand, slicked back his hair, and took a deep breath.

'Of course, everyone breaks. Cruz and his sidekick knew this. So did Shattner. When Diego was cutting him, he lunged *inside* not away, and the knife went too deep. Diego said he was smiling as he died. They were kicking him and screaming at him as he lay there, asking him to confess.'

Chloe shut her eyes, willing her imagination to stay silent, not throw up images of Shattner broken and bleeding, the deep driving urge in him not to escape, but to die before the truth spilled out. She drew a deep breath and looked at the men around her, the cold, hard light in their eyes comforting her.

She rested her head against Bear's shoulder, which was hard as a rock. 'The kids. Elaine Rocka. They need to know he wasn't a loser.'

Bwana's voice rumbled in the vehicle. 'They will. We would've been proud to know him.'

'What've you done with them?' she asked after a long time.

'They're alive, but Broker came up with a unique disposal system,' Roger deadpanned, lightening their mood.

She looked curiously at him and turned to Broker.

'Eric's taking them.'

'To Oborski.'

Chapter 38

'Five of them, hundreds of us, and look where we are,' the speaker said softly. He didn't need to raise his voice, not when he was Agon Scheafer. Scheafer's hawk eyes surveyed the four of them seated in front of him around a small conference table in the dim lighting of a hotel room.

The room had hitters outside the doors, in the corridor, and a few of them in the lobby, looking just like hitters should, reinforcing the message to guests and onlookers that the hotel wasn't a place they should spend too much time in.

A fifth chair was empty, which Cruz would have occupied. Cruz had dropped off the grid for more than a day. The last they knew was him heading to New Jersey for a deal. And then silence.

The gang had scoured all parts of Gloucester City and within a radius of a hundred miles, but had come up empty-handed. The New York chapters had banged doors, knocked heads, and hadn't had any success either.

'Is HE worth all this?' Hamm ventured, choosing his words carefully. He had seen Scheafer disembowel another chapter head in front of them and sip delicately on a glass of claret as the man died.

The full force of those eyes turned on him. 'That's not for discussion. You haven't answered me. How have five people done this to us?'

Hamm had once been in a firefight with three SWAT agents and, after running out of ammunition, had taken them on with just a blade. He had come out on top. Just. His entrails tied back in with his shirt, he had walked a mile to the nearest residence, killed the occupants, and had called for help.

Feeling that gaze on him, he preferred taking on that SWAT team again than sitting in that room, answering to Scheafer.

'Our size doesn't count for much when you consider their abilities and that they're always on the move. They attack directly, and our men aren't used to that. They're used to cops crashing down doors, other gangs picking them off at night, but these guys attack swiftly, in the open, disappear before our guys have woken up, and when they do, they're dead or dying. They use lures and decoys, and our guys get sucked in. We tried taking them down at our sites, but they attacked us so fast and so unexpectedly that they got away.'

'All I'm hearing are excuses. You know how I view failure.' Scheafer looked intently at each one of them. 'We've recruited guys with military experience. These tactics shouldn't be a surprise to them.'

Kelleher, Sancada, and Morales fidgeted in their seats but kept quiet, happy for Hamm to take the heat and continue talking for them now that he had the ball. In any case, their chapters hadn't been hit so far.

'Their military experience doesn't count,' Hamm said, biting back the *for jack shit* that nearly slipped out of his mouth. 'Except a few, including us, none have served more than two years, and they were the worst soldiers. Against other gangbangers, their experience counts, not against these guys. These guys... you blink and you're dead. You don't blink, that's because you're already dead.'

He considered his words for a moment. 'I warned you this might happen, many years back.'

'You seem to be full of admiration for them.' The hawk eyes burned, sighting prey.

'They've ruined my chapter, brought heat on me, made a fool out of me,' Hamm replied savagely. 'I want to rip their hearts out and drink their blood. Admire them? Fuck no. But I have *respect* for them.'

The eyes didn't move, staring at him, and he wondered if those were the last words he'd utter.

'We should go nuclear, but there's a risk,' Hamm suggested cautiously. If he had to die, at least it would be after having his say.

'Speak.'

Hamm outlined his plan, and they considered it silently. Scheafer looked at it from different angles and then finally nodded.

'Set it up. I shall warn our friend.'

As they were leaving, Scheafer said in a silky voice, 'I hope, for your sake, this plan works. If it doesn't...'

He didn't have to complete his sentence. They all knew the price of failure was death, and not an easy one. Scheafer had many ways to cause a slow, painful death and enjoyed inflicting them.

'We'll hit Hamm's garage again; it's reopened now,' Broker announced.

Chloe looked at him skeptically. 'Won't they be sorta expecting that? For us to retaliate for taking me.'

'Yup, and that's why we won't hit immediately. We'll wait a week. Let them stew.'

They were back at their base, relieving Pieter and Derek, Rocka and the kids able to have some kind of normal life as the kids had started going to a nearby school. Broker had thought about moving base again, but this house was so well located that the benefits outweighed the risks. They had decided that the five of them would spend the least time in the house. Tony, when he was ready, Eric, Pieter and Derek would provide protection for the family.

Broker made another announcement, more triumphantly. 'My boy's come up with something more.'

They looked at him, puzzled. Broker scowled back at them. 'You think Werner doesn't have feelings just like us? It responds to motivation just like us.'

Bwana whispered, 'Next he'll be feeding spinach to the computer.'

'I heard that.' Broker waggled a finger at him.

'You were saying something.' Roger brought him back to the subject. Broker could go on for hours extolling the virtues of Werner, giving it human traits, if he was allowed free rein.

'Floyd Wheat changed a pattern about three years back. He started going to a café on the way back from his station.'

342

He paused, waiting for them to congratulate him. He got astonishment.

'That's fucking it?' Bear, normally not given to swearing, asked him.

Roger rolled his eyes, and Bwana went further. He threw his hands up and mentioned something about a straitjacket.

Broker sighed. 'How can I expect you guys to connect dots the way I do. Any change in pattern is what we look for since that could be a clue to something that's a life change, a motivation change, a behavioral change.'

'We get that, Broker.' Chloe played peacekeeper. 'Hard as it might be for you to believe, we are able to think for ourselves.' Chloe defending a couple of Mensa members.

'But this is so insignificant... it means nothing. He could've just liked the look of a barista there... you mentioned he was divorced and single. I remember I used to frequent one, back in the day, because the server had a nice smile. Just as I was nerving myself to ask her out, I got deployed. Maybe he liked their brew. There's no way of extrapolating a coffee-drinking habit into a mole's activities,' Bear rumbled.

Broker, his arms crossed across his chest, sat back and listened to them protest. When all of them had their say, he waited another beat. 'You guys done quibbling? Well, hear this...'

He stopped when Bwana raised a hand. The sight of the six-foot-plus hulk behaving as if he was back in school made him smile. He erased it, got in the groove, and pointed at Bwana. 'Yes, boy?'

'You got that because he used a charge card, right? Or a credit card, at that café.'

'Yes, boy, and before you go further, Wheat used plastic *everywhere*. Newsagent, McDonald's, cafés, grocery stores, home furnishing, car... wherever he had to spend, the card came out. He always used cards right from since when time began.'

Bwana deflated and gestured at him to carry on.

'Thank you, boy. Now what I was going to tell you before you questioned my deduction was that all those transactions are within a day or two of the bad busts the FBI was involved in. *All of them.*'

He smirked as they fell silent. 'Still doubting me? Here's another. He went to that café *only when* there was a bust coming up.'

'That still isn't conclusive, Broker,' Chloe protested, though with less steam.

'Agreed, and Isakson will want to have everything covered before he can make a move, all the I's dotted and the T's crossed and all that. Now I'm speculating here, but I think the café was either a meeting place or some kind of dead drop. For all we know he could have used the disposable cup to write a message that got picked up later.

'I'm more inclined to think it was a dead drop,' Broker said after a pause.

Bear caught on. 'Because if he had met anyone, then Isakson would have known. He had all these guys shadowed for a long while.'

'So, we check out the café and ask them if they remember his habits? If he was a regular over three years, chances are he'll be remembered,' Roger added.

'*Exactement*,' Broker beamed.

He brought up a map of the city and pointed out the café's address. 'Just off Hell's Kitchen. I have no idea if that's significant, but let's assume it's not and was on his way home. He's renting in the Upper West Side and drives a rather noticeable Camaro, purple in color with afterburners and vanity plates.' He recited the number.

'The café might, just might, have CCTV cameras inside and outside,' Bwana mused.

'Yeah. I knew my brains would eventually rub off on you guys.'

He produced postcard-sized photographs of Wheat, different angles, and handed them over to Bwana, who passed them onward.

They drew straws on who would go to the café, and it fell to Bwana and Roger.

They took the same Escalade again, which now featured new number plates and sporty white streaks running down the doors on both sides. *Makes it a different car*, Broker had commented when he tossed the keys to them.

They set out in the evening, Batman time, bright light and golden hue in the city, and finally their luck ran out on Ninth Avenue, the law of averages working for the gang.

At the Garment District, the traffic had slowed due to a bottleneck created by a police cruiser stopping another car, lanes narrowing to two, their ride in the outer lane. They passed the slower-moving vehicles on the left, Bwana rolling down the window on the passenger side to get a better look at the offending vehicle.

They passed a rusted brown Ford, its windows down, driver and passenger nodding their heads as they talked with each other. Roger overtook them slowly, and it was the sudden double take of the driver at Bwana that registered on him through the corner of his eye. He raised the tinted window and tracked them through the mirror, saw the passenger pointing at them, the driver slapping his hand down, talking furiously.

The Ford slipped in their lane, a car behind, and matched their pace.

'Rog,' Bwana warned him, Roger needing no warning. He had noted Bwana's stillness and had caught the car in his mirror.

'Nix the café. Let's give them a tour of the city and see if they have any more friends.'

He swung left at the next set of lights and headed to West End Avenue, and the wheels behind followed them, making no effort at concealing themselves. Half an hour of weaving in and out of traffic, sudden turns and using trucks and buses as cover, luck was still evading them.

'They've been on the phone,' Bwana said, pulling out his phone and donning his headset and mic.

'Maybe they've ordered pizza.'

Bwana punched a number. 'Broker?'

Broker responded immediately, 'What's up?' and listened without interruption. They could hear him punching keys, bringing their trackers up on a real-time map.

'You need backup?'

'Nope,' drawled Bwana, 'we'll see what happens, but you just might want to leave that place and find other digs.'

Broker was silent, knowing what Bwana meant. If they were captured, the gang could find out where they were holed up.

'We'll be out in half an hour. I'll get Rolando to get a couple of cruisers to run interference, but you guys... give them the slip and get away. If they get more hitters, you'll be in a tough place.'

Roger nodded, accelerated, looked in his mirror, and saw the Ford had disappeared. It appeared in the corner of his eye and overtook them slowly. The hitter closest to them was staring at them, his fingers made into a gun aimed at them.

Roger looked back in his mirror – a silver car had slipped behind them, its driver boring holes at them through the darkened glass of the Escalade.

There was one passenger up front, and another in the rear, both of them armed, automatic rifles visible through the windshield. These were harder looking men with short hair, and even in the distance, through the traffic, Roger could make that aura.

'These the A-team?' Bwana ventured.

'Possible. Certainly seem better than the military dropouts we've come across so far.' He opened the glove compartment and tossed a cap and gloves to Bwana. The black balaclava cap was tight on Bwana's head, the gloves snugly fitting. He supported the wheel as Roger donned his, and they bumped fists.

'Evade first, action a last resort,' Bwana commented, and Roger nodded.

The Ford slipped ahead of them, boxing them in, but he ignored it. A box worked only if it covered all sides and you respected them, and when he swerved in an alley, the car ahead was left with its occupants looking back at them.

The silver Nissan was a different proposition, handled by an experienced getaway driver. He followed them through all their tricks and turns, a determined wasp up their tail.

On a narrow street temporarily empty of any traffic, its windows rolled down, a hitter loosed off a few controlled shots aimed at their tires, all of them missing.

Roger headed back to traffic-heavy streets and noted the way the hitters concealed their weapons when they passed close to other traffic. *Professionals. Don't want to invite unnecessary attention.*

He joined West End Avenue, glanced sideways, and saw Bwana taking another gun, its steel frame and barrel glinting dully in his lap.

'Is that what I think it is?' he asked, keeping an eye on his mirror.

Bwana nodded, checked the magazine, and slipped it in his shoulder holster.

Roger drew on, passing several traffic lights, slowing at each of them, the Nissan closing the distance whenever Roger decelerated.

Their ride was the fifth vehicle from the next red light, and he inched forward as the cars ahead wheeled off at green. Bwana waited for amber, ignoring the honking from the long line of vehicles behind him, and just when it turned red, he floored it.

Horses lunged forward under the bonnet, surging their car ahead, raising another chorus of honking as vehicles from the sides came to a sudden stop furiously. He dropped speed once the junction was crossed, and in the distance he saw the Nissan move to the head of the line at the light behind.

Traffic flowed around them, ignoring their slow amble, and then six cars behind, he saw the flash of silver.

Timing was everything now.

In the distance he saw the next set of lights, about five minutes away, and six cars behind, the Nissan. He steered sedately, scanning the cars behind him, a white van and a people carrier behind it visible in their immediate wake. They followed him for a while, impatiently wheeled out and overtook him, and others slipped in their place. The flash of silver was now four cars closer.

Roger crossed the light, steered to the slow lane, allowing them to narrow that down to three cars, and then maintained enough speed to keep the train of cars in line.

They had their next break when a harried executive cut in behind them driving a Land Rover Defender, its tall body filling their mirrors temporarily. Roger gassed it to make space and saw that the Nissan had used the opportunity to fall behind the Defender.

349

He sped up and maintained a steady pace and the two cars behind followed suit. The business executive was oblivious to those ahead and behind him, oblivious to the weapons visible in the hitters' hands.

Roger nudged their ride to the side, bringing the driver side of the silver car into their mirrors. Now that side of the Escalade was visible to the heavies too.

The light ahead was green, and he slowed, taking his time, and then it turned amber, and Bwana slipped out, opening the door a crack.

He ducked beneath their sight line, ran back, slipped in front of the Defender, and tapped the Escalade to let Roger know he was in position.

Roger opened his door and climbed out, his hand going near his shoulder holster, drawing his gun, capturing their attention, their windows rolling down, doors opening, weapons straightening at him, passersby screaming, shouting, ducking, cars swerving.

Bwana climbed on the Defender's bonnet, ignoring the executive's shouting, raised his balaclava-clad head above its roof, his Grach leading his eye, felt time and space slowing as the driver and passenger swung their eyes and rifles back to take this new element into account. That split second costing them as the Grach in his hand bucked, its armor-piercing bullets punching large holes in the windshield, fissures decorating the holes, punching through the first two hitters, a third shot going in the back. Bwana flowed down the Defender, glided back to the Escalade, and Roger gunned it through the lights and away from the Nissan, which was slumped tiredly to a stop.

The city's traffic and honking came back into focus and moved swiftly under their wheels. Roger drove hard, cut through several lanes, circled several blocks to shake off any possible pursuers and finally slipped into a garage that Broker guided them to.

Wheeling into it, they jumped off, shut the metal gates behind them, and spent the next hour stripping the seats out of their vehicle. They would be incinerated, and new seating would be installed. The car would be fully valeted, spray painted with a new color, new plates, and back at Broker's service the next day.

Chloe swung by in the late evening to pick them up.

'Were they good?' she asked.

Bwana shrugged. 'We're still here.'

Chapter 39

'We'll go tomorrow to the café,' Roger told them when they joined Broker and Bear. This time Broker had found them a couple of rooms very near Hell's Kitchen.

'Nope.' Broker clapped him on the shoulder, swiftly running his eyes over both of them. They had said they came out uninjured, but the two often carried minor injuries that they never declared.

He saw Bwana scowl. 'It's not the first time you've uttered an ethical lie.' He shook his head. 'I'd never heard that term till you coined it.'

'The café – it's not improbable that the gang is watching it. They aren't stupid, and if Wheat *is* their guy and all that coffee drinking was a cover for passing messages, they might have some hoods hanging around it.'

'So we just give up?' Bear growled, his voice filling the small room they were in.

Chloe looked at him impatiently. 'Let's go to Isakson with this. They can put feet and eyes on the café.'

Broker's phone rang just as he reached out for it.

'Speak of the devil.' He thumbed it, accepting the call, holding a finger up to hush them. 'Isakson?'

He listened for a minute without interrupting. 'No, not there. Somewhere else.' He held the phone away as a torrent of words poured out.

'I can't confirm or deny that,' he said, winking at the others. 'Don't waste our time. Find a neutral place for us to meet, and we'll be there in an hour.'

He shook his head mournfully at them when he'd hung up. 'Isakson is a good agent; he's just too bureaucratic.

'Let's move. He's got some news of some meth changing hands, the gang buying.'

They separated, took two cabs, and met Isakson at a midtown Starbucks, Broker liking the anonymity offered by it.

'Easier to detect a hitter carrying an Uzi,' he said when Isakson asked him about the location.

He made a 'give' motion with his hand. Isakson sighed, looked around, and leant forward.

'Two million dollars' worth of ice is to change hands in two days; the gang is buying from a Puerto Rican outfit. Ice is—'

'A purified form of meth. We know. Carry on,' Bear interrupted him.

Isakson glanced at him, swallowed his retort, and soldiered on.

'We've been watching a gang safe house for the last week and have seen the Puerto Ricans slowly build up a stash there of meth. We were planning to raid the place but held back when we heard talk of a deal happening. Three days back, we caught a couple of gangbangers talking on their mobiles, and using lip-reading experts and long-distance electronic surveillance, we know they're selling the stash to 5Clubs. That deal is happening midday in two days' time.'

He leant back in satisfaction. 'This time no snitches, no intermediaries. Good policing and persistence has brought this to us. We aren't going to screw it.'

'You've cross-checked this with any chatter?' Roger asked him curiously.

'You don't get a lot of gang chatter. It's not as if gangbangers hit the Internet the way extremists do. However, from the street, we haven't got a lot of talk from our snitches. I'm not surprised. Given the way you guys have been going hard at them, I fully expected both gangs to keep this as quiet as they can.'

'How many are in the know?' Broker asked him casually.

He grimaced. 'The joint task forces, my team... a lot of folks. This came up through the task force; there was no way we could restrict the information flow.'

'Your thirty guys been involved?'

'Twenty-six. Four of them have been away for more than a month for various reasons.'

'Which four?'

'Santiago, Wheat, and two others. Santiago is expecting another child and is on maternity leave. Wheat plays basketball with a bunch of guys, dislocated his knee, suffered a hairline fracture, and will be out of play for some time. The other two had personal stuff come up.'

'How does this work? Are these four kept in the loop even if they're out of action?'

Isakson shook his head. 'Nope. We don't drown agents in stuff if they're not able to do anything with it. Not one of them knows about this deal.'

He looked at them keenly. 'Any of those four on your shit list?'

'We don't have a shit list yet. When we have one, you'll be the first to know.' Broker wasn't ready to reveal his hand yet.

Broker was a great poker player, and Isakson's probing look bounced off his game face.

'Why don't you guys join me as we crash that deal?'

They stared back at him in surprise and bemusement.

'What value would we add?' Chloe asked finally.

'Why didn't you tell him about that café? He could have checked it for us,' Chloe demanded once they'd gathered back.

Broker gave a slow smile, letting her figure it out for herself.

'Right. If this also turns out to be a no-show, then we cast a wider net?'

He gave her a thumbs-up. 'I asked my East European guys to check if that café had cameras or if there were any in the vicinity. They trawled the dark corners and have come up with quite a few and are now running those through a face recognition program. Let's see what they come up with.'

He gaped as Roger and Bwana left, returned with a large bag that clunked softly, opened it and started stripping and cleaning their hardware. 'Starting a war somewhere?'

'I always have a rifle in one hand and an olive branch in another,' Bwana said piously as he posed with the Barrett and a white cloth in either hand.

'I doubt you'd recognize an olive branch if it bit you on the ass,' Broker retorted. 'Seriously, though, where exactly are you guys going?'

'Why, aren't we going to watch the takedown?' Roger asked innocently.

The gang apartment was in South Jamaica, Queens, sitting atop a boutique, facing a block of apartments and offices on the other side of the street. Stores lined either side of the street, selling everything that anyone would ever need, and some selling stuff they wouldn't ever. The boutique was sandwiched between a Greek deli and a Laundromat. The Laundromat shared store space with a tax consultant and a storefront that proclaimed, 'Come Clean.'

Broker had looked at street maps and building plans, had shaken his head in frustration, and had suggested they do a recce to get a feel. Hiring two family sedans, they had driven down the street from both ends, noting likely hides.

'Isakson's men and the cops will be doing the same thing. We don't want to be tripping over them.' Broker looked down in a cup of what passed for coffee, and spoke in the wind.

Chloe nodded as she tried on wigs in a store, Bear patiently watching her, and realized Broker couldn't see her. 'We aren't going to engage unless they get ambushed.' She wasn't asking.

They waited for Bwana and Roger to chip in, a long wait as Roger navigated around a drunk, and Bwana perused the Greek deli, came out with a brown bag, and looked at the block across. 'Probably best to be in one of those apartments or offices. The cops will have taken vantage points on rooftops, and the street will be crawling with them.'

'We'll need the space for the whole day; would be good if we could take the neighboring offices too,' Roger added. If they had to open fire, the less innocents in the vicinity, the better.

Tony, recovered now, had rented two offices for three days, offices with windows that overlooked the street and had a good view of the gang apartment entrance, by the time they returned. He turned red when Chloe congratulated him on the fast work.

'Go easy on the praise,' Broker growled. 'He's bagged a date; those injuries came in handy. We wouldn't want him to be full of himself.'

Bwana and Roger bivouacked in the office the night before the takedown, setting up the Barrett on a stand deep inside, lining the walls with double layers of mattresses that Tony brought in a truck. The mattresses didn't get a second glance. Jamaica had seen everything and took everything in stride. The QDL suppressor knocked off a lot of sound, but not all of it; the mattresses would further deaden any noise.

The sun shone down brightly the day of the deal, shining equally on the cops and the gangs, indifferent to their affiliations. The first cops came, some of them as cab drivers, some of them street-side vendors, part of the ebb and flow on the street but obvious to their eyes. The way they held themselves, the loose yet tailored clothing giving them away.

'You guys in position?' Bwana asked.

Bear and Chloe were in a van sporting a courier company's signage. Bear wondered idly if Tony had minions who churned out the vehicle guises. 'We're here, finding it hard to stay awake, since we have no role to play here.'

'We go to the cavalry's rescue if they're in trouble. I'd like to see Isakson's face if that happens.' Bwana sighted down the Barrett one last time and then relaxed, settling for a long wait. Roger was a drunk lying in front of one of the shuttered stores, not in a position to join in their banter.

He could sense the tension creeping on the cops below as noon approached, could imagine the radio chatter, furtive checking and rechecking of weapons, Isakson and Rolando at some command absorbing the flow.

Noon came and went, and then another hour passed and then another half hour, and he could sense the frustration in the cops below, deflation and doubt in some of them. He could imagine orders being barked, some wiseass saying these are hoods, not known for their punctuality.

The ebb and flow in the street didn't change; in the midst of the traffic a black Chevy Impala nosed its way from right to left, another decrepit car among the many others below. The Chevy made a return pass twenty minutes later, and interest rippled below, several eyes following it, trying to see through the darkened windows in the rear, paying attention to the two in the front. The two were alert, their eyes flicking constantly from side to side, mirrors to front, slowing fractionally in front of the boutique. Invisible currents connected the cops when the car made a third pass, and on its fourth pass, it nudged into a parking space as another car exited. *Another gang car?* Bwana mused.

The car stayed in position for a long time, the front two watching the street, their lips moving occasionally. The passenger got out, stood behind the door, ducked below, and said something to the driver when he was satisfied. The driver brought a phone to his mouth, said a few words briefly, heard the other person out, and nodded once at the passenger.

The rear doors split open, spilling two men, average build, one stocky, the other leaner, their hands close to their bodies. Stocky led the way to the apartment entrance, passenger in the middle, Lean in the back, who walked backward for some time, watching the street. The driver didn't look at them, his attention on the street, ahead, behind and around him.

The three disappeared in the shadow of the entrance, forty-five minutes passed before the feet of Stocky appeared, then the rest of his body, a black trash bag in his left hand. The passenger and Lean had similar bags, all three hurrying to the Chevy. The driver opened the trunk, and as the first man threw his bag inside, the street exploded.

Cops ran to the car, guns drawn, shouting, wearing the ESU vests of the NYPD's elite Emergency Services Unit, some sporting FBI jackets. Some of them broke away, entering the apartment after calling out. Other cops formed a second perimeter fifteen feet away, training their guns on the hoods. A third perimeter kept onlookers back. One of the hoods, the passenger, made a move to his waist, triggering a burst of firing in the air by the cops. His hand fell away, then skyward, his second hand joining it. The driver, sucking on a Colt shotgun thrust through his window, kept his hands motionless on the wheel.

The ESU team leader tore open the trash bags, riffled through them, and sporting a broad grin, waved a thumbs-up in the air. The cops from the apartment returned, pushing three cuffed hoods ahead of them; all of them were bundled in a police wagon.

By now the media had arrived, TV cameras and reporters surrounding the team leader, other less fortunate reporters interviewing onlookers.

Bwana stripped his rifle down and put it away, lowered the windows, and spent fifteen minutes scrubbing away all traces of his presence. He hit the street, turned swiftly away from the scrum, and made his way to the courier van.

Roger was already there in the rear and helped him stow away the rifle, and they headed out.

'Hold it, guys.' Broker's voice came over Bear's phone. 'Pick me up first. We're joining Isakson.'

Broker was in a café a block away, and their original plan was for them, leaving separately, to rendezvous back at the apartment.

Half an hour later, they were in a NYPD police van driven by a cop, Isakson and Rolando in the second row.

Isakson beamed at them. 'Fifty Ks. That's the biggest haul of ice in recent NYPD history.' He looked at Rolando. 'Your guys did a fantastic job, Rolando. You should be proud.'

Rolando acknowledged with a brief nod. 'It was a joint task force operation. The FBI deserves credit too.'

'So where are we heading?' Bwana interrupted the love-fest.

Isakson mentioned the name of a downtown hotel. 'I want to hear your theories – I know you have some – and see how today's bust affects them.'

He broke off as the van turned in the driveway of the hotel.

The takedown was so smooth, so slick and deceptive, they couldn't have planned it better.

Isakson, Rolando, and Broker were bunched together as they walked to the lobby of the hotel.

A doorman came from behind his stand, reached under his uniform, and shots rang out

Chapter 40

The shooter pumped two into Isakson, shifted slightly, and put another three into Rolando.

As Broker and the others dived, reaching for their guns, they were hit from behind by bellboys coming out of hiding, Tasering them to the role of helpless spectators. Bwana and Bear resisted longer, their big bodies absorbing the shock and weathering it, and just as their hands neared their guns, they were felled, the stock of a M16 crashing in their heads.

Bwana's vision dimmed, and just before he faded into darkness, he saw the doorman, a narrow- faced man, teeth bared viciously, slashing down on Chloe.

He came to when his head banged against the side of the truck they were dumped in, jouncing on country roads. He lay still, and ran a mental check – his wrists and feet were cuffed, wrists behind his back, his head hurt, but nothing was broken. He raised his head and met Roger's look.

'How long have I been out?' He tested his wrists and ankles and found no give.

Roger shrugged. 'Woke up myself just seconds ago.' The others stirred at the voices and raised themselves awkwardly, supporting themselves against the sides.

'We're in deep shit,' Broker croaked, cleared his throat, and continued. 'How did that happen?'

He answered his own question before the others could. 'They must have followed Isakson or Rolando, and must have had some kind of bug on him or his vehicle.' He thought for a while. 'That was some organization at the hotel. They must have had gunmen inside keeping everyone at bay, and a rapid switch of personnel to give us the warm welcome.'

'What about Isakson and Rolando?' Chloe asked.

Bear's voice was low and savage. 'It's likely they're both dead. The shooter was just a few feet away from them.'

Roger smiled grimly. 'Let's focus on the here and now, else we won't be around to figure out how they did it.' He nodded at the truck they were in. 'Middle-of-the-road Ford series, not new, suspension could do with a replacement, but sturdy. We won't have much luck breaking through the floorboards. Any of you have any blades on you? Anything to cut through the plastic?'

They all shook their heads; the hoods had cleaned them when they were out.

The truck was bare, a thick rubber sheet between them and the floorboards, the side walls bereft of any upholstery, just metal covered by black rubber sheets running from floor to roof.

'It's to carry bodies.' Broker divined Bear's thoughts as he looked around inside. 'The rubber sheets are easy to wash, also absorb any sound.' He had to shout over the truck's rumbling over the country roads.

Bear grunted, rolled around to have his feet against the wall, and kicked with both feet. He slid a foot back, colliding into Roger, the rubber beneath them slick with sweat, his feet losing purchase on the walls.

Roger rolled to lay beside him, joined by Bwana, Chloe and Broker lying at their heads, perpendicular to act as a stopper, and on the count of three, they all kicked.

After half an hour of vigorous kicking, the rubber and the side wall continued to mock them, the jostling of the truck robbing the power of their blows. In frustration, Bwana sat up and half crouched, looking for any sharp edges on the roof.

The truck swerved suddenly, throwing him on top of the others, and by the time he had rolled off them, the rear doors were jerked open.

They peered out and, against the dark sky, saw the barrels of automatic rifles appear first; then two dark shapes appeared, roughly hauled them out, and dumped them on the ground. They rolled over to absorb the impact and struggled to their feet.

They were in a small clearing surrounded by dense woods, with the tiniest patch of sky looking down on them, the cold light of the stars offering little comfort to them. *Harriman Park. If we have to die here, it'll be with the sky above my head*, Bwana thought.

The two figures were joined by three others, all heavily armed, standing in front of them in a loose curve.

'Why have you—' Broker began and fell back as one of the men swung his rifle, hitting him on the side of the head. Broker, sensing the blow, turned along with it, softening the blow, but it was still hard enough to split his temple and bring him down.

He coughed, shook his head, a thin stream of blood flowing darkly down his face, slowly got to his feet, swayed and steadied.

'Not in the face,' came a calm, pleasant voice. Hamm stepped forward from the group and looked at them pityingly.

'A good run while it lasted… and you caused us heavy losses.'

Broker's heavy breathing broke the silence.

'We found Cruz and Diego, severely tortured, dead, of course. By the time we found their bodies, the Russians had attacked and taken over a lot of our stashes. I guess you guys are responsible for that too.

'No brave words from you guys? No pleading? Nothing? I guess when you're facing death, you're no different to anyone else.'

He came closer, a victor inspecting his spoils.

'Now this one, maybe we won't kill. We need some entertainment.' He pointed his gun at Chloe.

Bear and Bwana launched themselves horizontally, their shoulders aiming for him, and fell heavily as Hamm took a long step back and two men clubbed them down hard. They crawled to their feet and fell again as the two again clubbed them between the shoulders.

They lay there for a while and then struggled to their feet, this time untouched, and then heard a heavy blow, and Roger fell gasping.

Roger had been moving to the right, inching away from them, but the hitters had seen his move and clubbed him.

'The Warriors,' Hamm mocked them, 'reduced to this. You must be wondering why I want your faces intact.'

'Not hard to figure out, asshole. You want us to be recognized,' Bear snarled.

Hamm held a hand up to halt the advancing hitter, and nodded.

'Why here? Why not in the city?' Broker asked him in genuine curiosity.

'This is my killing ground. I like my kills in the open.' Hamm shrugged. 'Enough talking. I have a chapter to run.'

He stepped back and raised his gun, pointing first at Bwana.

Bwana stared back at him, relaxing his body. *This was always going to come one day. We weren't meant to die in our beds.*

Hamm sighted at him, his finger tightening on the trigger.

His body flopped to the ground as a bullet took his head out like a watermelon.

Before realization had set in, another hitter fell forward, then a third and a fourth. The last turned around, spraying blindly in the dark. His body jerked twice, and he fell and twitched a last time.

Silence fell in the woods, a deep silence that swallowed thought and logic, broken by Bwana's deep sigh.

'Guess that memo of yours reached an angel,' he told Broker.

Broker held his hand up, gesturing him to be quiet, but they heard nothing, saw nothing. The tree line was thirty feet away, the trees tall and dense enough to hide an army in the dark. The shots could have come from anywhere, but Bwana worked out angles from how the bodies lay, and looked high and to his right.

He saw nothing and hadn't expected to see anything. They hadn't heard the shots, so not only was the shooter using a suppressor, he was a distance away.

He glanced at them and saw they were looking at him expectantly. He shook his head. 'Too dark, too far.'

He grinned, his teeth flashing white in the night. 'Looks like our time has not yet come. Maybe hell is too full, or even they've rejected us. There's still time for me to land a girl.'

They waited in silence for another twenty minutes, but their rescuer hadn't lost his shyness.

Chloe sagged against Bear, the adrenaline leaving her in a rush, her brain giving up processing their survival. 'Is it him?'

'Who knows? But who else could it be?'

Roger hopped to Hamm's body and knelt beside it. 'I don't know about you guys, but a return to the city and a warm shower sounds great to me.'

They joined him, two of them turning the bodies over, the remaining searching the bodies for a knife, any sharp edge to cut through the ties. An hour of grunting later, they stood panting, flexing their wrists and ankles. Roger checked Broker's head and temple, which was caked with blood, thin drops sliding down his face, parted the hair to see a horizontal gash, not deep enough to cause any damage, but would get infected if unattended.

They washed his face with a can of water they found in the truck, bandaged it using strips made from tearing Bear's shirt, pocketed the phones and guns they found on the hitters, and set out on the rutted road back to the city.

Bwana and Roger, having been to the forest several times, guided Broker back to the highway, where they joined the rush to the city, a magnet sucking up surrounding traffic.

'Loads of numbers on this.' Chloe looked up from Hamm's phone. 'It doesn't have any names in the directory, just initials, and there aren't many of them. There are several numbers in the recent call history.' She frowned at Bear. 'Make any sense to you?' She thrust the phone at him.

Bear studied it and saw a pattern of incoming calls from a number, followed by one or two outgoing calls to that number, repeated every two days with a new originating number. He looked at the growing dawn, the traffic falling silently behind them as Broker cut a swathe through it.

'Disposable numbers. They probably buy a batch and change the number regularly. Hamm knows the new number only when he gets a call. They probably have some rule about the number of calls made *to* the number.'

'Has to be Scheafer. No one else would be this paranoid.'

'Why can't it be the mole?' Roger argued.

'It could,' Broker replied, 'but Scheafer is a control freak, and I would be surprised if his chapter heads had direct contact with the rat. Is there any number that looks like one of those messaging numbers?'

Bear read it off and got a nod from Broker. 'Sounds like the number we got off the gangbangers in Arizona.'

A thought struck him. 'How long ago was the last incoming call?'

'Eight hours back. No other calls since then.' Bear went through the text message folder and found it empty.

Broker turned on the radio, searched for a station, gave up and growled at Bwana, 'Find a news station.'

They listened to the bulletins in silence, getting Broker's drift. 'Nothing. The cops must have hushed up the takedown. Now the million-dollar question is, will he call?'

No call came by the time they approached Central Park.

Broker used a hitter's phone to call Pizaka. 'Yes, obviously I'm alive,' he replied, rolling his eyes. 'Isakson, Rolando?'

'That bad?' We'll be there in forty minutes.'

'Fucker didn't want to say anything about those two.' He honked savagely at a trucker that cut in ahead of him. He overtook him and stuck his finger out, flooring the gas. 'Says we should meet for a debrief. As if we were planning to fucking disappear in thin air. We called him, for crissakes.'

Bwana met the eyes of the others in the mirror and winked. Broker's high regard for law enforcement, especially those who insisted on going by the book, was legendary.

One PP was crawling with cops when they arrived, many of them pushing paper, killing time, to have a look at them. Pizaka met them, his eyes going over them swiftly, lingering on the strips around Broker's head. 'You want to tidy up?'

They shook their heads impatiently, wanting to know the condition of the cop and the FBI man. Pizaka led the way to a conference room, which had three other occupants. Chang rose, greeted them, and introduced them to the other two.

Commissioner Forzini and Director Murphy looked like they hadn't slept for a while. Sleep was a luxury they couldn't afford, not when their respective number two men had been shot by a gang.

'Tell us,' Broker demanded, waving away their enquiries.

Forzini looked at Murphy, giving him the lead. 'Isakson took two in the shoulder. He's come out of surgery and should recover. Fully.

'Rolando was less lucky. The three shots he took; one missed his heart, the other two went through his lung. He too was operated on; the doctors have done all that they could. Now it's down to him, his body, his mind. He has a fighting chance, they say.'

Bwana's eyes were on Forzini's fists as he spoke, opening and clenching, his steady voice not masking his rage.

'Why did you hush up the attack?'

'We didn't, but we didn't share all the details either. The media and the public know there was a gang attack in a hotel. What they don't know is who was involved, and we have managed to control that. Luckily no guest or onlooker was able to see what went down exactly. We were hoping you guys would perform a miracle and get back alive…' Murphy replied. Murphy had come through the ranks, starting his career as a field agent, and little fazed him, but even he couldn't conceal his pain and anger.

'Lay it all out for us,' he commanded.

Broker laid it out for them, Pizaka and Chang making extensive notes as he elaborated, stopping him several times, getting him to repeat.

He didn't tell them everything.

They had come up with a plausible escape story, embellishing and glossing over some details on their way back, the least they could do to keep the ghost invisible. He saw Pizaka's and Chang's eyes go over them, assessing them, as he described how Bwana and Roger had launched themselves at their captors as soon as the truck doors had opened, and in the scuffle, Bear and Chloe had slipped out and overpowered the remaining. They were all martial arts experts in various disciplines – Broker wasn't, he regarded himself as a gray matter expert – and their story held.

'We'll want to take separate statements from all of you.' Pizaka's shades tilted at them.

'The shooter is dead?' Forzini asked hopefully, his lips twisting briefly in a grim smile when Broker nodded.

'Bodies are in the van in the parking lot below.'

Forzini looked at Chang, Broker tossed the keys to him, and once he'd left, Broker asked the Commissioner, 'How did they do it?'

'The gang probably owns the hotel through a shell company, to launder their money. We're still sifting through the chain of ownership. They closed down the lobby and reception for the day on the pretext of a film shoot, and then it was like stealing candy from a child. We've taken the manager and other staff into custody and are questioning them, but we doubt any of them are involved.'

'We suspected something like that might have happened, but how did they organize themselves so quickly? How did they know we were going there?'

Murphy sighed heavily. 'Something we've been debating. We think they had a tail on Isakson, a tail so good that he didn't spot it – remember these guys were the gang's A-team. They could've had a bug on Isakson's ride, but we took it apart and didn't find it. The FBI vehicles are searched every day, so a bug is unlikely. Our money is on a tail.'

'They might also be watching this place, and if they are, they'll know you guys are back,' Pizaka added.

Broker thought about the phone in his pocket and the possibility of a call and shook his head. 'We thought about that too. But if they know we've been taken, it's unlikely they'll waste any gangbanger on any more surveillance.'

They fell silent as Chang re-entered the room, nodding at the Commissioner.

'What exactly are you guys working on?' Pizaka couldn't direct this question to Director Murphy, so he smartly addressed it to Broker.

'Need to know. Way above your pay grade,' Broker growled, deliberately insulting him, telling him to shut up in his inimitable way.

Murphy scribbled something on his notepad and tilted it for Forzini to read, who nodded silently.

'Tell them,' Murphy looked at Broker. 'Forzini should know.'

Broker launched into a second narrative, this time shorter, keeping many of the principals out of the picture, and gave them time to digest it, knowing exactly what the next question would be and who from.

Pizaka didn't disappoint him.

'This has worked?'

He looked at Murphy and got a nod in assent. He met Murphy's gaze and recounted everything, right from the events in Arizona. He felt Chloe, sitting beside him, tense minutely and relax. *I've held back mentioning the messaging system described by Shattner, and she noticed it. Until we know who the mole is, that bit is not becoming public knowledge.*

'We narrowed the thirty names to a smaller set, and then we found an anomaly. An agent whose pattern changed ever since he was working on this case.'

'Who?' Murphy had gone still, his eyes fierce and hard.

'Floyd Wheat.' Broker explained his habits and how they correlated to the dud busts.

'These guys' – nodding at Bwana and Roger – 'were heading to the café when they were attacked. They got out of that jam, and then when Isakson told us about this ice deal, we put the café on hold to see how this deal panned out.'

'We busted that deal, though.' Chang being Mr. Obvious.

'Yeah. But Wheat didn't know you were planning to. He's been away for a month due to some knee injury and has been cut off from the information flow.'

Broker could see the Director writing Wheat's name on his pad, his pen digging deep in the paper, willing it to reach out and hurt him.

There was warm appreciation in his eyes when he'd composed himself. 'Clare said she'd trust you with her life. Or her career. Now I know why.' He nodded at himself. 'Now we'll get the bastard. We'll pick this thread from here and tear him and his life apart.'

Chloe tapped her watch, looking at Broker. He brought out Hamm's phone and placed it on the table. 'There's more,' he said.

The call came an hour later, this time from another mobile number.

Broker put it on speaker and held the phone up for the NYPD geeks to note the number and start tracing it.

There was silence from the caller, dead silence, not even breathing. Broker allowed the silence to last for a minute before breaking it. 'Yo, Scheafer, this is your friendly neighborhood Broker. I guess you've heard of me. You know this go-silent thing of yours was aped by Hamm. You must've been a real hero to him. Yeah, that's right. Hamm *was,* not is. Guy's rotting away in a NYPD morgue now. Overrated if you ask me. Oh, that was a neat trick at the hotel, but here we still are, and there he is.'

The silence continued. He looked at the tech guys, and they shook their head.

'You're down now how many chapter heads? Two, right? And the Russians are taking back territory. Didn't Hamm tell you there was an easy way to end this? Just tell us who your inside guy is.'

Scheafer hung up.

'Got anything?' Forzini barked at his men.

They shook their heads in frustration. 'One of those voice over IP calls.'

Forzini pounded the table in anger.

'We've enough to crack this now,' Murphy said mildly, calming him, knowing Forzini's desire to strike back.

'Director, did Isakson discuss the other matter with you?' Broker asked Murphy softly.

'Rocka and the kids?'

'Yes, sir.'

'That'll be taken care of,' Murphy said, and Broker sighed in relief inside. They had demanded that Elaine Rocka and her wards be placed in witness protection and the damage to her house be compensated. 'The danger to her doesn't go away even after we nail the mole. The gang could come after them. New identities and a new start for them is the least you can do,' he'd told Isakson.

'What now for you guys?' Murphy asked them a few hours later after they'd finished with Chang and Pizaka.

'We'll use our powers of persuasion on Scheafer.'

'Broker.' The Commissioner's voice rang out as they headed out. Broker turned, saw Forzini glance at his companions, gave a slight nod to them, and stepped forward, walking alongside him deeper in the building.

'Rolando's a good friend of yours?' Forzini asked him, fully knowing his answer. 'I'm godfather to his daughter. Lovely girl, going to Stanford this year. His wife makes the best pasta, but don't tell my better half.'

Broker kept silent, letting him take his time, form his words.

'Pizaka and Chang are good cops. They know how modern policing works. They'll go far.' He stopped, looking up and down the corridor they were in, empty but for them. He placed a hand on Broker's shoulder, a hand that had turned to a fist earlier. 'Me, deep down, I'm old school.' He looked searchingly in Broker's eyes, nodded once, and walked away.

'What?' the others asked when Broker joined them.

'We got carte blanche.'

Chapter 41

Shawn threw himself at Broker and Roger when they – showered, shaved, smelling nice – met the family in another anonymous apartment. He bumped fists with both of them, and when Lisa kissed them on the cheek, Roger grinned. 'Whoa, princess, that's some welcome.'

She looked at them seriously. 'My dad calls me that. Have you found him?'

'We're working on it, honey,' Broker told her, signaling Rocka with his eyes.

She understood, led them away and, when they were alone, asked in her direct manner, 'He's dead, isn't he?'

They nodded; Roger went on to tell her everything that had happened since they'd found his last page. Silence fell like a weight on them, the distant laughter of the children accentuating it. Pieter glanced in when he felt the quietness, nodded in understanding, and left them alone.

Elaine Rocka drew a deep breath, her eyes bright. 'It won't be over till you find this guy, will it?'

'Ma'am, for you and the kids, the gang remains a threat whatever happens. But there's a way out of this for you all to lead normal lives.'

Broker explained how WITSEC, the Witness Security Program, worked and what it would mean to their lives, but stopped when she smiled briefly and held a hand up.

'You forget, I work in the mayor's office. I know about this. Has this been signed off by the Commissioner, the FBI?' she said tartly.

'Yes, ma'am. We'll need to complete lots of formalities, but it's all done.'

She stood up abruptly. 'Do it. My babies need to get their childhood back.' She stalked away, a lioness protecting her brood.

'Remind me never to cross her.' Broker looked wryly at Roger as they left.

'It can't be done. Not unless you mount a full frontal attack and cut off the rear. We need a small army for that,' Bear said when they returned. 'Of course, Bwana and I are the equivalent of two armies' – he winked – 'but we'll need more than that.'

They were studying Kelleher's home in Queens, a mere ten-bedroom residence with a swimming pool and a surrounding wall. They were going to keep relentlessly on the gang till something gave, and the chapter head of Queens was their next target.

Broker drummed his fingers, going through their options. 'Let's try out some toys.'

They split up, taking three cars; Broker – shrugging off Bwana's look that asked, *Just how stinking filthy rich are you?* – led them.

He took them to an office block, with a basement parking lot, a corner of which was a tennis-court-sized walled-off block with shutters. Broker entered a code at the door, swung it open, flipped on the lights and gestured grandly.

One section of the block was a car mechanic's dream come true – a fully stocked garage housing three Escalades. The garage was not what had them gaping. The remaining section of the block had shelves that ran lengthwise, stocking gadgets and weapons.

Bwana went to one of the shelves and picked a model car – this model was electric and had a spy camera and a recorder fit in it. The device next to it was an inflatable weather balloon, one that conducted surveillance.

He closed his mouth. 'This yours?'

'Yes. Actually the whole building is mine.' He started to say more but held back, looking embarrassed.

'What?' Chloe asked him bemusedly; they had never seen him lost for words.

'It's ours,' he blurted out.

'Say what?' Roger shouted incredulously, his words echoing inside.

Broker shifted on his feet, refusing to meet their gaze. 'It's complicated,' he said finally.

Bwana and Roger pulled four folding chairs for all of them to rest themselves. 'Make it simple, Broker,' Roger said pleasantly, all the time in the world for them to hear Broker's astonishing revelation.

'You remember we rescued that girl in Morocco?'

They nodded, an assignment they remembered well.

They had taken down a terrorist cell in Morocco, and during the mission had discovered a hostage, a young girl who was shared among the men, a girl whose ordeal had turned her mute. They had freed her from the terrorists, wiping out most of them, taking the cell leader alive, and had brought both of them stateside for debriefing.

The cell leader had died during an attempted escape, but the girl had survived, and after two months of healing, medical care and psychiatric attention, she uttered her first words. Words that had a profound and positive impact on the Agency.

The girl turned out to be the daughter of a high-ranking royal in a Middle Eastern country, a country that the US was desperate to have warm relations with. The grateful royal met Clare and presented her with a check that made her raise her eyebrows. 'Shall I increase it?' he asked, reaching for his pen.

'He refused to take the money back, and Clare gave the check to Zeb and me to do as we pleased with it. We formed a company with the six of us as equal owners, invested the money, and a few years back, we bought this, outfitted it' – he waved his hand around – 'and this is it.'

'Why didn't you tell us earlier? Or Zeb, why didn't he?' Chloe regarded him curiously.

'There wasn't a right moment. Bwana and Zeb disappeared on assignments, Bear and you got assigned by Clare... then Zeb died. This is the first assignment we have all been together in a long while.'

'I was also scared,' he said after a pause.

'Of?'

'You guys are my family. I was scared this would alter our relationships with one another.'

He fidgeted under the weight of their gaze, all poise and sophistication deserting him, more nervous than he had ever been. He tightened as Roger stood and glanced at the rest of them and approached him. Behind Roger, Chloe giggled, and then Roger was doubling up, and they were all laughing.

He stared at them and staggered back as Roger punched him in the shoulder.

'For all those brains, you can be amazingly dumb. We *knew* all along about this place; we just didn't know where it was.'

It was Broker's turn to gape at them, his fog clearing as Roger explained, 'Zeb told us about the company and the investment, that time in the Catskills when you guys were camping with the Balthazars. He also told us you had this stupid fear of this impacting us, so we decided to play you along.'

He hugged Broker. 'We don't do this for the money, bro. This doesn't change anything.'

Behind him Chloe nodded vigorously. Roger was speaking for all of them.

'Right, let's see the toy I brought you here for.' Broker returned to form. He reached to the top of a shelf and showed it to them. It had wings, wheels, and various attachments.

'A drone, the latest in countersurveillance, has zoom video, all kinds of hearing gizmos that can hear a fly fart, and night vision. It can stay up for twelve hours, will self-destruct if tampered with, and noiseless from over ten feet away.' He patted it proudly and gestured at five other drones on the shelf. 'We've enough of them and can get more. The manufacturers also supply the NSA and Defense Intelligence Agency.'

Bwana inspected it, looking at the various attachments. 'Will it carry weapons? Can it fire?'

'Nope, too heavy, and remote warfare is not really what we guys are about.'

Kelleher's residence was in a relatively quiet neighborhood nestled snugly in its walled oasis, many large residences in its vicinity. A section of the wall ran along the street, leafy trees bordering it on the inside, carefully pruned to remove any overhang. The wall curved inwards leading to black metal gates, ten feet tall, which opened to a driveway that joined the street.

Most of the house was shielded from the street except for a few high windows.

'You've no other info on this residence? What kind of security? Dogs? Any idea about which businesses this chapter owns or runs? Bars, gas stations, anything?' Bear stroked his beard as he looked at the neighborhood map.

'If I had all those, you think I wouldn't be sharing?' Broker grumped. The chapter had little 'leakage' – information on its places of operation – which was a stark contrast to Hamm's gang. The only alternative available to them was to track Kelleher's movements, find a pattern, and then work out a takedown plan.

They needed to know which wheels he rode in.

A police cruiser whispered down the street at midnight, paused a moment outside the wall, and drove out slowly. If watchful eyes were around, they would've noticed a dark shape rising in the air, disappearing in the shadows of the trees.

That time of the night, the only alert eyes on the street were in the cruiser.

The cruiser crawled away, parking behind a DOT, Department of Transportation, truck that was parked a street away, in a perimeter of traffic cones. Roger hopped out of the cruiser and woke Broker in the truck, the warm smell of coffee enveloping him as the truck's window lowered. The drone could be operated by two pilots, each able to pass control to the other, and Broker's controls flickered to life as he took over. He'd connected the video and audio feeds to his laptop for detailed study.

The cruiser drove a block away and drew to a stop beside a Lincoln Town Car against which two figures were lounging, Tony and Eric. Roger and Bwana swapped vehicles with them and positioned themselves behind a row of parked cars, keeping the entrance to the street in view. At the far end, a similar-looking Town Car kept the exit in view, Bear and Chloe in it.

Broker did an initial pass of the grounds of the house, noting the armed guards with dogs patrolling the perimeter, swung the drone to the rear where the pool lay, its underwater lights splotches on the drone's night vision, moved around the back, noting the garages, tennis courts, and then brought the drone to the front, to the large portico and tall wooden doors, not shut in the night.

383

He counted eight armed guards outside, four of them with dogs, and in the portico, three SUVs, the darkness hiding their make. He had seen a pickup truck in the rear standing alongside a tractor, both near a rear entrance, which he guessed was the service entrance and also a possible exit route for the gang boss.

He sent a text to Bwana and Roger, asking them to check the rear out, giving them directions to the exit.

'The house seems to have twenty people in all, including Kelleher, a girlfriend – who seems to be seminude most of the time – house staff, and then the hitters. Ten of them, eight of whom patrol outside in the night, one acting as driver, and at any time there are three Porsche Cayennes that they use to ferry Kelleher to wherever he has to go to get his gang business done.'

Broker was reading from his notes in the late evening the next day as he grouped with the four of them, Tony and Eric relieving him on the drone, which was back in his truck.

They had spent the whole day monitoring the residence, Broker using the thick foliage of the trees as cover for the drone, Tony relieving him in spells while he rested.

Bear picked up the thread, 'Kelleher went to a strip club at noon, an hour away, spent three hours and then returned and has been holed up in his house ever since. He took the three rides, him in the middle, and had six thugs with him in total.' Chloe and he had followed the cavalcade once they'd exited the residence.

'The interesting thing is he doesn't use the phone much... he has incoming calls, but very few outgoing ones, and when he does, it's all in monosyllables and one-liners. This is one paranoid SOB. They must have learnt something from Cruz and Hamm,' Broker commented, stifling a yawn.

'Let's do this for two more days,' Roger suggested. 'Can your guys get us spare wheels? We don't want to be having the same rides for three days.'

'Do bears shit?' Broker snorted. 'He's already got spares lined up.'

At the end of the third day, they had a few more variables in the picture; Kelleher spent a few hours at a small warehouse the second day, and on the third he went back to the strip joint. He randomly selected a Porsche to seat himself in each day, sometimes the lead vehicle, sometimes the rear, no particular pattern to his choosing. He was away from his residence for four hours a day, but those four hours began anytime from noon to mid-afternoon.

'Those places are where he does business? A warehouse could be a neat cover for his drug distribution,' Chloe thought aloud.

Bear rejected the idea. 'Too obvious. Most likely the gang owns those joints, and he goes there to meet people or to put the fear of the gang in them.'

'Right, question time,' Broker announced. 'Take him down at the residence or at one of those joints? Why not the street?'

They debated the options, keeping in mind that there would be non-principals about at all the locations and the size of the force at the other locations was an unknown.

Bwana gazed at an out-of-state Subaru passing them, the blonde in it giving him a second glance.

'We don't do the takedown,' he said, staring at the Subaru's plates.

They stared at him as if he'd sprouted wings and horns.

'The Russians will do it for us.'

Chapter 42

Broker looked at him, dust particles bouncing off his dark skin, catching the sunlight, haloing him. He considered Bwana's suggestion. *Good idea. Why didn't I think of it?*

He mock-frowned at Bwana. 'We thought you wanted to take them out yourself, grind them into fine powder, and blow that powder away. You sure you aren't growing soft? How can we make it attractive to Oborski, though? While he disposed of Cruz for us, this will be like outright gang war, and while he's not averse to it, he will need a sweetener.'

Chloe remembered the decoy cruiser they'd used. 'If we tell him the cops will stand back? I guess they regard him as the lesser of the two evils?'

He acknowledged her with a salute. 'What I was thinking. Of course, we will have to put it in a different way to the cops. The Russian mob is *still* a gang they have to go after. Let me make some calls. While the Commissioner has given us a free hand, I am sure he wants us to be as subtle as possible and not create mayhem and bloodbath on the streets.'

Getting the Russians to play a hand turned out to be easier than they thought.

Oborski met Broker and Bear in a car wash that wasn't washing cars. It was thick with hard-eyed men with bulges under their shirts and jackets, who stared long at the two of them before a person called out from the office, allowing the two to progress.

Oborski was holding court in the shabby office, the gang boss relaxing in it as if it was the Great Kremlin Palace in Moscow, the Oriental girl incongruous in the surroundings, serving them tea. *If*

387

you are surrounded by ex-Spetsnaz hard men, you can treat any place as a palace, Bear thought.

Oborski regarded them coolly over his cup, smiling sardonically. 'You want us to do your dirty work, *da*?'

'Just helping you get an edge, my boy,' Broker replied in his plumiest accent. He, too, could posture.

'Maybe we don't need your help, *tovarich*,' the Russian replied. They had been planning an attack on 5Clubs once Cruz had been eliminated, and Broker's idea neatly fit in their plans, but he had to play hard to get. A gang boss wasn't a yes-man.

They danced around for another hour before agreeing on a plan, Oborski shrugging when Broker warned him about innocents and collateral damage.

Oborski had wanted to mount an attack on the residence when Broker had shared the surveillance video with him, but Broker had dissuaded him from that. The girlfriend and house staff had no role to play and didn't need to be endangered. Similarly the strip joint and the warehouse had been ruled out, at which Oborski had flung his hands up theatrically. 'You want us to lift him in the air?'

'Something like that.'

Broker nearly missed Kelleher's departure from his residence the day of the takedown, his attention momentarily distracted by a young shapely woman – *That must be New York's Finest Bottom*, he thought – walking past his window, and it was the growling of the engines on his laptop that brought his attention back.

Kelleher boarded the first Porsche and the other two swung behind him, scattering leaves and birds as they roared down the driveway, down the street, to the warehouse.

Behind them a tan Camry and a black Ford slipped in their wake and maintained a steady unobtrusive distance. A couple of lights later, four identical pickup trucks barreled past them, one split and cut in ahead of the lead Porsche, one slipped to their left, another to their right, in the neighboring lanes, and the last one slipped behind them.

Two other trucks slipped behind the ones on the left and the right, completing the box.

The trucks kept pace with the gang's vehicles, refusing to give way despite their repeated honking, staying in their lane, making other traffic bend around the mobile trap.

Lights came and went, and at one of them, a hood jumped out from the second Porsche, ran to the pickup nearest to him, slammed his hand against the raised window, and ran back when the lights changed. The pickup's dark window hadn't lowered.

At the next signal, a couple of hoods ran out and banged on the windows of the trucks in vain. The drivers of the trucks wore shades, scarves masking their lower faces, and stared straight ahead, ignoring the rage and fear beside them.

Two miles down, a Ford Mustang came roaring up, bristling with hoods, and fell behind the last pickup, and just as a head nosed out a window, three other trucks boxed it in from the side and behind.

By now traffic was giving them a wide berth, the Camry and Ford the only vehicles sticking to their tail, the only direction for the box to move, straight ahead.

Bwana smiled, a feral baring of teeth. 'Spetsnaz, huh? No wonder. How do you think this will end?'

Roger yawned mightily as he steadied the wheel. Action that didn't involve them bored him. 'Dark street or empty street, gun battle, the Porsches turned to broken glass.'

They followed a few more miles, saw that the box held despite various attempts to break it by the hitters, and when they reached the outskirts of an industrial area, they peeled off.

'Never to see them again,' came Chloe's voice over their satellite phones.

'Gang warfare,' screamed various headlines the next day as Broker consumed the daily papers with great relish. Bwana looked at him and the silent TV running in the background. 'You ever thought of negotiating a deal with these vultures? We're helping them sell. Feels like we oughta take a percentage of that.'

Broker hushed him up and read aloud, 'Anonymous sources say 5Clubs are holding something of value, which has caused the recent attacks on them.'

'Job done.' He smiled.

Exactly a week later, the message was acknowledged.

The next day, they were in Southport, Chloe guiding them to the site of her rescue past the abandoned buildings that even time had neglected. She pointed out where they'd been held captive, the locations of the hoods, and described the shoot-out and rescue.

They walked to the side of the building. Bwana ran his eyes down its length and up its height, saw the barrel still on its side, lifted it easily and set it upright, away from the force of the wind. Roger and he walked to the back of the building and surveyed it.

'Time me,' Bwana said and ran down the back of the site, around its far end, and then down the front to the main entrance, joining them from the other side.

They looked at the stopwatch in Roger's hand, and Chloe nodded. 'Feels right, but he didn't come round this end. He fired from the rear, then from the entrance, and then just vanished.'

She led them to brown stains inside the building. 'I noticed these when they brought us in, didn't pay much attention to it. Other matters were uppermost in my mind,' she said drily.

'Could be Shattner's,' Roger said. 'No way to tell, not without a forensic test. Diego told us this was their trading hub and also killing ground, so wouldn't be surprised if there were many such stains on the site.'

They walked to the waterfront and looked over the vast expanse of the Delaware River, hues of blue and green in the water, the entire area deserted but for them.

'Ideal spot for crime. Nothing happens here, no one comes here, except for joggers and the odd dog walker,' Broker commented as they looked around. He sighed. 'The bastards said they had weighed down his body and dumped it in the middle of the river, by boat. The river is about thirty feet deep, and nothing much would be left by now.'

Broker had asked the Commissioner to recover the body so that Shattner could be buried properly and more importantly with honor. Forzini had said he would burn the lines to his counterparts in New Jersey and get it done, but burning wires still took time, and bureaucratic red tape burnt slower.

It was dark when Bwana slipped out of their house, walked a couple of blocks, and as he was flagging a cab, he felt another presence by his shoulder. Roger.

'You didn't think I would let you have all the fun alone, did you?' The Texan's smile lit the night as he caught Bwana's answering grin.

Snarky had passed one last message to Broker before he had left the city to inflict his singing on another unaware town. Brownsville Autos was back in gang business, on a smaller scale, and the hood that had taken Cruz's place was a dirty piece of shit – Snarky's words – called Rajek.

Bwana and Roger had no specific plan in mind other than checking out the garage, but if they met any gangbangers, they would be welcomed with relish. A cab and a subway ride brought them three blocks away from the garage, and by the time they reached it, it was past bedtime for most residents of the city.

Gangbangers weren't like most ordinary residents, and the garage had lights burning, and they could see shadows crossing the lighted windows.

Bwana positioned himself beneath a streetlight outside the exit of the garage, leaned against an abandoned car, and waited. The wait went to midnight – for some reason gangbangers preferred the dark hours – when the garage turned dark, engines fired, and the first of three vehicles nosed out of the exit.

The first vehicle's beams illuminated Bwana for a few seconds as it roared away; then the second one bathed him in its lights and drew away. The third one slowed and stopped, leaving its lights on Bwana. A head cranked out of the passenger window, beetled brows furrowed in disbelief as the man took in the sight of Bwana standing nonchalantly in the light. The head disappeared. Bwana couldn't see against the light but could imagine excited chatter, heated swearing, and heads popped out again, doors opened, and four men spilled out wielding M4s.

Bwana raised his arms, prompting yells, the barrels turning toward him, and then the first crack sounded, and the gangbanger with the leveled rifle fell. The second crack took out the one on the passenger side, the cracks rolling and blending into one another, and from behind the vehicle, a louder report sounded, the rear window disappearing in spidery pieces, another roar put down the driver, and silence fell. Bwana looked at the fallen coldly, knowing the damage armor-piercing bullets did. *Ten seconds too quick, should've burned you bastards with a flame thrower first*, he thought.

He drifted back in the shadow, joined Roger on the other side of the street, and they walked away without a second glance. They heard the approaching sound of rapid footsteps behind them, and they still didn't turn. From the tread and timing, they knew who it was.

Bear came abreast of them. 'You bastards. You could've told me what you'd planned before slipping away.' He grinned and took out his gun. 'First time I've fired this, though I had heard about it. Nice weapon.' He handed the Grach back to Bwana and noticed the one in Roger's hand. 'You no longer a Kimber man now?'

Roger snorted. 'These pieces of shit are good for about a hundred rounds or so before they become useless pieces of steel. Russian-made stuff, what can you expect?'

A week after the Russians' box, they saw Broker approaching them as they were cleaning their weapons. Broker was wearing a beatific expression, almost floating in the air.

'St. Peters called you and confirmed a seat in heaven for you?' Bwana asked him sarcastically.

'Better,' Broker replied, the barb not even registering.

'They got Floyd Wheat.

'Dead,' he added.

Chapter 43

'Dead?' Bear asked stupidly.

'Yeah, you heard me right the first time. Cops found his body floating in the river, a hole in his head and a large part of his face missing, but enough to make him by his dentures and prints. Forzini told me they'd been keeping an eye on him, but he gave them the slip a couple of days back. Looks like he was summoned?'

'You think...?'

'Damn right I do, and thank God for that. One of us should, don't ya think?'

Chloe rolled her eyes and took up the cudgel. 'The gang did it? That would be confirming that he was their mole, wouldn't it?'

'That was sorta the point.' Broker leant back expansively, crossed his hands over his middle, and closed his eyes, a contented man.

Bwana and Roger looked at each other, thinking of their next camping trip. Bear caught their glance and laughed. 'Not so fast, guys. We still have unfinished business here. The family needs to be resettled, and then you guys can head for the hills. Broker, how're Rolando and Isakson doing? Plumb forgot about them.'

'Isakson's discharged and is up and about. I need to see him and wrap this up. Rolando is making a good recovery, still in the hospital, though. He'll be disappointed that this was over before he got back to the job.'

'We never figured out why Wheat turned traitor, did we?' Chloe mused.

Bear patted her arm. 'Let Isakson do some of the heavy lifting. They asked us to find their mole; we did that—'

'I've been thinking about that for some time,' Broker cut in. 'Traitors do their dirty work because of ideology, money, or because of coercion. I think we can rule out ideology in Wheat's case. Going by all the records Isakson has, the psych evaluations, he was a believer in law, hated gangs. Coercion — he didn't have anyone close to him to be coerced. Divorced, no kids, a mother, but he wasn't close to her, no other siblings. I guess money was involved, but we haven't been able to find any traces of money in his account. Of course, he could've been stacking wads of it in some hidey hole, in which case we'll never know. Cash is a bitch to track.'

'Or maybe he did it because he could. Got a kick out of it,' Bwana said.

Broker shrugged. 'That's the most difficult spy to unearth. The one who spies just because it gives him a trip. In any case, this is Isakson's shit to clean now.'

He rose and grumped at them, 'While you all enjoy the sun, I've got to bed things down with Pieter and Derek. We'll take over the family now and move back to my apartment.'

'What if Wheat wasn't acting alone?' Chloe called out.

'Isakson's problem. We were tasked with finding one mole; we gave them the bastard. If the whole danged FBI is infested, we can't do much,' Broker said over his shoulder.

Dupont Circle was throbbing with traffic and tourists, bright sun bathing the wide, clean streets. Broker grimaced. *They must have cleaned up just because I was coming.* It was hard, very hard to accept, but grudgingly he had to admit the city was cleaner than NYC. 'Of course, it's the capital; it would have to be clean,' he muttered to himself, drawing a curious look from a passerby. In New York, he would've shown the finger; over here, he smiled forcedly.

General Klouse was waiting for him, lounging outside the café, his security detail hanging around nervously, not comfortable with the National Security Advisor's presence in an open location. Broker grinned at their discomfort, recognizing a fellow maverick in the General.

He'd been to meet Director Murphy, who'd been relieved that their problem had been resolved, but also grimly determined to ensure his agency remained clean. He'd offered Broker a very senior position in the agency, to work with his intelligence people, an offer Broker had politely declined. He'd said he was too much of a nonconformist to fit into a rigid structure, smiling to take the sting out of his words. The Director had nodded in acceptance, expecting just such a response.

'No luck with the drones, sir,' Broker told him once he'd updated the General. The General would've been briefed by Director Murphy, but Broker felt obligated to bring him up to speed, since it was the National Security Advisor that had started the ball rolling.

'Chatter has gone silent for some time, in any case.' The NSA gave him his thousand-yard stare and smiled grimly at his companion. 'This isn't a business where we can relax, is it?'

Broker kept quiet, knowing no answer was required.

'I have told Clare we might need your help from time to time. Will that be a problem?'

'No, sir. If Clare is good, we're good too.' He paused. 'I don't work alone. I've a team.'

'Yeah, I heard about them. They the ones who tore up New York, right?' The General laughed for the first time. 'Commissioner Murphy was impressed… other than a few damaged vehicles and some angry media, you guys succeeded in cutting a gang in half.'

'Our advantage is we work in the shadows; we have fewer constraints,' Broker said modestly.

'You've made up with Isakson? He's an upcoming star, and a lot of eyes are on him.'

Broker didn't hide his distaste. 'I'm seeing him later today; he's in town. I'm sure he's a good agent, sir, but it's unlikely we'll be on each other's Christmas card lists. We're too different. Director Murphy now… he's as good as family.'

Broker made his way back to the J. Edgar Hoover Building and held himself back from jaywalking, reminding himself that this was a different town. They did things differently here. The ugly structure gladdened him; they didn't have such monstrosities in his city.

Isakson's warm smile belied his hollow and gaunt appearance, the shape of the dressings beneath his crisp white shirt visible.

'How does it feel coming back from the dead, Deputy Director?' Broker greeted him.

Isakson smiled wryly. 'I was in no danger of dying... Deputy Commissioner Rolando – now *he's* a fighter. I hear he's doing well. Been to see him?'

Rolando had been Broker's first stop once Wheat's body had been found. The cop had gripped his hand firmly and whispered, 'Looks like it was all worth it, Joe. The Commissioner was telling me all I had to do was lie here longer and you guys would clean up the city.'

Broker squeezed his hand, remembering a time in Mogadishu when Rolando and he, both attached to the Rangers, were jammed behind an abandoned car, exchanging fire with insurgents. It was during that tour that Zeb had saved his life. Rolando and Zeb were the only two who knew his real name.

Broker looked around Isakson's bare office, similar to the one in New York except for another print of the conquest of Mount Everest, this time Edmund Hillary atop it. 'You've got this at home too? You into climbing?'

'It's the conquest that interests me. Besides, that date and year have a significance for me.' He didn't elaborate. 'Wheat – the Director and Commissioner briefed me about your findings; we'll now rip his life apart and see what drove him to this. We owe you.' He gripped Broker's hand again.

'Mrs. Rocka and the kids?' he asked.

'They're back at my apartment. My guys are with them. How're things progressing with rebuilding their new lives?'

'I'll meet them and brief them in person on how this works, and then the Marshals will step in and take over,' he replied. Witness Protection was run by the US Marshals Service, and the FBI had no role to play in building new lives. 'You'll let them know I'll be coming?'

Broker nodded, and after another hour of discussions, he caught an evening flight back out of Reagan Airport.

It was when he was passing a bookstore at JFK, that a book cover caught his attention – a drawing of Gunnery Sergeant Carlos Hathcock, the most successful sniper in the Vietnam War.

Broker knew the story of Hathcock, the most famous Marine Corps sniper who broke just about every shooting record when he was in the Corps and won the Wimbledon Cup, the US Long Range High Power Championship.

Hathcock had 93 confirmed, witnessed kills in Vietnam, but he himself believed he had taken out upward of 300 enemy personnel.

Broker stopped and stared at the cover as it dug something deep in his mind and brought up images of marksmen, shooting distances, targets, and positions and close-range shooting. That thing in his mind that made connections between random events and discovered logic and reason and purpose, brought up numbers, and suddenly everything fell in place.

He remained oblivious of his surroundings for long seconds, the curses of passengers behind him lost in the air. He started jogging, then sprinting, and reached the exit and searched for a cab, all the while trying various numbers on his sat phone and finally got through one.

'Tony,' he shouted, 'get—'

A black van wheeled in front of him, its doors swung open, and Broker bitterly realized he was outwitted when he saw muzzles pointed at him.

The gunmen, masked and silent, snatched his phone, thumbed it off, and drove him to his apartment block. They whipped off their masks when they reached it and prodded him to the entrance, past his security code at the main entrance, up the passkey-coded elevator, and up to his floor.

He didn't recognize any of them, but recognized the build and their moves – they were the gang's best hitters, experienced mercenaries who'd joined the gang. He stood in front of his apartment door, ferociously thinking of ways out, hoping beyond hope that the one factor he was counting on turned out right, when a blow to his head from behind brought him to his knees. He was grabbed by his shirt and pulled upwards, his vision darkening, and a gun jabbed in his ribs. The message was clear, he had to disarm the security on his door and enter it.

A split second of hesitation and he was hit again, harder, almost losing consciousness, and pulled up again, the gun ramming harder in him. With shaky fingers, he entered the code, swiped his finger, and looked in the eye scanner, and the door swung open.

He was flung inside, stumbling, and when he looked up, despair flooded him.

The four of them were there in front of him, all bunched close together, several heavies behind them. Bwana and Roger had gone out, and he'd been hoping against hope that they hadn't returned yet and would be the rescue team. He saw Bwana shrug in resignation at his glance, and both Roger and Bwana fell as rifle butts hit them.

Another hood brought Broker to his knees with a rifle. Dimly, he heard a voice yelling at them, 'Don't fucking move a muscle.'

He coughed, a ribbon of blood spooling from his lips, sagged back as he was pulled up, and jerked once as cold water was poured over his face. He retched drily, wiped his face with his shirt, and breathed deeply, sight returning to him slowly. Bwana was still on his knees, though the hitters had stopped raining kicks and blows on him, his breathing loud and harsh in the silence of the room.

There were six hitters behind the four; Rocka and the kids were to the right of them. Lisa and Shawn were in shock, their eyes wide and blank, mercifully not comprehending the events before them. Beyond them, Broker saw the lighted skyline of the city through the darkened glass wall of his apartment.

There was one hitter with his gun aimed at the family, two behind Broker, nine heavies in all. Bwana, Roger, Chloe and Bear were not tied or restrained in any way, but were bunched so close together that any aggressive action was impossible.

Soft footsteps sounded, and a huge man glided into view, wearing a sports jacket over a tight T-shirt and jeans, his litheness of movement belying his size, a panther on the prowl, his hawk eyes inspecting the scene before him, a thin smile breaking on his lips when they lighted on Broker.

'Broker, I presume,' he said in a cultured voice. Scheafer, born and battle-hardened in Kosovo, had acquired a cultured accent and had slowed down the pace of his delivery. Murderer, rapist, thug, killer, and torturer, he might be, but who said refined speech didn't go along with that job.

'You've decimated half my gang. What I built in five years reduced to a fraction in less than a year,' he said, a savage expression crossing his face. 'It all ends today, though.'

'Maybe not for all of you,' he said, glancing at Chloe. 'This little one, now, I just might keep. That other one' – he nodded in Elaine Rocka's direction – 'is too old. No use for her.'

She looked at him steadily, her voice clear and firm. 'On the farm we used to put down rabid dogs and foxes. Your mother should've put you down at birth.' She fell heavily as he stepped to her and slapped her savagely.

'Bitch. In Kosovo, women knew their place. Fucking and children. That's all their purpose was. In your country, you've been given too much freedom.' He glared at her for a moment and turned back to Broker.

'Why're you here? Any of your thugs could've killed us,' Broker asked him, asking him anything to buy time. He didn't have a plan, *they* didn't have a plan, but every minute they bought gave them an opportunity to think of one.

'I brought him,' a new voice replied, and a figure stepped into view behind Scheafer, a hand on his shoulder.

A figure they knew very well.

Chapter 44

Deputy Director Isakson.

His professional façade was replaced by an air of contempt as he surveyed them all, his eyes flicking over all of them before swinging back to Broker.

Broker realized how it must've gone down. Isakson's presence at the apartment would have lowered the alertness of Bear and Chloe, with the Fed probably presenting Scheafer as a Marshal to them. Scheafer's men would've swiftly entered the apartment, overpowering them, and when Bwana and Roger entered, they would've been felled by the concealed heavies.

'You don't seem very surprised to see me,' Isakson sneered at him. 'Your guys, on the other hand... I think they're still not believing it.'

Roger and Bear turned their burning eyes on him, underlining his comment.

Broker answered him slowly. 'For a traitor, you did everything right, better than Hanssen. You probably wouldn't have been made.' He fought the urge to launch himself at Isakson and ram his smirk down his throat.

'I was at the airport, and it was a book cover that made the connection for me. I realized Hamm's gunman at the hotel couldn't have *missed* you, shouldn't have missed your heart or head. You were a couple of steps ahead of Rolando, closer to the gunman and just ten feet away from him. At that range, those shots weren't a lucky accident, not when Rolando's shots were more lethal.'

Isakson was silent, and after a pause Broker continued. 'The bullets went where they were intended to – your shoulder, injuring you, but not fatally. Rolando, on the other hand, got lucky. When I met him at the hospital, he said he'd stumbled just at the moment your gunman shot him – that saved him. Of course, then, I didn't attach any significance to his words.

'Then the poster and print of Mount Everest in your two offices – you had some fascination for that conquest. But it wasn't just that, was it? Everest was conquered in nineteen fifty-three, a year divisible by nine. The four digits added are divisible by nine. Twenty-ninth of May. Two, nine and five. Their product is divisible by nine. There are so many links to the number nine in that date that they should've jumped out and slapped me in the face the first day I met you.'

Broker grinned at Isakson through his split lips as he saw the FBI man's face tighten.

'Shattner's journal had one more page that we didn't share with you, since we didn't trust the FBI or the cops. That page referred to the "nine" the gang used to access messages. You probably made that code on the spot as you leant back in your office and your gaze fell on the date.'

He grinned wider when Isakson didn't respond, his silence acknowledging Broker's deduction.

'Why? You're the second most powerful man in the FBI? Why, you bastard?' Roger asked him, and if eyes could set fire, Isakson would've been ashes.

Isakson laughed. 'That's the most common question heard in law enforcement. You overrated assholes, I became the second most powerful man in the FBI just because of this.' He gazed scathingly at Roger.

'I came across Scheafer many years back, before he started the gang, during a drug raid. He was hiding in the garage, and I was the only agent to see him. We had a few words, and his proposal intrigued me enough that I let him go. I figured I had nothing to lose, and truth to say, I had already contemplated this idea. I didn't really think he would get in touch again, but he did, and from there, my career took off. I "busted" some deals of his, and in return I made sure we looked the other way when he wanted me to. It worked for both of us.'

He smiled arrogantly. 'You stupid fools, we played you all along. Wheat was *meant* to be found. He was a crooked agent, turned by Hamm, but the way we set up our drops with him, he was our decoy, and you guys fell into that trap. You'll find the floorboards of his home and car stuffed with cash. His Laundromat was where he collected the gang's cash. It was so simple that no one got it. Go in with dirty laundry, come out with clean laundry wrapped around his payment.'

'If that's the case, why this? Wheat is dead. There was no need for you to out yourself to us,' Broker asked as he edged closer to the two thugs behind him. Closer reduced the chances of gun use.

Scheafer snapped, 'We couldn't risk that you hadn't stop digging. I've never underestimated my enemies. That's why I'm alive, they're dead.' He glared at Isakson. 'Enough of this show and tell.'

He turned to bark orders to his henchmen and paused when Broker held his hand up. 'How'll you explain our deaths? There are too many powerful people who know about us and our involvement in this. They won't rest till they get to the bottom of our deaths.'

Isakson gave a chilling smile. 'I'll personally lead the investigation. I'll never rest till I find out who your killers are.'

He nodded at Scheafer, putting distance between them.

The glass wall shattered with a tremendous explosion, and a wave of air blasted in.

Something clattered on the floor, a voice shouted out, 'Flash-bang,' and the four of them threw themselves to the floor.

Chloe hurled herself sideways, bringing down Rocka and the kids, and covered them with her body. *We know this drill. We train in this manner*, she thought.

Isakson and the gang squeezed their eyes shut, bracing their body for the explosion, some of them covering their ears.

The five of them alone saw the masked, black-suited figure rolling in a split second behind the exploding glass.

The figure knelt, and two spits rang out from his shoulder, bringing down the hitters behind Broker.

The figure moved, and a shadow blurred through the air.

Chloe expertly caught the Sig, reversed it in one fluid motion, and took out the hitter over her.

The best of the Special Ops or SEALs have reaction and response times measured in fractions of seconds, training and combat honing them to knife-edge perfection.

The hitters were good, but their reflexes were dulled, and the deception slowed them down further.

By the time Scheafer had realized and opened his mouth to shout, Bwana, Roger and Bear were engaged with six of his men, hurling themselves underneath their rifle lines, Bwana flying horizontal, a fist going deep into a thug's midriff, doubling him over, almost going *through* him, his feet crunching the groin of the one next to him.

He smashed the head of Midriff on the floor so hard that the glass in the room trembled.

He rolled over on top of him, snatched the dead man's M4 and, holding it like a pistol, fired it point- blank in Groin's head, then took out two more hitters who were pointing their guns at Bear.

Still lying on the dead man's head, he swung the rifle on the remaining two thugs, and saw Bear and Roger had them well under control.

Bear had similarly gone under another hitter's rifle, and had grabbed it by the barrel and pulled it *toward* his own body, catching the man by surprise.

The gangbanger stumbled forward, and Bear used the momentum to strike under his chin.

One hundred and eighty pounds of Bear, all hard muscle and rock, met an unprotected chin. No contest.

Roger dispatched his hitter even quicker.

He struck lightning fast, using the momentum of the upward swinging rifle against the hitter.

His hand caught the barrel and flung it *up* and into the face of the sixth man, breaking his nose, and head-butted him into unconsciousness.

He winked at Bear, and they turned on Isakson.

Isakson was down, out of action.

Broker had staggered to his feet and had thrown himself at Isakson, wrenching away the FBI agent's gun from its shoulder holster.

All this before Isakson had realized there was no stun grenade, and by the time comprehension returned to him, Broker had hammered him on his chest and over his wound till Isakson lay bleeding and unconscious.

Scheafer was quicker and faster, a lifetime of war and danger bringing out the animal in him.

He spun toward the black-clad figure, his gun arm straightening, and staggered back and fell as a block of concrete – the Watcher's spinning kick – smashed into his head.

He crawled back, then whirled suddenly and grabbed and pulled Elaine Rocka as a shield in front of him.

He wiped his face on her shoulder, baring his teeth in triumph as he saw the Watcher sheath his gun.

He reached down his side to pull his blade from its ankle sheath, but she saw her chance in the split second his attention had diverted, and she sagged suddenly, letting him bear her weight.

Off-balance for a second, he let her fall, and then the Watcher was on him, raining a hammer fist on his right shoulder, numbing it, and another hammer broke his nose, spraying them both with blood.

The Watcher's left leg swung up and kicked Scheafer in the groin, and as the gang leader doubled over, another hammer fist slammed in the back of his neck.

Scheafer roared and bulled into the Watcher, head-butting him in his midriff, and his massive hands wrapped around the Watcher and squeezed like a vice, his barrel body exerting inexorable pressure.

The Watcher stepped backward to throw him off, raining blows on his back, but his heel tripped against Elaine Rocka's ankle, and he fell, twisting his body at the last minute so that they fell away from her.

Scheafer fell on top of him but didn't let go of his grip and, while falling, kneed the Watcher in the groin.

Scheafer pounced on the Watcher's upper body like a cat and pinned his right hand with his left hand the size of a bear's paw.

Simultaneously with a sinuous move, he pulled his knife and struck it at the fallen man's chest.

The Watcher desperately blocked his knife arm with his left, the two men straining, sweat and blood dripping off Scheafer and painting the fallen man's face.

The Watcher kicked up with his legs to dislodge Scheafer, but the 5Clubs leader held firm, his weight an immovable stone on the supine man's midriff.

Scheafer hissed, 'Now you die,' and put all his body behind his knife hand, his eyes glittering as they bored holes in the Watcher's eyes staring back through the mask.

The Watcher strained desperately, trying to free his mind from the white heat of the groin pain, trying to compartmentalize his ribs being crushed by Scheafer, felt his left arm give a millimeter, and then another millimeter, and felt Scheafer's mouth go wide as he scented victory.

He focused on the pain and wrapped it in a ball and made it smaller and smaller and then shaped it into a point and flung it deep inside where life and death began, and lanced the ball of fire within.

The ball exploded, drowning out the pain, and the fire streamed through him, and he sagged back suddenly, his left arm going slack, and Scheafer fell forward on top of him, his knife point piercing the Watcher's black skin suit.

Scheafer suddenly lost his smile and his eyebrows creased as the knife encountered resistance, the customized body armor underneath the Watcher's skin suit blunting its cutting.

The Watcher reared forward and head-butted Scheafer.

He followed it with another vicious head butt that split the attacker's right eyebrow, and blood flowed thickly down Scheafer's face.

Scheafer howled as the Watcher freed his right arm and struck his eye, another hammer-fist blow crushed his ear, a rapid double blow to his eyes took away his vision, and he fell sideways.

The black-suited man slithered from underneath Scheafer and gripped his knife wrist in steel and twisted and turned it around, breaking the joint, and his free hand clamped on Scheafer's neck.

He felt the ball of fire flow through him to his extremities, through his shoulders, down his arms and to his hand gripping Scheafer's knife wrist. The knife reversed deep into Scheafer, all one smooth fluid motion.

The Watcher leaned forward and whispered, 'I've been dead a long time.'

Bwana looked on awestruck – the two figures had been fighting so closely and so rapidly that they hadn't risked a shot at Scheafer.

He glanced quickly at his companions and saw the same expression on their faces.

When he turned back, the masked man had risen to his feet.

He looked back at them, his eyes dark and expressionless through his mask.

The city peered over his shoulder through the broken window, holding its breath, and time slowed, even the breeze slowed.

The Watcher took a step back toward the gaping hole, his gaze steady on them.

'Wait, who are…?' Broker's words were lost in a loud explosion as the entrance disintegrated, and a NYPD ESU team broke in.

When they looked back, the Watcher had gone, and through the shattered glass, the lights of the city winked at them mockingly.

Chapter 45

'Who is he?' they demanded.

It took three days for them to wrap up with the cops and the FBI.

Three days during which they went through the events over and over again with Pizaka, Chang, and Forzini.

Three days during which Isakson turned from arch villain to innocent and then back to traitor.

Director Murphy went through phases of rage and disbelief, with a constant undercurrent of shock.

Isakson was handpicked by him and was his number two. His being a traitor was a bitter pill to swallow.

They made Broker walk through his putting together the jigsaw at the airport and made him go through the chain of events – his satellite phone call to Tony, who'd listened in for as long as the line was open and realized what was transpiring and who then had placed calls to Clare, who in turn had lit a fire under the cops.

Pizaka and Chang pressed hard for Broker to reveal the mysteries of his entrance door, asked him how a simple code could disable all its security and render it into an ordinary New York apartment door and thereby make a forced entry easier.

Broker gave them an *in your dreams* look.

Isakson had suffered no damage other than heavy bleeding and had been interrogated separately by the FBI and the cops, and he'd mounted a vigorous defense: 'delusional, vested agenda, revenge' were words he used frequently.

Broker was stumped when it came to Isakson.

They'd no evidence to support his claim that Isakson was the traitor. Any competent lawyer would laugh out of court his charge against the FBI man.

Floyd Wheat's apartment had been broken into, and the money found as Isakson had said, but he explained it away saying that he'd investigated the agent once Murphy had told him about Broker's uncovering him.

Broker could see the doubt creeping in Director Murphy's eyes on the second day as Isakson hammered the point that they were out to get him for Zeb's death.

Commissioner Forzini was more receptive, but he, too, needed proof to act.

The hooded man remained a mystery no one could shed light on.

Clare shrugged when Murphy pressed her about his identity, and said she knew no one of that description. She let the steel in her show just once when Pizaka and Chang asked her again.

In the late evening on the second day, a bicycle courier delivered a package addressed to Director Murphy, and two other packages were similarly delivered to Commissioner Forzini and Broker.

Later, they questioned the courier, but the description he gave was so generic that it could've fitted several million men in the city.

Each of the packages had a memory stick that contained an audio and a video file. The files filled Murphy with such a raging fury that it was said his office looked like a hurricane had gone through it.

He had a short call with Forzini that ended with, 'If I could throw the bastard into Gitmo, I would.'

When Broker viewed the file with the others, he shouted, 'Holy shit.'

The audio file captured everything that had happened in his apartment right from the time Isakson entered it to the ghost's exit. The video file covered the events till the time the glass wall shattered, the explosion disabling the camera.

The files sealed Isakson's fate.

They inspected the window carefully, Bwana leaning out dangerously, and even though they knew what to look for, the bugs and cameras took them half an hour to locate; their size and color were such that they blended perfectly in the remaining glass.

When they'd recovered and disabled them, they went to the roof after having worked out how the ghost could've planted them.

The scaffolding rig was still in place, and Roger, lying prone on the roof, could just see the broken window far below amidst the smooth glass wall. 'Son of a bitch,' he said admiringly. 'All that security shit you've got, and he comes up with such a simple idea,' he told Broker.

Broker shook his head ruefully. The ghost had won his admiration long back.

The Marshals came and patiently endured the long wait Broker subjected them to as he checked and triple-checked their credentials. The first step to securing new identities for Rocka and the children was taken.

The children started counseling sessions with a reputed psychiatrist, the same one who had helped Rory Balthazar. The family would assume their new identities and new life once the counseling sessions ran their course.

Elaine Rocka glared at them when Chloe had suggested she undergo a few sessions herself, saying her only regret was that the ghost hadn't castrated Scheafer before killing him. She'd turned her eyes cuttingly on Bear, Roger and Bwana when she heard their attempts to suppress their laughter and had smiled softly when they couldn't hold back their guffaws.

The cops had matched the bloodstains in the abandoned site where Chloe and Tony had been taken, to Shattner, and had recovered Shattner's body from the river.

Elaine Rocka didn't want the children to witness Shattner's burial. Broker had agreed with her.

He had hatched a plan that would bestow honor on Shattner.

Broker, Bear and Chloe spent an hour with Commissioner Forzini, with Broker and Chloe articulating their plea while Bear sat silent, glowering at him. Forzini heard them out patiently, without interrupting, and when Chloe had finished, he turned over a sheet of paper on his desk and presented it to them.

'I authorized it last night,' he said simply. They left, embarrassed.

'You still dislike cops?' Chloe teased Broker when they left.

'Well, maybe not all,' he reluctantly agreed.

They hadn't yet told the kids the role their dad had played.

Elaine Rocka agreed with them that a formal occasion had to be made of it, one that stayed in their minds forever, a memory that would fill them with sunbursts of joy and pride whenever they remembered their father.

Clare avoided meeting them, knowing what they were after, ignoring Broker's calls and messages; she finally gave in when he showed no signs of letting up even after a month.

They stood in her anonymous office, ignoring her gesture at the seats before them. 'Who is he?' Broker repeated again.

'I didn't send anyone to shadow you or protect your backs,' she said truthfully.

They digested that, and Broker saw through it first. 'That's not what we asked. You know who he is. We too deserve to know who this ghost is.'

'I don't *know* who he is,' she replied, the faintest emphasis on the word.

Chloe pounced on it immediately.

'You can make a good guess, though, right?'

Clare had her game face on, which cracked finally when Bwana said with a straight face, 'We might have a job for him.'

She laughed and sat smiling at them, a strange expression on her face, letting the silence build, looking at Broker and Bwana the longest. Something in her gaze and posture sparked the air, electrons and protons buzzed furiously and silently.

'You know him well. Very well.'

Broker stared at her dumbly, then at Bwana, seeing the same uncomprehending expression in the other's eyes, and felt the flutter deep in his belly, a lightness in his head. He shook his head as if awaking from a deep sleep, looked across at Bear, Chloe and Roger, and saw the same disbelief warring with lurking hope.

'Zeb?' he whispered, forcing the words through a dry throat.

'But how?' he asked stupidly as her smile grew broader.

He flashed back to the night they'd mounted the rescue.

Carsten Holt was holed up in a three-storied house in New Jersey, with five of his hoods and the two hostages.

Two hoods were patrolling the top floor; two, the ground floor; and Holt and another hitter were watching over Lauren and Rory Balthazar on the middle floor.

Broker and Zeb decided to counterattack at night, just the two of them against six hard mercenaries.

Zeb would enter the house through a skylight in the roof, take out the two on the top floor, and go down to the middle floor, where he'd deal with Holt and rescue the hostages. Broker would take out the rest of the hoods using a long gun from across the street in front of the house. The sentries passed in front of windows, frequently – hence the long gun.

The plan worked perfectly. Up to a point.

Zeb dispatched the two hoods at the top and crept down to the hostage room.

He waited for the sentry's blind spot, and when it arrived, entered the hostage room, his Glock high and ready – and got the drop on Holt.

The plan fell apart then.

A door behind Holt opened, and a seventh gunman entered the room, firing at Zeb. He had to compensate for Zeb's position, who had crouched, and his first shot missed.

Zeb's didn't. Zeb double-tapped him, and his third shot creased Holt's right shoulder.

Holt dropped his gun, but his hand blurred behind his back and a knife split the air and buried deep in Zeb's shoulder, his gun clattering to the floor.

Holt charged at Zeb with another blade, Zeb parried, attacked and in the thrust and counterthrust, he dislocated Holt's right knee with a spinning kick.

Holt fell down heavily, but reached behind to grab a chair and hurled it at Zeb.

Zeb ducked, and as he was straightening, a steel band encircled his neck and a knife pierced deep in his ribs, searching for his heart.

The second hitter on the middle floor, who'd eluded Broker's sniping gun.

His brain went into autopilot, shutting down all nonessential systems in his body. He tried to pull away the hand choking him, but it was iron, cutting off his air, the knife going even deeper.

Through the fog creeping in his mind, he heard Holt laughing as he lay a few feet away.

Rage. Zeb welcomed it, stoked it, grew it into a ball of fire and hurled it deep inside, spreading through his body, reaching his extremities.

He moved toward his assailant, pushing the knife deeper into himself, trapping the assailant's knife hand between their bodies.

He twisted and grasped the knife hand with his right, squeezed, that ball of fire swirling in his wrist, squeezed and squeezed till the assailant cried hoarsely as his wrist snapped.

Zeb twisted to his left, sought and found the assailant's throat with his right hand and hurled himself back, dragging the assailant over and on top of him, his hand a vice crushing the assailant's neck. He ignored the hood's blows on his body, blanked out the knife going deeper in him during the struggle. Everything dissolved but for his hand around the hood's throat, squeezing till the hood's thrashing slowed and then stopped.

Holt lurched to his feet, picked up Zeb's gun and stood swaying over Zeb, watching him, listening to his harsh breathing.

'I wonder if you're worth a bullet now. Looks like you'll be at the pearly gates soon enough.'

Zeb whispered something.

'Praying? Shall I administer the last rites?' He lifted Zeb's gun.

The shot was muffled and could've been mistaken for a car misfiring. Except that the shot was in the room, and there was no mistaking the red, ugly hole in Holt's body.

Holt looked down stupidly, and Zeb fired again from beneath the dead gunman lying across him, through the gunman's body, using the gunman's waist gun that he had grabbed when falling backward.

His exertion had cost him all his life force, though; Broker saw it the moment he entered the hostage room and met Zeb's eyes. He saw the knowledge in Zeb's eyes.

He gripped Zeb's hand, not letting go even when the medics came, working desperately to revive him, ignoring Broker's screams and curses as he exhorted them to work harder, to do something, do anything to bring his friend back.

Broker was pulled back finally by cops, and Clare took charge, perfectly calm in the tornado of emotions in the room.

She spoke to him softly and asked him to take care of the hostages. She raised her voice when he stared at her blankly, not caring that she saw his tears and anger and bitterness and rage. She slapped him then, bringing him back to the present.

He nodded dumbly and moved to the hostages, the mechanics of activity pushing thought and emotion away.

Clare sat next to Zeb and held his hand.

She saw his cold pallor and looked at the medics and saw it in their eyes.

She stood numbly as they swiftly loaded the body, and followed them to the waiting ambulance below, shielding her face from the media who'd turned out in force.

Alone in the back of the ambulance, the two medics constantly attending to Zeb, she forced herself to think and plan, making up a story to spin to the media and to the FBI. The last vestige of her iron control deserted her then, and she sobbed deeply, uncaring of the medics' presence.

Zeb was her protégé.

She didn't notice the medics straighten, didn't notice them bend over the body, didn't see them rapidly attach various devices to his body, became dimly aware of someone calling her, and she turned around.

She looked into Zeb's open eyes. He whispered slowly, 'Don't tell anyone.'

It took him four months to recover. Four months of punishing himself to get back to the fitness levels that he demanded of himself, that his job demanded of him.

She tested him hard, threw him into the bear pit that was the Agency's training ground, where the best SEALs and Special Ops agents trained, and he healed. He became better than what he was before.

She spoke to the doctors, and they marveled at his recovery.

His body was in such fine shape, and his mind, a thing of beauty waxed one doctor, had shut down everything but the barest mechanisms to keep life alive. They thought all his martial arts training and mental conditioning had been responsible for that vital intervention. That, with the immediate and constant medical care, had led to his survival.

No, they'd said, his brain hadn't suffered any damage because it hadn't been deprived of oxygen.

He'd been adamant that he should be declared dead. 'I'm a magnet for trouble and will not put anyone else at risk again,' he'd said stubbornly. She urged, debated, threatened, and cajoled him, but he didn't budge.

'What about Cass?' she asked, playing her final card. Cassandra, his sister, who was close to Clare.

'I'm already dead. She'll survive,' he'd said harshly.

He was her best agent, and for all that he'd done for her and for the country, this was a small favor that she could grant, the deception not very difficult to maintain.

The doctors and medical staff were all sworn to secrecy – they never knew his real identity – and his medical records were altered to remove his existence.

Zebadiah Carter didn't exist anymore.

They stumbled to the chairs before her, struggling to grasp the enormity of the revelation.

'Where has he been all this time?' Bwana asked, the faintest tremble in his voice.

'You know I can't answer that' – she smiled to disarm the words of any offence – 'but he has been on some assignments… in Pakistan, those areas.'

Zeb had been undercover in Pakistan for several months, identifying several key Al Qaeda commanders, who were then taken out by drones based on his intel.

Color returned to Chloe's cheeks, anger tingeing her tone. 'We were,' she corrected herself, '*are* his unit. We deserved to know! This was such a massive deception for such a long time. We should've been in on it.'

'It was his to tell,' came the simple answer.

Clare could see what was coming, knowing them well, and fended off their growing anger, unable to hold back her laughter at one point when Roger threatened to make public all their projects. He looked embarrassed as soon as he finished. They just weren't wired like that.

Three hours later the standoff continued, the anger turned sullen, and she saw the first signs of hurt.

'You think he doesn't want to work with us anymore?' Bwana voiced their fears, not meeting her eyes, afraid of her response.

Clare sighed. For such an intelligent bunch, they sometimes didn't see the woods for the trees.

'You think he was shadowing you guys and saving your sorry asses because he didn't have anything better to do? You're his only family. He's got no other ties, bonds. Sure, he has Cass, but that's an entirely different relationship. Do you really think maintaining this lie was easy for him?'

Broker started to speak but stopped when she held her hand up. 'I know what you'll say. This is Zeb. He can control his emotions better than anyone and walk away without a second glance, without a second thought. That doesn't mean he doesn't *feel*, you idiots.

'He made this decision, right or wrong, but ultimately it was his call. He was the one who nearly died.

'Maybe you should get this through your thick heads; he disappeared not because he cared for you less. Maybe it was because he cared for you guys so much.'

She looked at them individually, saw it sinking in. 'Before you ask, he'll come when he's ready. You know the Zeb style by now,' she added drily.

Chloe brushed back her hair with fingers that trembled slightly. 'Do you have a number for him?'

'We have a number to leave messages for, and then there's a number for him when things go nuclear.' She gave them the messaging number. They'd been with the Agency long enough to know that the nuclear number was for just that.

Chloe looked at the number, back at Clare, a *may I* expression on her face. Clare nodded and watched as she dug out her satellite phone, looked at Bear and the others for assurance, took a deep breath, and dialed.

'Umm, Zeb. We heard you can come back from the dead. How about showing us you can walk on water?'

It was a brilliant morning with the sun smiling down on them, the skies azure and not a cloud in sight, when they made their way to Green-Wood Cemetery in Brooklyn.

Broker had acted very secretive around the family, and Elaine Rocka got her only clue when Broker asked her what kind of headstone they would like for Shattner.

On the day, Broker told the kids they'd be visiting their dad's final resting place, and when he drove into the cemetery, Elaine Rocka realized where they were heading and mouthed a silent, 'Thank you,' when she met his eyes in the mirror.

Broker had done his usual – negotiate, cajole, charm, convince – and secured a site at the renowned cemetery and had ensured that the grave and headstone was ready and in place. They'd decided, with Elaine Rocka's consent, that the children didn't need to be subjected to a burial service. It was far easier for them to visit the grave and mark closure.

The family got another surprise at the grave.

Commissioner Forzini, in dress uniform, was waiting for them at the grave, obscuring their view of the headstone, and after introductions, he smiled warmly at Lisa and Shawn, reached behind him, and presented them both with a folded flag.

On top of it was the New York City Police Department's Medal for Valor.

He stepped aside, letting them view the marker for the first time. It was simple and elegant with just his name and dates and two other words.

They saw Lisa's and Shawn's eyes go over the inscription, their lips moving silently, their eyes falling on the first word and pausing there for a long while, their mouths shaping the word. *Dad.*

Their eyes fell on the last word.

Hero.

Slow smiles came across their faces, growing wider and broader, bathing them in warmth and eclipsing the sun.

The Marshals were with the Commissioner, and when they'd finished at the cemetery, the family left with them.

Elaine Rocka surprised them all by hugging them tightly before she left.

Roger winked at her – 'Careful, ma'am, you've a reputation to maintain' – and blushed when she kissed him.

Bwana spotted the bottle first. It stood tall on the bonnet, glasses beside it.

They went closer, and Broker nodded approvingly when he saw the label, a Diamond Creek Gravelly Meadow Cabernet. He opened the bottle in silence, filled the six glasses, and they toasted in silence, taking turns to drink from the sixth.

They knew Zeb was watching them from somewhere.

The Warriors were complete.

Why not join the Warriors on their first outing in The Warrior, Book One in the series

Zeb Carter doesn't exist

The ex-Special Forces operative has no past and undertakes missions for a shadowy government agency that no one knows of.

A routine mission to the Congo to identify rogue mercenaries explodes when he witnesses barbaric acts that he can't walk away from. Plagued by the scale of the unspeakable crimes and its victims, Zeb does something he has never done before.

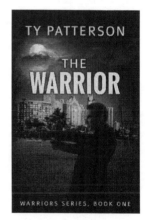

He breaks the mission rules and decides to hunt the ruthless perpetrators.

Disowned by his own agency and with just a maverick intelligence analyst, Broker, along with him, Zeb tracks the perpetrators to New York.

There he enters a grey world of conspiracy and hidden agendas, facing opponents not just those he's hunting and finds that he alone is interested in justice.

Everyone else wants the affair buried and Zeb along with it.

Praise for The Warrior

What a ride. Christine Terrell, Goodreads

Zeb reminds me of Jack Reacher but more real life and easier to connect to. Suzanne Bennett, Amazon review

I have read many suspense, mystery and special ops and The Warrior is one of the best I have read. CaryLory, Amazon review

Ultimately, it's a story of one man's desperate desire to chase away his own demons & how far he would go to do so. Terri, Goodreads

If you are a Jack Reacher fan then this book is for you. Tony, Amazon review

I liked this book and would recommend it. As good as Baldacci. Andrew Bedford, Amazon review

If one needs an adrenaline rush, then this book is definitely IT!!!! Ansuya, Amazon review

You'd better start early, because you will be staying up way into the wee hours of the next morning. Jane, Amazon review.

Coming soon

The Warrior Code

Warriors Series, Book 3

by

Ty Patterson

Chapter 1

The sound of a vehicle sounded in the distance, grew closer, and then faded away, disappearing in the deep silence.

Zeb lay still in the deep shadow of the bough of a tree.

The night light had given up the battle to reach the ground, and his camp 'fire', a few feet away, was bathed in darkness. He had made a cold camp and had a pile of wood and sticks handy, in case he needed to light them.

He had been stalking a grizzly all day, a large female just under seven feet and over five hundred pounds easily.

He hadn't seen a female bear this large, and when he'd spotted her snuffling for roots, he'd stopped and stared, forgetting momentarily that he was visible. Luckily he was downstream from the bear, and she didn't notice him.

He'd followed her all day, her and her cubs, watching the cubs frolic as their mother searched for food. If he was honest with himself, he was following them to also test his stalking skills.

He was in Yellowstone National Park, a vastness of almost three thousand five hundred square miles spread across the three states of Wyoming, Montana and Idaho, and home to Old Faithful Geyser. A vastness that put man in proper perspective.

He'd done the touristy double-loop attractions and had palled quickly of being around people and had broken out to the southeast corner of the park, one of the most remote areas in the United States.

He'd parked his drive in an isolated spot, covered it, and had set off hiking, breaking away from the hiking trails.

He'd been there for over two weeks, making his way through the remotest parts of the park and hadn't come across another human being, which suited him just fine.

Stalking the grizzly had brought him to where he was now.

Patches of shrub at chest level competed for air and sunlight while taller foliage ruled the skyline. There was ample undergrowth, which provided the bears with green fodder. There was a stream a klick away with the purest water and the best fish he'd had in a long while. The stream was half a mile away from a potholed track road through which the rare vehicle passed.

He'd felt the vehicle first before hearing it, its presence so unusual at that time of night that he'd stayed awake for some time trying to track its progress. The sound died about a mile away from him, and silence fell over the park.

He tried going back to sleep, but when that turned elusive, he gave up and decided to head to the stream for wildlife spotting.

He didn't have much to pack, a bedroll, a backpack that contained all that he needed, which wasn't much – water, rations, his guns, spare magazines, a Ka-Bar, binoculars, night vision glasses, and his sat phone. He checked his phone, not expecting any messages, and there were none. It was just past midnight when he set out.

A shot rang out.

He paused and peered through the darkness and saw nothing. He let the silence of the park become natural, and listened above it.

He thought he heard voices, but couldn't be sure.

Another shot rang out.

He ran.

Dimly he thought, *I should mind my own business. But then life would be boring.*

He became another shadow in the darkness of the park, moving from cover to cover, his feet rolling over the ground the way a panther's did.

He hoped the bears hadn't woken up and wouldn't be as curious as he was. Luckily, they had been heading south, and he was heading in the other direction.

The US Army had stats for everything, and one of those stats was for various age groups running a mile. Six and a half minutes placed the runner in the top one percentile for that age group. There didn't seem to be stats for running the remotest part of the park at night while at the same time keeping an eye out for grizzlies.

Zeb ran the mile in five minutes.

He heard the thrashing in the brush ahead, about two hundred feet away, before he heard the voices.

'Stop shooting, Steve. You want to get everyone's attention?' a male voice cursed.

'I'm trying to slow her down and scare her. Bitch. We should've killed her when we had the chance,' another male panted.

'You shit, all you had to do was bring her out of the back of the truck and to the open where we could question her. Now we have to chase her tail in the darkness.'

'She kicked me in the nuts and took me by surprise. Once I get my hands on her—'

'Shut up. Stop. Do we even know which direction she's gone?' the other hissed angrily.

Zeb drifted closer, a hundred feet away from them and could hear their harsh breathing as they tried to listen over themselves. It was too dark for him to make them out clearly, but they seemed to be about five feet seven in height, dressed in dark clothing. And out of shape.

He turned his attention to the woman they were chasing, and laid the map in his mind, calculated time and distances and visualized how it might have gone down.

Four hundred feet away was an open patch where a truck could come in, and he guessed that was where it was parked now. The woman had given the two pursuers the slip there and headed toward the denseness of the park.

Maybe two minutes of wrestling with the men, five minutes of running through the open patch... he turned a full circle and set out cautiously in the two o'clock direction.

He stopped every ten feet and listened, and at his third stop he felt her.

A presence at first, different from the surrounding park, and as he went closer, he could feel her moving softly away from all of them.

Her movement became faster as the pursuers stepped up their chase, and then she gave up the stealthy movement as the two pursuers heard her.

'I can hear the bitch now,' one of them grunted to the other.

'Wait, we just want to talk to you,' Steve called out.

That will make her stop. Zeb almost laughed, but he didn't do laughter.

He was the middle angle of the triangle formed by the three moving parts, and he stepped it up, closing the gap on the woman.

Zeb had worked out three things about the men chasing the women.

They weren't out to kill the woman. They might molest her, but not kill her. If they wanted to kill her, they'd have done that by now.

The one who had berated Steve was the leader of the two, though it was highly unlikely he was the one behind all this. The one who-was-not-Steve turned on a flashlight and aimed it ahead, trying to catch the woman in its glare.

The third was that these weren't professionals. Pros didn't fire needlessly nor did they attract attention in this manner. But that didn't mean these guys were any less dangerous.

One moment the woman was fleeing in panic, darting rapid glances over her shoulder, and the next a hand was clamped firmly over her mouth and she was lifted in the air and carried sideways, twenty feet away, behind a dense thicket.

The pursuers didn't see anything. All they heard was her rushing through the park and, the next moment, silence.

Zeb felt the woman draw a deep breath, and he squeezed, his hand an iron band around her waist, trapping her hands, and the other pressing deep against her mouth, not allowing her lips to move. The deeper she breathed, the tighter he squeezed, till she relaxed when she realized screaming wasn't futile.

It was impossible.

He held her there, making sure her pale face wasn't visible, and watched the flashlight disappear along with the soft thudding of the two men. He hoped they didn't come across the bears. He didn't want to be the one to clean up their remains in the park.

Three hours later, they were still there waiting silently and saw the flashlight come back, swinging in short movements, the anger and frustration in the two apparent in their tread.

He waited till he heard the vehicle start in the distance and drive away.

They'd be back in the daylight. He'd known hunters of their kind before.

'Will you scream if I remove my hand?' he asked the woman softly.

She kept stubbornly silent.

He waited patiently. He could outwait the Sphinx. After ten minutes he felt her nod.

He still didn't remove his hand. 'If you scream, chances are they'll hear and come back, and then you'll be in deeper trouble.'

She nodded again, and he removed his hand.

He stepped in front of her and looked at her closely for the first time.

She was a young woman, black or brown haired – too dark to make that out – and about five foot seven. She was slimly built, but he thought he could detect athleticism and muscle structure in her build.

'Who are you?' he asked.

'Who the hell are *you*?' she countered, her voice trembling but strong.

'I'm the man who saved you,' he answered her simply.

She went silent for a long while.

'I don't know who I am.'

He waited for her to elaborate.

She said finally, in a small voice, 'I've lost my memory.'

Author's Message

Thank you for taking time to read *The Reluctant Warrior*. If you enjoyed it, please consider telling your friends and posting a short review, here: http://amzn.to/1tlUmpX

.

About the Author

Ty has lived on a couple of continents and has been a trench digger, loose tea vendor, leather goods salesman, marine lubricants salesman, diesel engine mechanic and is now an action thriller author.

Ty is privileged that readers of crime suspense and action thrillers, have loved his books, The Warrior and The Reluctant Warrior. 'Intense,' 'Riveting,' 'Gripping,' have been commonly used in reviews.

Ty lives with his wife and son, who humor his ridiculous belief that he's in charge.

Connect with Ty:

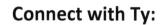

On Twitter: http://www.twitter.com/pattersonty67

On Facebook: http://www.facebook.com/AuthorTyPatterson

Website: http://www.typatterson.com

Mailing list: http://eepurl.com/09nyf

Made in the USA
Columbia, SC
27 May 2025

58511016R00264